Rowan Coleman

the Accidental Family

arrow books

Published by Arrow Books 2009

2 4 6 8 10 9 7 5 3 1

First published in Great Britain in 2009 by
Arrow Books
Random House, 20 Vauxhall Bridge Road,
London SW1V 2SA

www.rbooks.co.uk

Addresses for companies within The Random House Group Limited can be found at:
www.randomhouse.co.uk/offices.htm

The Random House Group Limited Reg. No. 954009

A CIP catalogue record for this book
is available from the British Library

ISBN 9780099525196

The Random House Group Limited supports The Forest Stewardship
Council (FSC), the leading international forest certification organisation. All our
titles that are printed on Greenpeace approved FSC certified paper carry the FSC logo.
Our paper procurement policy can be found at www.rbooks.co.uk/environment

Typeset in Garamond MT by Palimpsest Book Production Limited
Grangemouth, Stirlingshire
Printed in Great Britain by CPI Bookmarque Ltd, Croydon CR0 4TD

the Accidental Family

Rowan Coleman worked in bookselling and then publishing for seven years, during which time she wrote her first novel, *Growing Up Twice*, published in 2002. She left to write her second novel, *After Ever After*, and now lives and writes in Hertfordshire with her daughter.

Praise for Rowan Coleman

'A charming tale' *heat*

'A fresh, warm and hugely enjoyable read ... truly brilliant. Her captivating style leaps off the page, engrossing you from the first sentence' *Company*

'Highly enjoyable ... Coleman tells her story with bundles of warmth and humour' *Spectator*

'Touching and thought-provoking' *B*

'Highly amusing' *OK!*

'Emotionally satisfying page-turner' *Closer*

'At times laugh-out-loud funny, at others tear-provoking ... one of those books that makes you miss your bus stop.

For Adam

Acknowledgements

Thank you to the brilliant and patient Kate Elton and Georgina Hawtrey-Woore who are a constant source of support and inspiration and also to the whole team at Arrow and Random House who always work so hard on my behalf. Thank you also to my dear friend and wonderful agent Lizzy Kremer.

And huge thanks to the fantastic women who have supported me through an eventful year with glasses of wine, emergency childcare and a shoulder to lean on so many times – Jenny Matthews, Margi Harris, Kirstie Seaman and Catherine Ashley. Also to Clare Winter, Cathy Carter, Rosie Wooley and Sarah Darby. I feel lucky to have so many best friends.

And most of all thank you to my beautiful girl, my daughter Lily, a constant joy and delight and the light of my life.

A Bedtime Story

'Right ... um, well – once upon a time, not that long ago, there lived an exceptionally beautiful princess, who had long golden hair and was a size twelve as long she stayed off white bread and cake.

Princess Sophie lived in a very nice one-bedroom turret in an up-and-coming part of the kingdom and she owned an extensive and extremely stylish collection of shoes and one cat called Artemis. Actually she didn't exactly own the cat; the cat just lived in the flat with her. More like a flat mate really, or a flat cat ... *Anyway*, Princess Sophie thought that she was very happy because she had a very nice home and a lot of nice clothes and shoes.

The princess even had a very serious and important job that she was very, very good at. She was a career princess, one who knew that events management wasn't just planning a load of big parties. In fact, Princess Sophie was very good at most things except for being close to other people. She didn't realise it at the time, but she was actually quite lonely.

Then one day a very fat and badly dressed fairy godmother came to visit her from the land of Social Services. She told the princess that a very sad thing had happened. The princess's oldest and best friend Lady Carrie had died. And she had left behind two beautiful daughters who needed to be looked after.

The fairy godmother reminded Princess Sophie that once, long ago, she had made a promise to Lady Carrie that if anything ever happened to her, she would look after the two little girls.

Well, Princess Sophie didn't exactly know what to think. She was very, very sad about losing her friend, but also she was scared. When she had made that promise she never dreamt that one day she would have to keep it, and she wasn't sure that she knew how to look after two small girls. But when she thought about her lovely friend, Princess Sophie knew she couldn't let them down. And so the two girls came to stay. Their names were Bella and Izzy. Bella was an artist and pony expert who could fly as long as no one was looking and Izzy was a true fairy, which was easy to see because she always dressed as a fairy even when she went to bed, *even* when she had a bath.

At first Princess Sophie and Artemis weren't at all sure about Bella and Izzy, especially not when they turned her lovely white sofa into a green curry-scented one, ruined her make-up collection and got stuck down the loo. Princess Sophie thought that there was no way that she would be able to cope. But the two girls needed a friend to look after them and Princess Sophie was the only friend they had so she stuck it out.

And gradually day by day Princess Sophie got to like Izzy and Bella a bit more, and they got to like her a bit more too. And even though all three of them felt sad they were all sort of glad they had each other.

Then one day a handsome stranger called Prince Louis arrived at Princess Sophie's door; he was Bella and Izzy's daddy. He had been in a faraway land and as soon as he had found out what had happened he came back to look after his daughters. But no one had seen him for the longest time and Princess

Sophie didn't know if he was a nice man or not. Bella wasn't sure if after all that time she still wanted him to be her daddy. Only Izzy who had never even met her daddy before decided to like him right away – and you know what they say, first impressions are always right. And ever so slowly the two girls and Princess Sophie got to know Prince Louis.

One day it was time for Prince Louis to take Bella and Izzy back home to the Kingdom of Mermaids, by the sea. Princess Sophie felt very, very sad about them going, but she knew they had to. She knew that they'd be happy there, in the place that Lady Carrie had loved best. And so she took them all down in her magic chariot Phoebe, the Golf.

And when they were there Princess Sophie realised something wonderful and scary too. She realised that she loved Bella and Izzy, that she loved them with all her heart – and even more scarily she realised that she loved Prince Louis too.

Well, Princess Sophie didn't know what to do about that, because she wasn't used to loving anyone apart from her cat, who she wasn't all that sure loved her back. She didn't know how to show or tell the people she loved how much she cared about them and she didn't know if they would want her to love them. So when she saw how happy Prince Louis, Bella and Izzy were she decided to leave and go back to her turret, even though it broke her heart.

Once she got back she felt sad every day, even though she was crowned queen at her office and became the boss of everything which was really only what she deserved because she was so very good at her job. At night she lay awake missing the three people she loved best.

Then Princess Sophie's friend Cal told her that if she stayed in her turret pining away she would never be happy. He told her that she had to be brave, she had to go on a quest to the Land of the Mermaids and find Prince Louis and Bella and

Izzy and tell them that she loved them and that she wanted to be near them, come what may.

So she travelled down to the Land of the Mermaids and when she got there she told Prince Louis and Bella and Izzy how very much she loved them, and the best thing – the happiest thing of all – was that they told her they loved her back.

And Princess Sophie decided to stay in the Land of Mermaids for ever and ever.

The End.

Or if you really want to be picky – the beginning.'

Prologue

The room was dark except for the artificial orange glow that was cast by the fake coals of Louis's 1970s electric fire.

Sophie stared into the dusty coals, her head on Louis's chest as she listened to the rhythmic beat of his heart. His fingers had been gently smoothing her hair away from her face for the last twenty minutes or so and neither of them had said a word to each other, principally because there had been far too much kissing for small talk.

'You've been here for six hours and eleven minutes,' Louis said quietly, almost to himself. 'You've actually, physically, really been here and not just in my imagination for over six hours.'

'Have I?' Sophie lifted her head from his chest to look at him, finding two tiny golden reflections of the fire glinting in his dark eyes. The trouble was that whenever Sophie looked at Louis she wanted to kiss him and so for the last twenty minutes she had tried not to look at him. She felt, particularly given the circumstance of her arrival earlier that afternoon, that they should probably be doing less kissing and at least *some* talking about what was going to happen next now that she'd left her entire life in London behind to be with him and his daughters in Cornwall. Only kissing was so much nicer and it didn't involve her having to talk about all the things she

5

was thinking and feeling, which was always a plus where Sophie was concerned.

Still, there was something unseemly about the fact that the last six hours and eleven minutes had largely comprised of kissing with a break for tea and putting Louis's very over-excited daughters to bed. She was sure there should be more speeches, more declarations of intent and far less kissing. Sophie found herself worrying if Louis minded all the kissing and then she wondered how she would ever go about asking him such a question. Perhaps it was better just to kiss him and think about the consequences later; after all, it was that kind of rationale that had brought her here in the first place.

Sophie Mills was being uncharacteristically impulsive.

Just as Sophie was caving in to her desire to kiss Louis, he spoke first and for a fleeting second she was rather irritated with him.

'I think that six hours and eleven minutes is the longest time that we have ever spent together in one go,' Louis said. 'Apart from that night when . . .'

'Do you think I'm crazy, Louis?' Sophie asked him, twisting round to look in his eyes. Why she'd waited for him to start talking before she could think of anything to say she didn't know. And rather more worryingly, why did the very thing she thought of to say make her sound like a madwoman? She should have stuck to kissing. Kissing was safe territory.

'You probably are a *bit* mad,' Louis said, smiling fondly in the artificial light. 'I don't know many women who'd give up their job, their *career*, their home and their life in London to come and be with a single dad and his two unruly children in Cornwall.'

'Christ, I am mad!' Sophie sat bolt upright, feeling a chill rush along the parts of her body that were no longer welded to Louis's. 'You hardly even know me and I've just landed on your doorstep telling you that I'm here to stay! You must be horrified.'

Louis tapped one long finger on his thigh three times. 'Yes. Yes, I am.' He nodded. 'I'm totally horrified. Hence all this naked kissing; that's me in turmoil, that is. Look – getting to know you is one of the most wonderful things I have ever done and I feel like you know me better than anyone ever has. I don't know what Bella and Izzy would have done these past few months if it wasn't for you. You were there for them when no one else was and they need you in their lives. I think you need them, too, and hopefully, you also need me.'

'Do you mind all that kissing, by the way?' Sophie asked him intently, silently cursing herself for her apparently boundless capacity to ask stupid and inappropriate questions that were far more likely to make a man fall out of love with a woman, than in.

Louis laughed. 'Like I said,' he said with a straight face, 'I'm horrified. It's dreadful kissing an incredibly beautiful woman for hours on end.'

'Are you being sarcastic?' Sophie thought it was best to double check.

'Of course I'm being sarcastic! Good God, woman, I *love* kissing you!'

Sophie found herself smiling, her shoulders relaxing again as she leaned into him, her thigh resting against the length of his.

'I do love the girls,' she said thoughtfully. The realisation of this fundamental truth still shocked her, but it was inescapable. Two small lost children had inspired emotions in her that she had never believed possible – and the children weren't even hers. 'I do love them. And I'd do anything for them, but . . .' Sophie's mouth went dry. Declarations weren't really her thing and she'd already made one today, which was one more than she had ever made in her entire life, but now that she was here she felt she had to say something important and *momentous*. 'I came here for you, because I, you know, love you and stuff.'

'And stuff?' Louis repeated, his voice full of warmth.

'Yes, and stuff,' Sophie said, holding his gaze defiantly. 'And *stuff*.'

'Sophie,' Louis picked up her hand and stroked the back of it, 'thank you. Thank you for leaving your life in London to come down here for me. And I really mean that because I am stupidly, wholly, utterly grateful to you because I *love* you. I love you *and* stuff, if stuff is a requirement. I haven't said it before now because for the last six hours and' – he checked his watch – 'twenty-two minutes I've been wondering if you're really here or if this is all some bizarre illusion I've conjured up for myself because, God knows, all I've done since we parted is daydream about having you near me.' Louis kissed the back of her hand. 'But now that you've told me that you love me "and stuff" I know it's really you. Only the real Sophie Mills would say that. Maybe it's impossible for two people to fall in love after only a few months and maybe we are crazy, but you being here has made me the happiest man this side of Plymouth and probably beyond. I love you, Sophie Mills.'

Sophie put her hand over his and found there were tears in her eyes.

'I'm glad,' she said. 'Because I would have looked like an awful idiot if you hadn't.'

'You really are here, aren't you?' Louis said, reaching out and touching her cheek with his fingertips.

'Yes, it appears that I am.' Sophie leaned her cheek into his palm.

'And look,' Louis told her earnestly, 'I want you to know that I'm here for you all the time. The second you have a worry or a doubt or feel like freaking out because you've realised that no one wears a kitten heel on a weekday around here, then all you have to do is come to me and I'll talk you down because—'

'Louis.' Sophie stopped his mouth with her finger.

'Yes?' Louis said against her skin.

'Shut up and kiss me.'

Chapter One

Six months later

'Cream teas are the devil's work,' Sophie said out loud as she inspected herself in her latest pair of jeans. Technically she was still a size twelve but if she was honest the almost daily trip to Carmen Velasquez's Ye Olde Tea Shoppe had pushed her hips to the size's upper limit, something she'd have to sort out eventually, particularly if she was going to wear so much purposeful denim.

Once, before Bella, Izzy and their father came into her life, Sophie had owned only one pair of jeans, which she seldom wore. She had been an occasion dresser, with a fondness for a sequin on a work day and a rule that a heel should never dwindle below three inches. But since she'd come to stay in St Ives not only had she not bought a single pair of unfeasibly high heels, but she'd also collected four pairs of jeans, two denim skirts, an assortment of casual tops and an anorak. Sophie loved her double-zipped all-weatherproof red and navy blue anorak, but it was a love that dared not speak its name, at least not when she was talking to her erstwhile secretary and good friend Cal on the phone about her outlandish new life in Cornwall.

'Have you got any wellies yet?' Cal would quiz her without fail during their weekly chats.

'Me, wellies? Are you joking? I have some standards,' Sophie would tell him breezily.

'Wellies mean you aren't coming back,' Cal took pleasure in telling her. 'Wellies are a sign of commitment to your new way of life. Wellington boots are the nearest that you, Sophie Mills, will ever get to an engagement ring.'

'Well, thanks, Cal. Thanks very much for boiling my entire romantic happiness down to a moulded rubber boot,' Sophie would reply. 'Besides, what would you, the king of commitment-phobia know, anyway? I might get married one day.'

Sophie gazed out of her bedroom window at the grey and stormy sea beyond the harbour below. Before she had left London to come here she had never once daydreamed about getting married or being a bride. But during the last six months she'd spent with Louis she had found herself thinking about it more than once.

'To Louis?' Cal persisted.

'Potentially.' Sophie's mouth curled into a silent smile meant only for her. 'One day, you know . . . when the time is right.'

'Wellies first.' Cal was adamant. 'Once you've bought the wellies then he'll finally know that you're committed and he'll ask you. He's waiting for the wellies.'

But as yet there were no Wellington Boots in the original 1970s MFI wardrobe in Sophie's room at the Avalon B&B and at six months she was the second-longest-staying guest, second only to Mrs Tregowan who had been there for nearly a year after her husband died, deciding she could not bear to go back to her bungalow without him.

Sophie had been in the Cornish town of St Ives for most of the spring, for once feeling part of the burgeoning season, embracing the renewal of life as she felt herself awaken to the unknown possibilities that the future might hold. On weekend mornings she and Louis had paddled in the freezing waters of the harbour with the girls till her city-soft toes turned blue, collecting interesting shells and bits of pottery. Sophie had let the cool, crisp sea breeze ruddy her cheeks and whip her fine blonde hair into a tangle. As they climbed over the rocks and stones to the harbour wall, their toes encrusted with sand, Louis would hold her hand in his, reviving her numbed fingers with his body heat till she felt the blood tingle and throb in her fingertips. She had stayed for the whole of the fickle summer, in turn drenched with warm rain and occasionally studded with jewel-like days bathed in sunshine. During the summer holidays when Louis was working building up his fledgling photography business, the girls gave her their own personal tour of the town: picnicking amongst the clover and daisies above the whitewashed town perched so haphazardly on the rocky cliffs which tumbled into the sea; dodging the tourists at the roller disco that took place every day at midday in the Guildhall, which Sophie found both exhilarating and humiliating in turn; and taking her to the Tate Gallery to show her the paintings there, Bella lecturing her with confidence on light and perspective; and leading her in and out of the maze of tiny cobbled streets to show her their favourite houses and window boxes laden with geraniums. And in the evenings, after Louis had got back from that day's assignment, they'd walk along the harbour wall until they found the family of seals which were always there, lounging on the rocks just out to sea as if they rather enjoyed their celebrity. Izzy would give them a new name every day and Bella would tell Sophie stories about them.

Now it was late September and things had stayed more or less exactly the same way since the week she had arrived: a charming mixture of novelty and routine combined with a kind of happiness she had never felt before and the sense that this wasn't really her life she was living after all, it couldn't be.

She felt as if she were walking through the pages of a romance novel or had suddenly been given the lead role in a movie because real life was never this easy.

She saw Louis and the girls every day. Since the start of the new term she had been taking the children to school; Izzy had turned four and had now joined the nursery at Bella's school. Every other afternoon she would pick Izzy up at one and they would enjoy a cream tea at Carmen Velasquez's Ye Olde Tea Shoppe before returning to school to fetch Bella at three fifteen. Then they'd go for a walk on the beach, making sandcastles and chasing each other with lumps of slimy seaweed if it was sunny enough or, if it was rainy, go back to Louis's house to make things out of dried pasta. Very occasionally they'd partake of a second cream tea at Ye Olde Tea Shoppe as it didn't seem fair that Bella missed out.

In the evenings, after the girls were in bed, Sophie and Louis would sit in front of the electric fire he kept swearing he was going to replace with a period fireplace to match the house's Victorian exterior and laugh and talk and share news and hold hands and do a great deal of kissing. And most nights the kissing would lead to touching and the touching would lead to the most wonderful and dazzling sex that Sophie had ever known. Louis's sofa had seen a lot of action over the last six months and his rug had seen a great deal more. But to date Sophie had never stayed the night.

'I'm fairly sure you could sleep over if you wanted to,' Louis had said one night as the pair of them lay sprawled in front of the fire, which they had switched on for old times' sake, even though it was August and a swelteringly hot night. He traced a finger along the curve of her breast that shimmered with sweat in the firelight. 'I'd love to go to sleep with you, Sophie,' he murmured. 'And to wake up with you. I'd like to see you in the morning with your hair all tangled up and sleep

14

creases in your cheeks. I'd like to have sex with you in the morning, while you're still half dreaming and biddable.'

'Well, you'd be unlucky,' Sophie told him as she stretched, and wriggled because the rug was a nylon mix and a bit itchy on her skin. 'Because I sleep like a princess and I never get tousled or creased. Besides, I'm only ever biddable when I want to be, which might be right now if you play your cards right.'

'Stay over,' Louis asked her gently, kissing her shoulder. 'Please.'

'I can't, Louis. What would they think?' Sophie pointed at the ceiling. Bella and Izzy were fast asleep upstairs.

'They'd think that you'd stayed the night and then they'd wonder whether, seeing as Daddy was in such a good mood, they could score Coco Pops for breakfast two days in a row even though they're only supposed to have them twice a week,' Louis said. 'They wouldn't care, Sophie. I think they'd be happy about it.'

'I can't,' Sophie replied uncertainly. 'It wouldn't be right. They aren't ready for that.'

'They do know we're going out together, you know,' Louis said wryly. 'All the hand holding and "I love yous" have given it away a bit. I think you are the one who's not ready.'

Sophie dropped her gaze momentarily. Perhaps Louis was right. Everything seemed so complete, so wonderful now, that she sometimes felt as if her happiness was balanced on a high wire. She was afraid of changing anything, including moving their relationship on a step in case the perfect peace she'd found here teetered and crashed.

Sophie was all too aware of her own double standards. Here she was naked and sated on the living-room floor with only a flight of stairs and a locked door keeping her and Louis from being discovered by his daughters. But staying over was something else; it was the next level and she wanted it to be about her and Louis taking another step forward together, not a way to have sex that would result in fewer friction burns. Sophie eyed Louis from beneath her lashes.

'So we are going out together, then?' She teased him instead. 'Only you've never formally asked me, so I did wonder. It's just that the children are only seven and four. I can't possibly stay over – not when we're not . . .'

'What?' Louis propped himself up on one elbow and looked at Sophie, his gaze travelling slowly upwards from the tops of her thighs, over her breasts and finally meeting her eyes with the kind of look that would have made her knickers fizz had she been wearing any.

'We're not, you know, thingy,' Sophie said, smiling as she wound her arms around Louis's neck and drew him down to kiss her. But his lips stopped short of hers by a hair's breadth.

'Marry me, then,' Louis whispered.

Instead of answering, Sophie kissed him hard, pushing him on to his back on the carpet and climbing on top of him with the kind of unbridled abandon that, had she stopped to think about it, she would have found rather embarrassing. But she didn't stop to think because one of the best things about being in love with Louis Gregory was that when she made love to him she didn't think about anything at all apart from how very wonderful it made her feel.

Still, as delightful a distraction as it had been, Sophie had not answered or even acknowledged Louis's question. It hadn't gone unnoticed but it did go unspoken about, because Sophie and Louis didn't talk about anything much except for the day's events and exactly where each other's bodies should be kissed next. Sometimes the thought would creep into Sophie's mind that all she and Louis knew about one another was how to make each other laugh and their bodies sing, but it was a thought that rarely stayed too long. Sophie would either be laughing too hard or melting under Louis's touch to dwell on it much.

At the end of each evening Sophie would spend a few minutes talking to her cat Artemis who, apparently, was not nearly as concerned about progressing things along as her owner was. Artemis had moved in with Louis on the very first day they had arrived from London, and the animal now lorded it over the resident ginger cat Tango with the ferocity and splendour of a feline Boudicca. Sophie would then get in her Golf if she hadn't been drinking, or take the local taxi if she had, and go back to the B&B to sleep alone.

It wasn't that she didn't long to wake up with Louis's arms around her, because she did. It was just that six months on she was still determined before she edged along that precarious high wire to be absolutely sure that what she was doing was the right thing and that she wasn't making a terrible, terrible mistake, the kind of mistake that would burst this wonderful little bubble she had been living in and let reality come careering in.

Cal would say that all the happiness, not to mention the general feeling of contentment and joy that had pervaded her daily life since she had come down to Cornwall to stay, should be proof enough for her to take that next step towards commitment. But then again Cal had been known to declare his undying love to a man simply because he admired the lining of his jacket so Cal's opinion was not, in this case at least, one Sophie felt able to rely on. This time she had to know for herself and although all the evidence supported a favourable outcome there was something, some small, tiny, indefinable piece of information that Sophie was waiting to fall into place before she could know for sure that she was meant to be here.

The problem was that Sophie wasn't entirely sure exactly what it was she was waiting for.

Less than a year ago Sophie had been working her way up the career ladder, within touching distance of the very top of her game, which was corporate events management in the City. She was second in command at McCarthy Hughes and about to step into her boss's shoes to run the whole shebang. The moment that she had been working for since joining the company fresh out of school was almost upon her.

And then her best friend, her dear, sweet, sometimes rash, but always loyal and lovely best friend Carrie, had been killed in a car accident leaving behind two small girls without anyone to look after them, except an ailing grandmother and a father who could not be found. Suddenly a drunken afternoon, long ago, when Sophie had promised Carrie that she would be the children's guardian had become horrifyingly real. Sophie had taken the two strange, sometimes quiet and frequently destructive little girls into her life, telling their social worker that it would only be for as long as it took to track down their good-for-nothing absent father.

There had been a lot of tears, several bed wettings, the incident with a laptop, the breakfast cereal and the hair serum that still made Sophie wince whenever she thought about it and, of course, the cat food debacle that Sophie had neglected to mention to the girls' social worker, not because she was trying to hide anything, but because her mother had told her that as far as she knew a few mouthfuls of Kitekat weren't lethal to curious three-year-olds.

It was fair to say that motherhood, as transient and as accidental as it had been, had not come easily to Sophie, particularly as she struggled to come to terms with the death of the woman she considered her closest friend, the woman who, it turned out, she had hardly known at all. So what had occurred next had been entirely unexpected.

The children had come to need her and trust her. And she had slowly begun to love them. A love that, despite its strength and depth, had crept up on her unawares. Slowly parts of her that had lain dormant since the death of her father had been revived and through their own grief the children had somehow reconnected Sophie to herself. They had set her heart beating again.

Which happened to be at just the moment her dead best friend's husband, the girls' father, walked back into his daughters' lives after a three-year absence.

At first Sophie wanted to hate Louis, but when it became clear that hating him was going to be impossible because he wasn't the heartless monster she had imagined him to be, and was in fact a rather sensitive, sweet, sexy man with an amazing body, she'd simply settled on not falling for him. After all, what worse possible choice could a 32-year-old woman make than falling in love with her dead best friend's husband? Sophie spent many a long night awake on her sofa while the children slept in her double bed trying to think of one, but none came to mind. She didn't even think a cork retro wedge worn with a full skirt above the knee compared when it came to an ill-judged decision made in poor taste. So Sophie tried, she really tried, not to want him. But as she got to know him, and saw how desperate he was to win back the trust of his children, she found out what had really happened to drive him and Carrie apart and eventually she understood and respected what he'd been through. It didn't help that whenever she looked into his eyes her heart beat like a drum against her ribcage and her knickers fizzed.

After that it was all fairly textbook – if the textbook you are reading is *Emotionally Repressed Women and How Best to Manage*

Denial. Sophie had fallen for Louis, she had pretended that she hadn't fallen for Louis, she had spent a night of unscheduled illicit passion with him, and then she had left, planning to torture herself for the rest of her life with an endless series of 'what might have beens' till Cal had told her to stop it and go and be happy instead. And six months ago, incredibly, she had done just that.

At the age of almost thirty-three Sophie Mills had thrown her entire carefully built-up life away to see if she could make things work with a man she barely knew. She worried about how it must look to people on the outside: she and Louis, two strangers who barely knew each other, thrown together by circumstance and, fond as he was of her, Louis perhaps regarding Sophie as a rather convenient replacement for the girls' lost mother, a replacement who came ready made with his children's trust and love already assured.

Now she thought about that last step on the high wire, the one that would lead her to a new and permanent life in Cornwall. That last step which would mean that she could finally call Louis's house her home.

It was a shame, Sophie thought as she squeezed the extra flesh on her hips between her thumb and forefinger, that she didn't have a similar problem committing to cream teas.

A knock at the door interrupted her thoughts and she quickly hid in the wardrobe.

'Aunty Sophie?' Bella called out as she pushed the bedroom door open. 'We're coming to get you!'

'You is going to get got!' Izzy giggled, galloping into the room after Bella like a herd of small but determined elephants.

Sophie remained silent in the wardrobe secreted between business suits and sequined party dresses that hadn't been worn in months. Her job on the days when Louis picked the children up from school and brought them round, was to wait to be found. And even though the girls knew exactly where she was hiding (there weren't that many opportunities for discretion in the tiny room), she had to wait nevertheless. Sometimes Izzy wouldn't be able to stand the excitement and she'd be found in less than a minute. On other days, it could take quite a long while and by the time she had been uncovered Sophie would have quite a crick in her neck and pins and needles in her calves.

'Is she under the bed?' Bella's muffled voiced suggested that she had crawled under it to check.

'Is she in the toilet?' Izzy's giggle bounced off the walls in the tiny en-suite and Sophie smiled to herself. Izzy had changed a lot in the last six months but her devotion to toilet humour had never wavered.

'Is she up the chimney?' Bella called out.

'Or on the lampshade?' Izzy suggested.

'Of course she's not on the lampshade, Iz,' Bella said matter-of-factly. 'The lampshade is tiny and small and made of paper and Aunty Sophie is *huge*!'

Sophie pursed her lips and silently swore off clotted cream scones for about the seventh time that week.

'I think . . .' Bella said in the tone of voice that meant Sophie had to prepare to be discovered. 'That she might be . . . in . . . the . . . wardrobe!'

In the second that Bella flung open the door Sophie jumped out yelling 'BOO!' at the top of her voice, an event that never failed to make both girls scream and giggle, as they leapt on Sophie and propelled her in one very girlish heap on to one of the room's twin beds.

'You got me,' Sophie said when she had got her breath back. 'Where's Daddy?'

'Downstairs talking to Mrs Alexander about sandwiches,'

Bella said sitting up, pushing her fringe out of her eyes. Sophie brushed the child's dark hair off her forehead and kissed her on the cheek.

'You need a haircut again,' she said. 'Your hair grows faster than anything I know.'

'What about me, do I need a haircut?' Izzy hooked her arms around Sophie's neck and rested her cheek against Sophie's. Sophie wound a finger into one of Izzy caramel-coloured curls. 'You have hair just like your mother's,' she told the younger girl, knowing how much she liked to talk about Carrie. 'You can cut it and brush it and wash it all you like but it will do exactly what it wants to do . . . which reminds me of the little person it's attached to!'

'I'm not little any more,' Izzy protested. 'I go to school now and anyway, are you coming for a cream tea?'

'Of course she is,' Bella said. 'Aunty Sophie always comes for cream teas.'

'I can't deny it,' Sophie said. 'But today is absolutely my total and utter last one.'

'You said that yesterday,' Bella reminded her.

'I know a thing,' Izzy said with big round eyes and a typically dramatic tone. 'A really, really specially secret thing that Daddy says I'm not to tell you!'

'Do you?' Sophie was mildly anxious. The last major secret Izzy had had involved Artemis and an entire packet of smoked salmon that Izzy had fed the cat under her bed in a bid to make the cat love her more than Bella. What Izzy had failed to understand was that Artemis would never turn down free food even from her worst enemy and it was a miracle that she actively liked any human at all. She had lived with Sophie for years in her flat in London and had barely ever spoken two words to her, so to speak. For some reason Bella was the only human whom Artemis loved, whether it was because the once mistreated cat saw something in Bella she recognised or because Bella was the only person on the planet who knew how to tickle her behind her ears the way she liked it, Sophie didn't know. But she did know that all copious amounts of smoked salmon would achieve was piles of orange fishy vomit deposited all around the house.

'Have you been trying to make friends with Artemis again?'

'No, it's even better than that!' Izzy said, giggling gleefully.

'It's not really,' Bella said firmly. 'It's not anything at all. It's really best forgotten about.'

'Yes, we are not to tell because Daddy says he has something very important to ask you but we mustn't say what it is,' Izzy said, wiping her nose on the back of her hand and then her hand on Sophie's fuchsia candlewick bedspread.

'Izzy!' Bella hissed, digging her little sister in the ribs. 'Shush.'

She smiled at Sophie; a wide toothy grin that Sophie had seen once before when Bella denied using Sophie's steak knives as tent pegs to make a den out of her best and, for that matter, only leather coat.

'Oh come on, girls, what are you two hiding? Is your dad finally going to strip that hideous wallpaper in the living room?'

'It's much more exciting than that,' Izzy told her. 'It's the most exciting-est, most massive-est thing *ever*!'

'No it isn't!' Bella tried to urge her little sister into discretion by waggling her eyebrows, which might have worked if her fringe hadn't been so long it obscured them completely. 'Daddy has nothing to say to you what-so-ever,' she pronounced the new and unfamiliar words that she loved acquiring so much with great care. 'I expect he won't want to talk to you about anything of consequence at all.'

'Except that he's going to ask her to—' Izzy began.

'Pay for the cake because he's lost his ... money,' Bella interrupted her.

'Or at least he hasn't got any monies left because he's spent them on this most beautiful-est—'

'Hat,' Bella finished for Izzy. 'He's bought a completely *enormous* hat.'

Sophie looked from one girl to the other. It could never be said that she was the world's most intuitive woman, it had taken her a rather long time to realise, for example, that Louis had loved her back and that the feelings she had for him weren't just an unrequited, slightly psychotic and rather ill-advised crush. Yet here was Izzy seething with secrets, talking about something exciting and massive that Louis wanted to ask her while Bella was gamely trying to cover up with a tale of a lost wallet and an enormous hat. A few months ago Sophie would have been wondering what on earth Louis wanted with an enormous hat, but she had changed from that blunt black and white woman and these children had helped her do it. That and the fact that they were dreadful at keeping secrets led her to believe that, unless she was very much mistaken, what the girls were trying not to tell her was that their father was going to ask her to marry him. Again.

Only this time she wouldn't be able to pretend that she hadn't heard him and there would be much less of an opportunity for distracting sex right in the middle of Ye Olde Tea Shoppe.

Chapter Two

Carmen Velasquez was the embodiment of her name. A few years older than Sophie at thirty-seven, she had olive skin, dark pool-like eyes and shiny black hair that fell in a neat bob to her shoulders. She looked, Sophie remembered thinking the first time she had met her, like a Spanish rose. Which was interesting because she sounded exactly like what she was: Essex girl through and through.

The story of how Carmen had come to be running a tea shop in St Ives was almost as far-fetched as the one that made Sophie the second-longest-staying guest at the Avalon B&B. Carmen had fallen for a strapping young man, thirteen years her junior, at the Club Twenty nightclub in Chelmsford. Carmen had been dancing on a podium when she had been literally whisked off her feet by a decidedly Nordic-looking young man who, without bothering to discuss either her name or marital status with her, had kissed her passionately up against a sticky wall till the fluorescent lights finally flickered on at two in the morning. They had spent a night of unbridled passion together, and she discovered that the young man's name was James, that he was on a stag night with his best mate from school, and that he was currently employed as a long line fisherman off the coast of Cornwall. Carmen Velasquez, who at that point in her life had been called

Carmen Higgins, had kissed James goodbye as the sun came up and sadly supposed that that brief but joyful intermission in her life was over and that she would never see him again. But she had been wrong.

Less than two weeks later James appeared at the office where she worked in human resources for a small children's charity and told her that he hadn't been able to stop thinking about her. After giving the matter some thought Carmen took the afternoon off and booked a hotel room in which they discussed the matter further. She'd told Sophie on the very first afternoon the two women had met that she probably would have have felt more guilty about betraying her marriage if it wasn't for the fact that they didn't have any children and her husband was a twat, to quote Carmen directly. From that fateful afternoon onwards Carmen and James shared various hotel rooms located around the southern half of the country for over a year, all the while Carmen expecting the younger man to go off her at any moment and leave her to brace herself and get on with her loveless marriage, in the knowledge that she had at least tasted happiness for a short while.

Only James didn't go off her. James fell in love with her and begged her to run away to Cornwall to live with him. Finally, after eighteen months of mini-bars and shredded credit card statements, Carmen had taken the plunge, left her husband and reclaimed her much more impressive maiden name.

Never one to sit about on her arse, as Carmen put it most succinctly, she had taken on the local ailing tourist-reliant tea shop, deciding at last to turn her passion for pastries and baking into a career, and had transformed it into a thriving year-round concern within her first year of owning it. And she and James were still going strong; something that Sophie would have found heartening if it wasn't for the fact that she believed in the law of averages and surely the chances of there being two happy whirlwind romances blooming into two successful long-term relationships in the same Cornish town seemed rather remote. But even if Carmen had dibs on the fairy-tale ending coming true in the district it didn't stop Sophie from liking her enormously. It wasn't only the quality of her jam that led Sophie back to the Ye Olde Tea Shoppe so regularly, it was that she could really talk to Carmen and Carmen could certainly talk back. Carmen had stepped into the void that Cal had left, and Sophie found her forthright friendliness a literal port in the storm as she discovered her feet in the alien town.

'He's gonna what?' Carmen asked her, her thickly mascaraed eyes widening as Sophie whispered her fears over the lace-doilyed counter to her friend as Louis and the girls were sitting only a few feet away. 'Never! What, here?'

'I think so,' Sophie said. 'Although, to be fair, I'm not one hundred per cent sure. It's just Izzy said he had a big question to ask me and that he'd spent a lot of money on something really special.'

'Right. Well, I love that child, but isn't she the one who made a mouse out of cheese and kept it in a matchbox under the bed until it grew actual fur?' Carmen asked her practically. 'I'm not especially sure you should build assumptions on what she has to say, bless her. What about Bella? Bella's the one who normally knows what's going on. Bella knows what's going on from here to Land's End. That girl loves information.'

'Bella tried to cover it up, going on about hats and stuff. Bella was *definitely* trying to keep something a secret – it has to be a proposal, it fits the facts and it's not as if it would be the first time . . .'

'Wouldn't it?' Carmen's eyes widened a fraction further. 'What? Don't say you've turned him down before?'

'Not exactly,' Sophie said, experiencing a rather wonderful flashback of exactly what had happened next for a split second. '*Anyway*, that's not important at the moment. What's important is *what am I going to do?*'

Sophie glanced back at Louis who was letting Izzy dress him with a hat she'd fashioned out of paper napkins and some secret bubble gum. It was a good job he wasn't precious about his hair style, Sophie thought fondly.

'Say yes, you idiot,' Carmen told her in hushed tones. 'That feller's pure class, love. If I didn't love my James, I would, let me tell you.'

'Would you?' Sophie watched Louis, trying to see him through fresh eyes. To her he was the most beautiful creature that had ever walked the earth in the form of a man but it always interested her to know how other women saw him.

'Look at him,' Carmen all but growled. 'He's sex on legs, that one.'

'Sex on . . . ? Oh, never mind. The point is that any moment now he's going to ask me to marry him and I'm going to have to say no, Carmen, I'm going to have to turn him down.'

'Excuse me? Turn him down? But why?' Carmen fired the three questions at her in quick succession, each one gilded with incredulity.

'Because this is too much, too soon, too fast . . .' Sophie faltered. 'We've only been together six months. And it's not much longer than that since his wife died and he came back to look after his estranged children and found me as their guardian. There should be much more of waiting three days for a phone call, dates and dinners before any kind of proposal. An eventual key swap, a toothbrush left in the bathroom, and perhaps my own drawer to keep a few bits and bobs in. We're still at the unbridled-sex-wherever-we-happen-to-be stage. Besides, how's it going to look to the outside world? It will look like Louis is getting himself a free nanny with added sex benefits. How can I marry him when I don't even have my own knicker drawer?'

'But you have got a key,' Carmen told her. 'And Louis'd give you all the drawers you wanted if you asked him. I can think of two reasons why you should marry him now: one, if you keep doing it on his sofa you're going to slip a disc, and two, you love him, you silly mare. Who cares about tradition and dates and knicker drawers? If you love him, marry him – *now*.'

'The point is that there is no need to rush things. He's not ready to get married, no way, is he?'

'*He's* not ready, you say?' Carmen said, twisting her mouth into a tightly sceptical knot.

'Of course he's not!' Sophie said. 'Look at him, he's confused!'

Just at that moment Louis was surrendering while both his daughters held him in a deadlock and tickled him until his laughter filled the entire café and probably echoed out across the ocean all the way to New York City.

'He does look miserable, now you come to mention it,' Carmen said dryly. 'Look, sweetheart, you don't know that he's going to ask you anything yet. This is probably just you imposing your own fears and obsessions on something those two little lovelies said. In fact . . .' Carmen gasped and clutched her hand to her chest. 'Stone me, I know what it is they were on about!'

'Does anyone really still say "stone me"?' Sophie asked her. 'Go on, then, what's your theory?'

'It's not a theory, it's definitely what Izzy and Bella were trying not to tell you. It's obvious! Him and James and some of the other lads have been talking about a boys' surfing trip to Hawaii for ages, haven't they? Well, James has got together the cash to go now, and he's trying to get the others to put deposits down so that he can book early and get a good deal. He asked Louis about it last night. I bet that's what Louis wants to ask you, to look after kids and cats while he's away living it up in the sun ogling fit young birds in bikinis.'

'Really? That would be brilliant!' Sophie said, seizing on the thought.

'I'm not so keen on the young birds in bikinis myself,' Carmen said primly. 'But if you find that preferable to a proposal, then who am I to disagree?'

'It *could* just be that, couldn't it?' Sophie mused aloud. 'His photography business is pretty much established now and he's always wanted to go to Hawaii. Plus it fits the facts, doesn't it? It *is* a big question to ask and it *would* cost him a lot of money and he'd definitely ask the girls if they minded before he'd go.'

'Yes,' Carmen said. 'And he'd probably be a bit worried about telling you in case you scarper back off to London while he's not looking.'

'I reckon it's that,' Sophie said with more than a little relief as Carmen piled a cake stand high with scones, pots of clotted cream and jam. 'That's what it is. Oh, I'm such an idiot.'

'I'm not going to try and fight you on that one, you nutter,' Carmen said. 'Now, is there anything else?'

Sophie looked at the cake stand.

'Well, as it's my last ever cream tea, how about another pot of jam?'

'What were you two gassing about, all cloak and daggers?' Louis asked her as she set a calorie-laden tray down on the red and white gingham tablecloth.

'Oh, nothing,' Sophie said, trying her best to look casual and unconcerned and exactly like the sort of girlfriend who was very relaxed about her boyfriend taking a holiday without her. 'Girl talk. You know Carmen.'

For a good half an hour the table was largely silent as cream and jam and scones and cake were liberally sloshed around in a tactile feast of delight, one that Sophie was just as involved in as the girls. And then, finally, the replete and hyperactive children climbed off their chairs and went to look for entertainment.

'So, anyway – good news,' Louis said a little nervously. They sipped tea in relative peace while the girls helped Carmen clear the tables of place mats and menus, as the café was about to close.

'Oh yes, what's that?' Sophie concentrated hard on sounding casual.

'Mrs Alexander's coming over to babysit tonight. I'm taking you out to dinner at Alba.' Louis had made a reservation at the best fish restaurant in town, the one that looked out over the harbour where the fish it served were landed and where, if you were lucky enough to get a window seat, you could see the town's collection of rather dashing lifeboat men (including James) take the boat out for practice runs dressed head to foot in yellow rubber outfits that gave Carmen palpitations.

'You're taking me out to *dinner*? I mean, just you and me?' Sophie asked him. In the last six months not only had she never stayed the night at Louis's house but they also had never been on a date with just each other. They had spent more time together than Sophie had ever spent with anyone ever, but there had always been two other delightful little people tagging along – unless you counted the evenings in front of the electric fire after the girls had gone to bed, which were wonderful, but not exactly dates. It wasn't something that Sophie had wondered or worried about, it was just the facts of their situation. When she had decided she wanted to be with Louis she had decided she wanted to be with his children too; her love for the three of them, although entirely different had become as one. So this evening would be only their second ever date and, considering that the first one had been a bit of an accident resulting in unplanned and complicated sex, technically it could be called a first date.

'Yep, you can put on a frock, if you like, and maybe some of those high heels you carted down here with you,' Louis said, with a hopeful raise of a brow which made Sophie blush.

It was clear to Sophie that Louis was buttering her up for news of his departure, but she didn't mind. She thought it was sweet that he was so worried about how she would take the news of his impending holiday and she wanted to dress up; she wanted to dress up because he clearly wanted her to and that made her feel kind of sexy. Louis was probably the first man she had ever known who made her feel sexy. Other men had found her attractive. Jake Flynn, for example, the New York businessman she'd had a near miss with around about the same time that Louis and the girls came into her life. Jake looked at her and she could feel his desire for her, but for some reason it didn't penetrate through her outer layer – despite his square jaw, strong arms and excellent teeth. For a long time Sophie had thought that her inability to feel passion had to be because of something lacking in her, and then one night, on her first visit to the Avalon B&B back when they still barely knew each other, Louis had kissed her goodnight on the cheek. It was nothing, his lips barely grazed her skin, but she could not sleep for the rest of that night because of the way his touch had made her feel. Suddenly she'd felt frighteningly, viscerally alive.

'She's said she'll stay the night at my place if you don't mind locking up the B&B doors at midnight and making sure Mrs Tregowan gets her cocoa. Nancy will let herself in and start the breakfasts in the morning,' Louis said directing his gaze out to sea. 'I thought I could stay over with you.'

'Stay the night with me?' Sophie asked him.

Louis laughed. 'Yes, I don't know why we haven't thought of this before; you don't have to worry about the girls being freaked out, and I can finally wake up with you and see if it's true that you sleep like a princess.' He leaned a little closer to her. 'And you and I can make sleepy early morning love.' Louis saw the hesitation in her face. 'Come on, Sophie, don't tell me you don't want me staying over with you now? That's what serious couples do, you know. They sleep together, by which I mean actually sleep, overnight, and in a bed and everything.'

'I know, I know . . .' Sophie covered his hand with her own, suddenly yearning for the warmth of his bare skin against hers. 'We are a serious couple, aren't we?'

'I've never been more serious about anything in my life,' Louis said, looking back at her, the promise of what was to come lighting his eyes. 'The girls are stoked about it; they reckon they're going to have a midnight feast.'

'They can try,' Sophie joked. 'But I don't fancy their chances much. Beware the fool that tries to come down for breakfast at anything later than seven fifty-nine a.m., let alone tries to eat in bed at any hour of the day. Mrs Alexander takes no prisoners.'

'So I'll pick you up at eight, then,' Louis said, testing the words that were so unfamiliar. 'Be ready?'

'I'll be so ready,' Sophie said.

'I love you, Sophie Mills,' Louis told her. He must have told her the same thing many, many times, but every single time she heard those words Sophie still couldn't quite believe her luck. She was too happy, everything was too perfect. Sooner or later something would have to go wrong.

Chapter Three

As it turned out Sophie was ready by seven twenty-nine so she went downstairs to sit with Mrs Tregowan who was the only guest who ever made use of the guest sitting room. Grace would sit in the floral Windsor armchair opposite the TV and watch ITV for up to eighteen hours a day. She didn't watch any of the other channels. The other channels, she had told Sophie once, were far too full of doom and gloom and grey people in grey suits talking about real life.

'Give me a paternity test any day of the week, or a nice grisly murder,' Grace had told Sophie.

The first time Grace Tregowan had sworn, Sophie had been mildly shocked. She had forgotten that little old ladies were once young women and she supposed that just because one day she would be old, it wouldn't mean that she would suddenly stop thinking or feeling or swearing the way she did now. Sophie had been known to use the odd choice swear word in her time – but she was nowhere near as foul-mouthed as Grace.

Over the last six months she had got to know the 89-year-old well and now nothing Mrs Tregowan said could shock her any more. Grace had had a colourful life, to say the least: a life full of lovers, danger, sex and husbands – four of them. So perhaps it was that passion-filled life that meant that Grace was so content to finish her days in the Avalon guest house watching ITV while her motley collection of cash-grabbing relatives who never bothered to visit or call clamoured desperately for their inheritance. Grace had told Sophie in one of their very first conversations that she was now mainly staying alive just to 'piss the fuckers off' and, as her chequered career and collection of husbands had apparently left her enough money to pay Mrs Alexander's bill indefinitely, she was doing just that in floral print and bone-china style.

'What do you think of my outfit?' Sophie said, walking into the sitting room as the opening bars of the *Coronation Street* theme music played. She twirled in a soft-pink beaded chiffon dress with a drop waist and a fringe of beads all around the bottom. She'd been wearing it the first night that she had met Louis, although it fitted her a little differently now to how it had back then. Her bosom had blossomed another clear cup size and her hips and bottom were more generously rounded beneath the sleek material than they had once been, so that the dress revealed an extra centimetre or two of cleavage and clung a little more closely to her bottom. The effect of the cream-tea-related weight gain wasn't necessarily a bad one, Sophie thought as she looked in the mirror in her bedroom. Perhaps it was because Louis loved her body so much, but, recently, all of the angst and worry she had indulged in over the bulge of her tummy or the fact that she'd never suit a hipster jean had melted away. Sophie felt as if she had grown into her curves, as if her body was merely answering the inner hum of her desires, and for the first time in her life she was utterly comfortable in every inch of her skin. She felt womanly, something she had never ever imagined possible, and, at the end of the day, if she had to put her finger on why, it was a combination of two factors: cream teas and sex. But mostly sex.

'You look lovely, darling,' Grace told her, examining Sophie as if she were appraising her prize cow. 'I had a dress not dissimilar to that before the war, you know, 1938, if I recall correctly. I was living in Paris, in Montparnasse, with this painter called Jacques Bellaconti; lovely man, enormous cock, but he did go on something rotten. Communist, he was, and I've never yet met a Communist with a sense of humour. He said he was a surrealist, but he didn't really have talent. Still, Jacques had lovely hands and he knew what to do with them . . .' Grace trailed off for a second and Sophie got the distinct impression that the old lady was fondly remembering at least one part of his anatomy in action. 'Anyway, I had a dress just like that, only I was as thin as a whip – there was nothing to me. That was the way they liked it back then. That was the way Jacques liked it, anyway, and he always preferred me with my clothes off. I expect your young man's the same.'

Sophie blinked and caught her refection in Mrs Alexander's gilt-framed mirror.

'He does, rather, but given that nudity isn't all that acceptable while out for dinner, do you think this will do? This is our first proper date in . . . well, since I came down here, really.'

Grace smiled at Sophie, her blue eyes still bright and clear. 'You look lovely, darling. So much better than when you first arrived. You were too thin, with all those dark shadows and anxious looks. The sea air must agree with you and all of the fucking, of course . . . sex is a marvellous restorative tonic. It's the principal reason I've lived as long as I have.'

'That'll be it,' Sophie said as Grace's attention drifted back to the TV. She went to the window and, after some moments rifling through Mrs Alexander's various layers of lace curtains, she tweaked back enough diaphanous material to be able to see out. It was dark outside and Sophie felt the skin on her arms prickle with goose bumps as she imagined the chill of the night air cutting through the thin material of her dress.

There was something else, too, prickling at the back of her neck.

It was fear, Sophie realised. She was full of first-date nerves. She hadn't felt this tense and high on adrenalin since that day when she had turned up at Louis's house and told him she wanted to be with him. Everything that had happened since had been something of a rollercoaster, and she had been speeding along up every incline and down every descent caught up in the euphoria of love. They talked, of course, but never really about anything, never about their pasts, their dreams or their fears, and much of the time the girls were there, twin suns for their conversation and attention to revolve around. And obviously they had large amounts of fabulous sex, but they had never been alone together in *this* way. There was something frighteningly formal about her and Louis going on a date, even if she had just been telling Carmen that she and Louis didn't date enough. What if they didn't have anything to say once they were dressed up and staring at each other over a flower arrangement and a tea light? What if, when it came to it, their relationship was based entirely on their shared love for the girls and really excellent sex? What if, without Bella and Izzy there, or the opportunity to kiss each other stupid, it turned out that they didn't like the same things, had no common interests, and didn't even find the same things funny? Cal was always telling Sophie that she was the least funny person he knew; what if Louis realised that she was really quite dull? What then? What if the man she was hoping was her soulmate discovered he didn't like the way she chewed her food? Sophie bit her lip anxiously as she waited for the security light in the porch to switch on as Louis walked up the pathway.

Soon she would really have to start thinking about what she was doing. She'd have to start planning again. In another six months her savings would run out and if she was going to stay in Cornwall she'd need to think about finding a way to earn money down here. Soon the short-term let she had on her flat would come to an end and she'd need to decide whether to let it again or put it on the market. Soon the demands of daily life would come crashing in and she'd need to know if the life she was leading now could be permanent or if it was just a castle of dreams which could be blown away at any moment by a passing gust of reality. But not yet, Sophie told herself as she watched the path. Not quite yet.

All she had to concentrate on tonight was being the cool, hip kind of girlfriend who looks after a man's children and cats while he goes on holiday with the lads, because Carmen had to be right, that had to be what he was going to ask her. Yes, there was the argument that she had looked after the girls and at least one cat on her own before and it hadn't been a problem (if you discount all the criminal damage), and that his going away for a couple of weeks hardly merited a special dinner and a nice frock, but perhaps he *would* make a big deal about asking her now. After all, their relationship was new. He might think she would take his going on a lads' holiday at this point as a bit of a snub, and, if it hadn't been for a warning from Carmen, she might have struggled with the idea of his being so keen to get away from her already, especially when she was still keen to spend every second of her life in his company. At least, she would have struggled at first because one of the other things she had discovered about being in love was that it made her far less sensible and prosaic and far more prone to emotional outbursts which, if a girl wasn't very careful, could make people think she was mad. Fortunately, Carmen had given her the chance to process the idea, to rationalise it and prepare. So that when Louis asked her, she could appear serene and reasonable. There would be no bursting into resentful tears on the spot, and she could hide all those impulses without him ever knowing about them. No, all she had to worry about was trying to be witty over dinner, chewing with her mouth closed, and whether or not Louis would fall down the gap between the twin beds in her room, because it was definitely the surfing trip he wanted to ask her about. That had to be it: the expense, the secrets, asking the girls' permission. That, most definitely and absolutely, was the only thing he could possibly want to ask her, Sophie told herself as she waited for the glare of the security light on the path.

'I tell you what,' Grace interrupted Sophie's thoughts. 'That Ken Barlow. I would.'

When the B&B security light blinked on it revealed that Louis was wearing a suit, causing Sophie to think two things: first, that her boyfriend looked really good in a suit, and second, that she hadn't even known he'd owned one.

'Well,' Louis said, looking around him at the chic modern interior of Alba, as the waiter poured their wine. 'This is nice.'

They had been given the best seat in the house, on the first floor in front of the floor-to-ceiling plate-glass window that looked out over the harbour and across the sea. It was dark and blustery outside, of course, but through the insulated glass Sophie could hear and sense the movement of the ocean only a few feet away, and all that fathomless power churning just on the other side of the centimetre-thick glass made her feel a little as if she were perched on the uppermost arc of a roller coaster that was about to plummet. Or perhaps it was something else that was giving her that feeling. She decided not to dwell on it.

'Yes, this is nice,' Sophie said, picking up her glass and sipping from it as she looked out of the window. For a second she stared at her ghostly reflection, a pale imitation of herself in the glass, and then away. She was very tense for a woman on a second first date.

The pair of them examined the menus in silence as Sophie listened to the noise of other people's conversations singing in her ears. It seemed as if the whole of St Ives was on a date tonight and they all had something hilarious and fascinating to say.

Say something, Sophie urged herself. *Go on, say something witty and charming and romantic that will make him smile and look at you through his lashes like he does when he's thinking about how to get you naked.*

'Mrs Tregowan says that sex is a tonic,' Sophie blurted out, seemingly at exactly the same moment that everybody else in the busy restaurant took a break from talking to drink or chew.

Louis examined his menu for one beat more and then glanced up at her. 'No wonder I'm so fit, then,' he said. Sophie could tell he was trying not to smile, which made her want to smile.

'Sorry,' she said, lowering her voice as she leaned towards him. 'I was trying to think of something witty and flirty to say and that's what came out.'

The two of them sat watching each other over the tops of their menus for a moment longer.

He should say something now, Sophie thought as she gazed into his black eyes. *It's his turn.*

But Louis didn't say anything, he just watched her face closely as if he were trying to decipher or decide something that lay somewhere in her eyes. Finally Sophie broke the moment by glancing down at her menu. When she looked back up she saw that Louis was staring intently at his menu, but she was almost certain that he wasn't really reading it. He was thinking. *What was he thinking? Surely breaking the news of a lads' holiday to her couldn't be this intimidating. Unless . . . unless . . .*

'Are you OK?' Sophie asked him despite the fact that Cal had reliably informed her that that was the second worst possible question to ask a reticent man, beaten only by 'What are you thinking?'

Louis looked up quickly as if she'd startled him, his skin flushing red across the bridge of his nose.

'It's just that you seem a bit tense,' Sophie prompted, deciding she couldn't bear the tension for much longer.

'Do I?' Louis said, polishing off his glass of wine in three long gulps and then topping it up before the wine waiter could get near. 'That's funny, because I'm not tense at all. I'm really, really happy.' He leaned over the table and picked up her hand purposefully. 'Actually, the thing is that I'm the happiest I have ever been in my whole life and it's all because of you. I really love you, Sophie, I hope you realise that. I hope you know that I love you and that I am committed one hundred per cent to making this work between us. I know that I haven't been the most . . . mature man in the past. I know I walked out on my children because I couldn't handle Carrie's affair. I know that I rushed into marrying Carrie because I didn't know what I wanted or needed back then. But I don't regret it. I don't regret anything because I'd never regret having known Carrie or having my two beautiful daughters in my life. And now I have you too . . . or at least I hope I have you. Look, I want to ask you something and I was actually going to wait until dessert but it seems that I can't behave like a normal person until I've actually said the words, so here goes . . .'

'Louis.' Sophie panicked. Suddenly she wanted very much for Carmen to be right. She wanted that to be the conversation they were about to have and no other. 'Look, relax. This is not as big a deal as you think it is . . .'

'What isn't?' Louis asked her uncertainly.

'Carmen told me what you were going to ask . . .' Sophie pressed on, hopeful that she could somehow manipulate the moment into the one she was prepared for and then go on to enjoy two fish courses before Alba's sticky toffee pudding which was famous for miles around without having to have made a decision that was any more life changing than whether she should have clotted cream or ice cream to accompany it.

'Carmen told you?' Louis looked horrified. 'I can't believe she'd do that!'

'Well, you know Carmen,' Sophie said extra breezily, her anxiety exacerbated by how dismayed Louis was. 'She can't keep a secret and, anyway . . . it's fine. I don't mind at all. I'm not in the least bit bothered.

'You're not *bothered*?' Louis's face froze and Sophie ploughed on, sure she could somehow blunder her way out of this.

'No, of course I'm not. I know what you want to ask me might seem like a bit of a cheek after us only being together officially for six months, but we're both adults – we can take it!' She grinned at him. 'So come on, out with it then. Ask me!'

'I'm not sure I want to now,' Louis said, his ruddy face blanched of colour.

'Oh, don't be so silly!' Sophie said carefully. 'I know what you want to ask me, and I'm totally relaxed about it. Fully chilled out and calm.'

'Fully chilled out and calm,' Louis repeated, topping up his wine again. 'I don't really know how I feel about that.'

'Well, what did you want me to be like?' Sophie told him, with more than an edge of hysteria sharpening her tone. 'All stressy and clingy and needy and freaked out, acting like a headless chicken caught in some massive headlights? I'm not like that. I'm not that kind of girlfriend. I can totally handle it.'

Louis's expression was stricken as he chewed on his lip.

'You look a little bit like you'd rather be anywhere else than here right now,' he said slowly.

'Fine, don't ask me,' Sophie said, crossing her arms and leaning back in her chair. 'In fact, let's not talk about this now at all, let's just have dinner and forget about it, shall we?'

'No.' Louis looked adamant. 'I've made arrangements and got prepared and took my suit to the dry cleaners . . . I mean, I still want to . . . it's just that this isn't how I pictured it going . . .'

'OK, let's sort this out right now,' Sophie said as if she was chairing a board meeting back in London. 'Let's cut to the chase and then maybe we can order some food because I'm starving. You don't have to ask me, because the answer is yes, OK?' Sophie smiled at a shocked Louis. 'Yes, yes, yes. I'm totally fine with it. I'm more than fine, I'm happy. So it's a yes to the question you were going to ask me. Now can we move on?'

'Yes?' Louis's expression was caught halfway between confusion and a smile. 'I mean that's great, but this is a bit weird. This isn't how I thought I would feel when you said yes at all.'

'How did you think you'd feel?' Sophie asked him, a touch impatiently, shaking her head.

'I thought there'd be crying and surprise and joy and . . . hugging,' Louis said.

'Louis, all you're doing is asking me to look after the girls, Tango and Artemis while you go on a lads' surfing holiday to Hawaii!' Sophie exclaimed so that more than a few pairs of eyes swivelled in her direction. 'That's all you're asking me, isn't it? That's what Carmen said. So why would I cry? I'm not mental, you know.'

'What?' Louis's jaw dropped. 'That's what Carmen told you?'

'Yes!' Sophie said, desperately. 'Now can we please move on? I think the kitchen closes at ten!'

'Er, yes, you see – that's not exactly the question I wanted to ask you,' Louis said, catching Sophie's gaze and holding it until her racing heart gradually began to slow and she found that she could look away. 'That might be what Carmen told you and that might be what you think you'd rather hear, but *I* think that you and I both know that isn't the question I want to ask you.'

'It's not?' Sophie's voice trembled.

'It's not, and I've never seen a more terrified and panic-stricken woman in my life before but I'm getting to know you and I know that sometimes you need to feel the fear and do it anyway – so here goes.' Louis stood up and patted his pockets before producing a small dark blue leather box and opening it to reveal a diamond ring, nestling in a midnight-blue exterior.

Sophie leaned back as far in her chair as its rigid back would allow her and felt her heart cease to beat as he dropped to one knee in front of her. Dimly she wondered how long that particular state of affairs could continue before she keeled over and died. And at that precise moment she would have been relieved if it was any time soon.

'Sophie Mills,' Louis said, commanding the attention of the whole restaurant, 'I love you and I want to be with you for the rest of my life. Please will you marry me?'

About fifty people held their breath as Sophie looked first at Louis and then at the ring. She knew that she had to say something, that now was the appropriate time to say *something*, but for what seemed like an eternity nothing would come out, not even the outward breath that her lungs were begging her to take.

'Um, right,' Louis spoke, looking around at the other diners.

'You might not like the ring, and if you don't we can change it. Only I thought you would. It's from the 1930s and is in a deco platinum setting. It's not huge, it's half-carat, but it's good quality and it took me ages to choose it. I thought it was classy and stylish and timeless and ... silent – like you. Say something, Soph, my knee's gone numb and everyone's looking at us.'

Abruptly Sophie felt her heart starting to beat again and she felt a rush of blood to her cheeks. She exhaled, and when she took another breath she felt tears brimming in her eyes.

'Oh Louis,' she said, her voice husky and taut.

'What?' Louis asked her with a hopeful smile. 'Are there going to be tears and joy and hugging, or just tears? Still feeling calm and chilled?'

'Not exactly,' Sophie half sobbed and half laughed. 'You've frightened me half to death!'

'Not the textbook response when it comes to proposals,' Louis said smiling. 'But it beats the dumbstruck horror I was getting.'

Sophie laughed and got up and took Louis's hand, hauling him to his feet so that they were both standing opposite each other.

'I feel frightened and nervous and a bit sick and quite giddy,' Sophie said. 'And a lot like a huge semi-psychotic idiot. Are you sure you want to marry me?'

'Despite your rather casual acquaintance with sanity I still want you to be my wife, Sophie,' Louis told her, his voice low and serious. 'So? Do you want to marry me?'

Sophie nodded her head. 'Yes,' she said. 'Yes, I think I do.'

Sophie sat bolt upright in bed, her heart pounding. It was a while before her eyes adjusted to the half-light and she took some deep breaths as she waited for whatever dream had woken her up frightened and full of panic to fade away. And then she realised. It wasn't a dream. Louis had actually asked her to marry him and she had said yes. She'd made a decision about the rest of her life. She'd said *yes*.

'Morning,' Louis mumbled sleepily. Sophie felt his finger drift up her bare back and gently wind a rope of her hair around his wrist, tugging her back down on to the bed. It turned out that she had been right to worry about the gap between the twin beds. After several attempts and one incident that could have sent the pair of them to Accident and Emergency with an awful lot of explaining to do, they'd given up on the twin beds and ended up curled up tightly together in just one of them. Exactly as they had done on the very first night they'd slept together, Sophie remembered. The night after they had brought the girls back to St Ives for the first time since they had lost their mother. It had been a difficult and dark day, a day full of pain but also breakthroughs and some joy. It had been the day when Sophie had finally said goodbye to her old friend, the day she really believed that she was dead. That night her jumble of attraction, anger, mistrust and longing for Louis had boiled over and she'd gone to bed with him, uncertain of what it meant or where it would lead because, for a few hours at least, she hadn't cared as long as he had his arms around her. The next morning she had woken with her heart pounding just as she had this morning. She'd run away from Louis and the girls and she'd tried her best to go back to her normal life as if none of this had happened. She'd tried and she had failed. Now, on this second morning in a single bed with Louis, Sophie recalled all the angst, anxiety and guilt she'd been plagued with that night, wondering if any trace of it tainted this morning, but there was nothing, so why was her heart beating like a drum?

She had never been happier, more filled to the brim with

joy, and yet at exactly the same moment she had never been more afraid.

Louis reached across her and picked up her left hand, looking at the ring that glinted faintly on her finger in the morning light.

'I always thought I liked you best when you were totally naked, but now I realise I like you to leave a little something on.' He brought the ring, and her hand, to his lips and kissed it. 'Don't ever take this off.'

'Really?' Sophie asked him. 'Only I was thinking, we probably don't want the whole world to know right away so it might be best if—'

'The whole world does know.' Louis smiled as he kissed her fingertips. 'After the performance that we put on last night it would be impossible for the whole world not to.'

'Well yes, that *is* true. All those people know, but I mean Bella and Izzy. Mrs Alexander. The school mums – they'll have a field day. And Carmen! Carmen won't shut up about it. Not to mention my mother and Cal! Cal will never believe it. Then there's Christina and the girls back home. And Carrie's mum, we have to tell Carrie's mum. There are a lot of people we need to tell so perhaps till we have I shouldn't wear the ring. Not until we're officially official . . .'

'Rubbish,' Louis said. 'Just tell everyone. That's what you do, you get engaged and then you tell everyone and everyone is excited and pleased for you.'

'Yes, I know.' Sophie stretched out her fingers to look at the ring. 'It's just it's such a public thing, isn't it? An engagement ring – people look at it and they know everything about you.'

'Well, they know that you're engaged,' Louis said, twisting the ring full circle on her finger. 'It's a little bit loose, though. I'd hate for you to lose it. I know, we'll take it into Newquay today and get it re-sized. We can take the girls, they will be so excited. They've been trying really hard not to talk about bridesmaids' dresses in front of you for two whole days but I must warn you, there's a fight breaking out between pink and lilac and there has been some mention of wings.'

'Wings?' Sophie said absently as she studied the ring that suddenly said so much about her. 'That sounds nice.'

Louis propped himself up on his elbow and looked into her face.

'Sophie, if there's *anything*, any worry or uncertainty that you have, then please, tell me now,' he said, a lazy smile on his lips which Sophie knew meant he didn't for a second think that she had a single one.

'It's only that the rest of our lives is a long time,' Sophie said slowly. She watched a slight frown form between Louis's brows and instantly she wanted to make it disappear again.

'I don't mean I don't want to marry you, I'm just saying are you sure, Louis? Are you sure you know me well enough? After all, we haven't been together very long and we're still in that first flush of sex-fuelled love. Maybe we should wait a bit . . .'

'What, until we start getting bored and stop making love?' Louis laughed.

'No, it's just . . . I never want you to regret me,' Sophie said, suddenly serious. 'I want you to be certain because I couldn't ever bear for you to regret me.'

'Sophie,' Louis traced a finger along the curve of her cheek, 'life goes by in a flash, in the blink of an eye, and then it's gone. I'm certain that I love you and that I need you and that for as long as I'm here on earth I want you to be with me. I couldn't be more certain. I certainly couldn't be more certain that I am going to kiss you right now.'

It was hard to concentrate as Louis kissed her, his hands

rediscovering her skin under the covers as he pulled her body hard against his and indeed, as she felt his lips on her breasts and his fingers between her thighs, Sophie found it hard to think about anything at all other than how much she wanted him. But there was still one question, just an ember of a query, flickering dimly in the corner of her mind. An ember which blinked out the moment she felt Louis move inside her.

The question she had asked herself and had forgotten in a second was: was *she* certain? There hadn't been time for an answer.

Chapter Four

It was a busy Saturday morning in Newquay. The tourists had fallen away but the students were back in town and even after a summer spent largely in a small town rammed up to its eye teeth with holidaymakers Sophie found the bustle of the vibrant town hard to adjust to, which was foolish because she was a city girl, a Londoner born and bred, and used to elbowing her way through crowds along with the best of them. But something in her had changed since Bella and Izzy had burst into her life. For the first time ever she felt vulnerable, as if the merest glancing blow would bruise her badly. The outside world seemed like a much more frightening place with danger lurking in every corner that Sophie had been mercifully unaware of before she had two children to worry about. Carrie's sudden and pointless death had given her a sense of her own mortality, but more than that it had made her see how fragile the lives of those around her were, too. How easy, if improbable, it would be to lose the people she loved.

Apart from this new constant nagging anxiety she was also finding it hard to adjust to her new persona. Sophie was aware that she wasn't Sophie Mills career-girl-about-town any more. She wasn't even former-career-girl-about-St-Ives now. She was Sophie Mills, official engage-ee. Or rather, fiancée, Louis reminded her, pointing out that the word engage-ee didn't actually exist.

'You are my fiancée and I am yours,' he'd told her happily as they walked up the garden path to his house earlier that morning.

'I know, I know,' Sophie said. 'It's just going to take me a while to get my head around that word being associated with *me*. I mean, for starters, it's awfully *French*.'

'OK, if you don't like fiancée, how about betrothed? How about I call you my betrothed?'

'Mmmmm.' Sophie sounded sceptical.

'What – too medieval?' Louis asked her.

'No, it's just that it's a very formal word,' Sophie said.

'I see where you're coming from, but I think getting engaged stroke betrothed is supposed to be a tiny bit formal,' Louis pointed out.

'I know, I'm just saying that there should be a third word, a fun word. A word that isn't quite so loaded.'

'Loaded?' Louis raised a brow. 'OK, I'll give it some thought.'

'Well?' Mrs Alexander opened Louis's front door before he could fit the key into the lock, her eyebrow cocked and loaded. She'd obviously been waiting for them by the living-room window.

'The Avalon has not burnt down and Grace is absolutely fine,' Sophie reassured her. 'How are the girls, did they run you ragged?'

'They did no such thing,' Mrs Alexander said. 'It takes a lot more than a couple of sweet little poppets like those two to get the better of me. That cat of yours, on the other hand, nearly had my eye out when I tried to pet her.'

'That's because she doesn't like people; I did mention it,' Sophie said, wondering if Mrs Alexander might consider letting them in any time soon. Sometimes she took her scary land-lady persona a little too far, especially as everyone who knew her, knew that she had a heart of gold beating under her housecoat. 'She likes her space and she's very protective of her privacy. She takes her time over forming relationships ... she's a rescue cat, you know. I've had her for years now and she still doesn't like me. I try not to take it personally.'

'Good job, by the sounds of it,' Mrs Alexander told her. She appraised Sophie with a cool blue-eyed gaze. 'So are you going to marry him?'

Sophie looked at Louis. 'Did the whole world know what you were planning?' she asked.

'More or less,' Louis said, shrugging apologetically.

'And are you?' Mrs Alexander pressed her, still barring the doorway as if somehow their entry was dependent on Sophie's answer.

'It seems that I am,' Sophie affirmed, feeling Louis's arm on her waist. Then, worrying that she hadn't seemed suffi-ciently happy she added, 'Louis and I are officially engaged to be married. It's very exciting.'

Mrs Alexander beamed quite unexpectedly, turning her habitually sour expression into one of pure delight that caught Sophie quite off guard. 'I'm thrilled for you, darling,' she said, hugging Sophie with surprising fervour and releasing her just as swiftly. 'I'll need a month's notice on the room if you're going to want your deposit back.'

'Oh, I don't expect I'll be moving out for ages yet,' Sophie said, avoiding Louis's eye.

'Anyway, the girls have been waiting all morning for you. They've got a little show prepared.' Mrs Alexander stepped aside to allow them into the house, smiling at Louis. 'I wanted to make sure everything was OK before I unleashed them just in case Sophie turned you down, love.' She fluttered her lashes at Louis, casting him her best 'come hither' glance which, if they didn't know Mrs Alexander, most people would find quite intimidating.

'OK, girls,' Mrs Alexander shouted up the stairs. 'Take it away!'

There was a burst of excited laughter from up the stairs, the yowl of a very angry grey cat that whizzed past and out the front door at a rate of knots with what looked suspiciously like a pink bow tied around its neck, followed in much more sedate fashion by Bella and Izzy as they paraded down the stairs humming a passable version of 'Here Comes the Bride', Bella hefting the much more submissive and lace-laden Tango under one arm.

The shower curtain had been detached more with force than care, as far as Sophie could tell as she looked at the ripped holes where the rings should have fitted through, and turned into a white plastic shiny cape. Bella's pink flowery bedroom curtain had been fashioned into a skirt worn over two or three fairy and Disney princess costumes, and what blooms of late summer had been found in the garden had been savagely hacked down and stuck into the girls' hair behind their ears. They had finished off their bridal look with a generous helping of Sophie's second-best make-up. (She had learned long ago never to leave her best stuff lying around.)

'We are your bridesmaids, Aunty Sophie!' Izzy shrieked as they finally reached the bottom of the stairs in one piece, which was a minor miracle in itself given that their trains contravened most health and safety laws. 'We are, aren't we? We ARE your bridesmaids?'

'Aren't we?' Bella reiterated, her expression a good deal more solemn and just a tiny bit more threatening than Izzy's, despite the two rosy dots she had lipsticked on to either cheek. Sophie knelt down and put an arm around each of them, glancing over her shoulder at Louis who was leaning on the banister at the bottom of the stairs.

'Do you think it's a good idea for me to marry your daddy?' Sophie asked them, aware a beat too late that she didn't really have a contingency plan if either of them said no.

'I do,' Izzy said nodding as she spoke. 'Because there will be a *massive* party and a wedding cake and I've seen a picture of a wedding cake and it was *massive*. And you love cake, Aunty Sophie, so getting married will make you really, really—'

'Massive?' Mrs Alexander offered.

'No. Happy, silly!' Izzy giggled and kissed Sophie on the cheek. 'You will be happy.'

'Excellent,' Sophie said looking at Bella and raising a hopeful eyebrow.

Bella twisted her mouth into the sideways knot that Sophie had come to learn often preceded a difficult question. She braced herself.

'I do think it's a good idea for you to marry Daddy,' she said slowly as if she were working out her thoughts as she spoke. 'Mostly.'

'Mostly?' Sophie asked her gently. 'What do you mean, Bella?'

Bella shrugged. 'I just mean mostly,' she said. 'I want you and Daddy to be married, mostly.'

'OK,' Sophie said, briefly pressing the palm of her hand against Bella's cheek. 'Well, if you think of what the mostly bit means then you will tell me, won't you? Because how you feel is more important to me than anything and anyway, as if I could ever possibly have any other bridesmaids apart from you two, even if I wanted to. Although I think we might have to work on your look a little bit.'

'I was thinking of wings,' Izzy said. 'Glittery ones.'

'And I was thinking of ponies,' Bella said, catching Izzy's

enthusiasm and making her momentary reticence seem like a passing whim. 'I thought we could ride ponies down the aisle. That would be really cool!'

The word aisle made Sophie think of a million different things at once. But principally churches, dresses, guests, an actual wedding which would result in an actual marriage, which would mean that she had made a real and life-changing decision that would be finally finalised in about the most final way that a decision possibly could be. With a legally binding contract. Suddenly she found that she was the one who was 'mostly' glad that she had agreed to marry Louis Gregory.

'Well, we can sort out all the details later,' Louis said, catching the look in Sophie's eyes and peeling himself off the banister to help her to her feet. 'For now we're going to Newquay to get Sophie's engagement ring re-sized,' Louis had said.

'Can we wear this?' Bella asked him, gesturing at her bridesmaid-meets-Vegas look.

It would have been churlish to refuse.

It wasn't a long journey to Newquay but it had been a very loud one.

'Aunty Sophie,' Izzy had asked, 'who will you be once you and Daddy are married?'

'Who will I be?' Sophie had glanced at Louis who was driving. 'I'll be me, of course.'

'Mrs Sophie Gregory,' Louis said proudly.

'I'm not changing my name,' Sophie said without thinking. She glanced at Louis, unable to read his expression from his profile. 'I mean, no one changes their name these days, plus I've got my professional reputation to think of. Sophie Mills has a reputation in the events industry. No one will have heard of Sophie Gregory.'

She didn't mention the other niggling anxiety that had popped into her head the second Louis mentioned her potential name. She'd already taken Carrie's children, admittedly at the wishes of her friend, and now she also had her dead friend's husband. To take her name, too, seemed a step too far. It was as if she were really trying to walk in the shoes of that mythic first wife, just like a latter-day second Mrs De Winter obsessing over Rebecca.

'How about Mrs Aunty Sophie?' Izzy hazarded.

'I like Sophie Mills,' Bella said, providing Sophie with an unexpected ally. 'And just because her and Daddy will be married doesn't mean that she won't be our Aunty Sophie any more.'

'Exactly,' Sophie said.

'But what if I want to call her—' Izzy began.

'GIRLS!' Louis had raised his voice to cut cross whatever Izzy had been about to say. 'That's enough questions, you're giving Sophie a headache! Look, we're here now. Stop shouting and show me how pretty and ladylike and bridesmaidsy you can be. Because only quiet, respectable, ladylike girls can be bridesmaids.'

'With wings,' Izzy muttered under her breath.

'At all,' Louis said.

'Except', Bella had told him, looking at him from beneath her fringe, 'that we are your daughters and so we are definitely going to be bridesmaids *at all costs*.'

Sophie followed the Gregorys through the shopping crowds at a slight delay. She knew that Louis had guessed that she was feeling a bit overwhelmed by the maelstrom of opinions and questions that the girls had thrown at her and she loved the fact that he knew her well enough to give her this small distance between them while she adjusted to everything that was happening. The very fact that he had discovered that about her gave her joy in itself. It was evidence, a tangible example that showed her how their relationship had deepened since they'd first met and, more than that, she had discovered that she wanted to make him happy, and that she'd do more or less anything to help him achieve that. That had to be love.

What she needed to do, Sophie decided, was to take baby steps. First step: she *was* in love with Louis Gregory. The wild leaping of her heart whenever she stood next to him proved that conclusively – she had already taken that step and she thought she'd adjusted to the news rather well, what with all the sex and happiness it entailed. Second step: she had very recently agreed to marry him, which would take a bit of getting used to, but she was confident that she would get used to it because, after all, she had got very used to step one alarmingly quickly. Third step: she'd have to think about some sort of wedding eventually although she'd read in an old edition of *Tatler* she'd found in the doctor's surgery when Izzy had a chest infection that long engagements were the latest trend, so perhaps it didn't have to be that soon. Fourth step: that would be the actually being married to Louis step, the part where she moved out of the Avalon and in with him and the girls. Then there was the fifth and final step. The fifth step would be the whole of the rest of her life with Louis and the girls. The rest of her natural life, being fully married.

As her heart was gripped by a sudden vision of eternity Sophie decided then and there not to dwell on any of the steps past one and two. One and two really were the only pertinent steps at present. After all, she hadn't even told her mother she was engaged yet.

As long as she had a little more time to simply enjoy the

being in love with Louis bit and getting her head around the being engaged to him, then Sophie was certain she'd be able to deal with the other issues eventually. She'd said yes now; there was no going back.

The ring would be ready and perfectly sized within a couple of hours, so Louis suggested lunch. Bella suggested brides-maid shopping and Sophie suggested the pub. In the end they compromised by going to the Bell which passed a Pronuptia shop on they way and served food all day. As Sophie sipped her gin and tonic she watched Louis and the girls: talking, chatting, planning, laughing. They, the Gregorys, were a family now. A proper unit, something that they had not been till very recently. And Sophie was proud that she had helped make that happen in some small way. Or in a rather large way, actually, she admitted to herself, quietly blowing her own trumpet. It was Sophie who had taken Bella and Izzy in when all she had to offer them was microwavable ready meals and a one-bedroom flat share with a maiden aunt and a neurotic cat. And it was Sophie who had employed a private detective to track the girls' father down after Carrie had died. It was Sophie who had stood guard over Bella and Izzy while she tried to work out if the wildly handsome stranger who happened to be their father was friend or foe, and it was she who had done her best to reconcile the three of them, even when Bella still insisted that she hated the father who had abandoned her. Sophie had bonded them back together and she had done it for Carrie, for her dear friend who, for so many years, had always been the best, most free and wildest part of her.

Sophie looked at Louis brushing a tangle of dark hair from his eyes, his smile casting shadows in his stubble as he laughed at something Bella said.

On many of the nights that she spent alone in the B&B

Sophie would wonder if she would ever have fallen for Louis if she hadn't met him in that way and at that time. Would she have fallen for him if he hadn't have been a confused man, a jilted husband suffering from guilt and loss? If she hadn't loved the woman that he had once loved, or fallen so hard for his strange, lost daughters?

'Hey, Wendy? Wendy Churchill, it *is* you!' Sophie was snapped out of her thoughts as Louis called after a woman who had been sidling passed their table. 'Don't try and pretend you don't know who I am!' Louis teased her jovially.

Sophie studied the woman's face as she slowly turned to face Louis. Perhaps a couple of years older than Sophie, she had reddish hair pulled back into a ponytail.

'Louis Gregory,' the woman said slowly. 'Last I heard, you'd moved away.'

'I came back.' Louis grinned as he stood up. 'And so did you, by the looks of things! Last time I saw you . . . well, it was over twenty years ago.'

Sophie blinked as her betrothed stepped out from their table and engulfed the woman in a huge bear hug. She was smaller than Sophie, qualifying as petite, with slender hips and narrow shoulders, and the sort of pretty girly elfin looks that Sophie hadn't realised, till that very second, that she despised. Abruptly Sophie stopped feeling womanly and sexually powerful and started feeling like an ungainly oaf, big and lumpy. She sucked her stomach in and sat up straight.

'How long since you lived up North?' Louis asked, glancing at his girls. Izzy was doing her best to get the entire contents of one mini-sachet of ketchup on to a single French fry. Bella, though, was staring hard at this Wendy woman from under- neath her fringe and listening intently to every word that was being said. Bella liked to know everything that was going on; she spent much of her young life trying to ensure that no piece of information, no matter how trivial it might seem, ever got past her.

'Moved back down here about a year ago, I've got my own business – running costs down here were cheaper and I missed it; it's always been home.' Wendy smiled. 'What about you? Where did you go and why did you come back?'

'Well, it's a long story but basically I lost my wife, in a car accident not so long ago. I came back to look after my two daughters Bella and Izzy ...' Louis gestured at his duet of daughters.

'Good afternoon,' Bella said gravely.

'They're yours?' Wendy Churchill said, glancing briefly at the two girls, without returning Bella's greeting. 'You're a *dad*?'

'Yes,' Louis laughed. 'No need to sound so shocked, Wend! Bella is seven, Izzy is four. I'm a dad twice over and after a serious false start I'm not doing too bad a job of it now. In fact, thing's are going really great and this—' Finally Louis gestured towards where Sophie was waiting to be introduced but Wendy ignored her. She keep watching Bella who, after a second, wrinkled her nose and then wrestled the pot of ketchup sachets from Izzy, choosing to ignore the stranger while she righted the injustice of Izzy getting all of the sauce.

'They're exactly like you,' Wendy said slowly, as if she were processing some other hidden piece of information.

'Are they?' Louis looked pleased. 'I can see it with Bella, but Izzy is the image of her mum.'

'No, they both look exactly like ... you.' Wendy stopped, glanced over her shoulder, and then seemed to collect herself. Suddenly she beamed at Louis.

'God, I'm sorry, it's just it's been such a long time since I last saw you. I still think of you as sixteen, the great tall, lanky lad that you were. Bumping into you now – a real grown-up man with kids is a bit of a shock.'

'*You* haven't aged at all,' Louis told Wendy, which made Sophie raise her eyebrows a little because if this woman was about Louis's age, some old school friend or something, then there was no way she could look the same as she had done at sixteen. Not unless she'd had wrinkles and roots back then, too.

'Daddy, who is this lady and what does she want with us?' Bella returned her attention to the stranger. 'And why is she staring at us as if we are animals in a zoo?'

Sophie beamed at her; she could always rely on Bella to ask the pertinent questions.

'This', Louis said, finally tearing his eyes off Wendy's face, 'is my old friend Wendy Churchill. We used to go to school together.'

'And we were a little bit more than friends,' Wendy said, smiling coyly, which Sophie found made her want to slap Wendy Churchill quite hard.

'Oh, well.' Louis chuckled and Sophie was dismayed to see him flush. 'You never wrote, you never called. You broke my heart, Wendy Churchill!'

'You never tried to find me,' Wendy added, her tone a touch more serious than Louis's.

'Hey, you were the chucker, I was the chuckee,' Louis said. 'And that reminds me, this is my fiancée, Sophie Mills.'

Finally Wendy removed her gaze from Louis's face and looked at Sophie.

'Wow, you don't let the grass grow, do you? I thought you said your wife only just died.' It was a comment that Sophie found rather hard to maintain her fake smile through.

Louis laughed awkwardly. 'Carrie I had been apart for three years when she died . . .' he explained, his smile faltering.

'Sophie was there for me and the children when it happened. She saved all of us.'

'Oh, I *see*,' Wendy said, nodding as if the mysteries of the universe had suddenly all become clear.

'Well, anyway, Wendy,' Louis's smile vanished, 'it was nice to see you again. Take care of yourself.'

'I've always had to.' Her reply implied something that Sophie could not fathom except that it was barbed, with just a hint of resentment. 'Goodbye, Louis.'

She stood there looking at Louis for a second longer than Sophie deemed appropriate and then shrugged and made her way out through the crowds.

'What a charming lady,' Sophie said, exchanging a knowing look with Bella.

'Who *was* that funny lady?' Izzy asked, emerging from her food and slinging an arm around Sophie's neck to kiss her, leaving a tomato ketchup cupid bow kiss on her cheek.

'She was a rude lady,' Bella said. 'I didn't like her.'

'She's just someone I used to know,' Louis said as he watched her go, but there was a look in his eye that belied his casual dismissal of her, a look that reminded Sophie she knew hardly anything about Louis's life before Carrie, he never talked about it. There were years, decades, of his life that were a mystery to her.

'When I knew her she never used to be quite that intense,' Louis leaned over and wiped away the smear of ketchup from Sophie's cheek with the ball of his thumb. 'I'm sorry, babe. She was pretty rude to you, blanking you like that.'

'Was she? I didn't notice,' Sophie lied, more interested in finding out more about this relic from Louis's past. 'Childhood sweetheart, was she? She's probably been pining for you all these years and is put out that you're with me; pure jealousy, and who can blame her, hey, bridesmaids?'

As Sophie predicted, the word sent the girls into paroxysms of hysteria and the Wendy interlude was soon forgotten as Louis had to catch Izzy as she raced around the pub in excitement, her loo paper bridal train fluttering behind her.

That afternoon, with Louis's electric fire on and the lights blazing against the driving rain that pelted the house's whitewashed pebbled exterior, Sophie sat near her cat Artemis and waited for Louis to come back from the kitchen with a cup of tea for her. She would have liked to have sat next to Artemis, but she had learned after many claw-related injuries that you never approached the cat, you waited for the cat to approach you. This afternoon Artemis was clearly not in the mood, so Sophie sat near her and missed her, because she loved her cat even if she knew Artemis could mostly take or leave her.

The girls had gone upstairs to draw some designs for Sophie's wedding dress, dragging poor old Tango with them just in case they felt they needed a mannequin to model dresses on, and Sophie was glad of a few moments' peace even though she wasn't too pleased about being considered the same body type as a blatantly tubby ginger tom.

'I'm glad you're happy here without me,' she told Artemis who tucked her two grey paws neatly beneath her and blinked in response. 'I mean, I wouldn't want you to miss me, or pine for me or go off your food just because I gave you a home when no one else wanted a psychotic and antisocial cat and we shared a flat for years and years. I'm glad you're emotionally independent.'

Artemis regarded her with a long, flat stare that Sophie was reasonably sure said, 'If you haven't got any food with you, you might as well leave.'

'What do you think about this Wendy woman, then?' Sophie asked Artemis. 'She fluttered all over Louis today, acting all weird and mysterious, and she *was* acting that way, I didn't imagine it. And *he* . . . he gave her this funny little look. This wistful look, what was that all about? Who was she to him? The trouble is I have no idea. I haven't got a clue. I mean, what do I really know about him or his life before he met Carrie? He never talks about it.'

'About what?' Louis said as he came in carefully carrying two mugs of hot tea. 'And why are you talking to that cat?'

'She understands every word,' Sophie protested weakly.

'Yes, but she doesn't give a toss. If you want to talk to a dumb animal, you should try me. I hang on your every word.' He sat on the carpet and leaned his back against the sofa, his shoulder brushing Sophie's knee. The glow from the fire tinted his complexion a ruddy orange as he passed Sophie her drink.

'OK, then,' Sophie said taking a sip of her tea. 'I asked Artemis what do I know about you? I mean, I know that you're lovely and an excellent kisser and fabulous in bed or on a sofa or whatever, and that I love you, but what do I know about you? I know hardly anything about your family . . .'

'Because I don't really have one,' Louis said, exchanging glances with Artemis.

'Or your past. I mean that Wendy from today, who was she?'

Louis sipped his tea, 'I told you. A girl I used to know at school.'

'You were more than just friends, she said, while she was ignoring me,' Sophie added rather pointedly.

'Oh God, I was sixteen, she was fifteen – it was that time when you're going out with one girl at morning registration and she's chucked you by afternoon break. Technically, I was "more than just friends" with half my year. The female half.'

Louis laughed but Sophie did not.

'Come on, babe,' Louis said, setting his tea down on the

coffee table and kneeling to face her. 'It's just someone I used to know. It's no big deal. I want to kiss you, I haven't kissed you in at least two hours, I'm getting withdrawal symptoms.'

One hand slid up her thigh as he took her drink from her and moved in to kiss her.

'No ... Louis, wait,' Sophie said. Louis waited, looking mildly surprised. Sophie stopping him from kissing her was entirely unprecedented.

'What, don't you want the cat watching? I have to admit she's putting me off a bit too,' Louis said glancing over his shoulder at Artemis, who, if she had lips, would have been pursing them in matronly disapproval.

'No, listen.' Sophie put her palms on either side of his cheeks and made him look at her. 'You and I are engaged. To be married and stuff.'

'Yes.' Louis smiled. 'It's great, isn't it? Especially the stuff bit.'

'Yes, it's lovely, but I don't know anything about you. Your life before you met Carrie, it's a complete mystery to me. And I want to know, I want know all about you, every little thing from your first memory onwards, because it's all part of what makes you you, and I love you and I think if I know more about you I'll feel more ... secure.'

'Secure? I've just asked you to marry me. How secure do you need to feel?' Louis asked her, perplexed.

'All right, not secure, then – closer to you. The more I know about you the closer I'll feel to you.'

'I've often found that naked kissing and stuff is the best way to achieve that.' Louis's smile was beguiling but Sophie was adamant.

'No, no kissing. I want to know, tell me about her. Tell me about Wendy, please.'

Louis sat back on his heels and sighed.

'Fine,' he said with a shrug. 'You want to know about Wendy. Well, Wendy was my first proper girlfriend – my first love, I suppose. I'd had this crush on her from the minute I set eyes on her when she first arrived at our school. I was thirteen and she was twelve. This gingery hair and ... well, she was the first girl in her year to have curves, put it that way. I saw her and I thought that's her, that's the girl I'm going to marry one day.'

'Oh.' Sophie was taken aback by the sudden flare of jealousy she felt in her chest. 'And?'

'And?' Louis shrugged. 'And that's it. Wendy was my first love. Who was your first love?' Sophie thought for a moment. Just then she didn't want to tell Louis that it was him.

'That can't be it; you met her when you were thirteen but you knew her for three more years. What happened next?'

'Do you want a daily account or monthly?' Louis's tone was sardonic. 'Only it was a long time ago and I might have forgotten some of the details How many sugars she had in her tea – that sort of thing.'

'Louis, I'm serious!' Sophie told him, trying to wrestle the frustrated tone out of her voice. 'You went out with her, for how long and when?'

Louis sighed and stood up, crossing over to the armchair where Artemis was perched. The two of them regarded each other for a second like gunfighters in a spaghetti western and then, realising who was by far the more superior animal, Louis sat down on the floor in front of the fire, crossing his legs like a schoolboy on a camping trip.

'So I carried this torch for her.' Louis smiled to himself. 'God, I loved her. She never talked to me, never looked at me. We weren't in any of the same classes or anything, so I had to try and bump into her in places where I thought she might be. I remember walking round and round this park near her house once until it got dark on the off chance she might turn up, but she never showed.'

'Which park?' Sophie asked him, hungry for details so that she could more clearly picture the lovesick thirteen-year-old Louis. 'The one near the Guildhall?'

'What? No. No, this was in Newquay. Me and Wendy grew up in Newquay.'

'Did you?' Sophie asked him. 'I never knew that about you.'

'It's not that important, is it?' Louis asked her. 'It's just a place. I don't think about it as home; this place is home. Wherever you are is home, which is why it would be so much better if you moved in here with me.'

'Tell me what happened next. How did you get together?' Sophie pressed him, even though in her heart she shied away from knowing. Louis's answering smile was fond and full of warmth.

'We were both at the end-of-year party. I knew she was going to be there and I knew that that might be the last chance I'd have to talk to her. I was leaving school and it was the summer holidays. Stupid, really, I gave myself a deadline – I'd either tell her I loved her that night or never at all, typical teen dramatics. It sounds silly now but when I think about it I can still feel it, that tight band around my chest whenever I thought about her or looked at her. I really did love her like crazy. Pretty much every waking moment of every day was filled up with me thinking about Wendy and those ginger curls and the way that—' Louis caught the look on Sophie's face which matched the thunderous skies outside the window and he checked himself.

'Anyway, I was very nervous, of course. This was my moment of truth. I decided to have a drink for Dutch courage, and another one and another one. Four pints of cider and black on an empty stomach while I was waiting for the right moment, the moment when I felt brave and handsome enough to talk to her. Only if it ever came it was lost somewhere between being petrified and incoherent and utterly, utterly drunk. I threw up in the garden and passed out on a bench. When I woke up the party had finished hours ago, my mouth tasted like a sewer, my head was banging like a drum, and I hadn't said two words to the girl I loved.' Sophie watched as Louis's gaze slipped from her face, looking instead into his past. 'God, I was gutted. I'd missed my moment, I'd blown it. I realised I'd have to live the rest of my life without her and when I thought about it I just cried. I sat on the bench and cried my eyes out. Eventually I decided to walk home and, out of habit, I suppose, I took a detour past her house, probably to get one last look at her window. When I turned down her road she was there, sitting on the wall outside her house smoking a cigarette.

'"You took your time," she said as I walked up to her really, really hoping I wasn't going to throw up again. "I've been waiting here all night. I was just about to go in before my mum and dad realise that it's pillows under my quilt and not me."'

Louis grinned to himself. 'I was all over the place, not entirely sure I wasn't still on that bench and dreaming. So I asked her, "How did you know I was going to come?" And she went all cool as a cucumber. "You always walk home past my house; I didn't suppose tonight would be any different. Never once knocked on my door, though, so I thought I'd better sit out here and wait for you, else you'd never get round to asking me out."

'"You could always have asked *me* out," I said, because I was a kid and a bit of an idiot.

'And she hopped off the wall and put her arms around my neck and said, "I'm the girl, girls don't make the first move."

And then she kissed me, this long, smoky cider-drenched kiss and we stayed like that, necking on her front wall till the sun came up.'

Sophie steeled herself against the disappointment she felt at knowing that Louis had ever spent hours kissing anyone else apart from her, but it was useless, the jealousy swept through her like fire through kindling. She knew he had a past, of course he did, but the idea of him ever loving anyone else the way that he loved her, even some fifteen-year-old decades ago, hurt her almost more than she could bear.

'For that whole summer we were inseparable,' Louis went on. 'We spent every day together, just the two of us. I didn't see my mates for weeks. It was an amazing time. It was like . . . it was like . . .'

'A wonderful dream you didn't want to wake up from?' Sophie asked him.

Louis nodded. 'Yes, except that I had to. She left, or rather her family left, almost overnight. I couldn't believe it. I didn't know a thing about it.'

'Even though you saw her every day.'

'Towards the end of the holiday she didn't want to see me so much, lost interest in me, I suppose. When I phoned her she was never in. And I never saw her in the town any more, none of her friends seemed to know what she was up to. Then I walked passed her house one morning, hoping she'd come out and it had a sold sign outside it. It was already empty. They'd gone. I knocked on a neighbour's door and she told me Wendy's dad had got a new job up North. He'd moved them all in one weekend, just like that. I never heard from her again.

'Never?' Sophie asked him.

'Nope.' Louis shook his head. 'I was heartbroken, destroyed. It took me ages to get over her, I suppose, because I really thought we were soulmates . . .'

'Soulmates?' Sophie asked. She had hoped that Louis was her soulmate, but if he'd already had one in his lifetime, she wasn't sure. She wasn't sure exactly how many soulmates a person could encounter in one life, but she got the feeling that if it was more than one then the whole concept was rather less special than she'd been led to believe.

'Yes, silly teen love crap, you know – plus, she was the first girl I had sex with. That was a big deal.' Louis dropped the bombshell casually as if it were the least important detail.

'You slept with her!' Sophie couldn't stop the betrayal in her voice.

'Sophie, come on, it was years ago. At our age we are bound to have a past; you can't be jealous, can you? After all, you weren't a virgin when I met you.'

Sophie wanted to say 'only technically' but she didn't.

'No,' she lied instead. 'No, of course I'm not jealous.'

'We've got it!' Bella ran in clutching several pieces of paper, closely followed by Izzy whose arrival caused Artemis to discreetly retreat to the top of the bookshelf were she was far less likely to have to ward off unwanted advances from a small girl who just wouldn't believe that the cat didn't love her.

'We've designed the perfect dress for you, Aunty Sophie,' Bella told her, delivering the sheets of paper into her lap. 'Only on here we've written the "purrrrfect" dress because we've drawn it on a cat. It's a joke that is funny, do you see?'

'Yes, I do see.' Sophie took the piece of paper and smiled at the confection of glitter glue and felt-tip pen that Bella and Izzy had presented her with. 'It's marvellous and I shall certainly bear it in mind when it comes to selecting a dress.

Sophie half listened as the girls began to chatter, filling her in on all the dress's design points, such as its secret going-to-the-toilet skirt-lifting device and refrigerated pocket for perishable items.

What was the point, she wondered, as she listened to Bella's plans for a pony-themed wedding, of telling Louis that everything about Wendy Churchill made her feel uncomfortable, tense and as if she was in exactly the wrong place, with the wrong man, at the wrong time? That, for a second, Wendy made her feel like the interloper in Louis's life she sometimes suspected she might be. It was nothing more than her usual paranoia and neurosis manifesting themselves in a new, cruel and unusual way. Other than a woman she didn't know being slightly rude to her, and Louis doing exactly what she had asked him to, recounting an incident from long ago in his past, nothing had really happened. And besides, it wasn't as if she would ever have to see Wendy Churchill again.

Later that night, as she lay in her single bed in the B&B gazing at the ceiling rose that circled the floral lampshade, Sophie found herself going over and over Louis's story that he'd related to her earlier that day, adding details and embellishments of her own, images of Louis and Wendy walking hand in hand in unknown sun-drenched cornfields. She closed her eyes and tried her best to think about something else, anything else, twisting her engagement ring which still felt alien on her finger in the dark, but still thoughts of Louis and Wendy crowded her muddled and foolish head.

Eventually she sat up, switching on the lamp next to her bed. Wearily she climbed out of bed to make use of the tea- and coffee-making facilities that Mrs Alexander so kindly provided in every room and made herself a hot chocolate, climbing back into bed to look once again at the wedding-dress designs the girls had made her promise that she would pin up above her bed. As she closely examined the drawings, reading all the labels that Bella had so carefully spelt out in her best and newly joined-up handwriting, picking up the more outrageous details that Izzy had added, Sophie felt the tension in her chest subside and a slow spreading warmth take its place.

Louis, her first love, her soulmate, had asked her to marry him, she realised, as if his proposal had only truly just sunk in. He'd asked her to be with him and his daughters for the rest of her life and she couldn't imagine anything more wonderful. It was everything she wanted, he was everything she wanted, and she was going to marry him. All at once Sophie felt a rush of adrenalin that had her sitting bolt upright. The time to sit on the fence and wonder about her future was over. Now was the time to leap right into tomorrow and embrace and enjoy the one thing she knew was going to complete her. She was going to be Louis Gregory's wife and she could not wait.

Chapter Five

Sophie arrived on Louis's doorstep at the crack of dawn, surprised to find him and the girls already up.

'Hello,' she said, kissing him warmly on the lips. 'I was coming over extra early to make you all breakfast.'

'Ah, well, you'd have had to sleep over for that,' Louis said, his arms encircling Sophie as the girls looked on, nudging each other and giggling. 'I've got to get my gear ready for that ruby anniversary lunch in Penzance tomorrow. I'm recreating the wedding photos of the happy couple outside the church they got married in, it's seriously sweet. You should see them, Sophie. Mr and Mrs Harris met and fell in love when they were fifteen, married before they were twenty, and are still as happy and as crazy about each other now as they were then. Who says young love doesn't last, hey?'

'Me,' Sophie told him happily as she sat down at the kitchen table with the girls who were making their way through their customary Sunday morning pile of toast and jam. 'I woke up this morning and I realised that hardly anybody knows that we are all getting married. And I thought we need to tell everyone we possibly can. We need to start making calls!'

'We do?' Louis said, sitting down next to her. 'You really want to tell everyone?'

'Yes, of course I do,' Sophie said. 'I can't wait for the whole world to know that I'm marrying you.'

Despite her enthusiasm, it was Louis who got to work on making calls as soon as he had cleared the breakfast dishes and settled the girls down with a box of Lego in the front room, trawling through his old address books and ringing round his friends. Sophie, on the other hand, paced the kitchen, her joy battling a barrage of nerves. She wondered why she found it so much harder than Louis to break the news. Perhaps it was because he didn't have a mother to tell, she thought. If he had a mother to tell he would be feeling much more nervous, because everybody knows that nothing is really real until you've told your mother. Of course he did have an ex-mother-in-law to tell, but as yet they had not discussed whose list that particular name should be on although Sophie guessed from Louis's carefree and joyous demeanour that he wasn't expecting it to be his.

What she was really scared of, Sophie realised, as she ran the ball of her thumb over her phone's keypad, was that the people she loved and cared about might not take her seriously. She needed them to understand exactly how happy she was, how serious she was about marrying Louis and, more than anything, she needed them to be happy for her.

Deciding she had to be alone to make her calls, Sophie took herself out into Louis's garden and sat at the bottom of it on the bench which the girls had nicknamed the fairy bower because it was located under a trellis and was smothered with a creeping rose bush which scattered soft silky pink petals on whoever was sitting below at the merest gust of wind. On this thankfully warm and dry Sunday morning with the last remnants of the summer's heat just detectable in the air, the remaining roses had already crumbled and shattered during an earlier shower, littering the seat, a faded pink confetti of petals.

As she scrolled through the names in her phone she made a mental list of who to call and in which order she would tell them. Then she crossed off the names she least wanted to tell until there was nobody left on her list and she had to start again. Finally she decided the only fair way was to do it alphabetically. Taking a deep breath, Sophie found Cal's name and pressed call.

'What now? Sick of sharing your lover with a sheep?' was Cal's friendly greeting.

'Oh, how very professional,' Sophie said. 'You can tell that McCarthy Hughes is going to hell in a hand basket – you never would have got that kind of rudeness when I worked there.'

'That's because you were always a rudeness-free zone – in all senses,' Cal said. 'And besides, it's Sunday morning and I'm still in bed. In fact, you're lucky not to be interrupting me mid-coitus with some lovely young thing. So come on, then, tell me which crisis of confidence are you having this week? Have you discovered you're allergic to clotted cream? Are you afraid the locals might try and burn you in a wicker man? Only you're going to have to hurry up if you want me to dispense my usual pearls of wit and wisdom as I have to prepare for a breakfast meeting with your old friend Jake Flynn tomorrow morning. He wants us to do the Christmas party again this year and it's got to be bigger and better than the last one and so far no one's had any ideas to top the cruise ship so … have you got any ideas?'

'You're meeting Jake?' When Sophie heard Jake Flynn's name she completely forgot about her news and Cal's question, which normally she would have pounced on in delight as tangible proof that McCarthy Hughes did miss her amongst its ranks even if Cal swore blind that her absence from the office went entirely unnoticed by everyone. Jake Flynn, a handsome New

Yorker with a chiselled jaw and perfect teeth was the man that Sophie had been endeavouring to fall in love with when Louis walked into her life. At the time Jake had been her most important client as she had been planning a huge Christmas party for his organisation on an ocean liner that regularly docked at Tower Bridge. She had been mildly attracted to him from the start but had been using their professional relationship as an excuse not to have to do anything about it. Once, before Bella and Izzy, Sophie had been the queen of not acting on her feelings, of living her life at arm's length. The old Sophie would have been quite content to have conducted her own particular brand of long-distance romance with Jake indefinitely – one that involved him not knowing about it at all.

When Cal had told Sophie Jake liked her, she had refused to believe him, but when Jake himself told her he was interested in her it became hard to ignore. He'd been sweet and patient and so understanding when Sophie had decided to take time off work to look after the girls. He'd even kissed her with all the charm and expertise that any woman could ask of any man. There had been face touching and no excess saliva. Except that by then Sophie had already met Louis and even if she didn't consciously know it, it was Louis who was constantly occupying her thoughts. She would never know what would have happened between her and Jake if she hadn't met Louis, whether a more quiet and conventional romance might have developed over time. The kind of relationship she had supposed she'd always have one day. Whether perhaps now, nearly a year on from their first meeting, there might have been an engagement announcement posted in the *New York Times*. Probably not, Sophie reasoned. There had been nothing between her and Jake except a sort of vague attraction. There had never been any heat and, with Louis, heat was a constant simmering presence on the point of boiling over the second he walked into a room. A heat that she could look forward to basking in till their own ruby anniversary and beyond. In a blink, Sophie forgot Jake and remembered what she was so desperate to tell Cal.

'Yes,' Cal interrupted her thoughts. 'Jake couldn't have been that broken hearted when you legged it because we didn't lose their account – it turned out you weren't remotely indispensable. Anyway, the Madison Corporation are having a big hands-across-the-ocean Christmas bash for their transatlantic offices which we're organising. It's a massive account and your ex-nemesis and my new boss Eve's given it to me, so I'm blossoming now that I am finally out from under your rather sizeable shadow. Life as your PA was terribly stunting, you know. I'm fairly sure Eve's going to promote me come the end of this year. She loves me, mainly because I'm not you.'

'Yes, well, she hated me because I was better at my job than anyone else there, so if she likes you ...' Sophie said, impatient and reticent about delivering her news all at once. 'Anyway, give Jake my love – I mean my best wishes – when you see him, won't you?'

'I will, but he won't care,' Cal replied breezily. 'He's got this uber sexy fiancée he brought with him when he was meeting with Eve; some New York chick, stacked like you wouldn't believe, groomed to within an inch of her life – stunning and slightly scary. You know the type.'

'Really? That's great,' Sophie said, more than a little surprised, considering the reason for her call, that she felt rather peeved. 'I'm happy for him.'

'Great, everybody's happy for everybody – so tell me what you've got to tell me so I can tell you to stop being so ridiculous and we can get on with our lives.'

Sophie's mind went blank for a moment and then she remembered.

'LouisaskedmetomarryhimlastnightandIsaidyes,' she gushed, keen to get the sentence out of her head and into the ether before she lost her nerve.

Sophie braced herself but nothing happened, except that there was a long silence on the other end of the line.

'And I didn't even have to buy any Wellingtons,' Sophie added with a touch of childish triumph that she supposed wasn't all that becoming of a blushing bride to be.

She waited for a response from Cal but he was silent.

'Cal? Are you still there?' Sophie said impatiently.

'Louis. Asked. You. To. Marry. Him.' Cal said each word slowly and heavily, each one weighted with disbelief. 'Bloody Fucking Nora.'

'Yes, it's great, isn't it?' Sophie prompted him. 'Isn't it?'

'But, *why*?' Cal asked her.

Sophie had been expecting many things from Cal: sarcasm, of course; a pretence that he had seen this coming from several miles off, despite all his declarations that Sophie would never get near an altar; and, finally, she had been looking forward to the kind of warm goodwill that characterised the real friendship that lay beneath the thin veneer of cattiness and sarcasm. But she had not expected this question at all.

'*Why?* Because I love him and he makes me happy – Cal, I've honestly never been happier in my life than when I'm with him. He was so sweet and nervous about proposing and you should have seen the ring he picked out for me. Vintage 1930s – it's perfect . . .'

'No, I don't mean why did you say yes,' Cal interrupted her. 'Of course *you* said yes. And of course he asked you, he's crazy about you. I mean, why did he ask you to marry him *now*? You've only been there for six months. You don't even have any wellies. Are you pregnant?'

'Cal! No, I'm not pregnant! And I don't need any wellies to know that I want to marry him, and he obviously doesn't need me to have any for him to want to marry me,' Sophie said. 'It's not as if either of us are feckless teenagers. I'm nearly thirty-three and he'll be thirty-six in . . .' Sophie trailed off. It did give her slight pause for thought that she wasn't one hundred per cent certain of the birth month of her betrothed, let alone the actual date. 'A few months.'

'Well, I have always thought that impending death is a good enough reason for a proposal,' Cal said dryly.

'Oh, for God's sake, Cal!' Sophie snapped at him. 'You're the one who persuaded me to leave London and come down here. You're the one who said I should be spontaneous and grab happiness and all of that. Well, I've done that and I'm still doing it – why aren't you happy for me?'

There was another pause and when Cal spoke it was with the warmth that Sophie had been hoping for. 'Of course I am. Of course I am happy for you, you silly cow,' Cal said. 'It was just a bit of a shock, that's all. One minute I'm fast asleep in my bed dreaming about my long-lost sex life and the next you're in my ear telling me that you, Sophie Frigid-pants Mills, are getting married, to a real live man who actually exists in reality and not just in your head. Oh, Sophie . . .' Cal trailed off and Sophie couldn't be certain but she thought she heard the faintest sniff.

'What?' Sophie urged him.

'It's just you, happy and in love and getting married. It's just brilliant and I'm delighted for you, which is odd for me, because I hardly ever care about anyone else's happiness. And who cares if it's quick. I've conducted whole relationships between breakfast and dinner on the same day!'

'And you are really, really pleased for me, aren't you, because Cal – I'm so happy and I'm so sure and you know that I've never been terribly good at being either of those things before.'

'Sophie Mills, you've done what so many people never have the guts to do,' Cal told her. 'You've chased down happiness, rugby-tackled it to the floor and pinned it there until it had no choice but to submit to your will or suffocate under your substantial weight. And frankly, as it was mainly me that persuaded you to move down there and go after Louis in the first place, making me entirely responsible for all of your new-found happiness, I demand that you make me your chief bridesmaid.'

'Ah,' Sophie told him. 'I think there might be some stiff competition for that role, although I will accept bribes.'

Christina, Sophie's last remaining single friend, actually cried when Sophie broke the news. And they weren't tears of joy. They were wet, phlegm-rattling sobs that required deep rasping inward breaths to sustain them, which Christina seemed to manage to be able to do indefinitely.

'Don't cry, Christina,' Sophie begged her. 'At least not in a bad way; you're kind of bringing the overjoyed and happy vibe down a bit.'

'I'm sorry, I'm not crying *really*; if I was crying really then what sort of a sad, clichéd single woman in her thirties would that make me?' Christina wailed. 'I'm premenstrual. They are irrational, premenstrual tears. It's my hormones that are making me cry . . . and really that should make me feel happy – at least I still have hormones – see, there's always a bright side.'

'Yes, it's a little different from the bright side I was thinking of, but still . . .'

'Now I really am the last one, aren't I?' Christina sniffed. 'I really am the final aged, single friend, the one who'll turn up in a BBC 2 documentary about women who can't find love and need specialist advice . . . I didn't think I would be the last one to find someone. I really thought it would be you.'

'It's so touching that everyone had such high hopes for me,' Sophie muttered.

'I suppose there's always Alison,' Christina said, referring to a woman Sophie had met briefly a few months ago. 'I mean, she's been married and had kids but now she's getting a divorce so *she's* single, and maybe it's worse being single and divorced than just single, but at least she's been married, even if it was to a total shit – what do you think?'

'I think you'll probably pull at my wedding,' Sophie said to cheer Christina up, suddenly thrilled at the thought of being able to set an actual date when she would be able to make Louis her husband. 'There'll be loads of fishermen and surfers and just men in general, hundreds of them.'

'Really?' Christina perked up considerably. 'When is it going to be, is it going to be soon? I know this designer that will make you bespoke personalised invites . . . He's single – well, when I say single, I mean he's not married yet which I think counts as single. I think men are fair game till they've got that wedding ring on, don't you?'

Briefly Sophie thought of the way Wendy had looked at her fiancé.

'No, I certainly do not,' Sophie said, a little more firmly than she'd meant to.

'Oh, sorry, forgot,' Christina said. 'You're on the other side now.'

Sophie thought for a long time before ringing her mother. She was aware that not only should her mother have been first on her list of calls to make, no matter where 'M' came in the alphabet, but she should probably also have gone home along with her betrothed to tell her face to face that her daughter was getting married.

Iris Mills barely knew her future son-in-law and although she had taken Sophie's sudden departure to Cornwall with good grace and was even pleased for her, Sophie wasn't sure how she'd feel about her making the move permanent. Her relationship with her mother hadn't been an easy one since her father had died unexpectedly when she was a teenager. There had been a distance between them ever since; a sort of nameless and entirely unfounded blame. Sophie was always cross and impatient with her mother and after the only man in either of their lives had gone Iris had seemed detached from her daughter, more caught up with the various waif and stray dogs that she collected from the streets of North London than with Sophie.

It was only when Sophie had taken on Bella and Izzy and she had turned to Iris for help, the first help of any kind that she had ever asked her mother for since she was fifteen years old, that, gradually, their relationship had changed and Sophie had found a way to relate to her mother again. It had been Iris who convinced Sophie that a small amount of cat food probably wasn't fatal to a three-year-old; Iris who had babysat the girls even though she knew that wherever the two children were the risk of fire and flood damage increased at an alarming rate; and it was Iris who had promised Sophie that she would be able to cope with whatever situation was thrown at her because if anyone could cope with two small bereaved children then it was her strong and capable daughter. For the first time in decades Sophie began to see that her mother admired her and slowly they had drawn closer together. Sophie had spoken to her about twice a week since she'd come down to St Ives, but they'd never spoken about anything serious. Her mum would always say how lovely it was to hear her sounding so happy and relaxed and then they'd talk about fleas, ticks or dicky-doggy tummy for the next half-hour.

But there was no getting away from it; a conversation about ear mites was not going to cut it this time. Sophie had to tell her mother that she was engaged in the business of getting married.

As ever Sophie had to wait for a cacophony of barking dogs to die down as her mother rescued the handset from the jaws of Scooby her Great Dane and clambered over a pack of hounds to the kitchen where she would shut most of them out so that she could talk in relative peace.

'Hello, love,' Iris said. 'It's not your normal day.'

'Isn't it?' Sophie had not been aware that she had a normal day to call but she wasn't surprised; her life had slipped into a soothing lullaby of a routine since she had arrived here. 'Well, that's because it's not a normal day!' she added brightly, pre-empting her big news.

'You're telling me,' Iris sighed. 'You remember Skippers, that little Jack Russell cross that was left tied up in a plastic bag in that skip on Balls Pond Road? Well, he got hold of next door's bins yesterday, had them out all over the street, so as you can imagine that made me popular with the neighbours again, but that's not the worst of it. He must have eaten an old dish cloth or something similar. It's coming out the other end, but very, very slowly. I'm wondering if I should give it a yank or would that make it worse – what do you think?'

'Mum . . .' Sophie paused and took a breath. Did she really want to tell her mum about her and Louis on the back of a constipated dog story? There was nothing else for it. 'Mum, I can't talk to you about the dogs today. I have some *news.*'

Sophie paused to let the weight of the word sink into her mother's dog-filled consciousness.

'News?' Iris asked. 'Oh, are you pregnant?'

'No!' Sophie was scandalised. 'No, I am not pregnant, but . . . oh, honestly, Mum – you've totally stolen my thunder. Louis and I are getting married!' Sophie paused for a beat but when Iris didn't immediately react she rushed on. 'And I am the happiest and most content and most alive that I have ever been, and you should feel really, really happy for me!'

'I'm am thrilled for you, darling,' Iris said a little hesitantly as soon as Sophie let her get a word in.

'Are you?' Sophie asked her uncertainly.

'Of course I am. If you're happy, I'm happy. I'm honour bound to say the sorts of things that mothers say, like isn't it a little bit soon and are you sure you know him well enough to marry him?'

Sophie paused. After all, these were only the doubts she had herself.

'Yes, Mum, it is technically a bit soon and no, I don't know every single thing about him. But I love him and want and need him now – and isn't it better to find out about the person you love as you go along together? Wouldn't life be boring if you knew everything about your partner right from the start? And I want this, I want it really badly. I didn't realise how badly I wanted it till I'd almost got it. I couldn't bear to lose him now.'

'Well, I can't think of a reason why you would,' Iris said. 'But believe it or not, darling, I do remember how you feel and I understand. You love him and he loves you and you want to grab happiness and cling on to it with both hands. OK, so you're breaking boundaries and stretching taboos . . . but who cares what the neighbours say, hey?'

'Am I stretching taboos?' Sophie asked her. 'What, because he's already been married to my dead best friend?'

'Did I say taboos?' Iris paused as she gathered her thoughts.

'I don't think you realise how proud I am of you. I much admired you for picking up and going off to Cornwall the way you did to be with Louis and the girls. It's so easy to sit behind your net curtains, watch your favourite TV all day, and just let life slip past you without any passion or promise. But you took a stand. You were determined not to let that be you leading a half-existence until you die and I don't think I ever told you how much you inspired me. I've wasted too much time since your father passed away and seeing you take that chance with Louis made me really think about my own life. Sophie, I—'

'Oh Mum, you don't know how much it means to hear you say that.' Tears sprang into Sophie's eyes and she realised exactly how much she had wanted Iris to be pleased for her.

'That man, those children, have made you so happy and so content,' Iris went on. 'I couldn't be more delighted for you. And listen, I know that how you got together was a little unconventional, but none of that matters. And darling, the thing is, I have a little bit of news too . . .'

'Scooby got another hernia?' Sophie asked her, resignedly.

'Like I was saying,' Iris went on. 'When you went down to Cornwall you really inspired me, you know. I looked around at my life and I thought, what have I got, apart from a load of dogs and a flea problem? I'm still quite a young woman, or at least I feel young inside. So I—'

'So you what?' Sophie asked her ominously.

'I've got a lover,' Iris Mills told her daughter. 'And I've never felt so good.'

'Did I mention that I'm getting married?' Sophie asked her rather absently as her brain tried to process the words that her mother had just uttered and failed. Mother and lover, her mother had a lover – no, the two concepts would not compute.

'Yes, darling, I know. And that is the most important thing, of course it is. It's just that I've been trying to tell you about Trevor . . .'

'*Trevor?* The same Trevor who works for the RSPCA? The one who helped you re-home that litter of mongrel puppies you found dumped by the river?'

'Yes! You remember him, he's a real dish, isn't he?'

'Um . . .' Sophie remembered Trevor. A big, capable man, who was surprisingly gentle with the tiny bedraggled puppies and who had an Afro-Caribbean lilt to his voice that he had never lost even though he'd told Sophie he'd lived in London since the 1970s.

'Anyway, I've been trying to tell you about him for a while now but all you ever seem to want to do is talk about the dogs and I thought that now would be the perfect time because you're engaged in a wild and passionate affair . . .'

'You're having a wild and passionate affair? Sophie all but choked on the words.

'Yes dear, I am,' Iris said. 'Trevor and I can't keep our hands off each other, but we aren't the priority now. You and your lovely Louis, those gorgeous girls and your wedding are, of course.'

'Thanks, Mum,' Sophie said slowly. 'And I'm pleased for you, Mum, I really am. I'm really glad you've found someone too. I can't actually quite believe it yet, and it sort of hurts my eyes to try and picture it, but Trevor seems like a really nice man and so if you're happy, so am I . . . I think.'

'Oh Sophie, I'm so relieved you're not cross with me,' Iris gushed. 'You've changed so much since you met Louis. I was really worried I'd get all that uptight old-people-can't-have-sex nonsense from you.'

'Sex? You're having sex?' Sophie squeaked, screwing up her eyes in an unsuccessful attempt to stop any kind of image forming.

'Marvellous sex,' Iris practically purred. 'I'd forgotten how great sex is, Sophie.'

'Um, so . . .' Sophie was so desperate to change the subject that, for the first time in her life, a discussion on ringworm would have been appealing.

'Sorry, Sophie – your wedding. Darling, you are my only daughter, my only child. Of course I will.'

'Of course you will what?' Sophie asked, full of trepidation in case her mother was preparing to offer her sex tips.

'Come down and help you organise it,' Iris said. 'I can't wait.'

There was one other person that Sophie had to tell, only this time she could not call. She had to find the right place to tell them and after some reflection she decided that she had to go alone. Louis was still on the phone when she pulled her trainers and rainproof anorak on.

'I'm going for a bit of a walk to get my head together,' she whispered to him. He nodded and smiled, crossing the room in two easy strides to plant a warm kiss on her lips and hugging her tightly, before saying into the phone: 'Yes, mate, I'm a condemned man and I couldn't be happier about it.'

It was blustery and cold on the cliffs that rose about St Ives. The sea was grey and foreboding, merging with a dark sky that threatened rain. The short autumn day was already darkening and Sophie found herself alone on the cliff top, the season's last remaining tourists chased away by the bite of the wind and the promise of tearooms.

Sophie had thought long and hard about where was the best place to go and tell Carrie that she was marrying Louis. Carrie didn't have a grave; she had never wanted anything so sober or depressing to be left behind for people to stand over or, worse still, forget. There were really only two places that Sophie could think of to find her friend. There was Carrie's little house on Virgin Street where she had started out her married life and raised Bella and Izzy – first with Louis and then alone after he'd found out about her affair. Or there was here, the spot where Carrie had loved to walk and paint and gaze out to sea daydreaming, planning her future. The spot where she had first met Louis.

Carrie's house was occupied now. A young couple had bought it. Louis had been determined to sell it to local people who would make a home of it and not keep it as a holiday let, and had let it go for much less than it was worth. They were a sweet young couple. Sophie remembered talking to the girl, Emily, while she and her boyfriend had looked around the tiny house. Emily had told Sophie that she'd met Steve in a nightclub in Newquay two years ago. They'd dated on and off and Steve had left her briefly when he thought that everything was getting too heavy. But a few months later he had found her again and had told her he realised that he loved her. Now they were buying their first home.

On that sunny afternoon in the tiny living room that Carrie had used to sit in and sing Manic Street Preachers songs to her daughters, Sophie found herself envying the couple. Theirs had been a slow and gentle romance, an easy approach to commitment that seemed full of assurance and certainty. They had a benign confidence in the future that, even as happy as she was, Sophie had lost a long time ago and thought she would probably never regain.

While Sophie thought the couple would have let her come in for a moment or two, she decided it wasn't the right place to find Carrie, especially now that her things would not be there. Carrie was never the kind of person to hang around in the past, she was always moving on.

It was here on the cliff top, watching over the wild wind- and rain-whipped sea that Sophie knew she would be able to find Carrie, where she'd be able to picture her and remember her most clearly. Carrie, who always seemed to have the wind in her hair, even indoors. Who always had a certain light in her eyes and a kind of restless grace that made you feel she was constantly on the verge of leaving. It was only when she was with her children that Sophie ever saw her friend become completely still, her lips pressed against their hair, her eyes closed as she held them. Carrie was like the sea she had always been drawn to. Always moving, always changing, often dangerous and sometime perfectly serene. Yes, it was here that Sophie would find her.

'Hello, Carrie,' Sophie spoke quietly into the wind that snatched her words away with urgent and greedy gusts as soon as they were uttered. A secret conversation conducted between her and the elements. She felt her stomach contract and realised how nervous she was feeling as she talked. 'I'm going to marry Louis. I'm going to marry your husband. There – I've said it, and no matter how many times I say it out loud it still sounds like a reader's true story in a gossip magazine. But there it is; it's happening . . . it really is happening. You know, ever since I met Bella and Izzy and Louis I've wondered what you'd think, how you'd feel about it if you were here. I tried to love your girls because I loved you, and that was a lot easier than I thought. And I tried not to love Louis because I loved you and I'm sorry, Carrie . . . but that was impossible. The hardest thing is that I know I would probably never have got to know how wonderful they are if you hadn't died. I would have probably gone on having my secretary send them gifts and cards every birthday and Christmas; Louis might have stayed in Peru. It breaks my heart that I had to lose you to find them . . . but Carrie, you knew that I would fight for your daughters, that's why you made me their guardian, and you knew that after quite a lot of stupidity and a serious amount of epiphanies that I would love them as much as I do. And I'll never let them down, I promise you.

'I don't suppose you expected me to fall in love with Louis. I don't suppose that *I* expected it. How could I, uptight, repressed me, ever be attracted to the man that *you* once loved? He took me by surprise, Carrie. But I do love him, I love him an incredibly frightening heart-stopping amount and I do ... I do want to marry him. I do. If being certain means you constantly feel like you've overdosed on caffeine and taken up permanent residence on a big dipper.' Suddenly Sophie had a picture of her friend laughing, her eyes sparkling, her hair tossed in the wind. 'Yes, you're right, I am terrified about it. I am scared stiff, but I can't see into the future. I can't know what's going to happen, can I? You and I know that better than anyone. All I can know is that at this moment, this hour, this day, I love him and I want to be with him. And right now I can't imagine that's going to change, and that's all I can know, isn't it?'

Sophie smiled and closed her eyes, spreading her arms wide to embrace the full force of the wind that battered and rippled her coat. 'We made each other a promise when we were girls – *always, for ever, whatever*. You made that promise to your daughters, so have I, and now I'm making that promise to Louis.' Sophie opened her eyes and looked into the silver-streaked sky. 'And I don't know where you are, my dear, dear friend, but wherever you are, I hope you'll be happy for us.'

Sophie held her breath, hoping for something, a beam of sunlight cutting through the grey sky, a sudden drop in the wind – some sign that Carrie had heard her, but of course there was none. There was never going to be anything so concrete, Sophie had known that before she'd made her journey to the cliff top. Still, even in the midst of the building storm and as the rain began to break, Sophie felt better and calmer. She didn't feel alone.

Which wasn't all that surprising because at exactly that second a small but fast creature decked out from head to foot in an all-in-one red waterproof suit careered into her legs and hugged her hard around her hips.

'Izzy! What are you doing here?' Sophie exclaimed. She wouldn't have put it past the often adventurous child to have somehow come up here on her own, so when she glanced over her shoulder and saw Louis hanging back as Bella ran towards her, Sophie was relieved and touched.

'What are you all doing out here in this weather?' Sophie laughed, pleased to see them.

'Daddy said he thought he knew where you'd gone,' Bella explained, her face clenched against the rain. 'He said he thought you wanted to come and tell Mummy about the wedding and he was worried for you on your own. And he asked us if we'd like to come too, because it's all our wedding and our news as well. And we did want to come.'

'Yes, because we are bridesmaids,' Izzy said. 'And Mummy would be awfully interested in that.'

'She would be,' Sophie agreed, crouching down so that her body shielded their smaller forms from the worst of the elements. 'Your mummy loved to dress up and put flowers in her hair and find something sparkly in her ballerina jewellery box to put on.'

'We are bridesmaids, Mummy!' Izzy ducked under Sophie's arms and hollered into the wind and rain. 'It's ex-ter-reem-ly exciting!'

Her sister, looking briefly into Sophie's eyes, gave her a small smile and then followed, leaving Sophie to watch, her heart in her mouth as Carrie's daughters spoke to their mother across the sea.

'And we are going to wear wings!' Bella shouted at the top of her voice.

'And there will be ponies, I expect!' Izzy added. 'And cake – chocolate, hopefully.'

'And Mummy, we are very happy,' Bella yelled. 'Me and Izzy and Daddy are very, very happy, so you don't have to worry because Sophie loves us and she'll take care of us.'

'Although she doesn't like to tidy up much,' Izzy added. 'Or cook. But we still love her.'

'Also,' Bella called out, 'could you please make it so it doesn't rain? I'm not sure what day it will be, but I can confirm at a later date.'

'And we love you, Mummy,' Izzy said.

Bella put her hand in Izzy's and they glanced at each other before shouting as loudly as their young voices would allow: 'We love you – always, for ever, whatever!'

Finally they turned back to Sophie and ran into her outstretched arms, knocking her backwards so that she tumbled with a full thud into the cold, wet and wiry grass.

'There,' Bella said, kissing Sophie on the cheek. 'Mummy knows properly now.'

'Can we have toasted teacakes?' Izzy said thoughtfully. 'I'm starving.'

Sophie put her hand on Louis's chilled cheek as they approached him, his hands thrust deep in his pockets as he waited for them.

'Thank you,' she said, placing her lips next to his ear. 'You never stop amazing me with how well you know me.'

'It's only because you're not that mysterious,' Louis teased her gently. 'No, that's not true. You are quite often unfathomable. But I knew you'd never let anything this big happen without wanting to tell your best friend and the girls felt the same way. It was a brilliant idea, Sophie.'

'Shall we go down and get toasted teacakes and a cream tea off Carmen?' Sophie asked him. 'I'm cutting down, but I thought as it's the weekend I might as well wait till Monday . . .'

'I'll catch up,' Louis said, looking at the cliff top. 'I've got one or two things to say myself.'

Sophie looked into his eyes; she wanted to ask him what he was going to say, but she knew that whatever it was it was just between him and his memory of Carrie.

'We'll be waiting for you.' She kissed him lightly on the lips.

As Sophie walked back down the cliff-top path with the girls just in front of her, she turned a few times to look at Louis as he stood gazing out to sea, talking to the wife he'd left and lost and probably had barely ever known. She paused for a second to watch his solitary figure, feeling the icy wind rip through the insulation of her coat and a shiver that had nothing to do with the weather raise an army of goose bumps that marched down her back. She felt, as Carrie's mother was fond of saying, as if someone had just walked over her grave. And all at once Sophie was overwhelmed with the impulse that she had to marry Louis and soon, before something or someone took him away from her for good the way that Carrie had been taken so suddenly from all of them.

Chapter Six

What Sophie had not been prepared for when she had accepted Louis's proposal was just how quickly and how keen she would be to end her engagement to him and become his wife. Within twenty-four hours she realised that rather than having agreed to a vague if beautiful declaration of love she had committed to an actual event that she urgently wanted to make happen at the earliest possible convenience.

This full-throttle enthusiasm she felt was unexpected and as Sophie began to think of all the things that needed to be done in order to bring the wedding to fruition she felt a little as if she were having an out-of-body experience, as if she were floating just above the top of her own head watching this other woman, this alien, excited, joyous being who spent in excess of twenty pounds on bridal magazines and hours trawling the Internet for wedding locations, while the old Sophie, the Sophie who did not commit and wasn't especially fond of feelings, kept well out of it. But that was only now and then, when she'd catch sight of her flushed face in a mirror or realise she'd spent twenty minutes reading an article on the best tear-proof mascara. She'd laugh and wonder at how unlike her old self she was since she'd allowed herself to love Louis and how amazing it was to feel so awake. For the most part, though, she was there in the moment, fretting over which mascara would be best to avoid panda eyes on her big day, even though she had not yet bought a dress, booked a venue, or set a date.

On Sunday evening after the girls had gone to bed she had been kissing Louis in the door frame of the living room. This often happened; she'd be going somewhere in the house – from the kitchen to the living room or from the living room out into the garden – and their paths would randomly cross and suddenly Sophie would find herself pinned against a wall, a kitchen counter, or, as in this case, the door frame, Louis firmly gripping the tops of her arms as he pushed her back against whatever surface happened to be available and kissed her.

Sophie had been breathless and expectant when he broke the kiss to look at her.

'I still can't believe it's you,' he said softly.

'Why, who were you expecting?' Sophie asked with the hint of a smile.

'I mean, I still can't believe that it's *you*,' Louis whispered, scanning her face with his eyes. 'I still can't believe that *you* are here with *me*, that you are going to marry me.'

'I'm fine with that, check away,' Sophie told him happily. She closed her eyes for a second, breathing in Louis's proximity. 'Sometimes I can't believe it's me either, or that you are you or that we go so well together – but we do, don't we?'

She opened her eyes and searched his for affirmation.

'I seriously suspect that we are the two most compatible people in human history,' Louis told her seriously. He glanced up the stairs that were partially lit by the landing light he had left on for Izzy, who maintained that after dark monsters lived in every shadow, despite Bella assuring her quite firmly that they did not; they lived under beds and in wardrobes.

'I was thinking,' Louis spoke slowly, lowering his lids, 'now that you and I are officially engaged, could you stay over? Because, although being with you on the floor or the sofa or your single bed at the B&B or the kitchen or anywhere is *amazing*, it would be great to go out-and-out kinky and make love to you in a full-sized adult double bed. I might even wake up without a sex-related back injury or friction burns for once.'

Sophie laughed, but when he pulled her hand to follow him she hesitated.

'They're asleep up there,' she said.

'I know, it's great – they're flat out, come on,' Louis urged her.

'But what if they wake up, what if they hear us? What if – God forbid – they walk in on us?' Louis stood perfectly still looking at her for what seemed like a long time.

'Well, other couples with children must do it,' he reasoned eventually. 'Otherwise the world would be full of only children.'

'Look, I know, and I want to stay over too, but if I have anything to do with it we'll be married really soon and I just think it will be easier for them to understand. And if we're married, then everything will be proper.'

'Proper?' Louis thought for a moment and then nodded. 'I suppose you haven't had much that's "proper" in this relationship, but promise me this – once we're married, you will come to bed with me every night in our bed and not worry about anything except that you won't be getting very much sleep. I love you, Sophie, but I'm going to have to put my foot down about having sex in the bedroom once I've got that ring on your finger.'

'It will be different once we're married,' Sophie assured him, on a sharp intake of breath as he pressed the weight of his hips into hers against the door frame. 'I can't wait to be married to you.'

'And in the meantime I have an improper question for you,' Louis asked her as he kissed her neck. 'Sofa or rug?'

'Rug,' Sophie said, lifting her chin as he nuzzled her jaw

line. 'But first I have a question for you. How about we get married on New Year's Eve?'

Sophie couldn't wait to invite Carmen to come to a wedding show with her. 'Invite' wasn't exactly accurate – press-gang, co-opt or draft would all have been more appropriate. After dropping the girls off at school the following morning, Sophie had swanned into Ye Olde Tea Shoppe on the pretext of fancying an éclair for breakfast and showing off her ring. But the very second Carmen turned her back to froth a cappuccino Sophie had whipped out her pile of wedding magazines and fanned them out on the counter.

'We're getting married on New Year's Eve!' she exclaimed as Carmen turned round, nearly sloshing a jug of hot milk over herself when she saw the literature Sophie had brought to accompany breakfast.

'New Year's Eve – that's, like, practically next week!' Carmen said.

'I know!' Sophie said. 'Well, less than three months, anyway. There's loads to do between now and then, so we've got to get started. I've bought us these mags to go through to get some ideas and I printed out all this . . .' She slapped a ream of printer paper down on top of the magazines that repre-sented at least half a small Amazonian rain forest. 'It's infor-mation on venues I found on the net. First, I just searched Cornwall, and then I thought no, let's go crazy, so I did Devon too. There's traditional churchy-type stuff, manor houses, modern venues, hotels, and even one parachuting wedding because, I mean, Louis's a surfer, isn't he? He might like an extreme wedding, mightn't he? What do you think?'

'I'm thinking I should make this coffee a decaf,' Carmen said, pressing her lips together. 'Slow down, darling, you've only had the ring on your finger for five minutes. Last time I

97

saw you, you were all "Oh no, I can't possibly marry him." And now it's "I've got to get him down the aisle quick before he changes his mind!" What's changed? Are you pregnant?'

'No, I am not pregnant. Why does everybody think I'm pregnant?' Sophie said loudly enough to make two hikers look up at her from their full English breakfasts. 'Which reminds me, thanks very much for feeding me a false line about Louis and the bloody surfing holiday.'

'I know, I'm sorry,' Carmen apologised. 'It's just that you looked nervous and I wanted to help calm you down, get you to the restaurant so that the poor bloke could ask you at least. I had no idea you could be so . . .'

'So what?' Sophie asked.

'Enthusiastic.' Carmen shrugged, crossing her arms. 'I was fully expecting you would say no.'

'Me too,' Sophie said. 'I really did, right up till the moment he asked me I was thinking, Oh please God, don't ask me, and then he did and then I said yes and then . . .'

'What?' Carmen asked her with bated breath.

'Then I realised how I'd feel if I ever lost him, and worrying and waiting and wondering didn't seem important any more. Carmen, I'm getting married, of course I'm enthusiastic! Enthusiastic is the watchword of brides everywhere. Do you want to see my engagement ring?'

Sophie thrust her hand under Carmen's nose and wiggled her fingers.

'Of course I want to see the ring!' Carmen took Sophie's fingers in hers and peered at them.

'Babe, it's perfect. Not huge, mind, but who wants a huge one anyway? They're simply vulgar. My husband bought me a massive rock when we got engaged and it didn't make us any happier. Plus it's very you. Louis has really thought about it. You can tell.' She met Sophie's eyes as she smiled and then, without warning, she flung open the hatch that divided her from her public and engulfed Sophie in an icing-sugar-scented hug, sending the weighty glossy wedding magazines slipping and slapping on to the floor in slow motion.

'I'm so happy that you're so happy . . . you two, you're just perfect together.' Sophie was touched and a little surprised to see tears in Carmen's eyes.

'And so are you and James,' Sophie reminded her. 'You and James are one of the loveliest, happiest couples I know.'

'I know . . .' Carmen said, tears beading on her waterproof mascara. She seemed as if she might be about to add a 'but' but none came. 'And you and Louis will be, too – which is why your wedding needs to be perfect.'

'It will be,' Sophie said confidently, bending to scoop up an armful of magazines. 'We just need to get some venue ideas. Maybe we'll find one when we go to the wedding fair.'

'A wedding fair?' Carmen asked as if Sophie had just suggested that they hop on a bus to the moon.

'Yes, it's in Plymouth all this week – how lucky is that?' Sophie told her. 'The West Country Wedding Fair. We're going tomorrow, I've just booked the tickets, Louis is on a half-day assignment taking photos of pasties for a local produce magazine so he can pick the girls up from school, plus they give away champagne and cake by the truck load at those places, so we'll be laughing.'

Carmen shook her head and smiled. 'You really want this, don't you?'

'Of course I do,' Sophie answered. 'Which is lucky because we are getting married in *three months' time*.' She spoke the last words slowly because she found that she was enjoying the fear that was coursing through her body at the very idea. 'Just think, in less than ninety days from today I could officially be married at my own wedding!'

'Well, why wait?' Carmen said as she sat down at the table with Sophie and leafed through a magazine. 'Where did waiting ever get anyone? If you're sure, you're sure and, let's face it, if you've said yes then you ought to be sure. Besides, the quicker it is the better it will be for those girls. If you wait much longer they'll explode from excitement for one thing, and for another, they won't be *quite* as cute any more – no offence, they are lovely kids – I'm just saying, for the photos, younger is cuter . . . ooooh, look at that dress! We're going to try on wedding dresses, I bloody love that.'

'We?'

'You. I mean you,' Carmen said quickly. 'Just think, Sophie, and remember this moment, because this is it – this is the beginning of the rest of your life.'

Sophie tried really hard to stop everything, even the beat of her heart, so that she could think with a clear head. One second of total clarity was all she craved, one moment of still-ness, so that she might advance confidently into a million moments of undoubted mayhem from this point, this moment where she finally left her old life behind her for good.

'Give me a cake,' Sophie said, pointing at a particularly fat éclair that glistened plumply in the fresh-cream chiller.

'A cake?' Carmen quizzed her, obliging nonetheless and plumping the éclair down on to a plate in front of Sophie. 'What's a cake got to do with it?'

'Well, if I'm getting married in ninety days, then I've defin-itely got to give up cakes and I want that one to be my very last one.'

Carmen had given her a side of clotted cream for luck.

'So you're getting married,' Grace Tregowan said to Sophie as she waited for Carmen to come and pick her up in her shiny black BMW four-by-four, skittish as a young colt on a spring morning. 'It's a lovely thing, marriage; I should know, I've done it four times.'

'Four times, Grace?' Sophie said dropping the net curtains and perching on the edge of the sofa as Grace awaited paternity test results on Jeremy Kyle. 'Four husbands, that's an impressive tally!'

'Well, some women would call me greedy,' Grace said, shrugging her frail shoulders with a rasp of cotton mix.

'Tell me,' Sophie asked her, 'did you love them all, or were three of them mistakes while you were waiting for the fourth one?'

'I loved them all, in different ways,' Grace said, sniffing and drawing her arms around her middle as if she had just felt the chill of the past. 'Take my Vincent, my first husband. I met him in France during the war. Special Ops found out that I'd lived in Paris and they sent me back out there because I could speak the lingo like a Frenchy. Three months' training then they drop you in a field in the middle of bloody nowhere and tell you to remember your name is Claudette. I was a wireless operator, sending messages back home. Vincent was running the local resistance, he was only twenty-two. These days that's nothing, you lot all still act like kids well into your forties, moaning about responsibility and mortgages . . .' Grace sighed. 'Vincent was just twenty-two, just a boy fighting for his country's freedom, fighting for his life. He was so young . . . so serious and so fucking handsome, Sophie, you should have seen him. Dark hair, so thick and curly you couldn't run your fingers through it, never mind a comb, and eyes as violet as the lavender in the lane. You have to try and imagine that we were frightened *all* the time; death was always just a heartbeat way. We saw it, smelt it, all around us. We saw our friends, people we loved, killed or taken from us. It's easy to love when you live that way – it's hard not to love, because when you love you know you are still alive. And I loved Vincent with all my heart. We didn't plan to get married, but then I fell pregnant. And he was a good Catholic French boy. We had a secret midnight wedding in a chapel in the town, but it wasn't legal because I never knew his real name and he didn't know mine. That didn't matter to us, though. To us it was sacred.'

'You married a man whose name you didn't know – but wasn't it sort of important to know that about him? Sometimes I think I don't know nearly enough about Louis, but at least I know his real name. Or at least I think I do.'

'It wasn't important,' Grace told her. 'All I needed to know about him was that he was there, his heart beating for me. At first I used to beg him to tell me, but he wouldn't and he never asked me for mine. I was angry with him, but then I realised he was only trying to protect me. He didn't ask me because he loved me. So the local priest risked his life to conduct the marriage. We always said that after the war we'd do it properly, but I think even then we knew that wouldn't happen, we knew that one of us wouldn't make it. I tried to keep the baby a secret but my controller found out I was up the duff and pulled me out. That was in 1944. I didn't want to leave him. I was desperate to stay, even with the baby.' Grace dropped her head, her eyes travelling unseeing over her blue-veined hands. 'I knew the night I said goodbye to him would be the last time I saw him alive. We clung to each other for the longest time in the darkness in the field where the plane landed to pick me up and he promised he'd be there when the baby was born . . .'

She trailed off, looking up into the middle distance at some long-lost face engraved with moonlight shadows.

'But he didn't make it?' Sophie asked her, breathless.

'Killed the next week. Shot by the Nazis,' Grace said. 'They always used to say that it's when you'd got something to live for, when you were afraid of dying, that you were in trouble, because you'd hesitate and make a mistake. They were right.'

'And the baby, is that Frank?' Sophie referred to Mrs Tregowan's eldest son, whom she had never met but who, from Grace's description of him, sounded frankly awful.

'No, that was my poppet, my little girl Claudette,' Grace said. 'Pneumonia took her before she was three months old.' She smiled at Sophie and patted her chest where her heart was. 'I keep her here now with her dad. I loved Vincent. I loved him with all of my heart. Would I have loved him if I'd met him on a normal day at a normal time when there weren't bombs falling out of the sky and death squads on the march? To be honest, I don't know. The trick is, Sophie, to love while love has you. Enjoy it, savour it, revel in it. So what if you're rushing into marrying a man you hardly know? Marry him while you love him. What's the point of waiting till he bores you rigid?'

'Grace,' Sophie said as she heard Carmen's car pull up, 'did anyone ever tell you how amazing and brave you were and did anyone ever say thank you to you?'

'What for?' Grace sniffed, looking at the TV. 'I did my bit, that's all, and I could have told her he's not the father of her baby; look at the nose on it, ugly little bugger!'

'Bloody hell,' Sophie said as she and Carmen walked into the Plymouth Pavilions where the wedding fair was being held. The huge space had been decked out with white and gold balloons and there was stall after stall of wedding paraphernalia from dresses to table favours to romantic dove-release hire and helium-balloon sculptures. The vast room was crowded with women of all ages, mothers and daughters, sisters and best friends, all of them with that faintly manic glint in their eye, that special glow that said, 'I'm going to have a great big massive party that's all about me and there's nothing you can do about it.'

As she scanned the heaving mass of people Sophie spotted a few beleaguered-looking men, mostly fathers, she guessed, but possibly the odd groom-to-be trailing along after his woman like a relic from a former age when men weren't necessary for anything other than standing at the altar and saying 'I do.'

'Look at all this wedding stuff and look at all the people here looking at all the wedding stuff. Who knew that so many people got married?' Sophie said.

'I know, and they all look a little bit scary to me,' Carmen said, hooking her arm through Sophie's. 'What is it about weddings that make women go all feral?'

'I don't know, but what if one of that lot gets to my dress before I do?' Sophie replied, that manic glint lighting her eye. 'We need to get in there now.'

'We can do this,' Carmen said as if they were about to go over the top of a trench. 'I'm a pastry chef and you, you were the premier corporate events organiser in London, Europe and North America. You know everything there is to know about planning parties.'

'You're right,' Sophie affirmed. 'I'm the woman who once organised a book launch in a hot-air balloon and two years ago I did a satellite link-up with the Russian space station for a Russian energy company. I'm Sophie Mills, none of these other bitches stand a chance.'

'Dress stands twelve o'clock,' Carmen said pointing across the vast hall.

'Marvellous,' Sophie said. 'Cover me, I'm going in.'

'I need cake,' Sophie said, emerging from the dress section of the exhibition, with her hair tousled, her lipstick smudged and her shirt buttoned up wrongly as if she'd just had secret sex, except that what she had been doing was a million times better than that. She'd tried on every single style of wedding dress that had ever been brought into existence. From the giant puffy meringue to a white lace thigh-length minidress with a detachable train, Sophie had tried them all on and then so had Carmen for good measure. 'Look, there's the wedding cake section. Let's go over there and score hardcore fuck-off cake. Do you think you can snort cake? I need to mainline cake.'

'I thought you were giving up cake, because you need to if you want to wear that minidress,' Carmen said as she followed her.

'I am giving up cake, I'm just exhausted from all the lace and sequins. I can feel my blood sugar levels dropping and we haven't even started yet. I need emergency cake. It's medicinal.'

'I like the last one with the bustle and the sleeve,' Carmen offered as she hurried after Sophie, struggling to keep up with her friend's purposeful heels as she tottered beside her in her heeled ankle boots.

'God, no! That one made me looked like sheep's carcass dressed as mutton!' Sophie responded, her eyes locked purposefully on baked goods.

'OK, well, that gold one with the bows and the glitter effect was really something.'

'Yes, it was something. It was something that a lady does not repeat unless she's stepped in it. I mean I loved it, I loved trying on all of the dresses, especially the pink one with the butterflies and the diamanté . . .'

'And the one with the neckline that was so plunging the vicar could get a good look at your navel . . .'

'But none of those dresses was the right dress, Carmen. I need the right dress and I need it today or tomorrow. What am I going to do? I need to find the right dress and I've just tried on every single wedding dress in the history of wedding dresses and I haven't found the right dress and ... I really need cake. Now. Look over there,' Sophie said clocking a stall that had a sign hanging over it that read: Celestial Cakes – Bliss in a Bite. 'That's what I'm talking about.'

'The main thing is that you looked stunning.' Carmen trotted along trying to keep up with her. 'Truly you did. In every single gown, even the hideous ones, you glowed. You're so lucky getting to marry the man you love.'

'You could marry James if you wanted to, couldn't you?' Sophie asked her, stopping suddenly by the Celestial Cakes stand so that Carmen bumped into her.

'Not really – I'm still married.' Carmen shrugged.

'Then why not divorce your ex?' Sophie asked her.

'I don't know,' Carmen said, sighing as she looked over the cake samples that were on display. 'I'm waiting, I suppose ...'

'Waiting for what?' Sophie asked her. 'You've moved down here, you live with James. St Ives is your home now. What is there to wait for?'

Carmen thought for a moment and looked as if she were about to say something more. Then her eyes slid past Sophie to something behind her and widened.

'That's your dress,' she breathed. 'That's the perfect dress for you.'

Sophie turned round to see a model walk past serenely in an ivory satin dress, simply cut so that it skimmed her hips and swished around her feet as she moved, like the froth of an incoming tide. The scoop neckline and low back was edged simply with seed pearls and the light reflecting off the material seemed to make the girl's skin shine.

'Want that dress,' Sophie said suddenly monosyllabic. 'I really need to follow that dress and get that dress. I wonder what size that model is because that's the dress for me. Maybe I could have her dress and take it home today, what do you think, do you think they'd do alterations on it today, you know, stick material in where her hips and thighs should have been because I need that dress and I've only got ninety days . . .'

'Oh my God . . .' Carmen picked up a square of iced fruit cake from the Celestial Cakes table and shoved it in Sophie's mouth. 'Get your gob round that and calm down, woman.'

Sophie was appalled at Carmen's silencing tactic, but the cake really was rather delicious so she decided against spitting it out.

'Eat the cake, love the cake, think only of the cake and relax. In a minute we'll go over to where they are having the catwalk and we'll find out who makes the dress, and you can try it on. Everything will be fine,' Carmen talked as Sophie munched. 'Now, I don't know what your policy on hats is going to be but I'm thinking of a fascinator for me as your head bridesmaid, what do you think? You can swallow before you answer that.'

The two women stared at each other for several seconds longer till Sophie finally swallowed her cake.

'Ah yes, well, you see, the issue over head bridesmaid isn't quite fully resolved yet,' Sophie said, thinking of the three adults and two children who were so far vying for the post. 'Not because I don't love you or anything but more owing to the fact that, due to the principal reason of the fact that . . . oh, thank God, there's Louis! What's he doing here?'

She felt a rush of relief as she saw the back of Louis's head and shoulders at the wedding underwear stand a few stalls away. For some reason he seemed to be rifling through a box of frilly knickers.

'Louis!' she called out but he didn't turn around.

'Are you sure that's him?' Carmen asked her, momentarily

diverted from her bridesmaid pitch. 'What on earth would he be doing here unless he's got a thong habit that he wasn't planning to share with you till the wedding night? Why's he got his head in a box full of knickers?'

Sophie began to hurry over towards where he was standing.

'Well, he said if it wasn't for the pasty shoot he'd have popped down with us to do some industrial spying on the wedding photographers, find out their rates and things. Maybe the shoot finished early and he's come to find me. Come on, let's get him and show him that dress . . .'

'Over my dead body,' Carmen gasped, stopping Sophie with a hand on her shoulder. 'You do not show the prospective groom the prospective wedding dress! Don't you know anything about basic wedding etiquette? You know, stuff like asking your only adult female friend who comes with you to wedding fairs to be head bridesmaid, for example. Besides, that's not Louis, since when has Louis worn low-rise tight black jeans and a studded leather belt?'

Sophie stopped and looked again at the figure. Carmen was right, it wasn't Louis.

'But he really looks like him, doesn't he?' she said. 'His hair, his shoulders, even the way he's standing there. It could be . . .' Her sentence ground to a halt as the subject in question turned round. 'Louis.'

He was a young man, perhaps twenty or twenty-one, he still had the edges of acne around his chin, but he stood with the confidence and self-assurance of a much older man, without that kind of awkward posture that some young men have when they haven't quite worked out how to get all their limbs moving at once. And he looked almost exactly like Louis.

'He *does* look like him,' Carmen said, digging Sophie in the ribs. 'Here, take a photo on your phone, we can tease Louis about having a secret love child when we get home.'

'He must be a relation,' Sophie said, watching the young man as he hung bits of frilly underwear on a stand without even a hint of self-consciousness. 'A cousin or something. He has to be. Look at his mouth . . . those lips are just like Louis's. I have to ask him because Louis's got no family that I know of. I bet he'd be really excited if I found him a cousin or something. A long-lost relative – it would be the perfect wedding present.'

'I wouldn't mind him for Christmas,' Carmen breathed, as they watched the young man effortlessly flirt with a bride and her mother over blue and cream frilly garters.

'Hands off, Carmen,' Sophie said, feeling unexpectedly territorial. 'Your younger man quota is fully filled. This one's mine.' Brushing cake crumbs from around her mouth and briefly running her fingers through her hair, Sophie approached the young man, feeling oddly a little bit as if she had stepped back in time and was getting the chance to meet the love of her life when he was new, before he had baggage, when he was fresh.

'Hello,' she said smiling at him. His answering smile was confident and attractive. Sophie struggled to contain the confusion of butterflies that went off in her chest and found herself colouring.

'You really are a blushing bride.' He smiled, holding her gaze. 'Come on, you can tell me what you're after – I'm unshockable.'

'Actually, it's you I'm interested in, not your thongs,' Sophie said, surprised to find herself flirting with him, not least because she had never flirted with anyone – she wasn't even sure if she'd ever flirted with Louis. It just wasn't something that came naturally to her.

'Best news I've had all day.' The boy grinned at her.

'Do you mind if I ask you your name?' Sophie asked him.

'Probably best, if we're going to be going on a date,' the boy said. Sophie found herself giggling, but Carmen's raised eyebrow brought her back to her senses.

'Seth,' he told her holding out a hand. 'And you?'

'Seth,' Sophie repeated his name. 'I'm Sophie Mills and I'm not asking you out on a date – it's just that you look an awful lot like my boyfriend ... fiancé ... betrothed. I'm still not really sure what to call him.'

'So we've established I'm your type, and hey – I like an older blonde, especially one with curves,' Seth told her. Sophie was ashamed to feel heat rising in her belly. Standing here with Louis from the past, a past before he'd met Carrie or run off to Peru, was really very confusing. She glanced sheepishly at a very sour-looking Carmen and made an effort to pull herself back together.

'You are very confident, aren't you?' Sophie told him concentrating hard on remembering that he was not her fiancé. 'How old are you?'

'Twenty,' Seth told her, tipping his head on side to appraise her figure. 'Too young for you?'

'No, I mean yes, I mean you really do look like him.' Sophie frowned. 'Do you know anyone called Louis Gregory?'

'Nope,' Seth said. 'Should I? Is he likely to want to fight me for you?'

'I thought you might be related, cousins or something – he doesn't have much family.'

'Neither do I,' Seth told her with a shrug. 'It's just me and Mum. Nan and Granddad live up North. I don't know about cousins or uncles. Look, if that's all you're really interested in, you're better off talking to Mum when she gets back.'

'Seth!' The young man looked up and sighed. 'Here's the boss now. She's going to want to know why I'm flirting with the bride instead of selling her themed hen-night knickers.'

He treated Sophie to a slow grin. 'The things a student will do for cash. Come back at five and I'll take you for a drink.'

'Seth, I thought I told you to get all the stock out; it's not going to sell in a box, is it?'

Sophie turned around at the sound of the oddly familiar voice and came face to face with Wendy Churchill.

'It's you,' Sophie said bluntly. 'You work on the stall?'

'It's my business – and you are?' Wendy raised a brow which let Sophie realise that she knew exactly who she was but was choosing to pretend not to.

'Louis's fiancée, Sophie Mills,' Sophie told her with her best corporate smile. 'We met the other day . . . I was just chatting to Seth because I wondered if he might be related to Louis in some way. He told me to ask his mum – do you know where she is?'

There was a beat of silence between the two of them when everything slotted slowly into place and Sophie felt her stomach plummet through her toes.

Wendy held her gaze for a moment longer and then the tension in her mouth and eyes relaxed just a fraction revealing the hint of a smile which told Sophie what, suddenly, she already knew.

'I'm his mum,' she said, keeping her voice low so that it couldn't be heard above the hum of the chatter-filled hall. 'I had him when I was sixteen.'

Sophie looked over at where Seth was expertly flirting with Carmen over a lacy cream basque.

'He works for me part time while he's finishing his degree.' Wendy paused and eyed Sophie with her cold, grey eyes. 'And yes. Yes, Louis is his father. But he doesn't know that. And Louis has never known anything – he didn't even know I was pregnant. I haven't seen Louis in over twenty years – until I bumped into him the other day. Look, Sophie, me and Seth are fine. We are happy without him. We are doing really well. And if you and Louis are getting married then I guess that you must be happy too. Nothing has to change, does it?'

Sophie looked into Wendy's eyes. About ten thousand thoughts were chasing around in her head, each one screaming to be heard, not a single one of them making sense in the mêlée. But she knew one thing. Wendy was asking her to keep quiet.

'Wendy, you've just told me that the man I'm going to marry has a son he knows nothing about, are you seriously suggesting that I shouldn't tell the man I'm about to marry that he's got a child – a grown man of a son walking around less than fifty miles away from where he lives?'

'I am,' Wendy said flatly, her eyes glassy and reflective. 'What would it hurt?'

'You must realise I can't possibly do that,' Sophie replied. 'I can't keep something that huge from the man I love, the man I'm going to marry. Besides, he has a right to know about his son!' Sophie fought to keep her voice down, reeling from the weight of the knowledge that she was suddenly burdened with.

'No, he doesn't.' Wendy's face was dark with fury. 'I didn't tell him then for a good reason and I'm not going to tell him now. Seth is *my* son, I've brought him up alone for all of these years and I have done bloody well for myself by working my guts out. He is *nothing* to do with Louis.'

'But why?' Sophie asked her. 'Why didn't you tell Louis about him, if not back then at some point in the last twenty years?'

Wendy shook her head bitterly. 'I had my reasons,' she warned. 'And they are none of your business.'

'Mum, I've got that gig,' Seth said, coming over again and grinning at Sophie with that same easy smile that his father had. 'If I don't go now I'll miss the sound check and I'll get fired. Again.'

'Go on, then.' Wendy smiled indulgently, taking some notes out of her back pocket and pressing them into his palm. 'See you tomorrow same time, OK? Don't drink too much and don't—'

'Mother, I am a grown man,' Seth said, winking at Sophie and stooping to kiss his mother on the cheek. 'It's the ladies that have to watch out.'

The two women watched him go, his familiar gait and even Louis-like flick of his hair leaving Sophie's heart in her mouth.

'Look,' Wendy said her face softening a little, which for some reason Sophie found even more intimidating, 'all I'm saying is that nothing has to change. And if you give yourself a second to think about it you'll realise that is the best option. You can go your way, have your wedding and your life and I'll go mine. No one will ever know.'

Sophie shook her head. In the space of twenty minutes everything she thought she knew had changed and there was no way to put things back to how they had been before.

'Wendy, I'm sorry, but I love him, we've been through a lot to be together and what kind of person, what kind of wife, would I be if I kept this from him?' she said.

'Then you'll regret it,' Wendy told her quietly. 'I can promise you that. The cosy little life you think you've got for yourself will be over for good.'

Chapter Seven

Sophie stood in the playground waiting for Louis and Izzy to arrive to pick up Bella. She and Carmen were supposed to have been gone for the whole day so Louis had made sure that he had the afternoon free to collect Izzy at one and Bella at three-fifteen. It was the first place where she was certain he'd be and she knew she had to see him as soon as she possibly could so that she could tell him about Wendy and Seth. So that she could tell him about his son. She had no idea how she was going to tell him, how the necessary words would form into a coherent sentence and emerge from her mouth, but she knew she had to tell him at the first opportunity because otherwise she would lose her nerve and the consequences of that happening were unimaginable. For whatever reason, Wendy had tried to intimidate her and warn her off telling Louis the truth. But really, there was no alternative – she had to tell him no matter what happened next, even though it seemed certain that whatever it was it was going to change everything.

She had been driving back with Carmen towards St Ives when she came to the realisation that her knowledge of Seth and Wendy was simply not something she could keep to herself. No matter how much she might want to.

'Who was she, then?' Carmen had asked her as soon as they

were out of the car park. 'You looked like you wanted to deck her and I've never seen you want to get out of a place so quickly, especially not a place where they have free cake and your dream wedding dress.'

Sophie thought for a moment. It wouldn't be right to tell Carmen about Seth before she told Louis, but she knew if she told her even one piece of information about Wendy and Seth then Carmen's busy female brain would assimilate the rest in a nanosecond and she would work it all out herself.

'That woman was Louis's ex-girlfriend,' Sophie told Carmen. 'I met her when we bumped into her a few days ago. They went out together one summer, back when they were teenagers. She was his big first love, his first . . . everything.'

'Was she really? So what's she got to do with . . . Oh my bloody fuck. Louis is Seth's dad, isn't he?' Carmen asked her, taking her eyes off the road for a second to stare at Sophie.

'And he doesn't know a thing about it,' Sophie said, looking out of the passenger window at the countryside slipping by at a dizzying rate.

'And now you've got to tell him,' Carmen stated.

'Yes, I have, haven't I?' Sophie glanced at Carmen, whose eyes were now fixed firmly on the road ahead, a frown slotted between her eyebrows. Fear clutched Sophie's stomach and her conviction wavered. 'I do, don't I? I have to tell him.'

After a second Carmen pulled the car over and turned off the engine. She twisted in her seat to look at Sophie.

'Let's think about this,' Carmen said tapping the leather-covered steering wheel with one long enamelled nail. 'Do you have to tell him? Because, after all, if you hadn't bumped into Wendy or if she hadn't happened to have a wedding lingerie business that her son was helping out with, then you would never have known any of this. You'd have gone and ordered your dream dress instead of running out, we'd have come home tonight, and we'd have been none the wiser.'

'I know, but I *did* bump into Wendy and I *did* see Seth and I *do* know,' Sophie said twisting her fingers in knots. 'I do know and how can I know something so profound about Louis as the existence of his own flesh and blood while he doesn't? How can I possibly?'

'I don't know.' Carmen shrugged. 'Does he know everything about you? Do you know everything about him? Look, that Wendy woman and her kid must have been living around here for months at least, only a few miles from where Louis lives and nothing happened. Maybe nothing needs to happen now. Maybe you don't have to do this.'

Sophie shook her head. 'Would you tell James if another woman had had his child and he didn't know about it?'

Carmen's face dropped and she dipped her head. 'No, I wouldn't,' she said. 'I'd be too scared of losing him.'

'Really? You really think that there's a risk I'll lose Louis if he finds out about Seth? But how, why?'

'Children change things,' Carmen said. 'Kids, big ones, little ones – they change things especially if they belong to someone else. I mean it wouldn't be just you and Louis and the girls any more. It wouldn't just be you and the girls and Seth. There'd be that Wendy woman, she'd be there for the rest of your life too. Think about that.'

'Bella and Izzy haven't come between us, so why would Seth?' Sophie asked her.

'I don't know . . . I don't know anything about him or his mother, I just know that this is a massive thing, Sophie. You have to think about this before you go through with it.'

Sophie stared out at the road ahead as she tried to imagine

having a conversation with Louis about his unknown son.

'The thing is,' she said slowly, 'I can't marry a man I'm keeping such a huge secret from. I might want to, I might want to carry on and pretend I didn't see Wendy or Seth, but I can't. Because what if Louis finds out about Seth another way, maybe even bumps into him and Wendy the way I did? Cornwall is not a big place and they both work in the wedding industry – it's only a matter of time. What if he finds out that I knew and I didn't tell him? No one can get married on that much of a lie, Carmen, it just wouldn't be right. So I've got to tell him, haven't I?'

Slowly Carmen nodded, gently placing her palms on either side of Sophie's head and turning her to look at her.

'Mate, you're right – you've got to,' Carmen said. 'There's no way out of this one.'

Izzy spotted Sophie first, still in her uniform from morning nursery, only now it was bejewelled with splodges of paint and possibly jam and what Sophie hoped was chocolate spread.

'Aunty Sophie!' she cried out happily, running up to Sophie who picked her up and hugged the child's sticky cheek against her own as she noted Louis caught at the gate by one of the mothers who was no doubt arranging a play date. Louis was very popular with the mothers, a lone father struggling on with his children. They all loved him. Oddly they hardly ever spoke more than two words to Sophie and she always supposed it was because she wasn't a proper mother, not officially in the club as she hadn't ever given birth. She could be wrong, of course, but sometimes standing in the playground waiting for the girls to either go in or leave school was far more intimidating and clique-ridden than actually being at school had ever been.

'Hello, poppet. How was school today?' Sophie asked her,

careful to keep her voice cheerful. Woe betide anyone who referred to Izzy's half-day at nursery as anything less than school. The four-year-old took it very seriously and considered herself to be just as much a schoolgirl as her big sister.

'We learned letters and did role playing,' Izzy told her. 'And for show and tell I did "I am going to be a bridesmaid with wings and a big skirt." But I had to mostly tell as I didn't have anything to show.' She tipped her head to one side, her cascade of curls tumbling across her face. 'When exactly can we get my wings and how often can I wear them? Do you remember my fairy dress, Aunty Sophie? I miss my fairy dress, what happened to it?'

Sophie did indeed remember the garment that the then three-year-old Izzy had been wearing when she arrived at her flat more than a year ago to stay with the guardian aunt she barely knew. It was an item of clothing that she refused to take off at any cost. At one point Sophie had even resorted to bathing her in the outfit in a bid to get it clean. Izzy had clung to the dress with the determination and wilfulness that only a small child can have, and it took Sophie a long time to realise that it was her comfort blanket, her familiar thing in a world full of strange faces and places. In a world where one moment she had been sitting in her mummy's car singing along to the radio and the next her mother was dead and she was all alone. When the dress could take no more abuse Sophie had replaced it, but since they had come back to St Ives she'd thought Izzy had grown out of her obsession with it. Should she worry that the little girl mentioned it now? Could it be a sign that she wasn't as happy and secure as Sophie hoped?

'It's in your wardrobe, sweetie,' Sophie told her. 'Do you want to put it on when we got home?'

'I was just thinking that I could use the wings to practise

with,' Izzy said. 'Till you get me my real wings. Will I be able to fly?'

'Hello.' Louis caught up and kissed Sophie on the cheek. 'I didn't expect to see you here. Wedding fair a wash-out?'

'It was . . .' Sophie hesitated. 'It was unexpected. It made me think that we have a lot of things to talk about, Louis.' Which was true, but the knowledge of Seth must have given her voice a heavier edge because Louis's face dropped.

'I don't like the sound of that,' he said. 'I don't like the whole "we've got a lot of things to talk about" line. What does that mean?'

Sophie bit her bottom lip as she looked at him unable to find the right words to reassure him.

'Soph!' Louis's laugh was uncertain. 'Don't tell me you're getting cold feet?' he asked her anxiously.

'No . . . no, not at all. But you and I do need to talk.' Sophie looked into Louis's eyes and decided now was not the moment to bring up Seth. So she released her other concerns that had been building before Seth eclipsed them all. 'Especially before my mother gets involved and Cal sticks his oar in, otherwise we'll end up having a three-ringed circus instead of a wedding and that's not what I want. There was so much to think about at the wedding fair and so much still to do. I want to marry you on New Year's Eve but it's so near and we'll never find a nice place—'

'Ah, but I have found a nice place,' Louis cut her off with a grin that reminded her of standing opposite Seth less than two hours ago and made her feel guilty for changing the subject as if nothing at all had changed – which of course, for a few more precious moments at least, which Sophie mourned as each once passed, it hadn't.

'Really?' Sophie asked him, hopeful that this was a sign that everything was going to be OK, no matter what happened.

'Yes, subject to your approval, of course,' Louis said. 'Finestone Manor, up on the moor. It was where I was doing the pasty shoot, believe it or not. Home-made mince-filled pasties on a big dark oak sixteenth-century trestle table – all very historical, you know. Anyway, it's an amazing place. They only started doing weddings last year because the upkeep of the place was getting too much and they do the whole lot. Wedding ceremony, catering, accommodation for guests and in the winter there are log fires and little candles everywhere; it's meant to be really magical. I was talking to the owner while the food was getting fluffed and he said he'd give me a thirty per cent discount if I did some publicity shots for him free of charge, plus he offered a deal on wedding photos to his clients. I've done some sums in my head and I think we can do it as long as we keep the guest list down ... I'll show you photos when we get back ...'

'Louis, that's brilliant news,' Sophie said, hugging him so hard that she winded him.

'Blimey, I was wrong about the cold feet, wasn't I?' Louis said wrapping his arms around her. 'I'm glad you're pleased – you see? It's a sign. It's a sign that everything is going to be brilliant. I promise you.'

'I know ...' Sophie thought of those words rattling around in her head that she'd have to spit out sometime. 'I know. Whatever happens, everything between you and me will be fine. Nothing can come between us.'

Louis's smile faded into a frown but before he could press her further Bella arrived carrying her book bag and a rather elaborate cardboard hat, with feathers and sequins glued on to it. She examined Sophie closely. 'Why is everyone here? It's very unusual. Are we going to Ye Olde Tea Shoppe for tea? Is that why everyone is here? That would be acceptable.'

'That's a lovely hat and normally we would go out for tea,'

Sophie began, glancing at Louis. 'But Daddy and I have lots of things to discuss so probably we'd better go home ...'

'But please, please, *please*!' Izzy begged. 'I am starving, I *neeeeed* a scone!'

'You *neeeed* some vegetables and fruit and stuff,' Sophie pointed out, hoping that the real mums still in the playground would overhear and realise that even though she had never given birth she knew how important it was to get five portions of fruit and vegetables into a child – even if she had no idea how to actually do it.

'Strawberries are fruit,' Bella pointed out. 'Strawberry jam is fruit.'

'We can go for cake, can't we?' Louis said, smiling coaxingly as he tucked a strand of Sophie's hair behind her ear. 'I'm glad you're keen to see Finestone but the photos can wait a while. It's nice us all being together.'

Sophie tried to picture herself pretending everything was fine for another hour or two and she couldn't.

'No, Louis.' Sophie hesitated for one second, not wanting to say the words that would start the chain of events she could not predict a conclusion to. 'I have to talk to you about something else.' Her serious tone caught him off guard.

'What?' he asked her warily.

'Not here,' Sophie began, glancing around her and the now near-empty playground, and uncomfortably conscious of Bella's gaze.

'Sophie,' Louis's tone darkened, his coaxing smile evaporating in an instant, 'if it's not the wedding you're worried about, then what? Just tell me now, please, I'm not in the mood for games.'

Sophie looked at the girls. Mercifully Izzy had jammed Bella's hat on to her head and was shrieking with laughter as she tore away from a furious Bella who raced after her. Perhaps in the middle of a school playground wasn't the best place but then where was the best place to tell Louis he'd had a child he didn't know about for over twenty years?

'I saw Wendy Churchill at the wedding fair,' Sophie said, leaning close into him so that her voice was barely more than a whisper. She paused, breathing in his scent and the heat of his proximity. For some reason she felt it would be harder to be so close to him after she'd told him what she knew. 'She was there with her son. She has a twenty-year-old son, Louis.'

Sophie waited but Louis's male brain was not making any connections.

'She must have got pregnant when she was fifteen.' Sophie looked into Louis's eyes before pressing her lips against his ear and whispering. 'He looks just like you. Louis, he's your son.'

Back home, after Louis had stalked out of the playground, making it clear that a visit to Ye Olde Tea Shoppe was most definitely not on the cards, Sophie cooked the girls tea while Louis stood in the garden staring very hard at his decaying flower beds. Sophie's culinary skills had come on a long way since the first tea she had made them, which had been two microwavable meals mixed together to avoid argument. Now she was able to grill sausages and mash potatoes without having to concentrate hardly at all although admittedly that was because the girls rather obligingly liked her lumpy – or, as Sophie preferred to call it, 'textured' – mash.

Louis had not said a word to her since the playground, leaving Izzy to fill in the gaps with her usual endless stream of consciousness punctuated occasionally by Bella's sage-like asides such as 'Fairies live in dells, not groves, idiot' and 'No, the tooth fairy doesn't collect toenail clippings. The toenail-clipping fairy does that, obviously.'

Sophie had not pressed him to talk. She had no idea what he was thinking or feeling or if he'd even really understood what she had just told him. Now she watched him through her own reflection in the kitchen window as he stood in the twilight, perfectly still, just standing there, staring into the soil as the sky dimmed.

'Sophie, when you and Daddy are married where will you sleep?' Bella asked her suddenly, dragging Sophie's attention away from the window.

'In a bed, hopefully!' she said brightly even though she knew that Bella would never be satisfied with such a trite answer. For a seven-year-old Bella had a particularly effective questioning technique and a dogged determination to gather as much information as she could about whatever might touch her life in some way. Sophie had been expecting these questions but she had rather hoped not to have to answer them today.

'And where will the bed be?' Bella asked her intently.

'Well, I'll sleep here, in this house with you,' Sophie hedged, suddenly wishing she'd delayed her bombshell till after the girls were in bed so that Louis might be here to help her field these questions.

'Which room will you sleep in?' Bella asked her slowly. 'Because I don't want to share with Izzy again, she's a very restless sleeper.'

'I am not,' Izzy said, through a mouthful of sausage. 'That's not me, that's Tango. He's a very restless sleeper especially when you cuddle him up.'

'No, I'll sleep with . . . I mean I'll sleep in the same room as your daddy when we're married. That's what normal married people do, they sleep together in the same room with each other,' Sophie said. She stood Bella's searching gaze for a second more before springing up to cool her cheeks in the freezer while she looked for the blackcurrant sorbet the girls had recently become obsessed with.

'Will you do kissing when you're married?' Izzy asked her, giggling through her gravy-stained fingers. Bella rolled her eyes.

'They already do kissing,' she told her little sister. 'That's allowed because they are in love.' Sophie paused as she took two bowls off the drainer. Louis was still there, still in exactly the same spot. She had gone about this in the wrong way, she shouldn't have just blurted it out in the playground like that. What had she been thinking? Yes, Seth did look remarkably like Louis but she didn't have any proof that he was Louis's son, only her own expectations and Wendy's word. And there was something about Wendy that Sophie didn't trust. She was self-aware enough to know that she didn't like her because she was yet another part of Louis's past that she would never have access to, a part that was clearly so precious and important to him, but it wasn't just that that made her mistrust her. Something in the way she'd looked at Louis that first time they'd met in the pub made her uneasy. There was something destructive about her.

'Sophie?' It was Bella again, with that same persistent tone that Sophie had learned signalled the child had something on her mind and wouldn't rest till she'd resolved it.

'Yes?' Sophie steeled herself, scooping out the sorbet into the bowls, one eye still on the garden,

'Will you and Daddy have babies?' Bella asked her. 'Will we have a brother or a sister? Well, really a *half*-brother or a *half*-sister.'

Sophie sat down and slid a bowl to each girl.

'Well . . .' She and Louis had never discussed having their own children. Sophie supposed in the back of her mind that perhaps one day they would have a baby, although, rather like being properly married to Louis, till recently she hadn't been able to picture it as a concrete event. But whether or not he wanted more children was another matter. Especially as he was just getting used to the idea of his twenty-year-old son. 'I don't really know, Bella.'

'Because if you had a baby with Daddy it would call you Mummy, wouldn't it?' Bella asked her, carefully taking the smallest spoonful of her sorbet so as to make it last longer.

'Well, yes, if I did have a baby with your daddy when it was big enough to talk it would call me Mummy.'

'And it would call Daddy Daddy?'

'Yes,' Sophie said.

'But we'd still call you Aunty Sophie,' Bella said. 'Because even though you'd be married to our daddy and living here and we'd have a half-sister or a half-brother who called you Mummy you'd still be our Aunty Sophie and not our mummy.'

'That's right . . .' Sophie said slowly, trying to work out exactly what it was that Bella was worrying about. 'You know that I would never ever try to take the place of your mummy. I couldn't do that and I don't want to.'

Bella looked at her for a long time with her grave dark eyes. She had come a long way from the quiet self-contained child that Sophie had first met a year ago, the little girl who was struggling to grow up because she felt there was nobody left in the world to look after her or her baby sister. Before her eyes Sophie had seen Bella blossoming into almost the child she had been before her mother was suddenly taken from her, funny, with an infectious giggle and a surprisingly dry wit for one so young. But sometimes she would still get that look in her eye that told Sophie she knew that the world could hurt you when you least expected it. That was a lost innocence that could not be recovered.

'Bella, darling,' Sophie picked up her hand, 'do you mind me marrying your dad and living here?'

'No.' Bella shook her head. 'I want you to marry Daddy and live here. I'm just not sure about what will happen when you've got a baby that calls you Mummy and we aren't calling you Mummy . . . will we be split in two? Will you prefer your baby to us?'

'Will you?' Izzy who up till that point had been rather physically involved in her sorbet to the point that she was wearing most of it like a beard. She paused, mid-spoonful, her eyes suddenly brimming with tears.

'No . . . no, of course not. That could *never, ever* happen, I'll always love you exactly the same amount that I do now, which is a gigantic amount, by the way,' Sophie told her, trying not to be distracted by the sound of Louis coming in the back door.

'Is that as much as a proper baby?' Izzy asked her.

'She means your own baby,' Bella said.

'I think it would be impossible for me to love anyone alive on this planet more than I love you two,' Sophie said. 'I mean, yes, I love your dad, but you two – you made me happy again when I didn't even realise I was sad.'

'Will you love the baby as much as you love us, then?' Bella asked.

'Baby?' Louis snapped as he sat down at the table. 'Good God, there's nothing else you want to tell me is there, Sophie?'

Sophie could see by the angle of his shoulders that he was tightly wound and tense. When he was angry he almost seemed to fold in on himself, armouring himself against any assault of reason or affection She took a breath before she spoke, concentrating on keeping her tone light as if it were a perfectly normal day and she hadn't just told Louis about his secret love child, hopeful that if she kept on acting as if everything was OK that soon he would relax, unfurl and be the man she could talk to again.

'We're just talking about what would happen if we had a baby after we're married,' Sophie said carefully, keen for him to tune into how sensitive the girls were feeling.

'Oh, you don't have to worry about that,' Louis's laugh was harsh. 'I think I've got more than enough children to last me a lifetime; we won't be having any more kids.'

Sophie dropped her gaze to the table top aware that Bella was watching her closely, surprised at the sting of tears in her eyes. She felt as if Louis had physically hit her, the pain of his announcement was so sudden and unexpected. He was angry and confused about Seth, and his instinct was to shock and hurt her as much as she had him but, nevertheless, she found discovering his opinion on any future children hard to brush off. They had never talked about having children. It was one of the many things she didn't know about the man she wanted to marry, one of the things that she had so confidently told her mother and Cal and anyone who would listen that she'd find out about him after they were married, part of the big adventure of life with him. But what if he was serious? If he really didn't want children, what then? Sophie didn't even know if she wanted children, but the thought of someone telling her she wasn't going to have any made her feel cornered and angry, emotions she had to curb, at least for now, whether she liked it not.

'Sophie?' Izzy piped up, her face sodden with sorbet. 'I would call you Mummy if it wasn't for Mummy, because I do love you a lot.'

Sophie blinked back the threat of tears and made herself smile before she looked up, resting the back of her hand against Izzy's fruity cheek.

'That's a lovely thing to say,' Sophie said gently. 'Thank you, Izzy.'

'And now,' Louis said, picking Izzy up out of her chair and hoisting her under his arm, 'it's bath time. Bella, run upstairs and get out your jammies and find some towels, we need to get this monster scrubbed clean!'

Izzy shrieked with giggles as Louis tickled her and Sophie worried about the imminent re-emergence of the sorbet as he dangled her upside down by her ankles and swung her like a pendulum before setting her down and letting her scramble off upstairs.

'Are you OK?' Sophie asked him.

He looked at her for a long moment in the unrelenting glare of the kitchen's strip lighting.

'No,' he said. 'I don't think I am.'

Sophie watched Louis pace up and down his living room, every few paces taking a step over Tango who was stretched out on his back in front of the fire warming his belly after making off with two sausages that had been left on the grill. Artemis, who was perched on the top of the book shelf, watched Louis fixedly, her head following his journey back and forth as if at any minute she might pounce on him and attempt to wrestle him to the ground, something which Sophie wouldn't entirely put past a cat who still hadn't got over missing out on the sausages.

The girls had been silent for twenty minutes or so, which usually meant that they were properly asleep and not engaged in some impromptu late-night craft activity or staging of a musical. Normally by now Louis would have shooed Tango upstairs where he'd find the warmest spot to cuddle up in and sleep his food off, Artemis would be out in the cool night air disembowelling small mammals with abandon, and Sophie would be in Louis's arms. They'd be discussing their day in the short punctuation marks between long kisses. But that wasn't reality, Sophie realised as she watched him – this was. Trouble and trauma and working through things together. They had met under stressful circumstances, that was certainly true; it had been grief and loss that had brought them together. But for the last few months everything had been perfect, absolutely perfect, and it could have stayed that way if she hadn't bumped into Seth and Wendy at the wedding fair. But she had. This was happening and now she had to find a way for herself and Louis to face it together. The trouble was it seemed like the last thing he wanted was to talk to her. It even felt as if he'd rather that she wasn't there at all, and that somehow he blamed her for the conception of his son twenty years ago.

'Please, Louis, don't shut me out. Tell me what you're feeling,' Sophie begged him, wincing as she framed the words.

'What I'm feeling?' Louis's laugh was mirthless as he stomped over his prone cat once again. 'What am I feeling? Do you know, Sophie, I have no idea. No . . . no, that's wrong, I know exactly how I'm feeling. I'm angry, I'm really bloody angry. Sophie, why did you have to tell me then, like that?'

It came as a shock to Sophie to discover that Louis was angry at her.

'First of all, keep your voice down, we don't want to wake the girls, and second – I didn't want to tell you like that, but you said you wanted to know and you made it pretty hard for me not to tell you right then, Louis.' Sophie was reproachful.

'It's just . . . I can't get my head around what you're telling me; you're telling me I have a twenty-year-old son. How? I mean, how can that be?' Louis asked.

'Well, presumably when you and Wendy—'

'Once.' Louis's laugh was frenetic and fretful. 'We only had sex once. It was at this kid's birthday party. Me and Wendy had been going out for a while, I was so, so in love with her. I think I would have married her then and there if it had been legal. We decided that the party was going to be "the night". We were both terrified so we got really drunk on cider and ended up under the coats, in the parents' bedroom. I barely remember anything about it except that I wasn't one hundred per cent sure where everything went and it was over very quickly. Wendy cried. It was pretty awful, to be honest, but afterwards . . . I'd never felt so close to anyone before in my life. I really felt like I'd connected to another human being; we stayed there under the coats holding each other. I stroked her hair till she stopped crying.'

'But you didn't use any protection?' Sophie asked him, desperate to block out the image of him ever being sweet and tender with any other woman.

Louis looked at her and shrugged. 'I can't remember, but I was barely sixteen and out of my head on scrumpy. I'm guessing not.'

'And then what?' Sophie forced herself to ask him.

'Then? We saw each other a few more times and then she disappeared.' Louis scowled at Sophie. 'I told you all of this. Back then I didn't think I'd ever love again. But I've hardly thought about her in years . . . not till we bumped into her in the pub and now I find out she had my kid at the age of sixteen and I never knew anything about it? And she's been living less than fifty miles away for God knows how long and I've never bumped into her before.'

'Well, if you think about it, you've only been back in the country for a little while,' Sophie said, trying hard not to have heard the 'hardly' part of what Louis had just said. 'And I think she's only been back in Cornwall for a few months.'

130

'Maybe he's not mine,' Louis said. 'Chances are he's not – aren't they?'

'Except that you haven't seen him,' Sophie said, shaking her head. 'Louis, he looks just like you. I mean, he has your same mannerisms, your smile – he's pretty cute, actually.' Sophie attempted a smile but the black look she received in return soon quelled it.

'Sorry, Soph, I just don't think this is a joking matter,' Louis said, entirely distant, making Sophie feel like it would be impossible to reach out and touch him.

'I know, I'm sorry,' she said. 'So what's next?'

'What is next?' Louis asked her. She wished that he would sit down so they could talk properly, looking into each other's eyes, holding hands – between kisses, the way they normally did when they were alone. But he persisted in standing with his hands on his hips looking as if he wanted someone to blame. Looking at her.

'Well, I suppose the next thing is to get in touch with Wendy, to arrange a time to talk to her ...' Sophie suggested tentatively. 'Meet this head on and deal with it.'

'Yeah, I suppose. Did she say when would be a good time to call?' Louis asked her, running his fingers through his hair.

'Well, not exactly,' Sophie said slowly, finding that she was twisting her engagement ring around and around her finger.

'What did she say, exactly?' Louis asked her darkly.

'She tried not to tell me and then when it was obvious that Seth was yours she told me not to tell you. She said she'd got by for the last twenty years without anyone knowing and she was doing just fine. She said she was happy and she didn't want anything to change. She said if I told you I'd regret it.'

'She said that.' Louis was perfectly still for a moment. And then he exploded. 'Then why the fuck did you tell me, Sophie? Why the fuck did you do this to us?'

Propelled to her feet by shock and anger in equal measure, Sophie stood up to face him, aware that she was trembling.

'Louis, for God's sake, keep your voice down,' she hissed at him. 'What did you expect me to do? Did you expect me not to tell you? Did you expect me to marry you knowing about your son and not to mention it? Is that the kind of relationship you want from me, Louis? If you want to do this you have to realise it's about more than snogging in doorways and hand holding.'

'If *I* want to do this . . . ?' Louis trailed off.

'I'm the one who gave up my whole life to be with you,' Sophie snapped back.

'Yes, and you're the one who still lives in a B&B.'

'Because I'm trying to do at least one thing right,' Sophie protested, not sure how this conversation had turned so savagely on her. 'I want to marry you. I really, really want to marry you, but when you're like this . . .'

'Like what?' Louis asked.

'So angry and shut off and – I don't know how to handle you when you're like this, Louis, you're like a stranger to me.'

'You don't know how to handle me? Fucking hell, Sophie. I'm a man not an animal in a circus. Or maybe that's what you want me to be. Your performing poodle.'

'All I want is for you to be you, to be the man that I love and the man that I want to marry and the man that I can talk to about anything and who can talk to me. The man who must know I didn't have any choice over this. Think about it, Louis, how could you trust me, how could you marry me if I kept this from you?'

They stood there staring at each other for a second and

Sophie could hear all the unspoken words threatening to fly between them. Suddenly everything she had with Louis felt impossibly fragile, a beautiful web of silk that might be shattered any second by the glancing blow of a casual breeze.

'I'm sorry,' Louis said, his shoulders dropping. 'This isn't about you, I'm just shocked and angry and you're right, I'm taking it out on you. I'm sorry.'

Tentatively he reached out and picked up her hand. 'Of course you had to tell me about him. You didn't have any choice and I'm glad and grateful that you were brave enough to do it. Honestly I am.'

Sophie nodded and took a step closer to him and searched his face still stricken with remnants of anger. 'You do believe that I want to marry you, don't you?' she asked him. 'You do know how much I love you and how scared I am that all of this could be ripped away in a matter of seconds?'

'Scared?' Louis asked her, winding his fingers in her hair and pulling her lips towards his. Sophie resisted even though she was desperate for him to kiss her, desperate to be back in that familiar place with him once again.

'Things change, people change. You left Carrie once when things got tough . . . what if you leave me?'

'I left because Carrie was in love with another man – I know I shouldn't have gone, I know I shouldn't have walked out on my girls, but I'm a different man from the one I was then. Fuck, all I've done tonight is shout and blame you, no wonder you're scared. Maybe I've been waiting for something to ruin this for us, maybe I don't really believe that I can get this right. I haven't got that much else right in the past . . .'

'You have,' Sophie told him. 'You're doing so well with the girls, and building up the business from scratch . . .'

'Only because of you. Because I love you. And I can't lose you, Sophie.'

'You're not going to lose me,' Sophie said, wilfully snuffing out the small cold part of her that was still frightened that she might lose him. All she wanted now was the closeness between them to be restored, the safe little bubble they lived into be re-formed around them like a shield, even if it was only for a few more hours till the sun came up and reality rose with it. 'It's just that kissing can't be our main form of communication. We have to talk sometimes too.'

'I know, I know,' Louis told her. 'And I promise you that nothing is going to stop us from getting married on New Year's Eve. I promise you.' He pulled her close to him, holding her tightly.

'I really don't want you to go back to the B&B tonight,' he whispered. 'I really don't want to be parted from you. I need you, I need to be able to hold you tonight, all night.'

Sophie pulled back and looked into his eyes. Nothing about their relationship had conformed to what she had once hoped and expected for herself and now there was Seth to contend with too. Suddenly she was exhausted by clinging on to the last moments of her childhood expectations. She wanted to give him something, something to salve the anxiety and worry he was feeling and, more than that, she didn't want to leave him.

'I'll stay,' she whispered with a smile. 'I'll get up early before the girls so they won't even know. I don't want to leave you tonight.'

Sophie surrendered to Louis's kiss and felt her body burn up at his touch.

'And I'll help you, I'll help you get things sorted with Wendy and Seth,' Sophie breathed as Louis kissed her neck and pulled her T-shirt up over her head.

'I know, I know you will,' Louis said, running his hands down her bare back and unhooking her bra strap.

'And Louis,' Sophie forced herself to still his hand and made him look her in the eye, 'I love you so much.'

'I believe you.' Louis smiled at her. 'And I want you, right now.'

Chapter Eight

'And then what did you say?' Cal asked her breathlessly, as she sat in the guest sitting room with Mrs Tregowan, her mobile to her ear.

'I said, "Mum, if you're happy then I'm happy, and not remotely weirded out by the fact that you have a boyfriend."'

'And what did she say?' Cal pressed her.

'She said that Trevor wasn't her *boyfriend*, he was her *lover*. Her live-in lover of two months who, worse still, has told her he is happy to poop-a-scoop if she wants to come down here for a visit!'

'She wants to come and visit just when you've found out about the love child and the slutty ex?' Cal gasped.

'Exactly. I love her and everything, but the last thing I need right now is her down here making my already complicated life two hundred times more difficult to manage, plus I haven't exactly told her about her future son-in-law's unexpected offspring yet . . .'

'I don't believe this.' Cal sounded genuinely aghast for once.

'I know, I know, I should tell her, but it was only five minutes ago I was announcing my engagement and telling her how happy I was; telling her about Seth would just be so . . . so . . . embarrassing.'

'That's not what I can't believe. You not sharing vital information with the people you love, that's a given as far as you're concerned. What I can't believe is the sex that's going on,' Cal said bitterly. 'The end of the world is officially nigh. Your mother has got a lover, you have got a fiancé, and the only man I'm interested in ... well, let's say I haven't had a sniff of a dick in months, haven't even really looked at anyone in that way in ages. That's got to mean Armageddon – pass me a bible, I'm checking the Book of Revelation. What's wrong with me?'

'I'm talking about my life here, Cal; my fiancé, my wedding, my so-called happiness, my boyfriend's love child,' Sophie complained. 'The only thing that's wrong with you is that you're having a bit of a dry patch which, because you spend most of life situated in the middle of the damp patch, is freaking you out. I'm sure some foxy chap will catch your eye soon and you'll be back to normal.'

'I'm not so sure,' Cal sighed. 'Don't you see? It's like the butterfly effect. A man doesn't get enough shag action in London and a twenty-year-old love child turns up in Cornwall. It's chaos theory. It's because you and your mother are having sex and the universe can't cope. I've become a soulless sexless career girl and you and your mum are tarty shaggers! It's the Apocalypse, I tell you.'

'Cal,' Sophie said. 'If I had your sex life I wouldn't be getting married to one man. I'd be the only girl member in the fishermen's guild.'

'Suddenly you make the yokel life sound awfully appealing,' Cal said. 'But actually, Sophie, I'm sort of past that ... casual sex with strapping young men. I'm ready for something more.'

'How many times have I heard that before?' Sophie laughed. 'When you say something more you mean a one-night stand plus breakfast. Come on, Cal, you're not the settling down type.'

'You're probably right,' Cal said a little sadly. 'I'm probably not the sort of man you'd want to settle down with. Unlike your mum's live-in lover.'

'Anyway, this isn't about my mother's sex life, as much as I will need therapy for that at some point. Nor is it about your lack of sex life which I am sure is probably only a temporary glitch because for once you are making something of yourself and having a career. I've found out that Louis has a fully grown love child on the loose. And more importantly, he's just found out – and he's all weird about it and angry and tense.'

'I can see where he's coming from,' Cal said. 'I'd be angry and weird and tense if ever one of the little buggers that have surely been sired from my donated sperm ever turned up on my doorstep.'

'You donated sperm? When?' Sophie asked aghast.

'Oh, a few years back. I thought it was wrong to deprive the world of my superlative DNA just because the idea of impregnating a woman makes me want to heave. So I cut out the middle man, or rather put one in . . . anyway, if a child suddenly turned up *I'd* be angry and resentful and confused and desperate that they'd inherited my dress sense because, let's face it, the chances are their mother is a bit of a frump if she had to get her sperm from a bank. So God knows what Louis must be feeling.'

'No one knows what Louis is feeling, that's the problem,' Sophie said. 'He won't talk to me, not properly. He hasn't exactly got a good track record of dealing with difficult issues. The last time he had a major problem in his life he ran away to Peru.'

'True, but he came back when it counted,' Cal reminded her.

'And then there's this Wendy woman,' Sophie mumbled, picking at the hem of her sleeve. 'His first love and all that bollocks. You should see his face light up when he's talking about her. I think he still has feelings for her.'

'He still has memories of feelings for her,' Cal said. 'That's a different thing entirely, that's nostalgia, not love. Anyway, tell me more about the love child. He looks just like Louis, you say?' Cal mused. 'Is he straight?'

'I'm not dignifying that with an answer,' Sophie said tartly, smiling at Grace whose attention had briefly wandered from the TV. 'The point is I'm already marrying my dead best friend's husband whom I've known for barely a year. And now it turns out the countryside is littered with his progeny. Cal – what am I thinking?'

'Littered is a little bit of an exaggeration – at least, as far as we know,' Cal told her. 'And what do you mean, what are you thinking? Are you getting cold feet, Miss Mills? Has the love child put you off?'

'No!' Sophie protested. 'Well, not exactly – but . . . Cal what *do* I think about it? Why do I feel as if things have changed between me and Louis? Why do I feel that I've somehow ruined everything for us?'

'Things *have* changed between you and Louis,' Cal said, simply. 'The honest truth is you don't know that much about him . . . that doesn't mean you don't love him, I'm just saying you haven't known him for long. You've found out something about him, a part of him you hadn't seen before, and it's bound to change your perception of him slightly.'

'But it's not as if this was last year or even five years ago. He was a kid,' Sophie said. 'He made a mistake so why should that bother me?'

'Everything else shouldn't bother you, not if you're sure about Louis. All you should be worrying about is helping him get through this and getting on with marrying him. And you *are* sure about him, aren't you? You said so.'

Sophie paused for a long moment. She knew what Cal was waiting for her to say. She knew that as soon as she uttered even one word of uncertainty he'd pounce on it like Artemis on a injured bird and he wouldn't stop until he'd ripped her head off and spat it out on the bathroom mat. She glanced sideways at Mrs Tregowan who seemed immersed in the story of a mother who sold her daughter's baby to pay for drugs on the Jeremy Vine show.

'I am sure,' she whispered. 'I couldn't wait to marry him before all this happened and I still can't. I'm just worried, worried that somehow all this is going to ruin things between us.'

'You know what you need to help take your mind off things, don't you?'

'Vodka?' Sophie asked, hopefully.

'A hen night. A massive full-on London-based hen night organised by the nearest thing you've got to a best friend largely as a vehicle for him to finally get some hard flesh between his legs.'

'And how on earth will your taking me to a string of gay clubs help me take my mind off things in a way that won't mean I will require psychiatric help?'

'Because we won't only go to gay clubs and because once you're back in the Big Smoke you'll feel like yourself again. You'll have perspective, distance, decent shoes on, and most importantly vodka on tap. You could be here by the weekend.'

'Bizarrely enough that does sound quite tempting, but we're going to confront Wendy today,' Sophie informed him. 'Louis is coming by to pick me up any minute. I can't just say "Come on, darling, let's go and meet your secret love child's mother, oh, and by the way, I'm clearing off up to London for a drinking binge because the skeletons in your closet are freaking me out."'

'Well, you could, but as you won't, I'll bring the hen night to you. Well, I'll bring me to you, anyway; you drum up some hens. I'm coming down and I won't take no for an answer. Line me up some fishermen! I'll see you Friday night.'

'Cal, I'm just not sure that now is the time . . .'

'Oh come on, Sophie, I need to get away. This city is packed full of happy couples in love right now, including your mother, and I can't cope with it any more. I want to be with you, miserable, bitter, dysfunctional and doomed to romantic failure you, because you always make me feel better.'

'It's tempting when you put it like that but . . .'

'Book me a room with Mrs A, I'm on my way, darling!' Cal hung up.

Sophie stared at her silent handset and wondered why her life was populated so densely by a whole lot of people who thought they knew better what she needed than she did and concluded that it was probably a statistical inevitability given that most of the time she felt like she knew nothing at all.

'So today's the big day with the love child, then?' Grace asked her.

'Well, the love child's mother,' Sophie said. She should have known that nothing got past her fellow guest and that, besides, Mrs Alexander had been polishing the occasional table on the landing outside her room for quite some time while she'd been making arrangements with Louis about going to see Wendy.

'Of course Frank is illegitimate, although you'd never guess it to look at him, the pompous fool,' Grace told her, chuckling. 'He really is a bastard – the irony's kept me going for years!'

'Is he really?' Sophie asked her, glad to be distracted for a moment. 'After you told me about Vincent I always assumed that he must be the product of husband number two.'

'No; Sandy, my second husband, married me when I was

pregnant, but he always knew that Frank wasn't his. His dad was a German prisoner of war – he wasn't a soldier, he was interned here at the beginning of the war. After I got back from France, after the baby, I needed something to do to take my mind off things. I went up North and worked in the internment camps. They were nice fellers mostly. Not Nazis, just young men caught up in something they didn't really understand. Dieter used to carve tiny shoes out of bits of driftwood. He had strong hands and a firm grip and he kissed like an electric eel . . .' Sophie wrinkled her brow as she tried to imagine how an electric eel might kiss. 'I didn't love him, mind. But I needed something, someone, you know? I needed the sex. It was 1945, I was still young and beautiful, I needed to get over losing Vincent and my beautiful girl. We had a whole year together, they didn't send him back to Germany until 1946, but by that time Frank was growing in my belly.'

'Didn't he want to stay, or take you with him?'

'No.' Grace shook her head. 'It wasn't that kind of love, dear. It was just sex, really. If he'd have stayed we wouldn't have lasted.'

'So you had to get married to the first person who'd have you to save your reputation?' Sophie asked her. 'How awful.'

'Oh fuck, no,' Grace said. 'I couldn't care less what other people thought about me. No, I met Sandy and I fell for him, couldn't keep my hands off him even though I was six months' gone with Frank the first night we made love. And he felt the same way about me – we made each other feel happy and light. That was a good time . . . there was this sense of lightness in everyone, as if the sun had finally come out after six years. We still didn't have any food or any things. Times were hard, but we knew we were going to be all right, the dark times were over. There were blue skies over the white cliffs of Dover and it was possible to imagine a future again. And I think I loved Sandy that way, with his bright red hair and freckles. And he loved me, and Frank, too, as his own, not that Frank did much to deserve it – he always was a selfish little bugger.'

'How long were you married to Sandy for?' Sophie asked her. She was fascinated by Mrs Tregowan's husbands as if at least one of them might give her an insight into her own future marriage.

'Nigh on thirty years; I had my children with Sandy. Frank and Anna,' Grace told her, with the same little proud nod she gave whenever she told people her age. 'Yes, we stayed together till Christmas 1974.'

'It must have been hard losing him,' Sophie said, covering Grace's small hand with her own, afraid to squeeze in case she snapped her frail bones.

'It was; he gave me a fondue set on Christmas Day and then ran off with one of my daughter's friends on Boxing Day! Tarty little thing, she was, always in a plunge bra. He had four more kids with her and we never heard from him again.'

'Oh God, I'm sorry!' Sophie said. 'What a bastard – leaving you after thirty years of marriage.'

'It wasn't really his fault,' Grace said with a shrug. 'You see, Sophie, the thing about marriage is it's never certain. Not even at the beginning when you're just starting out and it's all hearts and flowers and you feel *so* sure of everything. Every day is a challenge, every day you have to make each other fall in love all over again and when he starts getting a bit portly, or losing his hair then that can be ... difficult. And I can't complain. I'd been having it off with the window cleaner myself.'

'Mrs Tregowan!' Sophie giggled.

'Well,' Grace said winking at Sophie, 'he had a very long ladder.'

143

'He's here!' Mrs Alexander, hovering anxiously by the front door, announced Louis's arrival.

'I'd better get going, then,' Sophie said, but as she made to leave Grace put a hand on her arm.

'As long as you remember to love him all over again every single day then you'll be all right,' Grace told her.

'I know,' Sophie said, smiling at the old lady, feeling a sudden surge of affection for her.

'And remember not to let yourself go. I'd recommend wearing your bra at night with tits like those, the big ones always get saggy if you let them swing.'

'I'll bear that in mind,' Sophie said.

'That's the trouble with smack,' Grace said directing her gaze back at the telly. 'It makes selling your grandkids on the Internet seem like a good idea . . .'

'All set?' Mrs Alexander asked Louis as she opened the door. Louis looked tense. His face was tight and drawn. Her own stomach was contracted into a tangle of knots but she was determined not to let her anxiety feed Louis's. She was going to be the calm one, the one who was strong for him even if she did feel like running a million miles in the opposite direction.

'I guess,' Louis said looking at Sophie.

'I looked her up on the Internet and I've printed off the address of her workshop,' Sophie said. 'All we do is go there and hope she's in.'

'Right.' Louis nodded. Sophie was surprised at exactly how much the prospect of seeing Wendy again terrified him, even considering the circumstances. She had seen him in adversity and he had never been like this. No matter how hard he'd found it when he came back to find that Bella hated him and Izzy didn't even remember him, he never lost his optimism or his confidence that he would work things out. It had been one of the things about him that had infuriated and impressed Sophie the most. But now he was genuinely frightened about seeing Wendy, this woman who had played such an important part in his life, whom he had loved so much and who had helped to form him into the man he was today. Briefly, guiltily, Sophie wondered if it was meeting his son that Louis was nervous of or seeing the girl he'd once been so in love with.

'I'm sure it will be fine,' Mrs Alexander said, rubbing Louis briskly on the back as if he had no more than a bad case of dyspepsia. 'You just tell her you want to meet your son and there's nothing she can do about it.'

'Right,' Louis said, pecking Mrs Alexander on the cheek because he knew it always gave her a hot flush.

'Do I?' he asked Sophie as he was about to get into her car.

'Do you what?' she replied.

'Do I want to meet my son?'

The workshop was on an industrial estate outside Torquay, one of thirty or so identical-looking units that looked like they'd been thrown together out of bits of paper and sticky-back plastic.

'It's unit thirty-seven,' Sophie said as she drove her Golf slowly down the concrete-covered road that ran between the units. 'Can you see the number? Louis?'

She braked and looked over at him. He was sitting stock still staring straight ahead of him, his fingers twisted in his lap.

'Is this really that bad?' she asked him, regretting the impatience in her tone immediately and working hard to curb her own misgivings about what they were about to do. 'I mean yes – yes, it is bad, I know, and it's a shock. But we'll face it together and we'll work out how best to handle it. If this is

145

what you want then I'm here for you. Or we could always just turn around and go back . . .'

'No, you're right,' Louis said, looking at her and reaching over to take her hand. He squeezed her fingers hard. 'This is something that has to be faced. I'm so glad you're here with me, Sophie. I haven't had anyone in my corner since . . . well, since Carrie.'

'So,' Sophie said, trying not to feel regretful that Louis didn't want to turn around and leave. 'It's not that bad, is it?'

'It's just . . . what if Wendy hates me? I wouldn't blame her. I got her pregnant and abandoned her when she fifteen.'

'You didn't abandon her, you didn't know till a couple of days ago! She never gave you a chance to do the right thing, whatever that would have been at sixteen. But now you have a chance to do *something* at least. She won't hate you, none of this is your fault.'

'You're right,' Louis said. 'I don't know why I'm so nervous about seeing her again . . .' Louis trailed off and Sophie knew that in that moment he was thinking about the summer he had spent with Wendy all those years ago. She dragged him back into the present, where he belonged to her.

'Look, that's unit thirty-three so it must be . . .' Sophie put the car into first and crawled along a few more units. She turned to look at Louis. 'We're here.'

The radio had been playing when Sophie and Louis pushed open the door. There were a couple of girls in their late teens packing underwear into boxes, probably to fulfil online orders; it was at bridebodybeautiful.com that Sophie had finally tracked Wendy Churchill down. She saw that Wendy guaranteed delivery within three to four working days for all orders made online. These girls must be in charge of delivering that promise.

'Yeah?' one of the girls asked them as they came in.

'You can't buy the stuff here,' another one said. 'You have to go to a fair or buy online.'

'We're not here to buy,' Sophie said. 'We're here to see Wendy.'

'Oh, right, out back,' the first girl said, nodding in the direction of a small office. 'WENDY, VISITORS!' she yelled, her powerful voice belying her thin frame.

'We'll go through,' Sophie said, pulling at Louis's hand and then pulling again when she realised that he didn't seem to be moving his feet.

Wendy's smile froze on her face the second that she saw who her visitors were.

'You told him,' she said to Sophie.

'I had to,' Sophie said, calmly. 'Surely you must see that.'

Wendy sat back in her chair and looked at Louis. Sophie waited for the hate and thinly veiled anger that she had experienced from Wendy at the wedding fair to be unleashed on her fiancé but instead Wendy smiled. It was a rueful, regretful smile. A pretty, flirtatious smile.

'You poor bastard, you must have been going through hell,' she said warmly.

'It's been a bit of a shock, I'll admit,' Louis said tentatively smiling back her.

'Look, I'm sorry I got all stressy with your girlfriend at the fair,' Wendy gestured at the one empty chair in the room and Louis sat in it. 'It was a bit of a shock for me too, having my deep, dark secret outed like that by some strange woman. I probably didn't handle it as well as I could have.'

'We understand, don't we, babe?' Louis said reaching up over his shoulder for Sophie's hand.

'Yes, we do,' Sophie said, trying, largely unsuccessfully, to repress the violent feelings of hate that Wendy effortlessly seemed to inspire in her.

'So – what do you want to do?' Wendy asked him pleasantly. Sophie wondered where her evil twin double had gone, where all the vicious threats and anger from the fair had gone and, more importantly, why? She told herself that it was just childish jealousy and resentment that made her feel so ambivalent about the woman. After all, Wendy had thrown a twenty-year-old six foot two spanner in the works of what was supposed to be Sophie's fairy-tale ending, but it wasn't just that. There was something about Wendy that troubled her.

'I don't know what I want to do, really,' Louis said, shifting uncomfortably in his chair. 'I mean, first of all I want to say sorry. I'm sorry I got you pregnant when we were kids. I was dumb, and drunk. I didn't know what I was doing.'

'Oh, I don't know.' Wendy raised a suggestive brow and Sophie had to work hard to stop her mouth dropping open in horror. 'I have fond memories of that night, and besides, it wasn't just your fault. I went to the same sex education classes as you. We were both young and drunk . . .' Wendy shrugged and the gesture seemed to throw off the last twenty years of single motherhood as if it had been no trouble at all. 'We both wanted each other so much.'

'But why didn't you tell me?' Louis asked her. 'I don't know what I would have done about it. I was a bloody stupid kid with no parents to help me out. But, I don't know – I'd have done something, got a job, maybe . . .'

'I didn't tell you because I didn't know, not straight away,' Wendy said. 'When you made it clear you didn't want to go out with me any more . . .'

'When *I* made it clear?' Louis looked surprised. 'You were the one that ignored *me*! I was heartbroken!'

'You were?' Wendy laughed. 'No, you've got that wrong. After that party I was so excited about seeing you again, now that we were lovers – you couldn't even look at me.'

'No, *you*'ve got that wrong – *you* ignored *me*. I thought I'd disappointed you so much that you'd decided to chuck me on the spot.'

'Far from it!' Wendy actually fluttered her lashes, which made Sophie what to shove her fingers down her throat and vomit. This was not going at all how she had expected. For starters the opportunities for her to be a supportive and understanding fiancée seemed to be negligible, particularly since Louis had carelessly let go of her hand. Plus, there had been a distinct lack of shouting or angst. Instead, there had been flirting. *Flirting*.

'I can't believe that,' Louis said, shaking his head as he smiled at Wendy. 'I pined for you for weeks.'

'Same!' Wendy exclaimed. 'Anyway, I didn't notice I'd missed my first period. I was never really that regular to begin with. Mum and Dad announced that we were moving for Dad's job, and I thought, why not? The only boy I'll ever love has chucked me – I might as well move on. I was a skinny little thing back then, really petite . . .'

'You still are,' Louis assured her, chivalrously.

'Oh, I don't know about that,' Wendy said coyly. 'But when I started to get a bit of a tummy, Mum said it was my hormones. Puppy fat! We'd been in Oldham for a couple of months when I felt it kick. Of course I didn't know it was a kick. I thought I had an alien life form inside me. He must have been moving around before then but I'd put it down to indigestion. But this – this was a really proper kick. I went running to my mum in tears, thinking it was cancer or worse. She put her hand on my belly and felt it and suddenly *she* was crying.

'"You silly, stupid, bloody foolish girl", that's what she said to me. I'll never forget it. Or what she said next. "You've gone and got yourself pregnant."'

Wendy shook her head, looking over Sophie's shoulder and

through the Venetian blind. 'But they were brilliant about it in the end.'

'Didn't they want to know who the dad was?' Louis asked her.

'Yes,' Wendy said. 'And I told them.'

'And your dad didn't come down here to kick my head in? Why not?' Louis asked her.

'My dad said what bloody use would a kid of barely sixteen be? He said we'd take care of it ourselves. And as for me, I thought you'd gone right off me. I didn't see the point in telling you, either. I must admit, when we moved back down about a year ago I wondered what would happen if we bumped into you. But we never did.'

Wendy and Louie gazed at each other across the desk with a kind of familiar fascination and wonder that made Sophie feel very uncomfortable. They looked as if they had just rediscovered a long-lost treasure that had once been very dear to them.

'And did he . . . did Seth never ask about who his dad might be?'

'We lived with my mum and dad till he was eight,' Wendy told him. 'My dad was still young enough and fit enough to play footy with him, run in the fathers' race. The subject never came up; I think because he'd never had a dad he didn't miss one. He did ask me when I met someone and got married, he wanted to know if Ted was his dad.'

'Wait, you're married?' Louis asked her.

'Not any more.' Wendy shrugged. 'It didn't work out. I tried to love him, but in the end there was always something holding me back . . .' She looked up through her lashes at Louis. 'Or someone, maybe.'

To his credit Louis broke Wendy's gaze first, clearly feeling a little awkward at the implication of her last comment.

'So what did you tell him?' he asked her.

'I told him Ted wasn't his dad, but that his dad was someone I'd loved very much once.'

'And he has no idea about me now,' Louis asked her.

'None,' Wendy said.

'And are you going to tell him?'

Wendy hesitated and Sophie waited for the same angry denial that she had experienced.

'No,' Wendy said, reaching across the desk to take Louis's hand. 'I think you and I should tell him together.'

Chapter Nine

As Sophie paced the single and largely empty platform at St Ives station waiting for her guest to arrive on the 16.46 she wondered two things: first, why Cal had never learned to drive and was forcing her to meet him at the station on the chilly and gloomy afternoon, and second, why Louis had arranged one of the most important and momentous events of his life without her.

After Wendy had made her suggestion Louis had just sat there for a moment. Sophie hadn't been sure exactly how he would react; she had expected something radical though – some kind of drama that seemed fitting for the occasion. But instead, Louis had merely sat back in his chair, his whole body relaxing as he ran his fingers through his hair, shrugged, and said, 'OK, then, when?'

He'd looked relieved, Sophie thought, glad that someone else was taking charge of the situation, telling him what to do. She couldn't blame him, she supposed, but she also couldn't help the feeling of unease that blossomed in the pit of her stomach. No matter how reasonable and sensible Wendy seemed now, Sophie found it hard to trust her and she was sure it was down to more than mild jealousy over Louis's past love. But whether Sophie liked Wendy or not, she was the mother of Louis's son and the realisation dawned as she stood in the tiny cramped office at Wendy's workshop that Carmen was right: once she was married to Louis, this woman would be in her life for ever.

Wendy had smiled, watching Louis's face closely. 'You two are so alike, you know. Of course I've known Seth for twenty years, he's my boy. I did my best to forget what you were like and I don't just mean how you look, but your mannerisms . . . your smile.' Sophie looked on as Louis and Wendy watched each other closely. 'Now I see you sitting in that chair and it's amazing. He's the spitting image of you.'

'Sophie mentioned that.' Louis's laugh was easy and relaxed as if suddenly he'd decided that discovering a child wasn't that big a deal after all. 'It's pretty crazy to think that's he out there, this son I've never met . . . so when shall we go and see him?'

'I need to pick the right time,' Wendy said glancing at Sophie briefly as if she were irritated by an eavesdropper. 'How about Friday? He's coming over to mine for dinner, he often does on a Friday, says he needs to get a good feed in before the onslaught of the weekend. How about you come too?'

'We could make Friday, couldn't we, love?' Louis asked Sophie, looking up at her. Sophie was momentarily thrown by the fact that he called her 'love' – a term of endearment he had never previously used and one she'd always thought was more fitting for couples who had been together for more than a hundred years.

'Well, Cal is supposed to be coming on Friday afternoon but this is much more important. I'll get out of it, he'll understand and—'

'Actually, I really think it would be better if it's just us; I mean just you and me, Louis,' Wendy cut across Sophie. 'It'll be enough of a shock for the poor kid without a load of strangers trooping in too.'

'Except that Seth's already met me,' Sophie retorted, before she could bite her tongue. 'I'm not the stranger, Louis is.'

'No, and you're not his father either,' Wendy said directly, addressing Sophie for the first time. 'Look, I'm sorry, you might have been the one to work out who Seth was, but as far as I'm concerned, for now Louis is the only one who gets to be there when we tell Seth who his dad is.'

Sophie had waited for Louis to object and to insist that Sophie should come with him, but he hadn't. He'd just twisted in his chair, looked up at her, and said, 'I think Wendy's right, love.'

Sophie checked her watch. Louis was right there now, at Wendy's house in Newquay. She'd invited him over at four-thirty, giving them time to work out how they were going to handle things when Seth arrived around six.

Sophie had been looking for the spare key in Louis's hall-table drawer for Mrs Alexander, who'd agreed to babysit, when she came across the brochure for Finestone Manor. It had only been a couple of days since she'd found out about Seth, since Louis had told her he'd discovered the perfect place to get married. They still hadn't looked at the brochure together and as far as she knew he hadn't booked it for any date, let alone New Year's Eve. She held the glossy folder in her hands for a few seconds counting backwards from ten, trying to snuff out all the irrational and childish feelings that surfaced in her when she considered that all of their plans had been so suddenly and carelessly shelved. Of course, discovering Seth was more important than booking their wedding day, but even so, as Sophie looked at the brochure tucked away in the drawer where Louis put credit card bills, bank statements and everything he didn't want to think about, she couldn't help feeling jealous and neglected.

Only a few days ago the whole world had been about them and the girls, about how she felt about Louis and how he felt about her and the new family they were endeavouring to put together in the best possible way. It had been about kissing in doorways and the awe and delight they found in each other, but now all of that was gone, and despite herself Sophie discovered she was angry.

'What about this?' Sophie had asked Louis as he came down the stairs. He'd dressed carefully in a blue shirt and jeans: shirt to err on the side of smart and dad-like, Sophie guessed, and jeans to show he was still young and cool. His hair was brushed off his face and tucked behind his ears and he'd shaved, too, which oddly made him look younger instead of giving him the responsible adult look that Sophie thought he was trying to achieve. He didn't look like himself. The tension, nerves and fear of the unexpected had altered his face somehow in small subtle ways so that his features were all slightly out of kilter and the face she had spent so many hours studying over the last few weeks and months seemed unfamiliar.

More than that he hadn't looked at her in the way she was used to him looking at her in several days. Instead, he looked at her as if he didn't really see her; it felt like suddenly finding yourself standing in the shadows when you had become accustomed only to basking in the sun.

'What about what?' Louis asked her.

'This.' Sophie held the brochure up under her chin, peering at him over it, like a child peeping over a table top. It seemed to take Louis a second or two to register what it was.

'Oh . . . that,' he said. 'I haven't booked it.'

'I guessed as much,' Sophie replied, putting the brochure back in the drawer. 'And I understand why . . . it's just – do you still want to get married on New Year's Eve? Because if you do, then we should probably sort it out, that's all.' Her voice was edged with unreasonable anger that Louis registered with a sigh.

He picked up his keys and looked first at his watch and then at the front door. Sophie knew that he didn't want to discuss it now. She knew that he wanted to drive to Newquay and be on time to meet Wendy and then eventually his son, she knew all of this and yet still she asked him. She discovered she couldn't stop herself.

'Of course I still want to get married ...' Louis said, frowning at the front door as if he could somehow will it to open using only the powers of his mind.

'Still on New Year's Eve?' Sophie pressed him uncomfortably.

'Well, yes, why would that change?' Finally Louis focused his attention on her and looked her in the eyes, reaching out to cup her cheek in the palm of his hand. 'I love you, Sophie,' he told her, with just a shade of impatience. 'All this secret son stuff is doing my head in, but it doesn't mean I don't love you or don't want to marry you any more ...'

'Really?' Sophie heard herself sounding insecure and needy, felt the muscles in her gut wince. She rested her hand on Louis's chest, feeling the beat of his heart against her palm. 'I'm sorry – I know that this is a really important day for you and that you have to go now and that the last thing you need is me asking you if you still feel the same but I can't help it, I can't ...'

Louis engulfed her in a hug, the kind of all-encompassing embrace that had been absent for the last few days.

'You nutter,' he said gently, kissing the top of her head. 'How I feel about you hasn't changed, *nothing* can change how I feel about you. I really want to marry you more than anything and preferably before they chime the New Year in. I promise you I'll ring them tomorrow, because I'd be gutted if we lost out on our New Year's Eve wedding for any reason. But right now I have to go and meet my adult son that I knew nothing about and who has no idea I exist.'

Louis sucked a thin breath in through his teeth as he framed the reality of what was happening in words.

'I'm so sorry.' Sophie looked up at him, nipping at her bottom lip. 'I've behaved like a selfish brat . . . and I feel like an idiot. Of course nothing is more important than getting to Wendy's on time.'

'I actually kind of like it that you care enough about the wedding to bring it up now, just at the very second I'm going out to meet Seth.' Louis's smile was wry. 'I like the irrational, vulnerable bit of you. I *love* all of you and I am going to marry you as soon as I have sorted this, OK?'

'OK,' Sophie said, allowing a small smile to insinuate its way into the corners of her mouth. 'But at no point did I openly admit to being irrational.'

'And remember,' Louis kept his voice low as he kissed her temple. 'If the girls ask, I'm going to meet a cousin and you're out with Cal.'

'You're sure you don't want to tell them about Seth right away?' Sophie asked, risking starting another conversation again, but only because she wasn't at all sure about Louis's decision to keep the news of a half-brother from the girls. However difficult it might be to tell them now, Sophie was worried that with all the people who already knew, including Wendy, Grace, Cal and even Mrs Alexander, they'd find out some other way and if they did she wasn't sure how it would affect them, especially Bella who had struggled so hard to trust her father again in the first place.

'I am sure.' Louis nodded. 'It's too much for them to take in right now. I'll tell them in my own way when the time is right.'

'OK, then,' Sophie said.

'OK, then,' Louis repeated. He kissed her on the cheek, smiling briefly. 'Wish me luck.'

'Good luck, and Louis . . .' Sophie hesitated, unsure if she should risk skewing the equilibrium that had been so delicately restored between them. 'Just be careful of Wendy. I know she seems friendly and open but . . . she was a whole different person when I spoke to her at the wedding fair. She didn't seem very . . . nice.'

The description was something of an understatement but Sophie thought that calling her a 'threatening, viscous, hatchet-faced old harridan' might not be terribly tactful at that precise moment.

'Don't worry about Wend,' Louis said, shortening her name with frustrating familiarity. 'I know her – she's great and, more importantly, she's handling all of this amazingly well. I expect she was shocked when you found out about Seth and that made her act all angry and protective. I know she's a bit strange around you but that's probably just because she's a little bit jealous—'

'Jealous?' Sophie snapped. 'Of what?'

'Of you.' Louis shrugged, his hand on the door latch. 'But you don't have to worry because it's you I love . . .'

'I wasn't worrying till then!' Sophie lied, wondering if Louis had spotted her silently seething whenever Wendy came up in conversation. 'It never crossed my mind she might be after you, but it's crossed yours, I see.'

'It hasn't!' Louis insisted. He looked at his watch. 'I'm sorry, but I haven't got time for this now, it's just stupid! I've really got to go.'

'I know,' Sophie said miserably, feeling the peace between them wash away again.

'There is nothing to worry about,' Louis told her firmly as he opened the door.

Sophie knew she should just have smiled and nodded and hugged him and sent him on his way at least feeling that everything was OK between them before he faced his son. But she felt disjointed, confused, angry and anxious, so instead she simply looked him in the eyes and said, 'Isn't there?'

He slammed the door on his way out.

Finally the train pulled slowly into the platform a total of eleven minutes late. Sophie hugged herself and waited for Cal's tall, elegant frame to emerge from one of the carriages. On this cool early October evening he was easy to spot amongst the five or six passengers who stepped off the train because he was the only man wearing a grey cashmere over-coat over a tailored suit finished off with black patent leather winkle pickers, but even if he had arrived in the heat and turmoil of a mid season he would have stood out a mile. Cal was one of those people whom other people looked at. At some point in his life as part of his evolution into an adult being he had made a decision to stand out from the crowd. It had nothing to do with his looks, although he certainly was striking, or that he was gay; it was something even more funda-mental than that. Cal had decided that life was too short for him to try and blend in; he was put on this earth to be seen, regardless of the consequences. And no matter how much they argued and bickered, it was the part of Cal that Sophie had always admired and aspired to the most.

That part of her, the part that had loved clothes and wore high heels religiously, had faded since she'd come to St Ives. She still had all of her glamorous clothes in her MFI B&B wardrobe (bar the red patent Jimmy Choos that she had lent Bella with uncharacteristic largesse when she was playing *Wizard of Oz* and had never seen again since, except during seemingly endless renditions of 'Somewhere Over the

Rainbow'), but she'd only ever had occasion to wear any of them once, and that was the night of Louis's proposal.

She would have liked to have blamed her newly sensible look on the fact that she was living, literally, at the very end of the country now, where fashion was an irrelevance, except that alongside its history of fishing, artists and tiny working-class cottages, St Ives was an utterly stylish place, chock full of designer shops and as many well-dressed and well-heeled people as you could hope to see anywhere on the streets of London. Sophie could easily have worn heeled boots and a pencil skirt to do the school run and not looked out of place, but she didn't. She'd frequently told Cal that there was no point in wearing anything nice when you had two girls hell bent on painting the town red and she had evidence of many a ruined item of soft furnishing and irretrievably stained garments to back that up from their time living in Sophie's one-bedroom flat, but that wasn't it either.

Sophie had always believed, although she hadn't told Cal because he'd laugh in her face, that when she'd come to Cornwall to be with Louis she had shed everything about her life that was inconsequential and unimportant. That she had pared herself down to her bare minimum, unless you counted the extra cream-tea pounds, and shown Louis the essence of herself – because that was the kind of courage that truly loving someone required. The fact that he still loved and desired her when she wasn't tottering about in some beautiful heels or trussed up in a tight top only affirmed how right and how liberating her decision to come here had been. But as she watched Cal walking down the platform towards her, Sophie considered for the first time another reason why she had let her devotion to glamour and shoes slip so easily away. Had she lost herself here? Had she lost herself in Louis and the girls and let her identity slip and bleed into theirs? All at once

Sophie missed the hours of preparation it took simply to leave the flat every morning, she lamented the dedication to shaping her brows on a daily basis and shaving her legs. She missed the fact that her nails used to be long and were never chipped and that the balls of her feet always burnt with gratifying pain that said 'these shoes are fuck-off gorgeous'.

As soon as Sophie saw Cal striding towards her she felt better, a little more like her old self again. She felt as if he'd brought more than just himself and a cerise Yves Saint Laurent suitcase on wheels. He'd brought her a little bit of herself with him too. The little bit of her that wanted the world to sit up and take notice.

'Good God, where the hell am I, and why?' Cal asked as he tolerated a hug from her. 'Because I know we are friends and everything, but I can't possibly like you *this* much.'

'Gucci?' Carmen asked Cal, with a raised eyebrow, nodding at his shoes.

The first place Sophie had taken him was for an after-hours cake at Ye Old Tea Shoppe to meet her best St Ives friend and see for himself exactly why hipster jeans, though never really an option for her in terms of style, had, due to a matter of taste and decency, now become totally out of the question.

It had been a mutual appreciation society between Sophie's two friends from the start. Carmen had handed him a slice of baked custard and nutmeg tart and admired the tailoring of his suit and he'd told her he'd never expected anyone so classically styled to be anywhere so far from civilisation, particularly not behind the refrigerated display counter in a cake-shop-cum-café.

'Now she', he said, nodding in Sophie's direction with a cursory glance, 'was always going to throw everything away

161

for a slim chance at happiness, that's desperation for you and, as I've always said, desperation is Sophie's middle name. But you, Miss Carmen Velasquez? You've got class written all over you.'

'That's because I'm from Chelmsford,' Carmen agreed with a nod. 'Say what you like about Essex girls but class runs though us Chelmsford girls like letters through a stick of rock.'

'Well, that's obvious,' Cal agreed. 'So tell me what brought you to the back of beyond?'

'It was love that brought me here,' Carmen said. 'Love for a much younger and very well-muscled man.'

'Seems reasonable.' Cal nodded, savouring the last forkful of his tart that he had been delicately demolishing in the same way that Artemis would polish off a bowl of tuna, slowly and carelessly as if she were doing you a favour by taking it off your hands, instead of the other way around.

Cal always maintained that he didn't really like food, which was why he largely survived on anything that could be impaled on a cocktail stick or ordered in a restaurant where he would never consider either a starter or a dessert. All food meant to him, he would often say, was fuel.

But once, after Cal had had a particularly wonderful weekend with a man who had then turned out to be married, he'd invited Sophie over to dinner to commiserate, telling her that her love life, which was even more sorrowful and emptier than his own, would cheer him up no end. Happy to oblige because at that point in her life the nearest she had to a relationship was an occasional round robin e-mail from her ex-boyfriend Alex, Sophie had assumed that dinner would mean pre-packed sandwiches, perhaps some mini-pizzas, if she were lucky. When she arrived, however, not only had Cal cooked enough courses and quantities to feed twenty, he had baked as well: cakes, muffins, cookies, tarts and more. It was like walking into a fine French patisserie. They had spent the weekend drinking wine and eating as much of the food as was humanly possible without actually rupturing their intestines and Sophie had let him hold forth about how terrible her life was because she knew that he didn't want to talk about his own.

'If you don't like food,' Sophie had challenged him, forcing down one final slice of chocolate cheesecake. 'Then how come you're a better cook than Gordon Ramsay?'

'I do like food, and of course I can cook. I am very accomplished,' Cal had replied. 'What I don't like is that I only ever eat when I'm miserable. And I don't want to be miserable, so I don't eat.'

Sophie had had to think about that for quite some time, during which she sampled just a tiny slice of Cal's Tarte Tatin to be polite and also because she thought the apples could feasibly represent one of her five-a-day.

'Wouldn't it be better to practise eating when you are happy so that you can have a healthy and happy relationship with food?' she asked him.

Cal had leaned back in his chair and narrowed his cornflower-blue eyes, as he looked down his impeccably chiselled nose at her.

'Well, obviously it would, but we all need a hang-up, Sophie, and this is mine. You, on the other hand, eat like a horse whatever the weather. I might be fucked up but at least I'm thin and fashion loves me.'

Sophie had never pressed him on how he felt about food again, because most of the time he did seem to be happy and thin and as far as she knew that ticked at least two out of three boxes on his list for a perfect life. But she knew that much as he might be pretending to be eating Carmen's tart out of politeness only, he was finding it just as delicious as

Sophie always did and she wondered if here, in the bosom of the coast with the sea air in his lungs, he might stop thinking about eating food equating with misery and just allow himself a little bit of happiness in a tart. Which, under other circumstances, was his personal mission statement.

'So where are we going?' Cal asked Sophie as he sipped the double espresso that Carmen had made him with some aplomb, once he'd lusted after the outrageously expensive and rather beautiful Italian coffee machine that she had invested in for the café – even though it was neither Olde or had anything to do with tea. 'Where's the hot banging be-seen-there-or-die venue in this town? And where, more to the point, are the hens?'

'Um,' Sophie looked at Carmen. 'Well, to be honest, what with me not having lived here very much and spending most of my time with Louis and the girls, I am rather limited on hens, in that Carmen is it. Unless you count Mrs Alexander, but she's babysitting and I would have asked Grace if it wasn't for the fact that she's eighty-nine and quite likely to die if she gets too excited ...'

Cal blinked at Sophie. 'This is it. I've come eight hundred miles on a train without a buffet with a load of cu— country people for this, for *this*. Well, fine, I suppose I should have expected nothing less; you've never exactly been popular. As long as the gin is flowing, the music's pumping and the men are easy and preferably confused then I'm happy. So where are we going?'

'Well,' Sophie tried to muster some enthusiasm for the night out she didn't really want. 'There's a lovely art gallery on the harbour with a bar that opens late sometimes ...'

'Or a very, very nice fish place,' Carmen said. 'Very chic and the chef once worked in the Dorchester.'

'Chic?' Cal rolled his eyes. 'I haven't come down here for

chic, I've come down here for dancing, drinking and wild rampant sex in the surf.'

'You've come down here for that?' Carmen asked him. 'In October? You'll freeze your bits off.'

'Also, don't forget, you've come down here to support me through Louis's love-child debacle,' Sophie told him, glancing at her watch again. It was just after six. Seth, if he were anything like his father, which everybody kept saying he was, would be at least twenty minutes late. Wendy and Louis would be there right now in Wendy's front room. (Which, for some reason, Sophie pictured as garishly decorated, much like that of a low-rent hooker, although she accepted that that mental image could have a lot more to do with her personal feelings towards Wendy than with Wendy's interior-design tendencies – although, if she was going to bring any supporting evidence to the theory that Wendy's house would be tacky, she would submit the fact that Wendy made her living out of selling very cheap and nasty nylon-mix underwear that a prostitute wouldn't mind being seen in, apart from the fact that most of it had the words 'Just Married' glued on to it in diamantés, which probably wasn't the best advertisement should you happen to be a lady of the night.)

Wendy and Louis would be there waiting for the sound of the key in the lock, waiting for the moment that Seth walked in through the living-room door and found his father there. She felt her heart constrict with panic not only on Louis's behalf but also on his son's. She knew what it was like to live without a father and she knew, too, how shocking it was to discover that your whole life, everything you've believed to be unalterable and true, could be turned on its head in a second. Wendy had had twenty years to deal with what she knew, Louis had only had a few days, but Seth would have had no time at all, and she worried for him because, as confident and self-assured as he seemed, he really was still only very young.

'It will all be happening any minute now,' Sophie said, staring at her watch face. 'It feels wrong that I am here, thirty miles away, while Louis is meeting his son.'

'Feels like an episode of *EastEnders* to me,' Cal said. 'But anyway, I am here now and I have come down to help you deal with the love child, and in my considered opinion the best way for you to do that is to get me very, very drunk and find me a podium to dance on. So where are we going?'

'A podium, you say? Well, there's Isobar,' Carmen suggested half-heartedly. 'Although it's a very young crowd in there and from what I remember they do tend to wear a lot of sombreros ... but it is open till two tonight.'

'And drinks are only a pound before ten,' Sophie added.

'And?' Cal asked, waiting for other options.

'That's pretty much it for late-night nightlife round here,' Sophie admitted. 'But there are many lovely pubs with local flavour. No podiums, mind, but quite a few solid oak tables.'

'Oh God,' Cal thumped his head down on to Carmen's checked tablecloth. 'I'm in hell.'

'You're regretting coming to see me, aren't you?' Sophie asked him, perhaps unnecessarily given his last comment. 'It seemed like a good idea to get down here and take my mind off my fiancé's illegitimate love child, as you thought there'd be half-naked sexually repressed fishermen lining the roads begging for you to out them, didn't you? But now you've got here and all you've found is an off-season holiday town with one nightclub, you're wondering why you left your wonderful, vibrant, amazing city of London that loves you no matter what you do, aren't you?'

Cal looked up at her. 'Frankly, yes,' he said. 'No ... look, of course I'm not. I'm here for you, Sophie. I'm just tired and I really need a nice long cool and very alcoholic drink.'

'We could always get in a cab and go somewhere bigger,' Carmen suggested tentatively. 'Penzance is only a fifteen-minute drive away but I'm not sure that it will be that fun this time of year – how about we go crazy and go to Newquay? There are loads of clubs in Newquay and, after all, this is your hen night, Soph. We need to find you some action.'

'Newquay?' Sophie repeated. 'That's where Louis is, though. If I go to Newquay for my henless hen night he'll think I'm following him around and that I don't trust him anywhere near that manipulative scheming bitch.'

'Well, yes, he would, if you went to Newquay to go round to her house and invite yourself in,' Carmen said, rolling her eyes at Cal. 'But I'm not suggesting we do that.'

'Oh, aren't you?' Sophie sounded a little disappointed.

'Cal's come a long way and we all of us need our minds taking off things, yours off the love child—'

'Me off my non-existent sex life,' Cal added.

'And me off . . . well, off baking cakes, for God's sake,' Carmen said, looking around her for something to blame. 'If I sift another tablespoonful of icing sugar I'm going to kill myself.'

'I'm not wearing nearly the right thing for Newquay,' Sophie said, looking down at her jeans and trainers.

'You are never wearing the right thing,' Cal said. 'Look, let's go back to the B&B, I can have a shower, and then we'll bling up and blast off, whaddayasay?'

'OK,' Sophie said, but she knew even then, even before Cal had got back to the B&B and poured her into in a low-cut pale blue silk shift dress and silver slingbacks, that the evening was bound to end in disaster of some kind, and she was right. Except she could never have imagined quite how disastrous it would be.

Chapter Ten

Sophie never remembered that she didn't like nightclubs until she was in one. And then she realised that she hadn't ever actively enjoyed them, not even when she was twenty-two and actually knew what any of the music playing was. Now she felt rather inclined to say to anyone who could hear her over the din that the music was too loud and that the lyrics didn't make any sense. Besides, there seemed to be only two reasons that Sophie could discern to go to a large room full of men in tucked-in shirts and bad music: one was to find a random person to have sex with, which she had never been that disposed to do before Louis, and was certainly not interested in doing now, and the other was getting really, really drunk leading to a subcategory of reasons that came under the general heading 'Things I Want to Forget'.

The really annoying thing was that as soon as Sophie was in possession of her large vodka and Red Bull she didn't seem to want to drink it. Perhaps it was having one éclair too many at Ye Olde Tea Shoppe earlier, but even one sip of the drink made her stomach churn. So not only was she rubbish at being in nightclubs but it also seemed that she was a failure at drinking to forget, too, which just about summed her life up at the moment. She was even crap at being crap.

Earlier, while he had been doing her make-up, Cal had said

that it seemed that loving Louis meant embracing his baggage too, and that she had to work out how and if she was able to do that.

'The trouble', she'd told him, 'is that sometimes I feel rather put out that I have almost zero baggage for Louis to have to embrace. If our emotional baggage was actual baggage then all I'd have for him to deal with would be a half-empty washbag, while he'd have me carting around a full set of three cases and a massive trunk, one of the ones you could probably fit a body in.'

'Well, that's your own fault for living like a nun for so long,' Cal had said. 'My point is that if you love Louis, then you have to love his baggage. You have to embrace it, you have to at least try.'

Sophie watched Carmen and Cal dancing together as if they were about to find some dingy corner and have mad crazy sex and they both looked great. Carmen had popped home while Cal had been demanding that Sophie pour herself into her glad rags and she had reappeared less than half an hour later in a black backless halterneck top and skinny jeans topped off by a lovely pair of stilettos. When she and Cal had snaked on to the dance floor of the Tall Trees Club and Bar, all eyes followed them for at least a few seconds and many more stayed to watch them dancing. They made a fantastic couple, rippling to the alien-sounding music as though they'd been partners all their lives, and when Carmen had indeed hauled Cal up on to one of the podiums there had even been a small burst of applause.

Sophie sighed and twisted on her chrome barstool so that her back was to the dance floor and concentrated on her drink. She really needed to get drunk; perhaps if she held her nose and downed it in one . . . Her stomach churned at the thought of it.

'Buy you a drink?' Sophie dimly heard the offer being made as she stared at her glass wondering exactly what alcohol went well with an over-indulgence of fresh cream cakes. A brandy perhaps? No, the thought of that actually made her want to vomit.

'Hey, you, I said can I buy you a drink?' Belatedly Sophie realised that the offer being made was to her.

'Who, me?' she said looking up at a blunt-faced young man, leaning on the bar and staring at her rather hard, like a dog who hoped that it could will a piece of meat off the table and into its jaws if only it could harness the power of its mind.

'Don't see anyone else here,' the man said. He smiled as he said it, but it was empty of any warmth. 'It's off season, slim pickings.'

'You know how to make a girl feel wanted,' Sophie said. She glanced back at the dance floor where Carmen and Cal were nowhere to be seen. 'Look, you don't want to buy me a drink. I'm engaged, and besides, I'm here with my friends.'

'I don't care if you're engaged.' The man shrugged. 'And I can't see your friends. Look, all I want is a laugh and a bit of fun. So let me buy you a drink. You won't be sorry.' He transferred his hungry gaze to her bust, which was burgeoning beneath the silk with much more gusto than the dress had been designed for.

'No thank you,' Sophie said.

'Let me buy you a drink, I said.' He stood up and although he wasn't much taller than Sophie seated, he was stocky and his stance was threatening. 'I only want to buy you a drink – where's the fucking harm in that?'

'Don't be a fucking wanker, mate. Leave her alone.'

For one moment, as Sophie caught a glimpse of her rescuer out of the corner of her eye, she thought that somehow Louis had found out where she was and had come to find her. But of course it wasn't Louis; Louis would never have been seen dead in a place like this. It was Seth.

'And what the fuck has it got to do with you, you fucking student?' The man poked Seth in the shoulder with a short, thick finger.

'I'll tell you what it's got to do with me,' Seth leaned down till he was nose to nose with the man. 'If you speak even one more word to either me or that woman then I'm going to rip your fucking head off and if you don't believe me, then try me, because I swear to you I've had the worst fucking night of my life tonight and right now killing you and going to prison for it doesn't seem like too much of a bad option.'

Sophie gasped, her eyes wide, as she sat back against the bar clutching her untouched drink, the condensation damp against the palm of her hand. She felt like she should do something, say something, but as the two men fronted up to each other she found herself glued to her chair by the gravity of Seth's fury.

The man stared hard into Seth eyes and then, shaking his head, stepped away, picking up his bottle of beer.

'She wasn't fucking worth it anyway, fat bitch,' he said, lumbering off into the darker recesses of the club, 'Fucking whore.'

'Shit,' Sophie breathed out and touched Seth's shoulder which was rock hard with tension. 'Seth . . . Seth, look at me. Are you OK?'

Seth turned to look at her and Sophie realised that he didn't remember who she was, he really had just turned up to pick a fight with a man who might have been shorter than him but who could have probably put him in hospital any day of the week if he'd wanted to.

'How do you know my . . . oh, you're the one from the wedding fair.'

The realisation didn't make him warm to her. The casual, free, flirty boy she had met previously was gone, probably swimming around in the copious amounts of alcohol that it looked like Seth had consumed, no doubt hoping to forget that he'd just met his father for the first time.

'Sophie, my name's Sophie. I'm Louis's fiancée – your dad's—'

'Don't fucking say it,' Seth said, spreading his fingers wide as he attempted to sit down on the stool next to Sophie, only finding his centre of gravity after swaying first one way and then the other.

'It must have been a shock,' Sophie said as Seth picked up her drink and polished it off in one, before waving at the barman that he wanted another.

'You could say that,' he said, glancing sideways at her. 'I mean, have you seen him? He looks like proper dickhead. He turns up at my mum's house and just expects . . . I don't know what he expects. Where the fuck has he been for the last twenty years? Nowhere, that's where. I didn't need a dad when I was a kid and I certainly don't need one now that I'm a man. I don't know what she's playing at this time, I really don't . . .'

'Who do you mean, Wendy?' Sophie pressed him, as his eyes wandered back and forth without resting on any one thing. 'What do you mean "this time"?'

'It's like I'm an adult now, right? So why does she still treat me like I'm a kid?' Seth asked her. 'Springing that fucker on me out of nowhere, when she could have talked to me, told me about him, maybe even asked me what I wanted for once – but no, it's all about her. It always is. And he . . . Louis . . . just turns up like he thinks it's going to be happy families. Fuck that bullshit.'

'Look, I know it must seem weird, but it's not as if Louis knew anything about you before last week . . .'

172

'He's a wanker,' Seth said, lurching a little closer to her. 'Why the fuck are you marrying him? Marry me, I'm younger, and the sex will be better.'

'Seth, you're really drunk,' Sophie said pushing him ever so gently back into a perpendicular position. 'Are you supposed to be staying at your mum's tonight? Maybe you should get a cab back there.'

'He'll still be there,' Seth growled. 'All over her. Fucking idiot.'

Sophie felt herself tense with jealousy. Seth was drunk and angry, he didn't mean what he was saying, but she couldn't stop her body reacting to it.

'I'll ring him, if you like, see where he is. I just think you need to go home, to sleep this off and give yourself a chance to think.'

Seth looked at her for a long moment, his dark eyes searching hers. Sophie forced herself to continue meeting his gaze as he scrutinised her, feeling somehow that he was owed at least one person looking him in the eye.

'OK,' he said eventually. 'But will you come outside with me? I'm not sure I'll make it to the taxi rank in one piece.' His smile was sweet, youthful and entirely his own. Louis had never smiled at her that way; perhaps once he'd smiled at Wendy or even Carrie like that but by the time she'd found him that expression had either faded or been worn away. Sophie guessed it must be the smile that had melted many a young woman's heart, but she agreed anyway. This would be good, her helping Seth; this would be a way of bringing her into this so that she could be there for Louis, to help and support him. Although, as Seth put his arm around her shoulders and leaned his body weight into hers, Sophie realised that this was a particularly heavy piece of baggage.

*

Outside, Seth collapsed against a wall, his chin tipped up as he sucked in the cool night air. Keeping an eye on him Sophie took a few steps over to the road to find a cab and ring Louis.

The phone rang three times and then went straight to answerphone which meant that Louis had rejected her call. She stood for a second looking at the phone and thought about phoning him again, but if he rejected her call twice in a row then she would be angry with him again and she still hadn't had a chance to make things right after he'd left for Wendy's earlier that afternoon distanced from her, because of her inability to deal like an adult with what was happening. If she could help Seth, if she could calm him down and persuade him to talk to his father again, then that would show Louis that she was sticking by him, no matter what his past threw at her, and that she loved him, come what may.

One thing she could be certain of was that if he was rejecting her calls then he was still with Wendy. And she didn't think she could send Seth home while he was there.

'Right,' she said going back to him. 'Where do you live? In halls or something?'

'No,' Seth said. 'I've got a house with my mates. In Falmouth. I go to art college there.' He peeled himself off the wall for a second and then, as though he were afraid he might fall off the wall, pinned himself back against it.

'I don't feel so good,' he said looking around him warily, suddenly suspicious of gravity.

Sophie thought for a moment. The way she saw it there were three options. She could put him in a cab back to Falmouth, but even if the cab driver would take him the twenty-five miles or so she wasn't at all sure he'd be able to remember where he lived or get there without incurring some vomit-related cleaning costs. Or she could send him back home to his mum's, even if seeing Louis again would make things much worse and even more difficult for everyone. Briefly Sophie thought of accompanying Seth on this short journey to his mother's house, delivering Wendy's son back to her and reclaiming her fiancé at the same time, but as tempting as that was, she knew it wasn't a good idea. The last thing Louis needed now was her turning up and demanding he come home with her. She had to give him his space, and if while she was doing that she could somehow look after his son, then all the better.

The third option was that she *could* take him back to the B&B. After all, Mrs Alexander was at Louis's house and she knew that there were quite a few rooms free. She *could* pay for a single room for Seth to sleep in, feed him coffee and Nurofen and then, once he'd sobered up, try to talk to him about giving Louis another chance. For a few more moments Sophie thought hard about her plan, trying to detect if there were any fatal flaws, but, unable to see any, she decided to take him back to the Avalon. After all, she was practically his step-mother. In some small way he was her responsibility, and by looking after him she was showing Louis that she cared. That she could be wholly a part of his life, even as complicated and as difficult as it often seemed to be.

Sophie dialled Cal and then Carmen's number on her phone. Neither one of them answered, so she left a message on Carmen's phone telling her that she was going home and that she'd see them back at the B&B. She could have explained about taking Seth with her but it would have taken a long time and he was gradually sliding down the wall like one of those sticky little octopuses that used to be all the rage when she was at school.

'Come on, you,' she said hefting him up and on to her shoulder. 'There's a cab.'

'Where'm going?' Seth asked her in a blur. 'Don't make me go back there, cos if he's there I'll . . .'

'No, you're coming back with me,' Sophie said.

'Result,' Seth said, grinning at her as she folded him into a cab.

'Not in *that* way. I live in a B&B. I'll put you in one of the free rooms so you can sleep it off and if you want we can talk in the morning.'

'Or we could just kiss now,' Seth said sliding his hand up her thigh as she got in the cab next to him. 'I like older women, I like older women a lot.'

'Seth,' Sophie removed his hand from her thigh, 'just so we're clear, I am absolutely categorically in no way going to kiss you, ever.'

'We'll see,' Seth said, that same sweet smile curling his lips. And then he passed out.

'That him, then?' Grace Tregowan asked Sophie as she deposited Seth with some difficulty and a minor back injury on to Mrs Alexander's rose-printed sofa. 'The love child. He's a looker, isn't he? Perfect opportunity for you to trade up.'

'Mrs Tregowan!' Sophie exclaimed. 'He's barely more than a boy.'

But still, it was hard not to admire the sweep of his dark lashes as he lay there with his eyes closed, and the fullness of his lower lip, his mouth parted slightly as he slept.

'I tell you,' Grace said, looking Seth up and down with an expression that made Sophie think it wasn't his eyelashes she was admiring, 'if I were sixty years younger, I'd teach him a thing or two . . .'

'What are you still doing up, anyway?' Sophie whispered as Grace, in her pink fluffy slippers, padded after her into the kitchen, where Sophie planned to risk Mrs Alexander's disapproval by brewing a strong pot of coffee that was really only meant for the breakfast service (instant after eleven a.m. was the rule).

'The older you get the less you sleep,' Grace said. 'I think it's because you know that death is getting closer and the closer it is and the less of life you have left, the less of it you want to miss dreaming about times gone by.'

'You are going to live for ever,' Sophie said as Grace settled herself a little stiffly on to one of Mrs Alexander's kitchen chairs.

'I hope not, darling; it's getting harder and harder to find anyone to have sex with me.'

'Hot chocolate?' Sophie offered.

'I shouldn't,' Grace said, drawing her bed jacket a little tighter around her shoulders. 'It'll have me farting all night – but then again I shouldn't have done most things in my life and that's never stopped me. Go on, then.'

As Sophie switched on the coffee percolator, she took the catering-sized tub of chocolate powder down from the shelf and heaped several large spoonfuls into two of Mrs Alexander's mugs.

'How are your wedding plans going?' Grace asked her. 'Are you coping with all of these love-child shenanigans – and the other thing, too?'

'The other thing?' Sophie asked her as she took some milk out of the fridge.

'The wondering. Wondering if you're doing the right thing marrying Louis. That thing.'

'But I haven't been wondering about it, not at all,' Sophie said as she heated a pan of milk. 'If anything, I'm the one who wants to get married the most now . . .' She trailed off and thought of the brochure for Finestone Manor in the drawer with the unread bills. 'The funny thing is', she said

177

thoughtfully as she watched the milk, waiting for bubbles to break out on the peaceful surface, 'that since all of this happened, if anything, I've felt that I might lose him.'

'Well, that's obvious,' Mrs Tregowan said. 'You met him in a stressful situation, you fell for him during difficult times. When everything seems settled and peaceful, when you've had a chance to really listen to your heart, that's when you have doubts and you haven't given yourself time for that to happen. Now everything is kicking off again, there's another drama and another woman to boot, you don't have time to listen or think, and that suits you because now all you have time to do is to try and fix things for him and to try and keep him.'

'I can't work out if you think that is a good thing or a bad thing,' Sophie said, setting Mrs Tregowan's chocolate on the window sill to cool. Mrs Alexander had told her that last year Grace had burnt her stomach badly on a drink that had been too hot and too heavy for her arthritic hands. So Sophie and Mrs Alexander always took care to fill her cup only halfway and to wait for whatever liquid was contained within to be cool enough not to scald before they gave it to her.

'Well, it's a good thing if you just want to marry him and hang the consequences,' Grace said. 'But then, to feel happy, you'd have to create yourself a drama every few weeks just to drown out your real feelings and you'll end up on morning telly with that bloody awful man shouting at you.'

'That doesn't sound so good,' Sophie said, sitting down opposite Grace with her own chocolate as she waited for the coffee pot to fill.

'Better to find a quiet place, away from all of this, and to give yourself a chance to listen and feel, because the thing is, Sophie, I don't doubt that you love Louis – it's just that what with all this rushing and panic and drama I don't think you really believe it yet.'

'Maybe you're right,' Sophie said thoughtfully, tasting the thick chocolate that coated her tongue. 'Maybe it would be a good idea for me to get away for a bit. But I don't want to seem like I'm running out on him, leaving him and the girls when they need me.'

'It would only be for a few days; the girls would barely know you've gone,' Grace said. 'And as for Louis, give him a chance to miss you. It never did them any harm. I left my third husband for three months, went to Morocco with this charming young man I met in the supermarket. Meat aisle, it was. I can tell, you Donald appreciated me more than ever when I got back. I never had so much sex in my life, after that. Every time he looked at me he thought of me and that young man, which made him really jealous, which in turn made him want me even more. It worked wonders, I can tell you.'

Sophie spent several seconds trying to think of something to say but for once Grace had left her entirely speechless.

'So, did you leave this Donald for your last husband, then?' She asked her finally.

'No.' Grace's smile was rueful. 'He had a heart attack during sex. I missed him, the poor old bugger, but it was the way he would have wanted to go. I had ten years with him, and eight wonderful years of sex, so I can't complain.'

'So would you say that you can base a marriage on sex alone?' Sophie asked, thinking that certainly the last few months of her and Louis's relationship had been based on just that.

'Yes, as long as one of you dies before you stop fancying each other,' Grace said. 'Otherwise, once the sex thing wears off, you usually find you hate each other's guts and have nothing to talk about.'

It wasn't exactly the answer Sophie was hoping for.

'I'm going to take this coffee through to Seth,' Sophie said, filling the largest mug she could find to the brim. 'Want a hand into your room?'

'No thank you, love.' Grace smiled. 'I can get around perfectly well. But if you could hand me my hot chocolate before it goes stone cold that would be lovely.'

Sophie paused and looked at Seth sprawled out on the sofa, his head tipped back, his mouth open. He looked disconcertingly like Bella when she was in a deep sleep, given over to unconsciousness with such abandon that you could almost believe that she lived her real life in dreams. Any doubts or even hopes that Seth might not be Louis's vanished as she watched him; he even snored like Bella.

'Seth.' Sophie crouched down and lightly shook his shoulder. 'Seth, I've got you some coffee.'

His eyes flickered open and then fixed on her, dark slits beneath his heavy lids.

'Am I really at your place?' he asked her, his voice dry. 'Or did I dream that?'

'You are at the B&B I stay in,' Sophie said, setting down the coffee, taking his hand and pulling him into a sitting position. 'I've booked you a room for the night; you can go and talk to your mum in the morning when you've got a clear head.'

Carefully she handed him the hot coffee. 'I put sugar in it, I hope that's OK.'

Seth took a sip of the coffee, his hand cupping the mug like Izzy did when she was drinking hot chocolate. 'That's top,' he told her. 'You are very nice, you know. You didn't have to rescue me. You could have left me in the gutter to sober up. I've done it plenty of times before.'

'I couldn't have done that.' Sophie smiled, settling into a

kneeling position on the floor, leaning her elbow on the seat of the sofa. She had seen two sides to Seth, flirtatious and angry, and now she was seeing a third. He looked very young, like a blank page, and vulnerable – unprepared for what life might write on him. 'Besides, can you imagine what would happen if Louis found out that I'd walked away and left you in that state? I'd so be chucked.'

Seth sipped the coffee in silence for a moment, looking around at Mrs Alexander's guest sitting room through half-closed eyes. Sophie guessed that the cacophony of flower prints and menagerie of china animals was probably not the best décor to embrace a hangover in.

'Why are you going to marry him, then?' Seth asked. 'I mean, you are a very beautiful, lovely, kind, proper woman. What did he do to get you?'

Sophie mused for a moment on what the phrase proper woman meant, but decided it probably had something to do with her age so decided not to pursue it further.

'I was looking after his children, my best friend's children. Carrie – my friend – died and I was the girls' guardian. Louis had been overseas in Peru . . .'

'Ran away from the kids, then,' Seth surmised.

'No, well, not exactly – it's a really long story, but the short version is that I thought that about him too. I thought he was a good-for-nothing, low-life loser who abandoned his wife and children and then just turned up years later, thinking everything is going to be all right because now he's ready to play daddy. But then I got to know him, I found out his story – his reasons for doing what he did. I realised that he is a great person, a wonderful person. And his daughters found that out too. I think the three of us fell in love with him at the same time.'

'He's got you properly taken in,' Seth said, shaking his head. 'You look so clever, too.'

'Clever?' Sophie questioned him.

'I mean you don't look like the sort of woman to end up in some backwater, living in a B&B, following a man around. You look like you're your own person.'

'I *am* my own person,' Sophie insisted. 'I chose to come here. It's not like Louis hypnotised me to get me down here.'

'That you know of,' Seth said, his eyes widening. He and Sophie smiled at each other for a second.

'Let me ask you something,' Sophie said. 'Louis didn't leave you, he didn't even ever know about you – not till a few days ago, and as soon as he knew, he wanted to meet you. He wanted to work out how to be a part of your life. So how can you hate him?'

Seth shrugged. 'I've never had a dad, not really. Oh, there was Ted, the bloke who was stupid enough to marry my mum, but he didn't stick around for long. And I'm fine about it now, I actually don't give a toss about it. When I was kid, that's when it was hard to cope with. You know, the fathers' race at sports day, or the other kids going off to the footy or on a camping trip with their dads. I had my granddad and he did his best, but it wasn't the same, you know? Not the same as having your own dad around.'

'I know,' Sophie said, remembering her first Christmas without her dad. But at least she had known exactly what it was that was missing from her life, Seth had never had a chance to understand that.

'Anyway *that's* when it hurt, back then. But I got on with things. Mum did her best, never let me go without, and Nan and Granddad were always there. I got used to it, came to terms with it. But I couldn't help but think about him, this man – my father whom Mum had told me she had loved very much and who had loved her back. I used to lie in bed at night and try and imagine him and wonder why on earth he hadn't come to find Mum, the woman he loved so much, and his son. I used to wish for him, will him to turn up at the school gates one day or be on the doorstep out of the blue on a Christmas morning. And I imagined he'd fling his arms round Mum and kiss her and he'd look at me and he'd say, "Son, I'm never leaving you again." And I wondered and wondered if he was lying awake staring at his ceiling wondering about me too. But he never turned up at school or came round at Christmas and as I got bigger I stopped thinking about him. I worked out for myself how to be a man. And now I'm fine, I'm sorted. I've got my own place, I've got college, I've got the band, my mates, and as many women as I can get my hands on. I'm happy. I'm sorted and then suddenly there he is, my dad. There he is turning up out of the blue just like I'd always wanted him to.' Seth's laugh was mirthless. 'And not only has he not been thinking about me, or wondering about me, but he didn't even know I existed till a few days ago and all of those hours and days I spent wishing for him as a kid meant nothing because I didn't even exist for him. You ask me how can I hate him and the answer is I don't know what else to feel about him, not now. All this, it's ten years too late – I don't need a dad now and I'm not going to pretend that I do to make him, my mum, or even you happy.'

'I can understand that,' Sophie said, resting her chin on her hand as she looked up at him. 'You're in shock, you haven't really had time to think about what's happened. But you might change your mind if you give yourself a chance . . .'

'I don't want to,' Seth said, with a shrug.

'But you don't know anything about him, not really,' Sophie said.

'I don't want to,' Seth said, draining the last of his coffee.

'For example,' Sophie pressed on, 'when he was in Peru he was working for a children's charity . . .'

'So fucking what? If he couldn't be bothered to look after his own kids,' Seth interjected.

'And he likes to surf. I bet you do, too . . .'

'Hate it.'

'Well, you're studying art, aren't you? Louis is building up a photography business. Portraits, landscapes, weddings . . .'

'Weddings? Sell-out.'

'And he is a good dad. His daughters – your half-sisters – really love him.'

'They really love him now, after he comes back into their lives after years of leaving them to it? They're kids, they don't know any different.'

He looked at Sophie again, narrowing his eyes slightly as he examined her. 'I bet you had a lot to do with that. I bet you got the kids to like him again. You fixed that mess for him and now you want to fix me, don't you?'

Sophie sat back on her heels and shook her head.

'I wanted his daughters to be happy because I love them, and they are happy now. And I love him, so yes, I'd like to help him and you get through this and work out what to do, if you'll let me.'

Seth put his empty coffee cup down on one of Mrs Alexander's lace coasters that she had told Sophie were there for decoration and were under no circumstances ever to be used. He sat up and, reaching out, picked up one of her hands as she knelt before him.

'I like you,' he said, looking into her eyes. 'I'd like you to help me.'

'Really?' Sophie was relieved and disconcerted at the same time. 'Well, that's great. Just say what you want me to do and I'll— oh.'

Before she knew what was happening Seth's fingers were in her hair, pulling her towards him and he was kissing her.

For a second, perhaps five, Sophie did not resist, the shock of what was happening disabling her fight-or-flight impulse momentarily. But it was also the heat of the vodka-soaked kiss that pinned her to the spot; it was a very good kiss. Perhaps it was five seconds, maybe ten, that she let Seth kiss her but it was several seconds too long because she was still a fraction of a second from pushing him away when Cal and Carmen tumbled in through the door.

'Oh my giddy aunt!' Carmen exclaimed as Sophie finally broke away. She pointed. 'That's not Louis!'

'And when I told you to embrace Louis's baggage, this is not what I meant,' Cal added.

Seth sprang out of his seat, still a little unsteady on his feet, and swayed out of the room, crashing into furniture as he lurched towards the door.

'Seth, wait,' Sophie called after. 'What about the room?'

'The room?' Carmen repeated scandalised. 'The *room*?'

But Seth didn't speak, he simply found the front door and slammed it behind him, loud enough to dangerously rattle the Doulton figurines on the mantelpiece.

'Oh bloody hell,' Sophie said, sitting on the sofa and burying her face in her hands. 'Bloody, bloody hell – how did that happen?'

'What exactly *did* happen?' Carmen asked her. 'Were you drunk and confused?'

'We were just talking and then he lunged, there was nothing I could do about it,' Sophie attempted to explain, trying very hard to get the memory of Seth's fingers in her hair out of her head.

'It didn't exactly look like there was anything you wanted to do about it,' Carmen said.

'That's not true, he took me by surprise, that's all.' Sophie looked at Cal who was looking at her and shaking his head.

'Go on,' she said wearily, 'say it.'

'Only you,' Cal said. 'Only you could snog your dead best friend's husband's secret love child. Now what the fuck are you going to do?'

Chapter Eleven

Sophie had never been unfaithful to anyone in her life and she wasn't quite sure how to handle it. Technically a kiss lasting only a few seconds, even if it was several seconds longer than it should have lasted, wasn't the worst crime that one could commit against a loved one, but, as Cal insisted in pointing out to her, when that kiss was with your fiancé's son, it put a whole new spin on things.

She had run out after Seth, barging her way past Carmen and Cal, but he'd hailed a cab that was passing at the bottom of the street and before she could reach him the car had pulled away, taking him God knows where. Wearily Sophie had turned on her heel, taking a deep breath of chilled sea air before she slowly walked back to face her friends and try to explain to them what they had seen.

It had taken a lot of explaining. The three of them had sat up for what was left of the night, Cal and Carmen drinking Mrs Alexander's Christmas sherry while Sophie made herself hot chocolate after hot chocolate, hoping the sugar rush would help her work out the best thing to do.

At just after three a.m., Mrs Alexander came in and found them all in the sitting room, sitting on her best cushions scattered on the floor, like teenagers who had just been discovered having a party when they thought their parents were away.

'Still up?' she said pressing her lips into a thin line, which meant that she had clocked the coffee ring on her best lace doily.

'Catching up, you know – you don't mind, do you?' Sophie asked her. 'We thought it would be better down here than in one of our rooms – we don't want to disturb any other guests. We're being quiet and I'll replace the sherry and wash the . . . doily.'

Mrs Alexander nodded once, which was the nearest that Sophie was going to get to assent. 'Well, Louis got back home about twenty minutes ago, if you're interested.'

Sophie *was* interested. In the midst of everything that had been happening she'd forgotten that Mrs Alexander wouldn't be coming back until Louis got home. He'd been at Wendy's by four-thirty that afternoon, and she'd met Seth in the club just before eleven, and left shortly afterwards. Carmen and Cal had come in at two and now it was after three. He'd been on his own with Wendy for the best part of twelve hours. Why had Louis stayed there so long, why hadn't he answered her phone call or at least called her back and asked her to relieve Mrs Alexander? If he'd have called her back, if he'd come and helped her with Seth, than her life would be a lot simpler at this point.

'Is he OK?' Sophie asked Mrs Alexander.

'He was quiet,' Mrs Alexander replied. 'Looked drained. Perhaps you should go over and see how he is?'

'I've had too much to drink,' Sophie lied, nodding at the sherry she hadn't touched. 'I'll go in the morning.'

'Right, then,' Mrs Alexander said, looking disapprovingly at Carmen and Cal as if she suspected they might be guilty of a lot more than staying up late and drinking sherry. 'Clear up after yourselves.'

'That's going to be harder to do now that she knows,' Cal

whispered as they heard Mrs Alexander go up the stairs.

'Just don't ever, ever tell anyone what happened,' Carmen said. 'It's simple.'

'But what if Seth tells someone, what then?' Sophie said. 'I'll look like a cradle-snatching slut – what then?'

'Deny it, deny everything for ever,' Carmen added. 'It'll be your word against his. Besides, I'm the only cradle-snatching slut round here, I don't want you elbowing your way in on my territory.'

'Look, it won't come to that,' Cal said. 'The kid was really drunk, there's a good chance he won't even remember what happened and even if he does, he's going to be so embarrassed that he snogged an old bat like her that he's never going to want anyone to know.'

'Excuse me, I think kissing an older woman is probably quite impressive,' Sophie complained.

'And so does my James,' Carmen added, with a nod.

'It depends on the older woman, love,' Cal said. 'Anyway in the scheme of things, even though kissing your fiancé's son is potentially the worst thing you could ever have done, it's not that important. It doesn't change anything apart from how high you rate in the idiot charts. Just go home to Louis in a few hours and act like nothing's happened.'

'Like I didn't have Seth here at all?' Sophie asked him.

'Probably for the best,' Carmen agreed. 'Think of it all as a nightmare . . . or maybe a dream, talking of which – how was that kiss, you looked like you were quite enjoying it?'

'How many times! I was in shock, that's why I didn't pull away right away,' Sophie's voice rose sufficiently to cause her friends to shush her. 'And anyway, you're not supposed to lie to your fiancé. If it was OK to lie to your fiancé then I would never have told Louis about Seth in the first place.'

'You do still want to be engaged to him,' Cal said, 'don't you?'

'Of course I do!' Sophie said. 'I love him.'

'Then go round later, act like nothing has happened, don't say anything and play it by ear.' Cal cocked one eyebrow. 'And try not to snog any other relatives on the way.'

Sophie paused outside Louis's front door, just as she had done six months ago when she'd decided to come down here from London and see if she could make things work with him.

She had hesitated then, unsure what her reception would be like, not clear how he felt about her. It was strange, given all that happened and the ring on her finger, that she felt exactly the same way now, six months later.

Taking a breath, she slid her key into the lock and let herself in.

It was early, barely five a.m., and the house was dark and quiet.

Sophie had tried to stay at the B&B until later, to act as if this morning was a perfectly normal Saturday morning and as if nothing untoward had happened last night, but she couldn't. After trying to go to bed for over an hour and failing, spending several minutes tossing and turning and looking at the darkness where her ceiling ought to be, she had got up and stood in the tiny shower in her en-suite, her forehead pressed to the textured tiles, the warm water running in rivulets over her shoulders and buttocks. When that didn't seem to calm her she tried reading a book, even watching what little TV she could find in the early hours of the morning for a bit, but nothing calmed her; she felt restless and anxious and desperate to see Louis. So she'd woken Cal up and told him where she was going.

'You didn't have to wake me up too,' he complained, shoving his head under his pillow.

'I did, just in case you wanted to talk me out of it,' Sophie whispered to the pillow.

'OK, don't go now; it's far too early, it will look weird and, anyway, I thought you weren't supposed to be there when the girls woke up till after you're married, or some other spurious excuse, to make sure Louis doesn't find out about your snoring till after you've got a ring on his finger. Stay here and shut up.'

'No, can't; have to go,' Sophie said. 'I have to see him, I just have to. Everything is wrong and all pulled apart. If I wait till the sun comes up and it's officially another day, then everything that happened tonight will seem like a dream, it will seem unreal only it is real. I need to be with him now. I need to be able to touch him and put my arms around him and hear his heart beating and know that we are still just as close as we've always been. I'll get up before the girls do, like I did the other morning. I have to go Cal, I have— Cal?'

'Whatever,' Cal mumbled from under the pillow. 'Just please let me sleep.'

Carefully Sophie set her bag and keys down on the hall table and crept up the stairs. Ever so carefully she pushed open Bella's bedroom door and peeped round to check on her. All she could see was a fluff of dark hair peeping above the duvet, her small body curled up beneath it.

In Izzy's room all was also quiet, although Izzy had flung her covers off and lay there with her arms sprawled above her head, knees bent up, one toe pointed as if she had fallen asleep mid dance move which, knowing Izzy, was entirely possible.

Then, ever so slowly, Sophie crept into Louis's room, the room which would one day be their room. He was lying face down. His clothes were strewn around the bottom of the bed as if he had just climbed into it and fallen straight to sleep. Sophie watched him for a second or two in the half-light, sorting out his features from his son's. As she looked at him, her heart in her mouth for fear that he'd wake up and find her there, Sophie realised that the two men actually looked quite different.

Louis's jawline was square, his cheekbones were a little more pronounced, and he had a bump in the bridge of his nose that Sophie loved to run her forefinger over, tracing a path to his beautifully shaped mouth. Seth's face in comparison was soft, not yet fully formed, his face more heart shaped, like Wendy's, his nose straight and narrow. He did have his father's colouring, though, and his mouth. He did have his father's exquisite mouth. Sophie took a breath, running her hands through her hair, unsure of what to do next. Should she wake Louis up and try to talk to him, explain what had happened with Seth? Or perhaps Cal was right, perhaps she should just turn around and go back to the B&B and wait to see what the dawn would bring.

Then Louis moaned a little in his sleep, the flicker of a smile briefly lit his face, and he rolled on to his back, exposing his torso. Sophie found she did not want to leave.

Slowly, quietly, she slipped out of her jeans and pulled her T-shirt over her head, shaking her hair out over her shoulders. After a second she unhooked her bra and slipped off her knickers.

In all the times that she had been with Louis in this house she had only ever got into this bed with him once, although he'd begged her to join him several times. Sophie had always told herself and Louis that she was waiting for them to be married, waiting for the children to get used to the idea, but as she stood naked on the verge of his bed, she realised that it had been about more than that. This place was a symbol, a final sign of commitment. And recently, when she should feel so close to him and yet felt so far away, it was the only place where she knew how to reach him.

Sophie held her breath, uncertain of how he'd react and then slowly, gingerly, as if there might be monsters lurking beneath the covers, she eased her way under the duvet, lying on her back next to him on the smooth sheet, which felt cold against the heat of her body. Slowly she turned her head to look at Louis's sleeping face, half obscured by the pillow. Wherever he was now he was probably far away from the son who didn't want to know him and she wasn't sure that he would thank her for bringing him back to that world. Sophie bit her lip and looked at the ceiling. She'd never done this sort of thing before, woken a man up for sex. She wasn't exactly sure of the etiquette or procedure. Should she give him a quick prod, she wondered, and then pounce? The shock might give him a heart attack. Should she whisper sweet nothings in his ear till he opened his eyes and smiled at her? Except that, despite her lack of experience of spending the whole night with him, Sophie knew Louis; once he was out he was out for the count. Once Bella and Izzy had treated him to an early morning serenade with their Barbie guitars and a set of drums made out of a Quality Street tin that Bella had found in the garden shed and Louis hadn't turned a hair. He had snored through the whole of their hard-rock rendition of 'Love in an Elevator'. It had fallen to Bella to fill the toothbrush mug up with cold water and tip it over her father's head in a bid to get her audience's attention.

The first thing Bella had said, Louis had told her later, when he had finally stemmed the shocked stream of expletives that had burst out of his newly conscious mouth was, 'Daddy, you are not supposed to swear in front of us.'

Sophie tensed as Louis shifted position again, rolling once more on to his stomach, one arm trapped awkwardly beneath him. At least if she pounced on him now she'd save him from a terrible case of pins and needles.

There was nothing else for it, Sophie told herself sternly. After all, she was here naked and in his bed. The only alternative to trying to wake him up was to slip out of bed and secretly put her clothes back on and leave, and although in the past Sophie could have been fairly accused of being emotionally cowardly at many points in her life, she was determined that this was not going to be one of them. Sex was the thing that she and Louis were best at. It was the cornerstone of their love for each other. It was the place where she would find that intimacy with him again that had somehow slipped just ever so slightly out of kilter.

Sophie Mills braced herself for seduction.

Rolling on to her side she slid her hand down his back stroking her palm gently over his buttocks. She watched his face as a frown flickered between his eyes and faded again. Sidling a little closer so that her breast brushed against his biceps, she repeated the action, stroking his back and bottom and this time softly kissing his shoulder and neck.

Louis's eyes flickered open.

'Wassat?' he murmured hunching his shoulder against her kiss.

'It's me, Sophie,' Sophie whispered. 'I missed you. I came to see how you were and whether or not you felt like having sex with me?'

Sophie screwed her eyes tightly shut for a second. She really was going to have to work on her sexy talk skills. Still, as hackneyed as they were they were effective. Louis was now wide awake.

He turned to face Sophie, reaching his fingers out to trace the curve of her cheeks.

'Are you really here or is this just a very vivid dream?' he asked her, his voice low and hoarse.

'I don't know.' Sophie heard the smile in her voice. 'Why don't you pinch yourself and see?'

Louis's arm encircled her waist and he pulled her body flush against his, moaning as her breasts crushed against his chest.

'I think I'll pinch you instead,' he said into her neck, his hand cupping her bottom. 'God, Sophie, it's so good to see you. How did you know I was missing you?'

'I didn't,' Sophie said. 'I just knew that I was missing you.'

'I'm glad.' Sophie felt Louis's mouth smile against her cheek. 'Two nights in a row – does this finally mean you've declared a bed amnesty?' he whispered.

'Yes – and it's getting light, so you'd better make the most of it. I want to be downstairs and fully dressed before the girls wake up,' Sophie replied, before kissing him so hard that she pushed him on to his back and rolled on top of him.

'Oh, babe,' Louis said. 'This is the best way to wake up ever.'

Sophie smiled into his eyes as she moved on top of him. Here in his arms, in his bed, in amongst his kisses and caresses, everything was perfect, nothing could touch her here where they were safe from harm and she could keep the outside world at bay for a few hours. As her hand travelled downwards between his thighs she briefly considered that perhaps sex wasn't the best basis for a serious relationship, but it was like Grace said – as long as one of them died before they got bored of each other then everything would be fine.

'Aunty Sophie, you are in Daddy's bed.'

Sophie sat up with a bolt, drawing the covers over her breasts, to find Bella in her pyjamas, her usually straight hair whipped into a frenzy, staring at her in shock.

'Oh God, I went back to sleep,' she moaned, more to herself than Bella. She looked at her watch. It was well past nine in the morning, which was the very latest that the girls ever slept in.

'That is *Daddy's* bed,' Bella repeated. 'And you are not married yet – are you?'

Sophie struggled to compose herself and even more crucially to form a coherent thought.

'No, no . . . um *yes*, yes – I *am* in Daddy's bed because I was so jolly tired last night that I didn't think I could get back to the B&B with out falling asleep on the way and sooooo . . . Louis . . . Louis, wake up. Wake up *now*.'

'What . . . again? Babe, you are amazing, but I am only a man – I need at least another half an hour . . . oh fu—flip – hello, Bellarina.'

'Sophie is in your bed,' Bella stated again, incredulous, as if she couldn't quite believe that no one else realised what was going on.

'Yes, I know,' Louis said. 'Sophie stayed for a sleepover.'

'I'm sorry, Bella, it must be very strange for you to come in and find me here like this, but like Daddy said I was very tired and so had a sleepover.'

'A sleepover, but when?' Bella asked her. 'Mrs Alexander was still here when we went to bed and I heard you come in and Sophie wasn't there then. She wasn't even here when you went to sleep and I know because when I went to the toilet I checked on you and she wasn't here then.'

Sophie trembled under Bella's concise interrogation technique, but Louis took it perfectly in his stride, draping an arm around her shoulder and smiling at his daughter.

'No, she came for a late sleepover, sometimes grown-ups have late sleepovers,' Louis explained. 'It was really more of a practice for when we are married and Sophie will be sleeping in this bed every night and we will get to see her every morning, which will be brilliant.'

'Well, it was a bit of a shock,' Bella said. 'I wasn't expecting it.'

'I'm sorry, Bella,' Sophie told her. She reached out a hand and to her relief Bella took it and climbed on to the bed, curling up against Sophie. 'It must have been a bit of shock to find me here this morning. I should have told you I was coming for a sleepover. I promise not to surprise you that way again. In fact, I won't be sleeping over again until after me and Daddy are married, I promise.'

'Do you?' Bella and Louis asked at the same time, both looking equally perplexed.

'Apart from the surprise, I don't think I mind you sleeping over,' Bella said. 'I like it and if you sleep over, then sometimes I can come and sleep with you like I did in London. Do you remember when we listened to the sound of the traffic and pretended it was waves?'

'I do,' Sophie said, recalling how both she and Bella had squeezed on to her two-seater sofa to curl up together whenever things got a little bit too much for them.

Bella twisted around to look at her. 'Did Daddy snore?' she asked Sophie, a hint of a smile playing around her lips.

'Yes.' Sophie nodded. 'All the time. I've never heard anything so loud in all my life.'

'Then sometimes you can come and sleep in my room because I don't snore. You snore, but only like a cat purring.

Me and Izzy say that Dad's snore sounds like a wolf growling!'

'It does, or an elephant with a blocked-up nose,' Sophie replied, sending Bella into fits of giggles.

'Hey, you two,' Louis protested. 'I do not snore.'

'You do!' Sophie and Bella giggled together.

'So, are you sure that you don't mind me being here?' Sophie asked her. 'That you're not upset or worried?'

'I like having you for a sleepover,' Bella said, suddenly serious. 'But it would be more fun if you were in my room. I've got a blow-up *High School Musical* bed which is designed exactly for the purpose of a sleepover. You wouldn't fit in it, but I would, and you could sleep in my bed except that Artemis probably wouldn't want to share with you and if she got in my blow-up bed then her claws might burst it so we'd have to shut her in the kitchen with Tango.'

'Don't you worry, I'm sure we'll work something out for my next sleepover.' Sophie kissed the top of Bella's head.

'But for now,' Louis said, his fingertip caressing Sophie's thigh under the covers, 'how about you run downstairs and get the Coco Pops out – it is a Coco-Pops day, today, isn't it?'

'No, Daddy it's a Shreddies day, which you know perfectly well. You don't have to worry. I don't need Coco Pops to make me feel better about Aunty Sophie having a sleepover.'

'Right – well, good.' Louis looked suitably chastened. 'How about you run and get the Shreddies out and I'll be down in a second.'

Bella stayed on the bed nestling into the crook of Sophie's shoulder.

'I'm glad I've got you, Aunty Sophie,' Bella said.

'I'm glad I've got you.' Sophie put her arms around Bella and hugged her gently.

'You are my B.F.F.,' Bella told her.

'And you're mine,' Sophie said utterly unclear as to what it was she had been told, only that whatever it was it clearly meant a lot to the child.

'I know,' Bella said. She cast a sideways glance at her father.

'Daddy, can we just this once have Coco Pops today even though it's not strictly speaking a Coco-Pops day?'

'Go for it,' Louis told her.

She hopped off the bed and ran into the hallway yelling, 'Izzy, get up! Aunty Sophie stayed for a sleepover and it's a Coco-Pops day!'

'Right on!' Izzy shouted as she thundered down the stairs after her sister a few seconds later.

'That was tricky,' Sophie said lying back on the bed and examining the ceiling. 'I was waiting for her to ask me where my pyjamas were ... we shouldn't have put her through that, or Izzy. I'm sorry, I wasn't thinking.'

'I thought she was pretty cool about it,' Louis said, sliding his hand up across her belly and coming to rest on her breast.

'I know she acts cool and together, but she's only a child; they both are. Children who have had a lot to deal with and precious little stability recently; they don't need any more surprises.'

'Do you mean finding out you had a sleepover, or do you mean Seth?' Louis sighed, withdrawing the warmth of his touch from her body as he flopped on to his back.

'Well ...' Sophie hesitated. Till that moment the whole of last night had gone out of her head, except for the part where Louis's body had been wrapped around her. Play it by ear, Cal had said. See what happens.

'How did it go with Seth, anyway?' she asked him tentatively.

'Badly.' Louis rubbed his hands roughly over his face. 'It went really badly. Wendy said we should come right out with it, no beating around the bush, she said. So he turned up to find me sitting in his living room – and when I saw him, Soph . . . It was so weird. I wasn't sure how I was going to feel, but I thought I'd feel something – like a spark of recognition, something in my chest. You know, that pulling feeling you get when you look at the girls. When I came back from Peru, the second I set eyes on Bella and even Izzy, whom I'd barely ever known, it was there, that ache that tells you that you love them. But I sat there and I looked at this . . . this *man* and I . . . well, there was nothing there. And he must have seen that in my face, he must have known.'

'So what happened?'

'It was like I said, he walked in, saw me sitting there, and Wendy said, "Seth, this is Louis, Louis is your father", just like that. For a second or two he was quiet, just looking from her and then back to me, and then he just said, "I don't have a father, I have never had a father, and I don't need one now. He's about twenty years too late." And he walked out without a second glance. I met my son for less than ten minutes and we didn't speak two words to each other.'

'It does seem a pretty brutal way to break the news to him; it must have been a shock – like Bella finding me here this morning. I don't think I'd react much differently. In fact, news of my mother's live-in lover did nearly give me a heart attack.'

'Wendy said it was best.' Louis shrugged. 'She said he appreciated her being straight and open with him and, after all, she's the one that knows him, not me.'

'So what happend after he'd gone?'

'Well, Wendy had cooked, so I stayed and ate and we talked

some more. Talked about the past, talked about Seth – tried to work out what to do.'

Sophie tried not to imagine Louis and Wendy sitting across a table that was, of course, candlelit as they talked over that glorious summer of love they had spent in each other's arms. This wasn't about Louis and Wendy, this was about Seth, and she had to remember that, otherwise she'd drive herself mad.

'What are you going to do?' she asked.

'Wendy thinks I should go to his college in Falmouth, try to talk to him again, but I wonder if he needs a bit of space? Like he said, he's done without out a dad for twenty years and now I turn up and what have I got to offer him? It's not as if he needs anyone to teach him how to ride a bike without stabilisers or play footy in the park.' Sophie felt a pang as she thought of what Seth had told her last night before the kissing incident. Of how he'd longed for a father to do just that with him.

'Maybe I should just let him know I'd like to meet him again,' Louis went on. 'Let him know how to get in touch with me and then give him some space to get used to the idea – what do you think?'

'I really think that would be the best thing,' Sophie said, remembering the look on Seth's face last night. 'He'd appreciate knowing that you will be there to talk to when he's ready.' Louis looked uncertain.

'But then again, Wendy is his mum; she should know best. If she thinks that I should really go for it, really try and make a relationship with him now, then maybe I should do that . . . I don't want him to think I don't care even if— the fact is, Sophie, I haven't know him long enough to know if I do care about him. And if he's angry and resentful, then whose fault is that? It's mine. I've fucked up the life of a boy without ever knowing about it and right now, right at this moment, I'm finding it really hard to feel anything.'

'You should do what you want,' Sophie said, letting her thoughts run away, out of her mouth before she had a chance to censor them. 'Maybe Wendy's got other reasons for wanting you to hang around so much; maybe she's not only interested in Seth . . .'

'Like what?' Louis turned to look at her, impatience threaded in his tone.

'Like she likes having you around in her life again, like she wants reasons to keep seeing you.' Sophie was painfully aware of how irrational and foolish she sounded.

'Don't be ridiculous,' Louis said, suddenly springing up out of bed and scooping up his clothes from the floor. 'I don't know why you have such a problem with Wendy. I thought you'd admire her, if anything. She's a single mother who's brought up her son, my son, on her own for twenty years and who just wants him to have the chance of knowing his father. What is your problem with that, Soph?'

Sophie wriggled awkwardly on the bed, feeling suddenly vulnerable in her naked state and hurt that Louis was quite so quick to defend his ex against the woman he was going to marry. She knew what she should say, she should say that she didn't have a problem with Wendy, that she was just being silly, but she couldn't ignore her instincts.

'I just don't trust her,' she told him despite herself, feeling the soft closeness that had existed all too briefly between them ebb away again at the mention of Wendy's name.

'Why ever not?' Louis exclaimed, pulling up his jeans. 'Last night, Wendy and I agreed to think things through and then talk again in a few days. Does that sound unreasonable to you? Does that sound like she's looking for excuses to get me to "hang around"?'

'No, but . . . Louis, please don't get angry with me. I'm just trying to look out for you!'

'You know, if you stopped trying to "look out for me", our lives would be a lot simpler right now,' Louis told her unfairly.

The two of them looked at each other across the bed, each one unsure of exactly what to do next. Just then the doorbell sounded and the relief on Louis's face was clear.

'Girls, don't answer the—' Louis ran to the banisters, grabbing a T-shirt as he went, but it was already too late, Bella had opened the front door.

'Dad,' she called up the stairs. 'That woman Aunty Sophie doesn't like is here.'

'Hi, Wend,' Sophie heard Louis greet his ex, all too aware that he was dressed only in his jeans, pulling his T-shirt on as he headed down the stairs. 'Hey, Bellarina, why don't you and Izzy watch your programmes on the kitchen TV for a bit?'

'I don't want to,' Bella complained. 'I want to stay here and listen to you and find out about this strange woman.'

'Well, this isn't a conversation for little girls, so go and watch TV please.'

'Yes, but, you see . . .' Sophie could hear from the tone in Bella's voice that she was in full negotiation mode. Normally Louis loved to engage her in lengthy, sometimes logically skewed but always entertaining, debates about why she should be able to do whatever it was that he didn't want her to, and about fifty per cent of the time she'd win him over. But Louis was not in the mood today and his tone was dark.

'Bella, do as I ask. *Now.*'

There was a pause and then Sophie heard Bella in the

kitchen saying very loudly to Izzy, 'We're going to watch cartoons even though they rot our brains.'

Like Bella, Sophie was unable to resist the temptation to find out what was going on. But even though she didn't think that Louis could send her away to watch cartoons she was also fairly sure he'd want to talk with Wendy on his own. Quietly she crept out of bed, dragging the thick and heavy duvet around her body and creeping to the top of the stairs where she could just about see Wendy's and Louis's heads without giving away her own position.

'So how is he?' Louis asked her. There was a reluctance in his voice as if he didn't want to know the answer.

'I don't know, that's the problem.' Wendy sounded upset, her voice shaky and strained. Sophie hazarded leaning over the banister, hoping to catch a glimpse of the other woman's face, trying to discern if her expression matched her tone. But Wendy's head was bowed, her hair screening her features. Sophie could see Louis's hand on Wendy's shoulder, the long fingers that had only moments ago been caressing her thigh, rubbing her skin in slow circles.

Choosing not to examine how that sight made her feel, Sophie dropped the duvet by the banister and darted back into the bedroom, plucking her clothes off the floor where she had discarded them what seemed like a lifetime ago now. Hurriedly she slipped her underwear on, straining to hear the continuing conversation below, hurrying back to the banister in bare feet, the rest of her clothes tucked under her arm in a bid not to miss anything crucial.

'I haven't heard from him since he stormed off last night,' Wendy was saying. 'He's not answering his mobile. None of his friends seem to know where he is. I thought he might have gone back to Falmouth but no one there has heard from him. He gets very emotional when he's upset.' Sophie pulled on her jeans, certain that the rasp of denim over her thighs could be heard in Penzance, never mind at the bottom of the stairs. 'I don't know where he is, Louis. I'm really worried about him – anything could have happened.'

Sophie held on to the banister as she pulled on first one sock and then the other. She knew; she knew where he had been at least up until two a.m. that morning, up till the point where he tried to kiss her or actually had kissed her depending on how much in denial she was feeling.

'He'll be OK,' Louis reassured Wendy. Sophie watched as he drew her into a hug, her chest tightening as she saw his arms around another woman. 'It's not as if he's a kid. He can look after himself.'

'I know.' Wendy's voice was muffled by Louis's shoulders and Sophie knew exactly the scent that Wendy would be breathing in; a mixture of sweat and sex and the last traces of yesterday's aftershave. 'It's just like I said, sometimes he can be a bit rash – acts before he thinks. He's got a temper on him, he gets really angry and self-destructive. When this girl he really liked finished with him last summer, he went out on a bender and ended up in a fight with three other men. He got four broken ribs and a dislocated knee.' Sophie heard Wendy take a ragged breath. 'What if he's in some gutter somewhere?'

'OK . . .' Louis hesitated and Sophie knew he was trying to work out exactly how worried he should be. 'Have you rung the hospital? Police stations?'

'No. I couldn't bring myself to do it. That's why I came here.' Sophie couldn't see her but she just knew that at that precise moment Wendy was looking up at Louis with tear-stained eyes made all the more bright by her crying. 'Perhaps I shouldn't be bothering you with this now but I didn't know who else to turn to – I hoped we could do it together?'

Sophie's heart sank. She was going to have to tell them that she *had* seen Seth, and he *had* been very drunk and in a brawling mood. If it hadn't been for the fact that she had seen Seth and experienced his rash behaviour with her own eyes and even lips, then she would have thought that Wendy was making the whole thing up, or at least exaggerating the situation just to get close to Louis and the hot, raw and irrational part of her still felt that way. But Wendy didn't need to make up complications to get to Louis, if that was what she wanted at all. She had his son and that was reason enough.

Despite her mixed feeling towards Wendy (a mixture that consisted of one-part hatred, two-parts loathing and one-part irritation), she could not withhold information about a child from his mother, not even when the child was twenty years old and had recently made a pass at her. Sophie might have been new to motherhood, she might have experienced it only by proxy, but she knew how much worrying about the children you loved could tear you to shreds and she found she couldn't let Wendy go through that. As she thought about how she'd feel if Bella or Izzy were lost, she was all at once overwhelmed with an unexpected empathy for Wendy, and emotional up-swell tightened her chest and sprung tears in her eyes. Sophie touched her fingers to her eyes and felt the damp of the unexpected tears on her fingertips. Suddenly she couldn't bare how Wendy was feeling and she wanted to do all she could to help her. Sophie didn't understand the intense rush of emotion that gripped her, or how she could feel so suddenly sympathetic to a woman she couldn't bear, but equally she couldn't fight it.

Brushing the unwarranted tears from her eyes with the heels of hands and fighting to control the shock of sobs that shook her shoulders, she took a breath and descended the stairs.

'Oh, you're here,' Wendy said when she saw Sophie.

'Yes – look, I couldn't help overhearing,' Sophie said, fighting to keep her voice steady and free from emotion. 'My friend Cal was down last night from London and he wanted to go clubbing; he, Carmen and I all caught a cab into Newquay for a bit of an early hen night, although there weren't any hens to speak of and—'

'And what's that got to do with anything?' Wendy asked her impatiently.

Sophie fought hard to maintain her empathy, which, when actually confronted with the world's most annoying woman, threatened to turn on a sixpence at any second into extremely violent impulses.

'If you'll let me finish ... We went to a nightclub and I saw Seth—'

'You *saw* him?' Louis asked her in disbelief. 'You saw Seth and you are only telling me this *now*?'

'I know, I was going to tell you but I didn't exactly have time, what with one thing and another ...' Sophie hazarded a small smile. She knew that wasn't true. She could have, should have told him about seeing Seth as soon as she had woken him up this morning, there had been more than enough opportunity, but she had chosen not to because for those few precious hours she wanted her bubble back, her and Louis's little world where nothing could touch them. 'But anyway the point is I saw him and he was really drunk and pretty angry so I ...'

'Why didn't you call me?' Louis challenged her, exasperated.

'I did, but you weren't picking up,' Sophie snapped back, incredulous that suddenly she had to defend herself.

'You could have left a message,' Louis countered.

'I would have but I thought it was best to get your son out of the road before he got flattened by a taxi.' Sophie felt cornered but she took a breath and pressed on, determined to deliver the information she had even if it was a little late. 'Like I said, he was really drunk, angry – a bit punchy. He tried to pick a fight with this guy and I thought it was best to get him out of there before he got into any trouble. But he refused to go back to Wendy's and I didn't think I'd find a cab that would take him all the way to Falmouth or that he'd be able to remember where he lived when he got there so ... so I took him back to the B&B to sober up.' Sophie rushed out the last part of the sentence in the vague hope that Louis and Wendy wouldn't hear and she'd be able to gloss over that part.

'You did what?' Wendy asked her. 'You took my son back to your B&B? What for?'

'To sober him up, what else?' Sophie replied, the memory of that foolish kiss weakening the conviction in her voice somewhat.

'Wait a minute,' Louis ran his fingers through his hair that was still tousled with sleep and sex. 'I need a second to get my head around all of this. You knew where Seth was and you didn't tell me? I don't get it, Sophie, why didn't you tell me?'

'I don't know,' Sophie lied. 'I suppose I was waiting for the right time. I'm sorry, OK? I should have told you sooner, but I'm telling you now.'

'So where is he?' Wendy demanded. 'Is he still at the B&B?'

'Um well, no ...' Sophie felt her heart sink. Not only had she withheld information from worried parents, she also had to break the news that she had single-handedly lost Seth again. 'He fell asleep on the sofa while I was making him coffee, but when I woke him up he seemed a lot better, a lot more together. He drank the coffee and we were having a bit of a chat about things when ...' Play it by ear, Cal had said. He hadn't figured on two recently reunited and not to mention angry parents hanging on her every word. It was definitely not a good idea to mention that Seth had kissed her and that she had been a few seconds tardy in breaking off the kiss. It was, on the other hand, an excellent idea never ever to mention the kiss and to pray hard that Seth was either too drunk to remember or too mortified to ever want to mention it again.

'When what?' Wendy asked her wearily, as if she were dealing with a very stupid person.

'When he just got angry again. He stormed off just as Carmen and Cal came back from the club. I went after him but he'd got in a cab before I could reach him and besides, I don't think he would have wanted to talk to me any more.' Not with the whole attempted snog thing, Sophie thought.

'And what time was this?' Louis had his hands on his hips the way they had been when Izzy had decide to paint his white Renault with her poster paints to cheer it up a bit.

'Just after two,' Sophie told him reluctantly. 'But at least we know he'd sobered up a bit and slept off some of what he'd drunk by then. I bet you the only reason he's not answering his phone is because he's probably just sulking.'

Louis looked as if he were about to say something that Sophie really didn't want to hear when there was a shriek from the kitchen and the clatter of cereal bowls on the kitchen tiles.

'Dadd*eeeeeeeee*!' Izzy yelled in the tone that usually indicated that she had sustained some minor injury that required rubbing or kissing immediately. 'I've fallen off my stool *again*!'

'She has,' Bella confirmed. 'And a bowl is broken.'

'I'm coming, poppet.' Louis looked from Wendy to Sophie, his face strained and tense. 'Go through to the living room. I'll sort the girls out and I'll be back in a second.'

Sophie glanced warily at Wendy as she led her through to the living room and indicated that she should sit on the sofa where not so long ago she and Louis had been having unbridled and carefree sex.

'Look, Wendy,' Sophie began attempting to build some kind of bridge. 'I *should* have said something sooner about seeing Seth but please believe me when I tell you I was only trying to help him.'

'Trying to interfere, more like,' Wendy muttered, staring out of the window at the metallic grey day.

'No, not at all. The poor boy was clearly really shocked – I just wanted to help him.'

'Why?' Wendy's head snapped round and Sophie got the full benefit of her Medusa glare. 'What has any of this got to do with you?'

Sophie was no longer able to prevent the exasperation that Wendy inspired in her slipping into her voice. 'If it wasn't for me, Louis still wouldn't know a thing about Seth and besides, I am marrying him. This has got everything to do with me.'

'Oh yes, that's right, I forgot,' Wendy said, a mirthless smile edging her lips upwards.

'Forgot what?' Sophie asked her.

'Louis told me all about you last night, he told me everything. How you moved in on your dead friend's life, like a vulture. Picking off her husband, her kids – even her home. What's your problem, Sophie? Can't you get a life of your own? Did you really have to wait for someone to die before you could get a man?'

'You *bitch*,' Sophie growled the word, the full force of her fury boiling over in her guts. 'How dare you judge me. You know nothing about me. Nothing about what Carrie and I meant to each other, and you certainly have no idea what Louis and I went through together and how much we love each other and those children.'

'I know that barely more than a year has passed after your so-called best friend died and you're marrying her husband and taking her kids. Well, you can forget about trying to do the same thing with me. Seth is mine and Louis's and he hasn't got anything to do with you.'

'Yours and Louis's?' Sophie's laugh was harsh. 'Funny how now, after twenty years, he's suddenly yours and Louis's. What's changed, Wendy? Why are you so territorial now when only last week you were asking me not to tell Louis anything and to forget I ever met Seth.'

'But you did tell him, didn't you?' Wendy hissed. 'You did tell him, even though I warned you that you would be sorry if you did.'

'What do you mean?' Sophie asked impatiently. 'How am I going to be sorry for telling Louis the truth?'

'I've been on my own for a long time now.' Wendy's smile was icy cold. 'I'm still young. And I was the first girl that Louis ever loved, that's a powerful thing. Besides, unlike you, I actually am the mother of one of his children.'

'What?' Sophie was aghast. 'Wendy, wake up! Surely you don't think that you can waltz in here and break me and Louis up just to get back at me for telling him about Seth? A week ago you didn't want anything to do with him.'

'But now I do,' Wendy said. 'And he wants something to do with me too, I can see it in his eyes.'

Unaware that she had moved at all, Sophie found herself leaning over Wendy, her finger pointing millimetres from her face.

'Well, you can forget it,' she threatened Wendy, her voice low and dark. 'Because if you think that I am going to let a jumped-up manipulative little tart like you anywhere near—'

Sophie crashed to a halt as Louis opened the door, his eyes blazing as he caught Sophie bent over Wendy, her face transformed by fury. Wendy's face crumpled.

'Please stop attacking me, Sophie, I'm only trying to look out for my son.'

'What's going on, Sophie?' Louis asked her. 'Leave her alone.'

'But I—' Sophie straightened up, feeling her cheeks blazing. 'Louis, this is ridiculous. You didn't hear what she was saying about me.'

'All I want is to find out where our son is,' Wendy spluttered. 'I thought as Sophie had already kept so much information from us that she might be able to tell us a bit more.'

'Louis – that's not it, she was saying stuff about us, about Carrie!' Sophie looked at Louis but his face was blank, shuttered, as if he simply couldn't absorb any more information.

'Look, I think you'd better go,' he said. 'Let me and Wendy sort things out here.'

'*Me? I've* got to go?' Sophie was incredulous.

'I think it's for the best,' Louis said, looking at his shoes, sensing some kind of betrayal. 'I'll call you later.'

'Fine, if you want me to go then I will go,' Sophie heard the warning in her voice and wondered if Louis heard it too.

Suddenly the door slammed open and the girls appeared in the doorway staring around the room anxiously, hoping to find answers in the faces of the adults.

'Why are you shouting?' Izzy asked, one or two Coco Pops still glued to her cheeks, her usually sunny disposition clouded in shadow. 'Is this lady being mean to Aunty Sophie?'

'No, no, not at all,' Sophie said as she held out her hand to Izzy, aware that she was countering her own story to calm the child. 'No, we're not shouting we're just worrying.'

'Worrying?' Izzy asked, going to her. Sophie sat down in the armchair that normally only the cats used and pulled Izzy into her lap. The child's eyes filled with anxiety. 'Is someone dead again?'

'No.' Sophie pressed Izzy's tousled head into her shoulder and kissed her hair. 'No one is dead and no one is going to die, I promise,' Sophie said.

'You can't promise that,' Bella told her, eyeing her father and Wendy warily as she went to join Sophie and Izzy, squeezing on to the seat next to Sophie.

'Bellarina, sweetheart, don't worry,' Louis said, crouching down next to the armchair. He put one hand on Bella's knee and brushed her fringe out of her eyes with the other. 'Everything is fine.'

Bella tossed her head, shaking off his touch.

'You told Sophie to go,' she stated bluntly. 'We were outside the door, we heard you.'

'Only because I have some important things to talk to Wendy about,' Louis tried to explain.

'What things?' Bella asked him.

'Things you don't have to worry about.' Bella and Izzy exchanged glances. Izzy leaned back against Sophie's shoulder and stuck her thumb in her mouth, her left finger winding its way into her curls just as it always did when she was either too worried or too tired.

'We need to know things, don't not tell us things,' Bella said, unhappily. 'Is everything changing again?'

'No, no – nothing is changing,' Louis assured her, despite the look that Sophie gave him over Izzy's head. 'Sophie is just going back to the B&B for a bit, aren't you, Soph?'

Even as she opened her mouth to affirm the statement, Sophie thought of the conversation she had had with Grace the previous night and her suggestion that Sophie take a break for a few days to clear her head. Feeling cornered by Louis and Wendy, suddenly Sophie couldn't think of anything she wanted more than to get away from all of this. She looked into Bella's eyes and shook her head. 'No.'

'Yes you are, because Wendy and I have a few things to talk about, remember?'

'I know,' Sophie said, careful to keep her tone even and calm. 'Don't worry, I'll get out of your way. But I think I'm going to go back to London with Cal for a few days. I've got a lot of things I need to sort out down there and now seems like a good time for me to go.'

'Sophie, I didn't mean you had to—' Louis began.

'No!' Izzy exclaimed, wrenching her thumb from her mouth. 'No, you can't go, Sophie!'

'I don't get it,' Louis said. 'That's not what I meant. You don't have to go back to London.'

'Don't I?' Sophie asked him. 'This is clearly something that you need to sort out with Wendy on your own without me around interfering. I wanted to try and help but you don't want me here, you want me out of the way. So I will get out of the way. And anyway, I need time to think.'

'Think?' Louis and Bella said simultaneously.

'What about?' Louis asked her, his voice jagged with frustration. 'Come on, Sophie, this is just silly. You're overreacting – I mean seriously, do you have to do this now?'

'Don't you love us today?' Izzy asked her, unhappily. 'Is that why you're going away?'

'No – I do, I do love you. I love all of you so much. But a lot has happened recently and it's all happened so fast that

I haven't had time to think. I just need a little time to think. To breathe.'

'But you are going to come back, aren't you?' Bella asked her. 'You will definitely come back.'

Sophie looked into her eyes and felt the weight of a promise that she had made her months earlier. She'd promised Bella that she would be there for her always, for ever, whatever.

How everything had disintegrated so quickly from this morning in Louis's bed to this moment Sophie could not fathom, but that is exactly what had happened. All the rushing, she realised, all the excitement and the urgency to be married to him had been her attempt to prevent this, her desperate attempt to make their relationship into something solid and genuine before reality came crashing in and smashed their bubble to pieces and suddenly the truth and strength of their feelings for one another were tested. And, ironically, she had been the one who tested their love by bringing Wendy and Seth into their lives and now their bubble was burst, now they had real problems to deal with, she wasn't at all sure if their relationship could stand it. Louis asking her to leave so that he could sort things out without her didn't help reassure her.

'Can you give us a minute, please?' she asked Wendy without looking at her.

'But what about Seth—' Wendy began.

'Wendy, just wait in the kitchen,' Louis told her without taking his eyes off Sophie.

Seeing that she no longer had Louis's attention Wendy complied, closing the living-room door softly after her.

'Sophie,' Louis said gently taking her hands in his. 'You're angry with me and you've a right to be. I shouldn't have asked you to go. Look, nothing's changed. I still love you. All this – it's got nothing to do with you and me.'

'It does, it has everything to do with you and me and how you see me in your life,' Sophie told him. 'I'm supposed to be your wife soon, the person who is always by your side and yet – Louis, you never talk to me, you don't tell me anything about yourself unless I drag it out of you and as soon as Wendy turns up on the scene I might as well not exist . . .'

'Don't tell me you're jealous of Wendy?' Louis asked. 'For God's sake, Sophie, grow up! Wendy and I were over twenty years before I even met you. This isn't about her, it's about . . .' Louis looked at his daughters sitting curled up side by side. 'It's not about Wendy.'

'You might not think it's about her but she certainly does,' Sophie said bitterly. 'And yes – yes, I am jealous of Wendy, I am jealous of every second of every minute of your past that I don't know about because it means that I don't know you. I really don't know you at all.'

'You do know him,' Izzy said unhappily. 'He's Daddy, Aunty Sophie!'

'And besides,' Sophie went on, 'you need to work out what to do about Seth . . .'

'Who is Seth?' Bella asked, suddenly. 'And why is he making you go away?'

'I just think', Sophie said, 'that it will be easier, that we both need some time.'

'But you are coming back?' Louis asked her anxiously. 'You are coming back to marry me on New Year's Eve?'

Sophie looked at him, removing the fingers of her right hand from his so that she could rest her palm against his cheek, feeling the stubble graze her tender skin.

'You haven't booked it yet,' she said simply.

'I'll book it now, right now,' Louis said. 'I'll make the call now.'

'There are more important things you need to sort out first,' Sophie told him.

'I want to marry you, Sophie,' Louis said. 'You do still want to marry me, don't you?'

'I don't know,' Sophie said very softly. 'I know that I am so in love with you and I love Bella and Izzy more than anything. But honestly? I don't know yet if the way we love each other is enough, if it's strong enough or real enough to make a marriage work.'

'I can't believe this is happening,' Louis said, sitting back on his heels. 'Only a few hours ago we were . . . is this really just because I asked you to go home while I talked to Wendy?'

'Look, I love you. All I'm doing is going back to London for a bit to give us both some space. Just because I'm not sure about marrying you it doesn't mean we can't be together like we were before.' Louis was silent. 'Does it?'

He looked into her eyes. 'I don't know. I don't understand any of this.'

'Please don't go, Aunty Sophie,' Izzy spoke softly. 'Please can we still get married. I want to wear my wings.'

'I know,' Sophie said. 'And I'm so sorry, darling, but I have to go.' She cupped Bella's cheek in the palm of her hand. 'You understand, don't you, Bella?'

Bella looked at her for a long moment and then ever so slowly shook her head.

'This is all your fault,' she said to Louis without a trace of anger or childish petulance. 'You've ruined everything again.'

She pulled away from Sophie and walked out of the room, her stamps as she raced up the stairs the only external clue to how she was feeling. Louis stood up and walked to the window turning his back on Sophie.

'Right,' Sophie said, a sense of unreality washing over her as she kissed the four-year-old on the head. 'I'll see you really soon and you can call me any time. Remember my number?'

Izzy automatically recited Sophie's mobile number that she had taught both the girls during the summer when all the beaches were packed with holidaymakers and it would be very easy for a small person to get lost.

'Good girl. I'll see you soon.'

'How soon?' Izzy asked. How long will you need to think? Do you think you will have finished thinking by Wednesday afternoon?'

'I don't know,' Sophie said. 'I'm not sure.'

'But you will come back?'

'Of course.'

'To live for ever and ever and be our . . .' Izzy stalled.

'What, sweetheart?' Sophie asked her, glancing at Louis who had his shoulders hunched as he stared out of the window.

'Be our sort of mummy,' Izzy finished, looking anxious as if she'd just asked for something she knew she was not allowed.

Sophie pressed Izzy's small body into hers and held her close till she wriggled to be free as she always did.

'I will always, always be there to look after you in every way that your mummy would have, I promise,' Sophie told her.

'Yes, but . . . if you don't marry Daddy, then there won't be any rings and I won't be able to say it, will I?'

'Say what, sweetheart?' Sophie asked her.

'Say Mummy to you,' Izzy told her, unable to look her in the eye.

'I am coming back,' Sophie felt her throat tighten. 'I'll speak to you tonight. Now go and give Bella a hug from me and tell her I love her.'

Sniffing and wiping her nose on the back of her hand, Izzy climbed off Sophie's lap and padded out of the room.

'I'll call you tonight,' Sophie said to Louis's back. He turned and crossed the room in one stride, catching her in his arms and pulling her to him.

'I love you, Sophie, and you love me. Please don't go.'

It took Sophie a huge effort of will to take a step back from the shelter of his arms but she knew that she had to.

'When you got back from Peru you wanted everything to be OK again as quickly as you could make it happen. You wanted to win over the girls, you wanted a job, a home . . . and maybe you wanted me because I was the nearest thing to Carrie that the girls – that you were ever going to get.'

'No, that's not it at all,' Louis told her. 'I wanted you because you are strong and kind and the most beautiful thing I have ever seen. Because I fell for you, because you make me a better man. I want to marry you because I love you with all of my heart. But if you don't want to marry me, then . . . I don't think I could be with you knowing that you didn't feel the same way.'

Sophie took a breath, feeling as if something inside her was tearing ever so slowly.

'Look, I know I shouldn't have let Wendy push you out . . .'

'No, you shouldn't have. The last six months have been intense and wonderful and magical but I don't know if they have been real. I think we both just need a bit of space to find out how we really feel.'

'I know how I feel,' Louis protested.

'I've got to go.' Taking a step forward, Sophie kissed Louis on the cheek. 'Please tell the girls about Seth, they need to know they can trust you and if they find out some other way then I don't know how they will react.'

'It feels like you're going for ever,' Louis said as she headed towards the door. 'Are you going for ever?'

Sophie didn't know what to say so she closed the front door behind her without saying anything.

Chapter Twelve

'There is actually no good reason why I can't stay with you,' Sophie said as she and Cal finally hit London just after eight that evening.

'Yes there is, my flat is very small and you are very large,' Cal said.

'I'd let you stay with me,' Sophie said miserably.

'Except you don't live anywhere and the one time I come miles and miles to visit you on a mission of highly uncharacteristic mercy you end up kissing your dead best friend's ex-husband's secret love child by mistake and I have to go home again the very next day. Some holiday.'

'Why do you have to do that?' Sophie complained as she pulled up at yet another set of red lights. 'Why do you have to sum up my entire life like it's a tabloid headline? This is really hard for me, you know, to leave him and the girls behind like that – I didn't want to come away but what else could I do? I couldn't just stay there feeling like an impostor in my own relationship, could I?'

'No, you couldn't,' Cal said. 'You did the right thing to get away for a bit. Louis loves you, he's just not used to loving you yet, if you know what I mean.'

'No, I have no idea what you mean,' Sophie said anxiously

as she cut up a four-by-four to change lanes. 'What the fuck do you mean?'

'I mean that for three years he had been his own man, he'd had no one to answer to except himself. Then he comes back to the UK and before he knows it he's got two daughters and a fiancée to think about.'

'Yes, but he's got us because he wanted us, because he fought for us,' Sophie protested. 'I didn't force him to propose to me.'

'I know,' Cal replied. 'And that's not what I'm saying. What I'm saying is that when you're in a relationship you have to adjust. You have to find different ways to live your life. After he'd left Carrie, before he'd found the girls and you, he dealt with everything alone. And he hasn't had a chance to get used to the fact that you are part of his life yet. That his problems are your problems and vice versa. He's still flying solo because that's what he's used to,' Cal said.

'Do you really think that's what it is?' Sophie asked him. 'That it's all just a bit too much too soon?'

'I think that's part of it, and I think with you out of the picture for a while he'll have a chance to miss you and think about things and I reckon things will be back on for the wedding before you know it.'

'But should they be?' Sophie asked him. 'I wanted it all so badly, so quickly. I wanted to rush it . . . why? Why was it so urgent?'

'Because you didn't want to waste another second of your life without the love of your life by your side?' Cal ventured.

'Or because deep down I knew that none of this was real. What if I knew deep down that it was nothing more than a glorified holiday romance?'

'Sophie, that's not how you feel. You love that man. That man loves you, you just need to work it out, OK?'

222

Sophie took her eyes off the road for a second to glance at Cal.

'Hang on a minute, where have all the witty one-liners and putdowns gone? Why are you so sincere all of a sudden?'

'I'm not, I just want you two to work out. There's got to be at least one couple in the planet that are destined for happiness and if it's not me then I want it to be you.'

'Cal, that's the nicest thing you've ever said to me.'

'Unless it *is* me, then I don't care about you,' Cal added.

'Please let me stay with you,' Sophie begged him.

'No!' Cal said. 'No.'

'But if I stay with my mother there will be questions and sex. And I won't be having any.'

'Well, if you stay with me there will be questions and sex and you won't be having any,' Cal said. 'At least at your mother's you get your own room, even if your chances of catching rabies are marginally higher over there.'

'Well, officially consider yourself out of the running for the position of chief bridesmaid,' Sophie shot at him as she pulled the Golf in alongside Cal's flat.

'I think I'll await confirmation that the position of bride has actually been filled before I start worrying about that,' Cal told her as he swung the car door shut with a slam.

As Sophie sat across the kitchen table from her mother, who was at that precise moment sitting on Trevor's lap, she considered bringing up the subject of tact and the social niceties of making out with your boyfriend when your daughter was in the midst of an emotional crisis. But Sophie had been in the same bubble as Iris was now and she knew when you were that happy, when you were that in love with another person, it felt as if the whole world should fall into step around you whether you were French kissing in the frozen food aisle in Asda or flirting with al fresco sex on the beach at sunset.

'If it helps, I think you've done the right thing, giving your-self some space,' Iris said, resting her head on Trevor's broad shoulder. 'If you aren't sure about marrying Louis and you needed to think about it, then why shouldn't you come home to your mother?'

Sophie wanted to say, 'Because looking at my mother kissing with tongues will send me blind', but instead she said, 'It would mean that I didn't love him if I wasn't ready to marry him. But he's more or less said that if I don't want to marry him then he doesn't want me any more. But if he loved me, he'd give me time, wouldn't he?'

'He's just hurt and scared of losing you,' Iris said, running the palm of her hand over Trevor's closely cropped hair, as if she were petting one of her dogs. 'Besides, this son of Louis's, that changes things, it's bound to; wouldn't you say, Trevor?'

Trevor's smile was sympathetic and it was the slight discom-fort and embarrassment in his eyes combined with complete adoration whenever he looked at Iris that meant Sophie was able to like him despite her mum's insistence on molesting him at every opportunity.

'None of this is really my business,' he said. 'But I can't think of a better woman to come back to in times of trouble than your beautiful mother.'

'Oh, Trev,' Iris exclaimed in the second before she fixed her lips purposefully to Trevor's.

'Christ in Heaven,' Sophie blasphemed under her breath before saying in a loud stop-kissing-now voice, 'I'm going to bed. I do have a bed, don't I?'

'Yes, of course you have a bed, in your old bedroom,' Iris told her as she gazed into Trevor's eyes. 'You'll just need to find some clean sheets and shove Inky and Tippex off the mattress. They've been using it as their bed for a long time now so it might need a bit of a brush down with a clothes brush and a squirt of Febreze.'

'Mum?' Sophie paused till Iris stopped looking into Trevor's admittedly rather lovely eyes and turned her attention to her.

'Yes, dear?'

'Is Trevor staying the night?'

'Yes, Sophie,' Iris said. 'Is that a problem?'

'No, it's just I might pop out to the late-night corner shop and see if I can pick up some ear plugs. And a maybe bottle of gin.'

Sophie's old room was not the comforting haven that she had hoped for. Perhaps it would have been odd if it had still boasted the Manic Street Preachers poster and the black lace shawls that she had taken to hanging over the lampshade in order to make it look a bit more gothic, but still, she had hoped for the sense of sanctuary that the room used to afford her when she was a girl and needed a place to hide. After her father had died suddenly her bedroom had become her whole world, a haven where she could plunge herself into the music she loved, curl up on her bed, and forget everything that hurt or confused her, which had seemed to be everything back then. It was in this room where she and Carrie had spent so many hours talking about sex, or what they thought they knew about sex, in hushed voices, laughing over the problem pages in *Just Seventeen* magazine and discussing every single boy they knew in exhaustive detail. It was here they had made promises to each other, here they had formed the bond that would one day lead Sophie into the path of Louis Gregory. It was in this twelve-by-eight-foot box with a window that Sophie's life had really begun.

Somehow it seemed an inauspicious place for a beginning,

particularly as the room was cold, the radiator had obviously not been switched on in years, and it smelt faintly of damp and strongly of dog. The hundred-watt bulb hanging from the ceiling was naked of a shade and its glare made the room seem unfamiliar and strange. With a heavy heart Sophie pulled on the same faded quilt cover decorated with pink and white love hearts that she used to have as a girl and wondered why she had insisted on coming back to London when she could just have gone back to the B&B where Mrs Alexander would have made her hot chocolate and Mrs Tregowan would have told her about her fourth husband and she could have watched Freeview on the TV that was bolted to the wall in her room until she'd fallen asleep, dreaming dreams inspired by late-night bingo and documentaries about people who dressed up as ponies for kicks.

Sophie never thought she'd feel nostalgic for her tiny room, her twins beds and candlewick bedspread, but just at that moment she was homesick for the Avalon, for St Ives and its constant cry of gulls. That room had felt like a place for a new beginning.

Carmen had told her not to leave.

Sophie had been throwing things into a case, while simultaneously brushing tears away from her eyes, while Carmen and Cal sat side by side on her spare twin bed.

'I'm just saying', Carmen had said, 'if this Wendy is as crafty as you say she is, then why are you going now and leaving her an open goal? You should be decking her, the silly bitch. I'll deck her for you, if you like. You don't diss a Chelmsford girl or her mates and get away with it, not unless you don't like having teeth. Better still, give me her address, I'll send her a cake laced with rat poison.'

'Can I just say,' Cal interjected, picking up one of Sophie's newly acquired practical T-shirts with a sniff of distain before slinging it one-fingered into her case, 'I'd still eat one of your éclairs even if I knew it was going to kill me.'

'Thank you, darling.' Cal and Carmen beamed at each other. 'But anyway, even if you won't let me hurt her, I don't think you should run away, Sophie. You should stay and fight for your man!'

'It's not Wendy that's the problem really,' Sophie said, pausing with a handful of knickers that made Cal look slightly panicky. 'It doesn't help that her and her love child turned up just after Louis proposed to me but, well, they did, and it's not exactly something that either Louis or I can pretend hasn't happened. It's more about Louis. He's supposed to be marrying me, I am supposed to become his wife and yet when one of the most serious and important things in his life happens, he doesn't want me around. I don't think he's thought past our wedding day. I don't think he's thought through what being married is really about.'

'Have you?' Cal asked her.

'No,' Sophie said thoughtfully. 'I don't suppose I have. I suppose that I've been just as caught up in the drama and the romance as Louis and I was looking for my fairy-tale ending. But that's not the ending, is it, getting married? It's only the beginning and it's then that you have to work out what marriage is really about.'

'I can tell you what marriage is really about,' Carmen said. 'I've been married, still am, technically, and let me tell you this: marriage is about compromise. It's about accepting your choices and dealing with the consequences. It's about waking up every day and making the decision to try your best even if your heart's not in it. That's what marriage is about and that's mainly why I left my husband for a younger man. That and the fact that he was terrible in bed.'

'Hang on a minute,' Sophie said as she jammed her case shut. 'A few weeks ago you couldn't wait for me and Louis to get married. You were practically dragging me up the aisle!'

'I know,' Carmen said. 'And that's because you two didn't look like you were settling for second best. You didn't look like you were getting married because you need something to talk about. You looked – *look* – like you were in love.'

'Love,' Sophie sighed as she attempted to shove another pair of scarcely worn shoes into her case, because she knew that trainers and boots would not cut it in the capital. 'What the bloody hell is love, anyway? What does it mean? And you don't mean that about marriage. You'd marry James, wouldn't you?'

Carmen sighed and looked down at the perfectly polished tips of her boots.

'James wants to marry me,' she said. 'But I won't let him.'

'Really?' Sophie asked, sitting down on the case with a bump so her clothes spilled out of the zip like so many lace-trimmed guts. 'Why, because you're still somehow married to your ex? James adores you!'

'Yes.' Carmen nodded. 'Yes, he does, he loves me and he adores me and I'm his girlfriend, his babe, the woman he loves. And I love him . . .' Carmen's smile was wistful. 'I have never been happier than since I moved down here to be with him. All those years before this, all those flat grey married years, seem like a dream, a life that happened to some other poor bugger. It's here and now that I'm awake and really living my life.'

'So why not ditch your husband and marry your toyboy?' Cal asked her.

Carmen shrugged. 'I'm thirteen years older than James, I'm still married and I . . . well, I can't have children. Not without a lot of bother and injections and IVF and even then at my age there's not much chance of it working. I've got fibroids, you see. I've known for years. It's never been on the cards. None of that matters to James now, he says all he wants is me and he doesn't care about kids. But he's only twenty-four. In another few years, two or three, he might feel differently. He might realise how much he wants to be a dad, he might meet a girl he can have children with. I can't tie him down to some old bird that might not be able to give him what he wants. So even though I'm the happiest I've ever been in my life I don't ever think about me and him as permanent. I think of him as my bit of luck that I must enjoy and make the most of until one day it finally runs out.'

'Oh Carmen.' Sophie reached across the narrow divide between the twin beds and picked up her hand. 'If James says he loves you and he wants to marry you and you love him and you want to marry him, then it's just silly not to let your-self be happy. We're only on this planet once; if we don't take chances, then what's the point . . .' Sophie trailed off as she listened to her own words. She had taken a chance, a huge chance, coming down to St Ives to be with Louis. And now, for the first time, she wasn't sure if it was a chance that was going to work out.

'Look, I'm as happy as I need to be,' Carmen explained. 'I love James. I've built the tea shop up so that it's doing really well, and I love this bloody stupid town whether it's stuffed full of tourists or empty and bleak. James has made me feel happy and alive and instead of waking up every morning knowing I've got to do my best to get through another day, I wake up looking forward to every second I'm going to spend with him.' She smiled at Sophie and squeezed her hand. 'And if you want to know what I think, I think that's love. Choosing to be with the only person that can make you happy come what may. That's love.'

'Or letting them stay for three nights in a row,' Cal interjected. 'Some people might consider that to be love.'

'Since when have you ever let a man stay at your flat for three nights in a row?' Sophie asked him, still looking at Carmen who bent her head so that her hair slid over her face.

'Never,' Cal said. 'But there's this someone. This someone who asked me round for dinner on a Friday night and I didn't leave till Monday morning.'

'I thought you said you weren't having any sex?' Sophie accused him. 'That you're off casual sex.'

'That's it,' Cal said. 'I am. We didn't have sex. We stayed up all night talking and watching films and eating and drinking and *laughing*. He really, really liked me – maybe more than any man has ever liked me, but you want to know the killer? Only as a friend.'

'Can't you seduce him or whatever it is you gay types do?' Carmen asked him.

'We do it the same way you older women do it,' Cal told her sweetly. 'Using alcohol as a lethal weapon and relying on soft lighting. But it didn't matter how drunk I got him. He still didn't fancy me and I . . . oh God, I'm in love with him.'

Cal looked as surprised by the revelation as everyone else.

'You love him?' Sophie asked. 'When you say you love him, do you mean you desperately want to shag him and that you are going to keep on chasing him till you get him naked?'

'No, well, yes, I do desperately want to shag him, but I'm not going to chase him. What I really want, what I find myself waking up and thinking about first thing in the morning, are ways just to be near him. He's funny and interesting and really sweet and he smells like fresh apples and sunshine. And when he talks the very tip of his nose goes up and down just ever so slightly . . .'

'Fuck me, you really do love him,' Sophie said, realising belatedly that she'd brought down the tone just ever so slightly.

'I really do love him,' Cal stared at her. 'And that, as you would probably put it, you sewer-mouthed tart – is a fucking first.'

'I don't see why he wouldn't love you back,' Carmen said, slinging an arm around Cal's shoulders. 'You're very nicely dressed and quite a looker. I would.'

'Thank you, sweetheart. But he's got a partner. A partner who's away working in France and who phones him every night and who he told about me and who I've spoken to on the phone and I promised to look after Steven for him while he's away. They are so sickeningly monogamous, Steven doesn't see me in a sexual way. I'm in hell and if you ask me, love is discovering for the first time the thing that you really, really want in life and realising you can't have it. But hanging around anyway because just being near him makes me a hundred times happier than being apart from him. That's why I had to come down here. He'd invited me round to his for a weekend of Grace Kelly movies. I wanted to go, but I was scared that if I did I'd do something or say something to make an idiot of myself and then he'd realise what a hopeless case I am.'

'I think this is probably a good thing,' Sophie said after some thought. 'I think it's a good thing that you are feeling love, even if it hurts. Remember what you told me when I wasn't sure about coming down here to find Louis? You told me I had to grab hold of life and take a chance, I had to be brave enough to let myself feel. And that's what you have to do now.'

'It kills me that my own words of wisdom are coming back to haunt me,' Cal said sadly.

'Are you sure you really have to go all the way to London to think?' Carmen asked Sophie. 'Are you sure that you can't just give Louis a ring, go over there later and get things back on track between you?'

'No . . . I want to, but I just don't think I can,' Sophie said.

'Then don't be gone too long,' Carmen said. 'I'll keep an eye on the girls and that Wendy slag while you're away but don't be gone too long. And as for you,' she ruffled Cal's hair, 'where exactly does this Steven's feller live in France? I'll FedEx him a rat-poison éclair.'

Sophie sighed and looked at her watch. It was just after ten. She knew that she'd promised to phone Louis but the girls would have been in bed and she wasn't sure that she'd have anything new to say to him. Instead she texted him. 'Got here safely, I love you. Speak tomorrow. xxxx'

She stood up and looked out of her window over the rooftops at the sky that always glowed orange over London's thousands of streets, swamping any hope of starlight. This is home, Sophie thought, pressing her hot palm against the cool glass of the window. Just out there on the other side of the glass was the town that was always open for business. The city she'd grown up in, the streets she'd known like the back of her hand all her life, pounding down them in her three-inch heels, insulated from life by the layers of grime and fumes and indifference that years of London living had built up, cocooning her from anything that might startle her out of her routine. Always dressed up to the nines, always ready for that last-minute conference call with the New York office, always ready to troubleshoot, to fix and to achieve, Sophie had once been the only woman within the M25 who knew where to get one hundred fairy lights within half an hour after five p.m. She might not have been happy here, if happiness meant feeling and loving and looking up at a sky full of stars, but at least she had known where she stood, and she was the master of her own destiny.

Sophie tapped one short and naked nail against the glass. It was just after ten on a Saturday night in London, in her suitcase she had her best pair of 1980s vintage Manolos, and she was holed up in her childhood bedroom like a refugee or a convict on the lam. What on earth was she thinking? She'd come back here to take stock, to feel like herself again, and the best way wasn't to be in her old room, entombed in the past. It was to be out there in the living, breathing, beating heart of the city.

Quickly Sophie picked up her phone and made a call.

'Christina? Hi, listen, I'm unexpectedly in town. What are you doing right now?'

It turned out that Christina was in the Light Bar in St Martins Lane Hotel at a private party, but as soon as Sophie had given her a brief synopsis of her situation she'd pulled some strings and had Sophie's name put on the guest list. It had taken Sophie just over half an hour to shower, change into one of the dresses she'd barely worn since arriving in St Ives, and slip on her cool and comfortingly uncomfortable designer shoes, shaking out her long hair and lashing on some lip gloss.

Opening her mother's front door she stood on the doorstop and inhaled London. Gone was the constant cry of the gulls and the incessant poetic crashing of the waves. There was no magical light here that was supposed to lift the human spirit. You couldn't see a scrap of green and if you breathed in too deeply you'd find yourself choking on traffic fumes.

Sophie smiled to herself; she was very glad to be back.

'So, what's the occasion?' Sophie asked as she settled herself into a booth with Christina and a luscious-looking mojito.

'It's my friend Alison's divorce party – do you remember her? You met her a while back, she was terribly impressed with your brave and impetuous decision to go to Cornwall in pursuit of a man. Anyway, her divorce came through and she's started a catering business that seems to be working out really well, so she's celebrating. That's her over there.'

Sophie glanced over to a blonde woman, around her age and groomed to within an inch of her life, who was laughing and talking to tall red-haired woman. 'She looks very happy to be divorced,' Sophie observed. 'It is slightly worrying, when you are on the brink of marrying someone, to see someone who looks quite so happy to be getting out of it . . .'

'Yes, but you are marrying the man of your dreams, your fairy-tale romantic hero. She married a dyed-in-the-wool bastard, with barely any redeeming features. She told me she feels like her life is just starting now, which is pretty impressive, seeing as she's got three kids to worry about.'

'I've got three kids to worry about,' Sophie mused more to herself than to Christina. 'And none of them are mine.'

'Besides, Alison is very happy, she got the house in the settlement. Sold it, bought a business, Home Hearths catering or some artsy fartsy organic country-type thing that ladies who lunch are into. And the moral of this tale is never get married in a hurry to a man you barely know . . . oops, sorry.'

'It's not the same,' Sophie exclaimed in horror. 'That Alison and me, we are nothing alike.'

'No, no, I know, and I wasn't saying that you were,' Christina reassured her hurriedly. 'Anyway, it's quite the thing, a divorce party, these days. But I've never heard of an end-of-the-engagement party. Especially not after only about five minutes. Come on, darling. Tell me all about it.'

'I don't want to,' Sophie said, watching Alison laughing,

looking so happy and free. 'I don't want to talk about it tonight, I just want to get drunk and have some fun.' Sophie brought her drink to her lips with gusto but for some reason the second she tasted it on her tongue she didn't want it any more and suddenly she felt homesick and lonely for one of Mrs Alexander's hot chocolates.

'Bloody hell, I'm even rubbish at drinking now,' Sophie sighed. 'And I used to be excellent at drinking, it was one of the things that you could always rely on me to get right. Have you got any class A drugs? I think that might be my only way to oblivion.'

'You don't do class A drugs,' Christina said. 'You are far too sensible. Oh babe, come on. You look lovely, you've got great shoes on, and you're in the most exciting city in the world! Let your hair down and live a little. How about we cut this party? There're no single men here anyway – which, if you ask me, is a travesty at a divorce party – and go clubbing? We could catch a cab to that nightclub in Kensington where Prince William hangs out. We could see if we could cradle-snatch some royals.'

'Not really in the mood for illicit aristocratic sex,' Sophie said, stirring her cocktail without enthusiasm.

'Admit it – you're missing him, aren't you?' Christina sighed. 'Look, why don't you go outside and give him a call? He won't mind that it's late and I'm sure you'll feel better once you've spoken to him. Sounds to me like this is nothing more than a bit of bridal nerves complicated by the full-grown love child – is he single, by the way? The love child?'

'You're right,' Sophie said, choosing to ignore the last comment because unlike herself Christina had successfully managed to imbibe several mojitos. 'I will call him. I'm sorry I'm being so lame after I begged you to come with me. I think all that sea air must have sucked the party girl right out of me. I'll call Louis and come back and down that bloody cocktail if it kills me.'

'And that's what I've always liked about you,' Christina observed as Sophie slid from her seat. 'Your natural *joie de vivre*.'

As she headed out of the bar Sophie passed the tall redheaded woman locked in the embrace of a long-haired man. They looked like newlyweds caught up in the first flush of romance, Sophie thought enviously. She could tell just by looking at them, the way they held each other and looked at each other, that they hadn't had to deal with any complications or problems, and she closed her eyes for a second, wishing ever so hard that she was back on the sofa in front of Louis's electric fire, not thinking about a single thing except each following second in his arms.

The lobby of St Martins Lane Hotel was minimalist, decorated almost exclusively white, with strange teeth-shaped seats and a large and seemingly random chess set out on the shiny tiled floor. Awkwardly Sophie perched on a tooth and took her phone out of her bag. Now that she had given herself permission to talk to Louis she couldn't wait to hear the sound of his voice, to tell him that of course she loved him and to find those few words that she hoped could draw them back together again and make her feel safe in the knowledge that he loved her despite everything that was testing them. She wanted to tell him she missed him and she'd drive back home to be with him in the morning.

'Sophie?' The sound of her name in an unfamiliar accent stopped her in her tracks. She looked up and watched as Jake Flynn walked towards her. Jake Flynn, the man who could have been the love of her life if things had been different.

'Sophie Mills, it really is you, you look fantastic – what are you doing here?'

'What are *you* doing here?' Sophie asked him. 'You're not going to the divorce party too, are you?'

'The what? No, my fiancée is staying here. I've been out of town today but I promised I'd take her out to a late dinner when I got back.' He gazed into her face. 'You really look stunning. Sea air, love and kids – it really suits you – you're glowing.'

Sophie felt a hot flush sweep across her chest. Jake always did have a way of looking at her that made her feel womanly.

'I think that's probably just because it's a bit hot in there,' she said, nodding in the direction of the bar. She beamed at Jake, surprised at how pleased she was to see his familiar face in this familiar place. For a second it felt as if the wheel of time had turned backwards and she found herself where she had been a year ago, working on an unrequited crush on Jake and desperate for the promotion that would take her to the top of her profession. It felt almost as if her old life had been waiting in suspended animation, holding its breath until she returned ready to pick up where she had left off in such a hurry. But she knew that wasn't true. Jake might have wanted her once but that was many moons ago and now he was getting married, and so – she reminded herself a little belatedly – was she.

'So what are you doing now?' Jake asked her.

'Oh well,' Sophie looked at her phone and slipped it back into her bag. 'I'll probably go back to the party, I expect, for a bit.'

'Come to dinner with me,' Jake pressed her.

'But what about your fiancée?' Sophie asked him. 'I don't suppose she's expecting a threesome, unless there's something you're not telling me.'

'Sophie Mills, are you flirting with me?' Jake chuckled.

'I don't know, am I?' Sophie asked him surprised; one thing for certain was that her life with Louis had changed how she felt about herself. Even though she was a little heavier than she used to be, she felt beautiful and desirable. And she knew that even if Jake had fallen for another woman he could see that in her.

'So how long are you in town for?' Jake asked her

'I'm not sure, I'm visiting my mum, so—'

'Have lunch with me, then? Before you go back, promise?' Jake's smile was a perfect balance of boyish and dashing. Sophie remembered that she had always loved his excellent teeth.

'Yes – yes, I will – that would be lovely,' she said, finding herself batting her lashes at him in a way that would have been impossible before she'd met Louis.

'God, you look great,' Jake said again as he slowly seemed to take in every millimetre of her face. 'Stunning.'

'Stop it, you'll give me a complex.' Sophie grinned, finding herself coquettishly winding her hair around her finger. 'Another one!'

For a second the two of them stood there smiling at each other.

'Jake, I thought you were going to come up to my room to pick me up!' A woman called out across the foyer.

'Oh, there's my girl,' Jake said, his smile dimming just a fraction. 'That's my fiancée, Stephanie.'

Sophie watched as an immaculate chestnut-brunette with hair a little shorter and a little thicker and a lot more styled than Sophie's marched over towards them on a pair of very high heels. She was wearing a grey pencil skirt topped off with a high-necked cream satin blouse that emphasised the shape of her bountiful breasts. As she approached she smiled warmly at Sophie and extended a perfectly manicured hand, which Sophie took rather self-consciously, suddenly aware that her fingertips had been nowhere near nail varnish in months.

'Hi, I'm Stephanie Corollo. Delighted to meet you . . . ?'

'This is Sophie Mills,' Jake said, kissing Stephanie on the lips. 'A former associate and good friend of mine who I've just bumped into.'

'Sophie, how lovely to meet you,' Stephanie purred. 'And may I say what fabulous shoes. Manolo, 1980s, am I right? You and I have a lot in common. Will you be joining us for dinner?'

'Oh no,' Sophie said. 'I'm supposed to be at a divorce party and besides, three's a crowd and all that . . .'

'Nonsense, Jake and I practically live in each other's pockets as it is and besides, I don't have any girlfriends this side of the Atlantic. I'm dying for someone to talk to about things with frills. Come to dinner with us, I'm sure Jake would love a reason not to talk about wedding plans for a few hours?' Stephanie's plea was charming and sweet and Sophie found her quite hard to resist but the fact that she had been, on more than one occasion, in a rather compromising position with her fiancé made her feel that she had to.

'I would love to, but I can't. A friend went out of her way to get me into that party and I can't run out on her. But it's been lovely to meet you, Stephanie. You and Jake make a fabulous couple.'

'We do, don't we?' Stephanie said, slotting her hand into Jake's and smiling at him. 'Well, come on, then, darling. They said they'd hold our reservation until midnight and after the day I've had I need at least two glasses of wine. Make that bottles.'

'I'll call you,' Jake said, interestingly not making any mention of their proposed lunch date.

'Do that.' Sophie nodded, watching for a while as Stephanie

strode out of the foyer and into the night trailing Jake in her wake.

Sophie took her phone out of her bag and thought about calling Louis. Suddenly the urge to speak to him had waned and it didn't seem like such a good idea any more.

Chapter Thirteen

'Coffee?' Iris asked Sophie as she emerged from her old bedroom at just past eleven, almost a week after she had arrived in London.

It had been an odd few days, a time where she felt as if she were walking between not only two lives, but two worlds, and just at the moment she wasn't sure which one she belonged in. After Jake and Stephanie had left, Sophie had gone back to the divorce party, but her heart hadn't really been in it. She had sat and watched as Christina drank more and more, eventually draping herself around a rather alarmed-looking Croatian barman and offering him practical English lessons. Sophie felt that was the optimum point to hook her arm through Christina's and pull her into a cab, delivering her friend home before finding herself back in her old bedroom at just past two. Her body had felt exhausted, trembling with tiredness, and she had gratefully crawled into her old single bed, feeling the chill of the wall against her back as she curled up against the cold. But no matter how her body longed for oblivion her mind would not let her rest. She kept thinking of the look on Wendy's face when she'd told Sophie that it was more than just a father figure for Seth that she wanted from Louis. And of how she had felt when Louis had asked her to go, brushing her aside like an inconvenience that was incidental to his latest personal crisis. Like she was yesterday's drama.

Sophie hadn't known when she had fallen asleep but at some point her muddled thoughts morphed into confused dreams where Jake waltzed her around at a wedding only she wasn't clear if it was his wedding, her wedding, or theirs.

The following morning, when she had dragged herself out of the morass of sleep, Sophie found a text on her phone from Louis saying, 'Glad you got there OK. We all fine.' There was nothing else, not a hint that he missed her, that he was worried about her or that he even wanted to talk to her. Sophie's thumb hovered over the call button for a long moment, but she resisted the urge to call him and to try and force things back into shape between them, even if afterwards it would almost certainly feel awkward and disjointed, like a square peg jammed into a round hole. She couldn't do that. She had to let him have his space and a chance to feel what life would be like without her, even if he found that he didn't mind it so much. Besides, she needed this time too, she needed to revisit what she had left behind.

She'd spent the rest of that Sunday in bed, or in her pyjamas sitting on her mother's sofa, eating cereal and watching whatever was on TV.

'It's just like school summer holidays all over again,' Iris had told her, drawing back the living-room curtains to let in some autumn sun that made Sophie blink and rub her eyes. 'You never used to want to go out and get fresh air back then either. I practically had to kick you and Carrie out of the door and tell you to enjoy yourselves. The last thing you need is to be sitting around in the dark moping. Why don't you go out for a walk? Take a dog or two. If you take Scooby he'll pull you along and you'll hardly have to put in any effort at all. You need some fresh air to blow away those cobwebs, that's what you need,' Iris assured her.

'What I need is a new brain,' Sophie told her mother. 'A new brain, one that knows how to process rational thought, and I need a new heart, a hard stone heart, not one that falls in love with the world's most inappropriate man at the drop of a hat, and most of all I need to not think, and sitting here watching whatever is on the telly is exactly the best way to do that. I need all of those things and nothing that is anything to do with fresh air. I've had more fresh air than any sensible lung can deal with recently and just look where that's got me.'

On Monday Sophie had been woken just after nine by her mobile.

'I miss you,' she'd breathed into it, answering it still half asleep and hopeful that it was Louis.

'Really? I haven't given you a second thought,' Cal's voice exploded in her tender ear. 'Look, I need you to come and take me to lunch today. I saw Steven last night and he was so sweet and kind and utterly uninterested in me. He even started suggesting friends of his who he might set me up with, oh the horror! I need to go to lunch somewhere really terrible. Like an Angus Steak House or a TGI Friday's. I need to be somewhere where the saturated fat flows freely and I can get off my nuts on an ice cream sundae and you're the only person I know who regularly eats that kind of muck, you have to come with me, it's your civic duty.'

'I don't know, Cal,' Sophie had yawned, stretching out so that her feet dangled over the end of the bed. 'I was thinking about having a duvet day. I've discovered that I like lounging around in my pyjamas watching daytime TV. And anyway my body's just realised that I haven't had a lie-in in six months and it's demanding I catch up with the deficit.'

'Oh no, you don't,' Cal warned her. 'No, you don't get to stay in bed moping. You need to be up and about and listening to me talk about Steven endlessly while I commit artery suicide with a double-bacon cheeseburger. You owe me, Sophie. I've lost hours of my life listening to you wittering on about Louis, debating if he is or is not the love of your life, blah, blah, blah, and I've never complained.'

'Er, excuse me . . .' Sophie began to protest.

'Barely ever complained. And now it's your turn.'

'OK, fine, you're right,' Sophie conceded. 'You are a good friend to me and I should be a better one to you even if I am in the middle of my own personal crisis. I'll get up and get dressed and come and meet you for lunch.'

'Great, come and pick me up from my office at one,' Cal instructed her.

'Well, I would but I don't really know if I want all the fuss of coming back into the office . . .' But Cal had hung up.

Sophie looked at her watch. There were at least two more hours before she really had to be awake.

After a very unsatisfactory, dribbly and barely lukewarm shower with a drain which was blocked with what look suspiciously like dog hair, Sophie had spent much longer than she had anticipated deciding what to wear for her first visit back to the offices of McCarthy Hughes, which had once represented so much of her life. She had to get her look exactly right and she had to do that with the haphazard collection of clothes she had thrown into her suitcase without any thought or forward planning. Somehow she had to find a look that said she was happy to have given up her hard-earned and well-paid career for a man she barely knew but that, given the need, she could step back into it at a moment's notice without even pausing for thought because her finger was still firmly on the corporate event-planning pulse. Sophie found herself thinking of Stephanie Corollo as she dressed, in the end picking a smart cream shirt, to top off her pencil skirt finished with a neat waistcoat that nipped just under her breasts. It took her an age to dry her hair with her mother's weak and dangerous-looking hair dryer, the very same one that Iris had been using to blow dry various animals since the seventies. When she came to put her make-up on she found that half of it was missing, probably having found its way into Bella's and Izzy's play make-up set. Eventually, though, Sophie was able to stand in front of the mirror and give herself the once over. She looked good. She looked like a woman in control, even if she wasn't entirely sure that some of the long blonde hairs that had strayed on to her shoulders didn't belong to an afghan hound called Marilyn.

Just as she was leaving, her phone rang. Sophie looked at the name that flashed on to the screen as she picked up her jacket and bag, expecting it to be Cal either complaining that she was late or changing his mind about where to eat. But it was Louis's name that appeared. He was calling her at last. He was missing her at last and most importantly, he was making the first move.

'Hello,' she said tentatively, an edge of uncertainty in her voice.

'Is this Aunty Sophie?' Bella's voice boomed out. Whenever she was on the phone she always had the tendency to talk twice as loudly as normal, which Sophie put down to the several months she had lived with her grandmother.

'Bella? Yes, it's me,' Sophie said, a rush of warmth sweeping through her as she heard the child's voice. 'Why aren't you at school, are you poorly?'

'I am at school,' Bella bellowed. 'Me and Izzy borrowed Daddy's phone out of his jacket pocket this morning and took it to school so we could talk to you. We put it in Izzy's book bag because nursery children hardly ever get searched.'

'I'm here too!' Sophie winced as Izzy's high-pitched shriek came through.

'Shush, or else we'll be discovered!' Bella urged her sister, who collapsed into a fit of giggles giving Sophie a mental imagine of Bella swooping the phone out of her sister's reach as she tried to grab it.

'Bella? You've taken Daddy's phone without him knowing and smuggled it into school?' Sophie asked her, anxiously.

'Yes,' Bella said. 'We wanted to talk to you and Daddy said not to phone you till you phoned us because you needed to think. We were going to call you in the phone box outside of school because we know your number but we needed money or a credit card so I borrowed Daddy's phone instead because I don't know how to use a credit card and he doesn't have any change.'

'You were going to leave the school grounds on your own and phone me?' Sophie asked, trying to quell the alarm that heightened her tone. 'Wouldn't your teachers have noticed?'

'Not at pick-up, it's easy to sneak past the teachers with all those people in the playground,' Bella said proudly, which didn't exactly reassure Sophie, but right now she knew the last thing Bella needed to hear from her was a telling off, especially if she was prepared to go to such lengths to talk to her.

'And where are you now?'

'We are in the playground, behind the scooter rack – it's lunchtime,' Bella told her a touch impatiently, bored with all the small talk.

'And are you OK?' Sophie asked her.

'We're not bad,' Bella said. 'Daddy seems quite cross most of the time, we haven't had a Coco-Pop morning in ages. And that Wendy woman keeps coming around. They keep talking without us being able to hear them but I know they are talking about Seth, who is Seth?'

'He's Wendy's son,' Sophie said uneasily, hating the position that Louis was unwittingly putting her in, forcing her to tell half-truths to the children.

'Well, I don't know why Daddy's so worried about him. Anyway, I miss you a lot.'

'And me, and me too!' Sophie heard Izzy in the background.

'I miss both of you too,' Sophie reassured them. 'I really do. But you know Daddy's going to be worried when he finds out his phone is missing, he needs it for work.'

'Except he's not working this week,' Bella told her. 'He's stopped all of his work to help that Wendy woman find that Seth person.'

'Has he?' Sophie asked, taken aback. She hadn't quite expected Louis to alter his life so radically the moment she wasn't on the scene. If he'd turned down or called off paying work right at the moment when his business was so fledgling and he was building a reputation, then what did that mean? Did it mean that she hadn't left a hole in his life at all for him to notice? Did it mean he was willing to give up everything he'd been building up over the last few months for his son, for Wendy?

'When are you coming back, Sophie?' It was Izzy who spoke this time, having successfully wrestled the phone from her sister at last.

'Um well . . . soon, I expect,' Sophie glanced at her watch. She was going to be late for Cal.

'Will it be tomorrow?' Izzy asked. 'Tomorrow is soon.'

'It might not be exactly tomorrow,' Sophie had told her, feeling her chest tighten. 'But it will be soon.'

'Do you promise?' Izzy asked her solemnly.

'I do promise that I will see you soon,' Sophie said hating to be vague, but knowing that with Izzy at least an open promise would be sufficient.

'Hey . . . !' Izzy yelped a protest as Bella came back on the phone.

'We have to go, there are dinner ladies at four o'clock,' Bella hissed.

'Oh . . . right, but Bella, listen – give your phone back to Daddy as soon as you see him, OK? I want to talk to him tonight. And promise me that you will not ever go out of the school unless it's with a relative or someone you know, OK?'

'OK,' Bella hissed. 'Got to terminate connection. Roger, over and out.'

Once the connection was severed, Sophie thought for a moment, feeling uneasy about the lengths that Bella had gone to talk to her. Nothing really bad had happened, but still, if the seven-year-old was prepared to consider sneaking out of school to make a call to Sophie then what else might she do if she felt under pressure? She'd certainly been happy to 'borrow' her dad's mobile phone. And she felt angry at Louis, who surely must know that no matter how much time she might need to think she would always have time to talk to the girls. He was being petulant, punishing her for leaving, and it was the children who were suffering. Sophie would have called him right then if he'd had his mobile phone, or at home if it hadn't been for the fear of finding out that Wendy was there, and told him exactly what she thought of him banning the girls from speaking to her, cancelling his work to follow wherever Wendy seemed to lead. But she didn't, and all in all that was probably a good thing.

*

Sophie looked up at the skyscraper where McCarthy Hughes was located and felt her heartbeat quicken. There had been something about her journey over here, the rumble of the tube train as it carried her into the heart of the City, the smell of the damp autumn air as she emerged a short walk away from her former offices, that had sent the adrenalin surging through her body, reminding her of the thrill that doing her job well used to give her.

The building that she stood at the foot of had been, not so very long ago, her entire universe, and she had been at the hub of it. And now she was back.

Sophie hadn't known quite what she was expecting when she walked into the open-plan office, but probably something not far off a crowd of her old colleagues mobbing her, each of them declaring how much they had missed her and how the old place wasn't the same without her around, at least that was how she imagined it whenever she thought about the job she had left behind. But in reality, not a single head rose from a single desk as she walked into the office and when Sophie stopped by Clara Hodgkin's desk to say hi it took her former workmate a long second to work out who was standing right in front of her.

'Sophie, how are you?' Clara had said. 'How's life in Scotland?'

'Cornwall, it's great, thanks.'

'And how is the little boy you look after?'

'Girls. Two little girls, they are fantastic, thank you.' Sophie smiled. 'And how are things here, working for Eve?'

Sophie was hopeful of a good deal of complaining and at the very least some eye rolling about Eve, her ex-arch-nemesis and rival who had become the boss at McCarthy Hughes when Sophie had given up her promotion to be with Louis and the girls. At this very moment Sophie was expecting to be told that things simply hadn't been the same since she had left. But Clara just shrugged and smiled and said, 'Same old, you know. Nothing ever really changes around here.'

Sophie slowed as she approached the office that had once been hers and was now Cal's. Leaning over his desk, in a tight black dress that showed every single one of her ribs, was Eve, examining something on Cal's computer screen.

Sophie stood in the doorway and looked around the office that had been her domain for so long. It was the place where she had tried so hard to be secretly in love with Jake Flynn and where she had first heard the news that Carrie had died and left two small children behind in need of a guardian. Cal had changed it completely as Sophie knew that he would. It had been painted a fresh white, he had moved a sofa in, there was a vase of ostentatious flowers, new blinds and artwork was hanging on the wall.

'A-hem,' Sophie coughed to make her presence known, even though she was fairly sure that both Eve and Cal knew she was standing there.

'Sophie Mills!' Eve said slowly a second or two before she looked up from the screen at Sophie. She treated Sophie to a thin red-lipped gash of a smile. 'You look very fat, I mean well, on country life.'

'And you look more and more like a Disney villain every time I see you,' Sophie commented back, sweetly. 'Are you hoping to get a part in a pantomime this year?'

'Well, you're the expert – after all, your entire life is a pantomime.' Eve raised an eyebrow. 'Tell me – how is life with your off-the-shelf family? Everything you hoped for, is it?' Eve asked her.

'And more,' Sophie said, shooting a look at Cal that warned him he better not have told Eve anything about her current issues.

'Yes, well, I suppose a twenty-year-old stepson probably is more than any new bride would ask for.' Eve's smile was serrated.

'And how are you?' Sophie asked her. 'Still totally and utterly alone?'

Eve smirked. 'Only on the nights I want to be.' She walked over to Sophie and held out a hand. 'It's good to see you, Sophie. We miss you around here. Total pain in the arse you might have been, but you were quite good at your job.'

'I was good at your job too,' Sophie reminded her.

'Well, listen, I have to get on, top job to do and all that, but just so you know . . .' Eve paused in the doorway as she was about to leave. 'If you ever do need a job then please come and ask me. You could have your old job back like a shot, any time, I really mean that.'

'Isn't my old job your current job?' Sophie asked Eve.

'You're old, old job. Any time. I'd love to have you come and work for me.'

Sophie nodded. As much as she'd like to be able to tell Eve to shove her smug job offer, she resisted.

'I'll bear it in mind,' she said instead as Eve slinked out of the office and across the floor like a black mamba in heels. She turned to look at Cal who was very carefully studying his nails.

'I want words with you,' she said.

'You never said don't tell anyone,' Cal said as they sat a little later over a mixed meat grill with onion rings and relish.

'I assumed that as my best friend you wouldn't tell anyone, because generally friends keep each other's secrets,' Sophie childed him. 'I've always kept your secrets.'

'I've never had anything secret till now,' Cal protested. 'And anyway, you can't have a go at me. I need your help. I'm in love and I need to stop it now before I lose my mind.' Sophie's expression softened and she pushed the bowl of fries they were sharing over to Cal.

'Unfortunately you can't just turn off feelings like that,' Sophie told him. 'If it really is going nowhere between you and this Steven then you just have to wait it out, wait for your feelings to go away.'

'But how long will that take?' Cal asked her miserably, stuffing a fistful of fries into his mouth.

'I don't know,' Sophie said. 'I think it probably depends on how much you love him. If you're not really that serious about him then probably a few weeks; if you like him a lot then a few months, and if you really truly love him then it could be years till you get over him.'

'Oh God.' Cal's head thumped down on the table top. 'I can't take this much more. I'm acting like an idiot. I keep making up excuses to phone him, asking to borrow books and DVDs when everyone knows that I never read or watch TV unless it's the *Coronation Street* omnibus. And I keep trying to bump into him, hanging around the deli that he uses in my spare time in the hope he'll have run out of pickled artichoke hearts, or walking in the park where he goes running with his dog. I can't stop thinking about him. It's literally driving me mad.'

'Perhaps you should tell him how you feel?' Sophie suggested, feeling a little hypocritical as telling people how she felt had never traditionally been one of her strong points.

'Are you joking?' Cal asked her. 'I can barely string a coherent sentence together when I'm around him as it is. If I had to actually say something profound and important to him it would come out as utter crap and he'd hate me for being an idiot as well as not fancying me. At least now he tolerates me. At least now he thinks I'm funny and sweet.'

'He thinks you're sweet?' Sophie asked. 'Is his dog a guide dog?'

'Not in the mood!' Cal chided her. 'I love him, Sophie, I love him and I don't know what to do about it.'

'Do you know what?' Sophie said. 'I honestly don't think there is a single thing you can do about it except ride it out and see what happens.'

Cal's forehead found its place on the table top once more.

That night Sophie shut herself away in her old room and resolved to call Louis. Now she had a reason to phone him, a solid, concrete and rational reason that wasn't purely about her wanting to hear the sound of his voice and hoping that he missed her constantly being at his side. She wanted to talk to him about Bella threatening to sneak out of the school gates and taking Louis's phone secretly into school to phone her. She steeled herself as she listened to the ring tone which rang for longer than the normal four it took to get Louis to pick up. When the phone was finally answered it wasn't Louis's voice that Sophie heard.

'Hello?' It was Wendy's voice. Sophie resisted the urge to instantly hang up. Realising that her name would have come up on Louis's phone, she didn't want Wendy to know that her being there on the end of Louis's number had rattled her in any way.

'Hi, Wendy,' Sophie said in an even tone, using her name to show that she wasn't remotely bothered. 'Can you get Louis for me please?'

'Sorry, he's ... a bit tied up at the moment,' Wendy said, deliberately vague. Sophie glanced at her watch. In all likelihood, Louis was with the girls, probably giving them a bath or reading them a story. It was just Wendy's tone and her own imagination that led her to picture him tied naked to the radiator in the living room while Wendy toyed with him. 'I'll tell him you called.'

'Thank you,' Sophie said. 'And please tell him it's important.'

'Of course it is,' Wendy said, before disconnecting the call. Sophie waited till gone midnight for Louis to phone back, but the call never came. Which either meant he didn't want to talk to her or Wendy hadn't given him her message at all. Sophie considered ringing him again, but the thought of it being Wendy's voice that answered kept her from calling again. It looked like she'd have to wait for him to contact her after all.

For the rest of the week Sophie had lived her old life, except that it now included long lie-ins and she didn't go to work every day although she did meet Cal at the office for lunch. She shopped for clothes that were entirely inappropriate for a seaside town in winter, taking her neglected credit card on a spree around the West End. She went with Cal to a poetry reading in a branch of Borders on Charing Cross Road because he thought he might bump into the Steven there. She spent ninety pounds in her favourite Covent Garden salon having her hair shaped and styled, leaving the stylist a ten-pound tip even though she'd just paid ninety pounds for her hair to basically look the same. As Friday approached she noticed two things acutely. Jake had not called her and asked her out to lunch as he had promised, and she had heard nothing at all from her fiancé.

And Sophie wondered how it was possible to go from feeling like the most wanted and loved woman in the world to feeling like an incidental irritation in the life of someone she had given up everything for. She knew that her old life, her comfortable closed-off city life, was still here for her, that she could even have her old job back if Eve was serious. But the problem was, the really big problem was, that now she'd had her space and her time to think things over, Sophie discovered she didn't want it any more.

'Coffee?' Iris asked Sophie as she sat mulling over the last few days. 'Come on, you need to get something hot inside you or else you'll waste away.'

Sophie shook her head; she had been grateful for the opportunity to sleep late over the past week, but she found it was taking her much longer to wake up than usual. Her head was fuzzy and she felt more tired and muddled now than she had when she went to bed. It didn't help having her mother fussing over her and forcing her to eat breakfast for fear that she might become an anorexic unless, of course, she asked for a bacon sandwich in which case the maternal concern would become the dangers of obesity while several smelly dogs milled about her legs. This morning, though, the merest thought of bacon turned Sophie's stomach. In fact, the idea of breakfast in general turned her off completely, which was most unlike her.

Iris waved a coffee pot under Sophie's nose as she entered the kitchen, still exactly the same as it had been when she'd left home, the walls lined with pine tongue and groove except for one which was covered with pearlescent wallpaper that shimmered in the morning sun and hurt Sophie's eyes. Sophie backed away from it, pulling down the corners of her mouth as she slumped into a chair.

'Got any decaff, Mum?' She yawned, burying her head in her hands, her fingers knotting in her hair.

'Decaff?' Iris asked her bowed head. 'You always said decaff was for losers who wanted to pay for coffee-flavoured water. I thought you'd want the real stuff after another night out on the tiles. What was it you and Cal went to see, some Russian play? I never had Cal down for a Russian-play fan.'

'He's not, but he is the fan of a Russian-play fan,' Sophie said, wondering exactly why she'd agreed to sit through hours of Chekhov so that Cal would be able to impress Steven with his knowledge of his work next time they saw each other, except that it was marginally preferable to sitting on the sofa and watching her mother and Trevor make out.

'And yes, we did hear you come in, thank you very much.'

'Well, it wasn't as if I was singing at the top of my voice or crashing around,' Sophie said, petulantly eyeing her mother between ropes of her own hair. 'I was as sober as a judge. All this stress has made me go off drinking, and no, it's not bloody ironic, it's bloody inconvenient. I mean, that's what we British do when things go a bit pear-shaped, we drink ourselves into oblivion and make ill-advised choices. Now I'm being forced – against my will, I might add – to think things through with a clear and rational mind. Although I'm not so sure about the rational bit . . .'

'You weren't drinking and you haven't had coffee once this week?' Iris asked her thoughtfully, still holding the coffee jug.

'No, Mum,' Sophie sighed wearily, feeling in mind if not in body every bit seventeen again. 'But you don't have to worry, neither of those things are classic signs of an eating disorder. If anything they show that I am super healthy. Apart from my cream tea and choux pastry addiction and frankly, when you live in the West Country that's practically a requirement.' Sophie looked around the kitchen that was mutt free, except for Tripod, her mother's three-legged Spaniel cross who'd come off worst in a collision with a bendy bus, who was happily grazing from a buffet of dog bowls left unguarded for a few blissful moments.

'Where are all the dogs, anyway?'

'The ones that can be trusted not to dig up next-door's dead gerbil are in the garden and I corralled Scooby and the others in the living room,' Iris said. 'I thought we should talk alone.'

'I might be mistaken but I think talking in front of dumb animals, generally speaking, does qualify as talking alone,' Sophie said.

'Those dogs understand every word I say and some of them are very sensitive. Little Miss Pickles knows immediately if there's something amiss and her hair falls out. I will not be responsible for a bald Pekinese. Anyway, you talk to that cat of yours.'

'Yes, but Artemis is not a dumb animal,' Sophie said. 'And besides, what about Tripod?'

'Tripod is deaf.' Iris rolled her eyes as she searched her cupboards till she pulled out a packet of herbal tea.

'I've got peppermint tea,' she informed Sophie squinting at the packet over the top of her glasses. 'It's best before 2002, but I shouldn't think it will kill you. Do you fancy that?'

'Peppermint tea? Do you know, that's exactly what I fancy,' Sophie said brightening up. 'I didn't know I liked peppermint tea.'

Iris pursed her lips and set about boiling the kettle.

'How about poached eggs for breakfast?' she offered her daughter.

'Poached eggs? No thanks, the thought of egg yolks makes me feel like throwing up. I'll just have some toast, thanks . . .'

Iris set a mug of steaming peppermint tea down in front of Sophie and sat opposite her at the table.

'Listen, Sophie,' she said. 'I haven't had a chance to talk to you properly since you got here. I told Trevor that you and I needed some mother-and-daughter time but you hardly ever seem to be at home and when you are you are usually asleep. But I want you to know that I am here for you and I know you wouldn't have come back here unless it was really serious.'

'It's OK, Mum.' Sophie smiled at her as she embraced her mug of tea, cupping it with both hands. 'I didn't come here expecting you to fix all my problems, it's just really good to know that I have got a place to come to if I need it. And you don't need to tell Trevor to go home because of me, I think it's sweet that you two are so close . . .' Sophie trailed off, feeling slightly nauseous again. 'Anyway, I'm really glad you're happy. I'm really glad you've found someone, and he's a lovely man if a tad oversexed for his age.'

'And he's dishy too, isn't he?' Iris prompted her.

'He is properly dishy, Mum,' Sophie chuckled into the aromatic steam of her tea.

'Anyway, I've told him to go back to his flat for a couple of days so that you and I can have a proper girls' weekend and talk about everything.'

'That's lovely,' Sophie said, with perhaps a little less enthusiasm than her mother was hoping for.

'So talk to me, darling.' Iris reached out and patted Sophie's arm. 'I'm all ears.'

Sophie studied her mother's Formica table top, and array of seventies-styled flowers spiralling in various shades of orange across its surface. When she had been a little girl she had sat at this very table discovering faces, creatures, and sometimes entire other worlds while her parents talked over her head. Her dad used to say she was always away with the fairies. Her dad used to make a smiling face out of bacon and tomatoes and pop the plate under her nose, making her laugh out loud. For a second, sitting in this kitchen, at this relic of her youth, the memory of her father was so strong that it almost felt as if he were standing beside her and Sophie missed him with a strength she hadn't experienced in the longest time, tears tracking down her cheeks.

'Oh sweetheart, is it really that bad?' her mother asked her, rubbing her shoulder vigorously.

'I don't know – it's not even that I'm crying about, I just thought about Dad and that set me off. I'm a mess at the moment, Mum, it's like someone peeled away a layer of my skin and I'm feeling everything a little bit more than I used to. I'm bursting into tears at the drop of a hat, making life-changing decisions without thinking about them. I'm very confused.'

'Well, this thing with Louis's son and his mother must have made you feel unsure,' Iris told her. 'Any woman would feel odd about her prospective husband's secret child turning up out of the blue, even if he is twenty years old.'

Sophie nodded, thinking about Seth distraught on Mrs Alexander's sofa. She had failed him; instead of helping him, all she'd done was make a difficult situation even more confusing and difficult for him. She barely knew him, it was true, but somehow Sophie felt he'd spent a lot of his life covering up for how lost and confused he was really feeling. It was something in his eyes that she recognised. Something she used to see in her own eyes whenever she looked in the mirror.

'And from what you've said this Wendy doesn't seem like the most sensible of women, trying to come between you and Louis when she should be worrying about her son.'

'She just hates me, that's what it is,' Sophie explained. 'She's got it into her head that she hates me and that she wants to take Louis from me and it's crazy. Crazy that she should think it and even more crazy that I should feel threatened by her. Louis likes her, I can see that – she was really important to him once. And he's trying to work out the best way to deal with discovering that he's got a son, but he wouldn't just drop everything we have for her, would he?'

'No. No, I can't believe that he would. He's sure, is he?' Iris asked her.

'Sure about what?'

'That this Seth is his son. Does he know that for sure?'

'Well, he hasn't done a test or anything, but you should see him, Mum. He looks almost exactly like Louis. A little smoother, a touch rounder in the face – but other than that . . . well, they have to be related.'

'All I'm saying is that it might be a good idea before the lives of so many people get seriously complicated to verify the facts,' Iris said. 'Louis is tall, dark and handsome and from the sounds of it this Seth is tall, dark and handsome. All that means is that the boy's mother likes tall, dark and handsome men.'

'No, Seth's Louis's son, I'm sure of it. He has exactly the same expression when he's angry, the same smile, he even kisses like . . .' Sophie trailed off, suddenly finding Tripod's attempt to get her to stroke him terribly endearing.

'How do you know how he kisses?' Iris asked her, as Sophie scratched Tripod under one ear so that the poor hound leaned rather too far to the left and toppled over on to the tiles.

'OK . . . I'll tell you as you clearly insist on dragging it out of me with your vicious interrogation techniques.' Iris raised an eyebrow. 'He tried to kiss me, OK? He actually did kiss me for a bit but he was very drunk and angry and I was very surprised so didn't react quite as quickly as I probably should have. It's not as if I fancy him or anything . . .'

'No, dear, because with your track record that would be a bad idea,' Iris said mildly.

'My track record?' Sophie exclaimed. 'What do you mean, Mother? I was practically a virgin until I met Louis.'

'I know, darling, I'm just saying. When it comes to forming relationships you always seem to pick the rather complicated route. On paper Louis was the last man you should have fallen for. Or the second from last, anyway, I'd say his son would definitely be the last.'

'I have not, am not and do not at any point intend falling for Seth. I was caught off guard and he is so like Louis, or like Louis would have been once, fresh and young and untouched by life. Just for a second I wondered what it would have been like to meet him then, when he was young and carefree and without a personal history to rival Henry the Eighth's.'

'From what you've told me it doesn't sound like Seth is very carefree to me,' Iris said. 'Sounds to me like he's a rather troubled young man with a mother who puts her own interests before his.'

'I don't know . . . I don't really know what Wendy's like. All I know is that she really hates me for rocking her boat and seems quite keen to get her own back, no matter what happens.'

Iris watched her daughter thoughtfully in the October sun.

'Well, leaving all of that to one side, you still love Louis, don't you?'

'I do,' Sophie said hesitantly.

'You don't sound so sure,' Iris said, pouring herself another cup of coffee and watching her daughter's face closely as the aroma caused Sophie to unconsciously wrinkle her nose for the briefest second.

'Mum, the thing is, how do you know the difference between love and just really amazing sex and fun and laughing and getting on really well? Because before Louis, I'd never had really amazing sex, I'd never really even *liked* sex. But now with Louis I can't get enough of it. And I know he feels the same way about me, I mean it feels like we can't be alone in a room together for more than five seconds without having to rip each other's clothes off—'

'OK,' Iris held up the flat of her hand, 'I'm delighted you feel that you can talk to me openly about this, darling, but you are still my little girl and that is rather more more information than I need to know. Thank God Tripod is deaf.'

'Sorry,' Sophie apologised. 'I just thought that now you and Trevor were so . . . active you might not mind.'

'I don't mind, but let's make a deal just to stick to generalisations and gloss over the details, OK?'

'Well, anyway, I'm head over heals in love with Louis,' Sophie went on. 'I'm infatuated with him. I can't think of a single thing about him that I don't love with a passion. I even like the way he snores, Mum. I even like his *snoring*. And I know that won't last, I know it's not real – what if in a year or two's time I wake up to him snoring and I realise that I hate it, and I hate him and the infatuation's worn off and all I'm left with is this man who I don't really know and who doesn't really know me, and all we have in common are his children who deserve so much better than another failed relationship? Nothing about us is normal. We didn't meet in the normal way, we didn't get together in the normal way and we're not starting out in the normal way. So how do we make this work, Mum? When nothing is normal how do you know what to do next? That's what I'm worried about.'

Iris studied her coffee thoughtfully, bending over to scratch Tripod's tummy.

'You always were far too sensible,' she said eventually.

'What do you mean?' Sophie asked her impatiently. 'How is it even possible to be too sensible?'

'I met your dad when I was sixteen, and he was eighteen,' Iris said, ignoring her question. 'It was at this Christmas party at the old youth club on Seven Sisters Road; it's not there now, of course, there's never anything for young people to do these days, no wonder they're all stabbing and shooting each other . . .'

'Mum, stick to the point – if you have one, that is,' Sophie prompted her.

'Sorry. I saw him playing snooker with his mates, full mod outfit – the suit, the tie the hair – and I melted on the spot. I fell for him so hard that I couldn't look at him, let alone talk to him. Whenever he was around I had trouble breathing, and the only way I could deal with it was to ignore him. This went on for about two years. He went out with every single one of my friends but never me; he never asked me out. I'd lock myself up in my bedroom at night and play my records and cry my eyes out.'

'Why didn't you tell him you fancied him?'

'I don't know, why didn't you ever engage in a proper relationship until you were in your thirties? I was shy and a bit repressed, I suppose, and a child, which is a pretty good excuse,' Iris explained. 'Besides, he was the best-looking, most popular boy in our group and I was a skinny kid with lanky hair and no breasts. I protected myself by staying away from him.'

'You and Dad didn't get married until you were twenty-three did you? What happened?'

'Well, for one thing I got breasts – but anyway, at eighteen Dad went off to university and I stayed in London, working in my mother's dress shop. You know, you don't get shops like that any more, little boutiques. My mum running up patterns in the back room, me out the front talking fashion with the girls . . . those were happy times.'

'OK, get to the bit where you met Dad again,' Sophie urged her. Remarkably, her mother had never told her this story before. Perhaps she hadn't been interested when she was a child and after her father died it was probably too hard for Iris to talk about; somehow the subject had never come up.

'So one day – years later, I was, let me see, twenty-two – I was at the cinema, can't remember the film, some piece of rubbish, black and white Northern kitchen-sink-type thing – I love a good musical, you don't get enough musicals any more . . .'

'*Mum.*' Sophie tapped the tips of her fingers on the table top.

'I was there with this other boy, Justin Parker, I think his name was, when I saw your dad in the foyer and all those feelings I used to have for him, the stomach-churning and the chest-tightening and the butterflies and the goose bumps, all just whooshed back and I felt like that silly skinny little kid again. He had his back to me and his arm around another girl. I don't know if he felt me looking, but he turned around and stared right into my eyes and he smiled, and I realised that he knew who I was – he remembered me. And in that second I knew that I was going to marry him. I knew it right then.'

'So how did you get together, then?' Sophie asked her, enthralled. 'What happened next?'

'He left his date standing there and came over, said hello like we'd always been old friends, and because I wasn't young or scared or shy any more and because a lot of lads used to ask me out back then and I knew I wasn't bad-looking, I suddenly found I could talk to him at last. We stood there just talking and laughing about old times till the foyer of the cinema was empty, his date had walked off and I had to tell mine to go.'

'What scandal!' Sophie laughed.

'We went to this little coffee place behind Upper Street, it was open all night and was full of cabbies and truckers and kids in black polo necks with too much eyeliner who thought they were cool. You don't get places like that any more . . .' Iris caught Sophie's expression and rolled her eyes at Tripod who seemed to be listening intently despite his deafness.

'Your dad bought me a lot of coffee – espresso, because I wanted him to think I was sophisticated so it might have been the caffeine that was making my heart race, except that it only happened every time I looked at him. We'd been in there for about an hour, laughing and joking, when he suddenly reached out and touched my hand and I felt this surge of electricity go through my body. It was so strong that I felt like I should have been jolted across the room and sitting in some cabby's lap with my hair standing on end! I'd never ever experienced anything like that before. He looked into my eyes and he said "Why did you never talk to me back then? I was crazy about you but you always ignored me. I went out with all your friends to try and get your attention but you never once looked my way." I just laughed and told him about my crush on him and we couldn't believe it, we couldn't believe that the pair of us had felt like that all those years ago and had never managed to do anything about it.' Iris trailed off, her tiny smile playing around her lips as she relived that night. 'He had a little flat on Balls Pond Road. Bloody horrible place, it was, cold and a bit damp, but he took me there that night and I stayed out till the morning for the first time ever. My mother had my guts for garters, I can tell you – but it was worth it.' She smiled at Sophie. 'That was the night that I found out I liked sex. We were engaged four months later, married within the year.'

'That's so romantic,' Sophie said, feeling the all-too-familiar tears building behind her eyes again. 'So when did that bit wear off?'

'I felt about him then exactly the way you feel about Louis

265

now, even though you're quite a bit older than me. I adored him. I couldn't think of a single thing about him that I didn't love. I even loved his hairy shoulders . . .'

'And so . . . did it go off once you were married for a few years?'

'Of course it did,' Iris said.

'See, I told you!' Sophie panicked.

'Well, no – go off is the wrong way of putting it – it changed, it *evolved*.' Iris nodded, pleased with the word she'd found. 'Life, money, children, work, that's all the stuff that can get in the way of love, the stuff that can push it to the back burner and make you forget that you are more than just co-parents and house-mates till one day the flame burns out, dies. The thing is, if you're worried about how to pay the mortgage or you've been up all night with the baby, if you can remember that love, that passion that brought you together, and allow yourself to feel it, no matter what else is going – then it grows, it deepens and becomes your strength, your fortress against whatever life throws at you.' Iris leaned across the table and stroked Sophie's face with the back of her hand. 'Sweetheart, it's so rare to be able to look at another person and say that's the one for me, and to know it with all of your heart. And sometimes I think that these days people are more afraid than ever to face how they really feel. You all get married later, you all have children late, all so worried about living your lives before any of that happens and that's crazy because loving someone, loving children – that *is* life. All the rest of it is just "stuff". You only get the kind of deep, strong, wonderful love that your father and I shared if you're brave enough to ride the waves that take you there. Your love for Louis will change and evolve – but if you believe in your heart that you do love him and you never let anything make you forget that – then it can only change for the better.'

'Mum,' Sophie said softly. 'That was really profound.'

'I know.' Iris nodded sagely. 'You see, I do know some things; you'd be surprised at how many things I know if you ever took the trouble to ask me.'

'I know.' Sophie's smile was rueful. 'So what about Trevor? Do you feel that way about Trevor?'

Iris grinned and Sophie couldn't help but mirror her expression when she saw the twinkle in her mother's eye.

'He makes me very happy.' She nodded. 'Sexually. But your father was the love of my life. I still regret those six years between the ages of sixteen and twenty-two that we were apart and I just thank my lucky stars I had him for as long as I did and that he gave me you.'

'Do you think I'm bonkers if I marry Louis on New Year's Eve, even if nothing about our relationship is normal?'

'What is normal anyway?' Iris asked her. 'Especially today. Sophie, life is complicated. I know you grew up with a certain vision of how meeting the man you love would be, but maybe that's why you've been alone for so long. Because you've been waiting for something that doesn't really exist. Life isn't a fairy tale, there are no neat happily ever afters. But if happiness comes your way then you should grab it and hold on to it, no matter how it arrives. And no, I don't think you're bonkers if you marry Louis at whatever time. Especially not now.'

'Especially not now, why?' Sophie asked her, finishing the last of her tea.

'Especially not now that you're pregnant.'

At that precise second Sophie's phone intruded noisily, vibrating in the pocket of her dressing gown.

Staring at her mother open-mouthed, she reached for it and answered. It was Jake.

'Hey, Sophie, sorry I haven't called before now – Stephanie has had me all over town running around doing wedding stuff.

This morning she feels it is necessary to buy out the whole of Heal's; I've left her haggling over a pod of designer tables – whatever that is – I don't suppose you could make lunch today, could you?'

'Oh yes,' Sophie said, perhaps a touch too eagerly to be seemly when talking to another woman's fiancé. 'Yes, Jake – fantastic. When and where?'

'How about a late lunch, say two? At J Sheekey's, do you know it?'

'Great, I'll see you there,' Sophie said, checking her watch and mentally calculating the exact amount of minutes she had to turn herself from aged teenage throwback to foxy girl about town. 'Look forward to it.'

'Me too, honey,' Jake said, before hanging up. 'Me too.'

Sophie set her phone down on the table and looked at her mother.

'I am not pregnant,' she stated, reinforcing her point with a slash of her hands. 'Mother? What on earth makes you think I'm pregnant?'

'You've gone off alcohol . . .'

'I'm stressed and my stomach's all churny, that's all that is. Besides, I do go off things, I went off Marmite for a whole year,' Sophie reminded her.

'When you were six. And the smell of coffee turns your stomach.'

'I never really did like coffee *that* much . . .' Sophie slowed as she remembered that till very recently she'd downed two cups of the black stuff before even opening her eyes. 'Anyway, that's probably living by the sea and not having to get up at five every morning to be in the office by six. I don't need caffeine any more, my body has weaned itself off it.'

'I thought you said you were stressed.'

'I am stressed *now*, my new fiancé had got a twenty-year-old secret love child who tried to get off with me, but I wasn't stressed when I went off ... gave up coffee.'

'And you keep crying ...'

'That'll be the stress and PMT, probably ...' Sophie said shrugging petulantly, a little like the teenager she was desperately trying to avoid reverting back to.

'And darling' – Iris added timidly – 'you've gained a little weight.'

'Ah well, yes, I know about that,' Sophie said. 'That's cream teas, that is. I eat a lot of cream teas, Mum. Besides, you don't put weight on in pregnancy till you're quite far along, so ...'

'So when *was* your last period?' Iris asked her carefully, accepting Tripod's paw that batted at her knee whenever she stopped stroking him and shaking it as if they had only just been introduced.

'Well, it was ...' Sophie trailed off as she thought. She had never been especially in tune with her body's biological rhythm, her cycle was never that regular, and she'd learned not to plan any event around it because, however much she tried to second guess it, it could always be guaranteed to turn up at exactly the wrong moment. 'I don't know, a few weeks ago. Three or so, I expect. Like I said, I'm premenstrual probably, that's bound to be why I'm doing all the crying and stuff.'

'Sophie,' Iris looked serious, 'think of a thing that you were doing the last time you had your period. An event, something you were doing with the girls, maybe.'

Sophie crossed her arms and huffed out a sigh, exactly as she used to when Iris would tell her to tidy her room, threatening that otherwise everything that was on the floor would be going out with the bins.

'Fine,' she sulked. 'I was at the roller disco with Bella and Izzy in the Guildhall, I remember because it hadn't stopped raining even though it was July and those two were whizzing around like maniacs and all I wanted was a hot-water bottle and a good book.'

'July,' Iris stated. 'When in July?'

'Just the other day, it was the summer holidays, Louis was doing this wedding out of town, it was a real big deal, his first big commission and that was July the seventh which was . . .' Sophie stopped talking as she completed the maths in her head.

'Over three months ago,' Iris finished for her.

'Oh God,' Sophie said very quietly. 'I'm having an early menopause.'

'No, you're having a lot of sex. Darling, I think you need to get a test.'

'I just . . . I don't feel pregnant and we are always very careful . . .'

'Do you have any idea what it feels like to be pregnant? And how careful? Were you on the pill?' Iris asked.

'No,' Sophie confessed. 'But we always use a condom . . . more or less.'

'More or less?' Iris asked.

'Well, maybe once or twice we got a bit carried away and . . . well, we went for the Catholic method instead – Oh God, Mother, I thought you said no details.'

'Darling, you need to go and buy a test today,' Iris told her. 'Babies come when you least expect them. Look at Tripod here. He was supposed to have had the snip but he still managed to get Miss Pickles pregnant. The vet said it was a modern miracle. Either that or Miss Pickles has been playing away with another black and tan spaniel.'

'I can't go and buy a test, I'm going out for lunch,' Sophie told her. 'In fact, I have to go and get ready now, so sorry, can't discuss this any more.'

'Sophie, I know that you like to push things to the back of your mind rather than face them full on, but . . .' Iris stalled as Sophie glared at her. 'Get a test on the way back,' Iris advised her as she dashed upstairs. 'And stay away from raw fish!'

Chapter Fourteen

As Sophie entered the wood-panelled finery of Sheekey's she shoved her mother's crackpot theory to the back of her mind. She was not pregnant, she would know if she was pregnant. There would be a feeling of some description, a prescient knowledge that she was about to become an actual full-blown biological mother to another human being. Something that profound, something that life-changing couldn't just creep up on you when you weren't looking, surely? It would have to announce itself in your psyche with some sort of intuitive fanfare otherwise it simply wasn't fair play. It was true that Sophie had not been especially clear on a lot of things that were happening in her life recently; she wasn't clear about love and what exactly that meant, about marriage or commitment or even, to be perfectly honest, about the boundaries surrounding kissing your boyfriend's secret son. But one thing she was totally, completely and utterly clear about was that she was not ready to have a baby. And so she dealt with it in the way she had always dealt with worries or problems that had overwhelmed her since she was a child. She decided not to think about it.

The concierge took her coat and led her to a table in the corner booth where Jake was already waiting for her, wearing his weekend uniform of light blue buttoned-down shirt topping off a pair of chinos.

'You look radiant,' he said, half rising to kiss her on the cheek as she slid into the booth next to him. Sophie had to admit that she did feel good, like her old self, only a bit hippier and with a new and improved cleavage. After her mother had aired her preposterous theory, which probably had a lot to do with Iris's longing for a grandchild and her HRT, Sophie had made a special effort to dress like a woman who was certainly not pregnant. She had slipped on her loyal and steadfast black Dolce and Gabbana heels, which she teamed with a black knitted dress that set off her pale complexion and blonde hair, her cake-enhanced curves filling out the dress much more satisfyingly now. The absolute truth was that she had tried on another skirt that she had brought with her, only she hadn't quite been able to zip it up and even if she had it would have made her newly round tummy look even bigger than it was. But even so, here she was – a modern, stylish woman. A woman who was most definitely free of any sort of reproductive type of condition of any kind.

'Hope you don't mind,' Jake said, 'I've ordered champagne and I thought we'd kick off with some Colchester oysters, a dozen are on their way, is that OK?'

'Um . . .' Sophie wanted to say, 'Yes, fine, oysters, I love them', but a little nagging part of her wouldn't allow it. 'The only things is, I've become allergic to shellfish.'

'No! Not now you live right by the sea where you can practically scoop crustaceans out of the sea with your bare hands?' Jake commiserated. 'You should have mentioned it when I suggested we came here!'

'I know, but I'm still getting used to the idea,' Sophie told him. 'It's come as a bit of a shock.'

'No problem, I shouldn't have been so presumptuous.' He called over a waiter. 'I'll change the order – how about their deep-fried whitebait? It's to die for. And you can enjoy the champagne.'

When Sophie thought about champagne, all she could think about was the taste of sweaty sock, and bile rose in her throat.

'Except that I'm on antibiotics,' Sophie said. 'I can't drink. I mean, I literally can't drink. I keep trying but nothing seems to go down.' Jake laughed and Sophie wondered what chemical outlets there were available for potentially gestating people and decided that probably there were none, unless you counted a hit of oily fish. Except that she wasn't a potentially gestating person. She was sure of it. Some women were obviously fertile, you could see it in the sway of their hips, the curve of their breasts – the way their hair shone; they looked like they had a body that could create life. Carrie had looked like that and Stephanie Corollo did; for all her New York City gloss it was easy to imagine her with a baby at her breast. But Sophie, well, till very recently she had always been a little bit uptight and closed off and she was certain that her uterus would be the same. Sperm might well be knocking on the door of her eggs but she had always felt they'd say 'shove off and mind your own business, we're washing our hair'. But that had been before Louis. Before suddenly she felt her body and her heart open up like a light-starved flower discovering the sun . . . but she definitely wasn't expecting. Not a baby, at any rate.

'So what brings you back up to London?' Jake asked her as she kicked herself for allowing that particular train of thought to develop; she was much worse at denial than she used to be.

'Oh . . . just visiting my mother, duty calls.' Sophie smiled. They were almost sitting side by side in the booth, his thigh barely six inches from hers. Sheekey's was a busy, exclusive place, this had to be a table that Jake had specifically requested and he would have had to have had some considerable clout with the management to get it at such short notice. Which meant that not only did he want to impress her, but he also wanted to sit as close to her as possible, a fact that Sophie found intriguing enough to distract her from the other matter.

'No trouble in paradise, then?' Jake asked her, with just the merest hint of hope in his voice. He picked up her left hand and looked at her ring. 'Wow, you're engaged too – congratulations. You should have said last night.'

'Oh well,' Sophie said, dropping her lashes coyly. 'I didn't want to steal your thunder. Congratulations to you – Stephanie is lovely.'

'Yes, she is, isn't she?' Jake smiled fondly. 'She's pretty stunning in every respect.'

'Why doesn't she stay with you at your apartment while she's in London?' Sophie asked him.

'Appearances. She's from a very old Italian New York family. She's got a great-grandmother who's about a hundred or something, who sets a lot of store by appearances, and that's filtered down to Stephanie. She's an old-fashioned girl at heart. We spend pretty much every night together but we need to do it at two separate addresses.'

'I think that's sweet,' Sophie said. 'I've started to think that no sex before marriage is probably an excellent idea.'

'Really? You surprise me, you don't look like a woman who's not—' Jake stopped himself, blushing. 'You look very happy.'

'So will you buy a house when you're married?' Sophie asked him, mildly disconcerted by the way he was looking at her while talking about his fiancée.

'Stephanie's got this amazing penthouse overlooking Central Park. We'll live there.'

'What, you mean you'll go back to the States at weekends or something?' Sophie was surprised.

'No, I mean I'll go back to New York, for good. Stephanie doesn't want to live in the UK. She'd miss her family too much and I couldn't think of anything to stay here for, much as I love this town and its people . . . especially some of them.' He paused to smile at her and Sophie found herself smiling back at him. Despite gorgeous, successful and independently wealthy Stephanie, despite the ring on Stephanie's finger and on her own, Jake still found her attractive and she found that at this moment, what with the late-period debacle and Louis's overly complicated personal life, she liked it. She liked it very much.

'She seems like a woman worth moving continents for,' Sophie said softly as Jake slid a few millimetres closer to her.

'She is,' he told her, leaning towards her a little as if he were breathing her in. 'She's the perfect match for me . . . which makes me wonder why . . .'

'Why what?' Sophie asked him in what she thought would widely be considered a seductive tone. She felt inordinately proud of herself, until very recently a seductive anything would have been well out of her reach.

'Why I've never quite been able to get you out of my head,' Jake said. 'You never really wanted me, we barely did more than kiss a couple of times, yet here you are sitting in front of me and all I can think about is how much I'd like to kiss you.'

'Well, I've got say I'm not surprised,' Sophie said, making Jake splutter a mouthful of champagne.

'No?' he asked her.

'Well, you know, there's this place, this table – oysters, champagne. This is not a lunch that one friend throws for another. It's a seduction lunch, Jake, whether you realised it or not.

You planned to get me here for one last little spin before you marry Stephanie. Next you'll be telling me you booked a hotel room so that we can have coffee in private.'

Jake stared at her open-mouthed for a second as if he were about to protest and then he laughed.

'You're right,' he said. 'I think that at the back of my mind I was hoping for something . . . but I promise you, I didn't plan it – there is no hotel room. It's just that you look stunning, Sophie, being in love really agrees with you and when I saw you it reminded me of how much I liked you, how different things would have been if you'd like me back, and that got me wondering, I guess. I'm sorry.'

'Don't be sorry,' Sophie told him, reassured that he still found her attractive despite herself because it meant that there was no way on earth she could have any type of bun in her oven. Pregnant women couldn't be beguiling and seductive, the two conditions had to be mutually exclusive, surely? Because Mother Nature wouldn't allow ladies to go round flirting when they had an actual baby inside of them, that would just be *wrong*. Sophie was certain that being knocked up meant that sexiness went out of the window. And she was definitely sexy, she was on fire with desirability. If only her so-called fiancé found her as hard to resist as Jake did.

'I think it's because you've changed.' Jake's voice was low. 'It's as if something or someone has switched you on, you look alight with life. You look incredible.'

'Thank you' Sophie said. 'It's the same for me, seeing you, you know. I think that if things had been different, if we'd met at another time, then maybe we would have rubbed along pretty well together. But I don't think we would have ever really been in love. Not like you are with Stephanie . . . not like I am with Louis.'

277

'Stephanie is amazing,' Jake said. 'And I do love her. It's just ... I really like kissing you, Sophie.'

'Perhaps it would be useful,' Sophie said thoughtfully, 'to have kissed someone else apart from Louis or ... any other Gregory man just to be able to compare and contrast. You know, to make sure that the feelings we think we are feeling for our significant others are real feelings.' Sophie raised her brows, surprising herself by what she had half suggested.

'Are you suggesting we kiss each other purely out of scientific research?' Jake asked her.

'Am I suggesting that?' Sophie hedged.

'I think you are.' Without warning Jake grabbed her hand and all but dragged her out of the booth and through the restaurant, turning heads as he went.

'We have to make a call,' he told the waiter, who looked astounded as he rushed past. 'Back in a minute.'

Sophie followed him, not absolutely certain of what was going on until they emerged into the alleyway outside.

Without pausing to take a breath, Jake put his hands on her shoulders and backed her against the buffer of a graffiti-covered wall. For a second he looked at her, breathing hard, and then he kissed her. And Sophie kissed him back in a way she would never have done before, her body hungry for intimacy and sex, responding to Jake long before her mind could process was happening. For several seconds everything about the kiss felt wonderful, incredible. And then Sophie realised – the lips that sought out her neck were not Louis's, the hands that had travelled down from her shoulders and across her breasts weren't the ones her body longed to be touched by and, most of all, she was standing in an alleyway kissing a man who wasn't the father of her baby. Not that she was pregnant, but if she was, then that would have been bad.

Sophie pushed Jake away.

'Wow,' Jake said. 'Not exactly sure the results of that experiment went the way they were supposed to.'

'Aren't you?' Sophie asked him.

'Not if I was supposed to discover that I don't like kissing you, because I do. A lot.'

'No, you don't,' Sophie told him, despite the evidence to the contrary that was quite clearly visible in his chinos. 'And neither do I. You love Stephanie, I could see it all over your face when you talked about her, and I love Louis. I really do, and I don't know what I'm doing kissing you in a back alley, because kissing you only makes me miss him more.'

'Ouch,' Jake sighed, picking up her hand and kissing it. 'You know, it kills me to say it, but I don't think I would have ever been the right man for you, even if Louis hadn't come along.'

'Maybe not – but judging from that kiss, Stephanie's a very lucky lady.' Sophie smiled tentatively.

'So can we still have lunch?' Jake asked her hopefully, holding her hand. 'We can swap wedding plans.'

'I'd love to have lunch with you. But I don't actually have any wedding plans yet,' Sophie told him as she followed him back into the restaurant rather conscious of her now-bare lips.

'Really? You're not like any bride I know. Listen, if it's not too awkward, you should talk it through with Stephanie. That woman is a wedding-planning machine.'

'Jake,' Sophie said as they settled back down into the booth.

'Yep?' Jake asked her, considerably more relaxed than he had been when they'd left.

'Thank you. It's so good to have you as a friend.'

His smile was perhaps a little sad as he kissed her on the cheek and told her, 'Sophie, I was always going to be your friend.'

Chapter Fifteen

Sophie stood in the chemist on the corner of Highbury Grove for a long time looking at its meagre selection of cut-price nail varnish. She thought of Stephanie Corollo's long, glossy red nails and then examined her own, broken and naked, still a little Cornish sand collected in their corners, and she picked up a bottle of 'Scarlet Woman' from a little wicker basket of bargain items located next to the copper arthritis bracelets.

The woman behind the counter watched Sophie closely, her facial expression set to mistrust and disapproval. Perhaps it was because she wasn't used to lengthy browsing in the tiny pharmacy where people probably usually knew exactly what they wanted when they popped in on their way home from work or while dashing the kids off to school. Perhaps, in her designer black-knitted dress and Dolce and Gabbana shoes, Sophie might look the type to try and run off with a bottle of nail varnish worth fifty-nine pence. Most likely, though, Sophie concluded, it was because the woman knew that Sophie had not come in to buy varnish, or a box of clear plasters, or an emery board or a hair net or indeed any of the other miscellaneous items that she was clutching in her hands, but the pregnancy-test kit that she kept looking at sitting on the shelf but which she hadn't yet had the courage to pick up.

It was foolish, Sophie knew, for a woman of her age and

in her circumstances to feel embarrassed about buying the item she needed. She was not some irresponsible teen or some good-time girl who'd end up on a morning chat show waiting for the results of a paternity test. She was a woman in her thirties and an engaged woman to boot, with a ring to prove it, even if she wasn't entirely sure how she'd left things with her fiancé. By almost anyone's standards in the modern world, she was probably perfectly entitled to be buying a pregnancy test without anyone judging her.

The trouble was that Sophie judged herself. If her mother was right about her condition she hadn't noticed any difference in herself for over two months. She was on the brink of motherhood and had taken about as much care over its approach as a lemming careering over a cliff – and what kind of mother would that make her? Once when the girls had first come into her life she had bemoaned to Iris her lack of any kind of maternal feeling, not to mention a total absence of the womanly instinct that people, mostly other women, harped on about incessantly, hinting that the female of the human species was ever so slightly psychic when it came to their offspring. Iris had told her that she had just as much maternal instinct as the next woman and that all she had to do was listen. Yet, for possibly two months, she had been potentially pregnant, and there had been nothing. Not the merest flicker in her subconscious to alert her to what would be the most pivotal life-changing moment in her existence on planet earth. And if she hadn't noticed something that profound, which directly involved her own body, then that didn't bode awfully well for the future. As she stood opposite the corn plasters and appeared to examine a value-pack of anti-nailbiting solution, Sophie was picturing babies left on buses, toddlers begging for breakfast at midday and five-year-olds reminding her it was a school day. She would be a terrible mother, the worst kind of mother on earth – what did she know about being a mother?

At that second her phone burst into life in her pocket, causing her to scatter her eclectic collection of items on the tiled floor and the woman behind the counter to sigh and fold her arms under her breasts, looking bleakly at her watch and then at the plastic clock on the pharmacy wall just in case her own timepiece had lied to her.

'Sorry,' Sophie mouthed to the woman behind the counter as she fished her phone out of her bag and saw Louis's name on the display. The sight of his name set her heart racing, but she was prepared for it to be anyone on the phone but him, including Bella or Wendy.

'Hello?' she answered, inwardly cursing the question mark in her greeting that could be considered either as reluctance to talk to him or that in the space of barely a week she had genuinely forgotten who he was.

'It's me,' Louis said. Sophie tensed; his voice sounded flat, distant, even as it nestled in her ear.

'I know,' Sophie told him, scrabbling about on the pharmacy floor, trying to make some amends for the chaos and disruption she was causing to what otherwise had been a blissfully uneventful afternoon for the woman.

'It is OK for me to call you, isn't it?' Louis asked her, edgily. 'Only you said you'd call and you haven't.'

'I have called,' Sophie said, despairing of the chill in her voice. 'Wendy answered, I left a message for you to call me back but you didn't.'

Louis was silent for a long moment. 'You didn't try again, though,' he said, not leaving Sophie any the wiser as to whether or not Wendy had passed on the message.

'Neither did you,' Sophie said. She wanted to talk to him about her call from Bella, about them taking the phone and almost sneaking out of the school gates but she knew that would be the worst possible thing she could bring up now. He had called her at last and she didn't want to overwhelm this fragile contact with a rush of information. Sophie paused, turning her back on the woman behind the counter only to find her face distorted by a convex mirror mounted high in one corner watching her all the same. She closed her eyes for a second and concentrated only on Louis.

'I'm really glad to hear the sound of your voice,' she said softly, desperate to draw them a little closer together, even over so many miles. 'I've missed you.'

'Have you?' Louis sounded uncertain, defensive, but perhaps just a fraction warmer. 'It's just that I wasn't sure if you'd walked out on me and the girls or not.'

'I would never do that,' Sophie promised him.

'So you've just walked out of marrying me?' Louis asked her tightly.

'Look, Louis—'

'Yes, I know – you need space. You don't need to explain anything to me, that's not why I'm ringing you. We've been looking for Seth all week but he's nowhere. One of his flat-mates says he met this girl who lives in London, in Tottenham, at a gig the other day, apparently he really liked her. He hasn't answered his phone all week or tried to contact Wendy – she says he can be a bit rash if he's upset about something. She's really worried, so we've got the address of this squat and we're coming up to see if he's there. We'll be leaving in an hour or so, hopefully the roads should be pretty clear so we'll make good time and get there for nine-ish. I thought I'd let you know in case we bumped into you.'

'Right,' Sophie said, fighting both the instant irritation that rose in her chest at the very mention of Wendy's name and the urge to point out that the chances of Louis 'bumping into' her anywhere in the capital city with a population of several million were slim to nil. But she didn't want to sound facetious and unreasonable.

'What about the girls?' she asked him.

'Well, Mrs Alexander's said she'll mind them. Hopefully, we'll get back by Sunday otherwise I'm not sure about school on Monday . . .' Louis trailed off.

'Look, Mum's house is sort of on the way to Tottenham,' Sophie said. 'Bring them to me. Mum would love to see them, I'd love to see them, they'd love to see the dogs. They can stay the night while you go and see Seth and then perhaps tomorrow I could take them to see their grandma, catch her up on the news.' Sophie, referring to Carrie's mother who lived in sheltered accommodation a short drive from her mother's house, wondered exactly what news she'd be catching Mrs Stiles up on. 'And if they miss one day of school it won't be the end of the world. If you and Wendy need to stay longer I'll take them back home.'

As Sophie said the last word of her sentence she felt a pull in her chest and pictured a sudden image of Louis's living room lit only by the electric fire. She felt homesick for a place where she didn't really fully belong yet. 'And perhaps we could have a few minutes to talk things over?'

Sophie eyed the pregnancy test selection on the shelf again. She wasn't exactly sure how Louis would take the news of yet another surprise child just at the moment and suddenly she felt very sad. If she was pregnant, if her body could possibly be playing host to a fledgling human life without having the common decency to drop her a line and let her know she was expecting company, then it should have been an occasion for joy, delight and wonder. A special time for both her and Louis. But as it was, the news would have to juggle with another new arrival, even if he was six foot two.

Louis seemed to have a surplus of children right now. And after what he'd said about not wanting any more children, she was sure that news of another one wouldn't give him any kind of joy at all.

'It's a long way to bring them for a couple of nights, but they would much rather be with you than with Mrs Alexander . . .' Louis said thoughtfully. 'Are you sure?'

'Of course I'm sure – and if you and . . . Wendy need a place to stay you could stay at my mum's too. Wendy could have the sofa – although she would have to share it with Scooby and he can get a bit frisky in the night. Mum said that last weekend he nearly knocked himself out humping his bean bag headlong into a brick wall!'

Louis did not laugh and, too late, Sophie realised that she had managed to sound flippant again.

'Thanks for the offer,' Louis told her. 'But I'm not sure what we're doing.'

Sophie swallowed her irritation at his use of 'we' without her being included in it.

'So I'll see you at Mum's, then?' Sophie asked him. 'Call me when you're nearly here.'

'Thanks, Sophie,' Louis said. He sounded as if the taste of her name on his tongue was unfamiliar.

'No problem, and Louis – I love you,' Sophie said. Seconds passed before she realised that Louis had already hung up.

'Right,' Sophie said, turning to look the shop assistant in the eye. 'This is ridiculous, I'm a grown woman. I do not need corn plasters or a hair net. I do not need any of these things.' She marched up to the counter and dumped the items she had collected on a display of cough sweets and, turning round, picked up the first kit that she could lay her hands on.

'I need a pregnancy-test kit,' she informed the woman with

all the confidence and self-assurance a person could muster, before she spoiled the effect just ever so slightly by adding, 'So there.'

Iris and Sophie stood outside the bathroom while they were waiting for the results of the test.

Iris had suggested Sophie bring the test out of the bathroom with her, but Sophie said that, pregnant or not, she had not yet reached a point in her life where she felt comfortable about walking around with a plastic stick that she had recently urinated on. Besides, knowing her mother's dogs, the odds were high that one of them would make off with it and bury it in the back garden at the first opportunity. The test, Sophie told her mother, could stay in the bathroom on the tiled window sill till they had the result and then it would go in the bin.

'All right, then,' Iris had said. 'Let's go downstairs and make tea while we wait.'

'No, I've only got to wait three minutes, less than that now. I'll have come back again by the time I get downstairs,' Sophie said, peering in through the crack she had left open in the bathroom door. She could see the test kit glinting innocuously in the autumn light. It just didn't look like it had the power to change your life completely, she thought. They should give them a look with more gravitas, perhaps a chrome trim and a red flashing light, something that said, 'Your life will never be the same again.' White plastic didn't seem to do it.

'Three minutes minimum,' Iris said. 'We could have tea and then come and look. Another five minutes won't make you any more or less pregnant.'

'No, Mum, I'm standing here, until the three minutes is up and then I'm going in.'

'I'll cover you,' Iris said, her smile fading when Sophie did not see the funny side. She crossed her arms and leaned against the textured wallpaper. Miss Pickles trotted up the stairs and eyed Iris for a moment before walking past, no doubt intending to catch a nap on Sophie's bed.

'I know,' Iris sighed, rolling her eyes as if she and the animal had just had a conversation.

There were several beats of silence, punctuated only by Miss Pickles throwing any unwanted items of Sophie's off the bed as she prepared for her sleep and then Iris piped up, 'Is it time now?'

Sophie glanced at her watch.

'Twenty more seconds,' she said, continuing to study the face. 'Ten.'

The two women watched each other, reflections of their pasts and their futures, and silently counted down the last ten seconds remaining between Sophie and her fate.

'This is it,' Sophie said and she pushed the bathroom door open.

'I'm not sure you should have out-of-date peppermint tea now that I know you definitely are pregnant,' Iris said, boiling the kettle, which was her stock response to most of life's up and downs. On the day her husband had died, Iris must have made a hundred cups of tea. Sophie remembered being sent out to the grocer's to get another box of eighty tea bags.

'I'll pop to the corner shop now and get some fresh ones,' Iris offered, picking up her purse.

'No, just give me a glass of water,' Sophie said. 'Don't go out, please.'

Iris put her bag down and filled a glass, setting it down in front of Sophie.

'Isn't it funny how things can change just like that,' Iris

said conversationally, snapping her fingers to illustrate her point.

'I'll say,' Sophie replied absently.

'Listen, sweetheart, I know it's a shock – but you know you love Louis and you're going to marry him. Perhaps a baby now is a little sooner than you might have planned, but I promise you, once you've had a chance to get used to the idea, it will be fantastic. It will be wonderful.'

'It's just so final,' Sophie said slowly. 'It's just so definite.'

'Yes, babies do tend to be quite definite.' Iris looked perplexed. 'What do you mean?'

'I mean that up until this point I still had choices. I could still have come back to London, got my old job back or one like it. I could still have flown off to New York and disrupted Jake's wedding. I could still have told Louis that I've had enough of him and his crazy ex and his secret son. In fact, up till this point I could have cut the last year out of my life at any time and never looked back, but I can't do any of that now. I definitely can't because I am that thing. The P word. Pregnant. That is me, I am it. Knocked up.'

'Yes, you are,' Iris said, sitting next to her. 'And I can see how it seems as if the world is suddenly closing in on you. But ask yourself – if you weren't pregnant, would you have really done any of those things? Would you have come back to London and worked in an office job that took over your life? Would you really have flown to America to break up the marriage of some man who I've never heard of, but who, I suspect, is the man you went to lunch with today? Would you really have left Louis because he's got an annoying ex or would you have helped him sort things out with Seth and stood by him because, even though it scares you to death, you love him? And most of all, Sophie, would you, could you, ever cut those little girls out of your life? Baby or no baby, I don't think you would have done any of that. Because that's not you, that's not my daughter who I'm so proud of.'

'Are you really proud of me?' Sophie asked her, surprised.

'Of course I am,' Iris told her, draping her arms around her daughter's shoulders. 'I didn't understand you, when you were working away all hours at McCarthy Hughes, never taking a breath to enjoy life, but I was always proud of you. And now, when I've seen how very brave you were taking on those girls and how much you fought for them. And how you risked everything to be happy ... I thought it would be impossible for me to be more proud of you, but here you are about to give me my first grandchild. Things couldn't get much better.'

Sophie nodded. 'I know,' she said. 'It's just that I'm pregnant. And it probably really hurts having a baby, and if I couldn't work out I was pregnant in the first place how in God's name am I going to deal with it when it arrives?'

'You did know you were pregnant, you just didn't know you knew,' Iris told her. 'You went off alcohol and caffeine, you put on a little weight. Your body was protecting your baby even if it took your brain a while to catch up with the signs. And it will be the same when the baby's here. You'll be amazed at what you know without knowing you knew it. You'll learn the rest and you'll cope and you will be brilliant at it. Look at how you coped when you took in Bella and Izzy. Look how much love you gave them and how they trusted and respected and loved you back and you'd had nothing to do with any children before then.' Iris kissed the top of Sophie's head. 'Look, darling, you won't be a perfect mother because there's no such thing. But you'll be a brilliant, loyal, loving, fun and fair mother, and do you know how I know that?'

Sophie shook her head. 'Is it because you've been on the dog tranquillisers again?'

'Because you already are, you already are a mother to those two little girls.'

Suddenly Sophie pictured Carrie with Bella in her arms, her lips pressed lightly to her firstborn's forehead, the look in her eyes one of shining contentment and joy. Sophie knew that whatever she had learned about love and trust from Carrie's daughters had been at her best friend's and Bella's and Izzy's expense. Precious stolen minutes, memories that the three of them would never be able to share together, snuffed out in a few minutes of arbitrary destruction. And as she thought about the tiny spark of life that had begun to burn inside her, she felt overwhelmed with all that Carrie and her children had lost.

'I'm not their mother,' she said. 'I never will be.'

'But you're the next best thing, and you love them every bit as much as you would – will – love your own. You think you were only ever meant for a normal, conventional life. That you don't know how to cope with complications. But I don't know anyone who could have taken on all of this the way you have. Only someone as strong as you could have done what you have. And if Carrie could be here now she'd thank you for giving them the love she can't give them any longer.'

Suddenly weary and indescribably sad, Sophie rested her head on the table and wept.

'That's it,' Iris said, rubbing her back the way she used to when Sophie was a very little girl. 'You let it out, you'll feel better for it, wait and see. And I bet you that once you've told Louis, he'll be overjoyed.'

'I am very pleased to see you, Aunty Sophie!' Izzy said as she flung her arms around Sophie, who was attempting to fend off a small pack of overexcited dogs. Louis must have stopped at some point on the way to change them into their pyjamas.

Izzy was wearing her favourite all-in-pink fluffy pony pyjamas with feet, and Bella had on her dark red flannel pyjamas that she'd chosen herself, all bundled up underneath a red and green tartan dressing gown that somehow succeeded in giving her the air of a Victorian amateur detective rather than a seven-year-old girl.

'Come here, Bella,' Sophie said, kissing her a little haphazardly on the fringe as Scooby shouldered Bella to one side, hoping that it was him Sophie was inviting for a hug rather than the child. 'Oh, I've missed you two!'

'This is Wendy,' Bella said to Iris, pointing and screwing up her eyes as Scooby gave her an inquisitive lick on the cheek. Wendy was standing in the living-room doorway just behind Louis, peering over his shoulder as if she were using him as a human shield. Louis looked a little awkward lurking in the hallway; he had never been to Iris's house before. And he looked as if he didn't know what to do or where to stand. 'Wendy is Daddy's friend who he used to go to school with, they did do kissing once but not any more because now Daddy loves Sophie. Wendy has a grown-up boy who has run away, although he is grown up, so . . .' Bella shrugged as if to say 'what's the big deal?' 'Daddy has brought us to London because he is going to help Wendy look for Seth. So that is why we're here. And to see you, Aunty Sophie. Not to visit you, because you only visit people you don't see very often, but we are still going to see you very often, aren't we? Because you are only visiting your mummy, aren't you? And then you are coming back to St Ives to be with us.'

'Yes, I am,' Sophie said, looking up at Louis, hoping to catch his eye, but he seemed to be studying the floor. Taking a breath Sophie smiled, hugging both girls to her chest amid a forest of wagging tails. 'It's been years since I've seen you!'

'It's been about a week,' Bella informed her, smiling all the same. Sophie dragged her bundle of girls on to the sofa out of the worst attention of the dogs and cuddled them to her. Apart from her need to know exactly where she stood with Sophie, Bella seemed quite calm about their unscheduled trip and Sophie knew that was because she thought she understood what was going on. Since her mother's death and ensuing upheaval that had wrenched her and her sister out of the world they had felt secure in and thrown them head first into a whirlpool of chaos and confusion, she had become a habitual gatherer of information if she thought it might have the smallest relevance to her or Izzy's life. Sophie was ashamed to admit that she didn't really know what Bella used to be like before Carrie died but she knew now that Bella needed to know everything that was going on around her; she was not a little girl who either enjoyed or coped with surprises. Yet it was clear that Louis had still only seen fit to give her an edited version of the truth and that worried Sophie. Eventually, he would have to tell his daughters exactly who Seth was and Sophie knew that Bella would feel hurt and betrayed and she was afraid of how she would react. If she could only have a chance to talk to Louis, to tell him all her worries and fears, then perhaps she could make him see that his daughters were going through all of this upheaval just as much as he was. Once again they were caught up in the affairs of adults, tossed and turned like landed fish on a constantly tipping deck. The two girls were all-but-powerless to control what was happening around them. But until she could sort things out with Louis all Sophie could do was to be there for them, be the person that they could always count on, always, for ever, whatever. As she looked at Louis, he seemed further away from her in her mother's house than he had been when he was in Cornwall.

Sophie had no idea what would happen between them next,

but she knew one thing; whatever it was, she could not let the girls down. She would have to always be there for them, even if it was as a single mother. They needed her and there was nothing on earth that would cause her to let them down.

Iris left the room and quickly reappeared with a plate of pink-iced biscuits that immediately attracted the attention of all the dogs and both the children, so much so that she had to hold them above her head, rather like a more domestic version of the Statue of Liberty.

'Now, I know it's late, but I thought just this once it would be OK for you to have a biscuit and some hot chocolate before bed. Not you, Scooby.' The girls giggled as Scooby made an attempt to balance on his back legs to reach the biscuits and Iris smiled sweetly at Louis. 'That's OK, isn't it, Louis?'

'Of course, Iris.' Louis advanced into the room for the first time, stepping over dogs to reach Sophie's mother and plant a kiss on her cheek. Sophie tried not to notice that he had kissed her mother before he'd come anywhere near her, but his apparent disinterest in her stung as badly as if he'd slapped her in the face. She dipped her head, burying her face in Izzy's hair, and closed her eyes until the threat of tears had passed. 'Thanks so much for having them to stay. They'd much rather be here with Soph and you than anywhere else.'

'It's no trouble,' Iris said, smiling fondly at the girls. 'You know, I think of you as family, and you two lovelies are the best little girls I know – yes, you are!' Iris chucked Izzy under the chin as if she were one of her pet dogs, and in fairness she did bear a striking resemblance to them because as soon as the biscuits had appeared she'd climbed down from the sofa and stood perfectly still at Scooby's side, her head not quite level with his, as both pairs of eyes fixed firmly on the prize.

'Well, you come with me, then,' Iris said. 'And you, Bella.

We'll go in the kitchen and let Daddy and Sophie have a few words.' She looked at Wendy and sniffed.

'Come through and have some tea, Wendy,' she all but commanded. Sophie looked at Louis's companion. She looked tired, her face was drawn, and there were shadows under eyes. It seemed like she hadn't slept much and nor had Louis. His stubble had grown halfway to a beard and he looked a little lost, a little like he had the first time that Sophie had met him on the night he'd flown back from Peru after finding out that Carrie had been killed. He was waiting for her outside her flat because he was desperate to meet the children he hadn't seen in three years and to make amends. That night Sophie had mistaken him for a tramp. Tonight, though, no matter how dishevelled and tired he was, there was no doubt that he was the man she loved and suddenly she was exhausted by all the thinking and the striving to be certain. All she knew was that she loved him and she wanted to do whatever it took to make him happy so that the tired lost look that tightened his skin over his cheekbones disappeared. And if that meant waiting for him to resolve things with Wendy and Seth, then she would.

'We haven't got much time,' Wendy said, glancing at Louis as she followed Iris towards the kitchen. 'I really want to try and see him tonight.'

'Won't be long.' Louis smiled reassuringly at Wendy as Sophie herded the last of the dogs out behind the other woman, shutting the door behind her. Finally they were alone.

'I've missed you,' Sophie said, standing an awkward three feet away from him.

'Really?' Louis asked her. 'I wasn't sure if you would.'

'Yes.' Sophie smiled cautiously. 'I know I shouldn't have just rushed off like that, I was tired and Wendy really did make things difficult and well ... Louis, it turns out I was very hormonal.' She paused, desperate to ask him if he had missed her too, but terrified at what he might say.

'It's OK.' Louis shrugged, directing his attention to the mantlepiece above the fire where her mother kept an array of her school photos from a cute and pony-tailed five-year-old to an awkward and lumpy teenager. 'It's all right that you need some space to think about us. I didn't want you to go, but I've had a chance to think about it since and maybe it's the right thing.'

'The right thing?' Sophie felt a cool wash of fear sweep through her. 'What's the right thing?'

'That we take a breather, have some time apart. Put the engagement on hold.'

'On hold?' Sophie asked him.

'Yes,' Louis redirected his gaze to the ceiling, and then the toes of his boots, seemingly preferring to look anywhere but at her. 'It's like Wendy said, the timing's not great. I need to get things sorted with Seth, I need to work out what's happening there and get that on an even keel. So maybe it is best for you to move in with your mum while I'm doing that.'

'Out of the way,' Sophie confirmed, her tone nudging at anger.

'No, that's not what I mean.' Louis frowned. 'Look, it was you who packed a bag and left without a moment's notice. All I'm saying is that maybe it is a good idea after all.'

'Because Wendy says so?' Sophie was desperate to bring things back to the point where she felt that she could reach out and touch and kiss him and tell him about the baby, but the more she wanted that the more she seemed to say the very thing that would push him away.

'No, not because of Wendy, because of Seth, and because it's what you want.'

'And what you want too.' Sophie fought to contain the

tears that came so quickly these days. 'When you say put the engagement on hold . . . what do you mean?'

'I mean exactly that,' Louis told her. 'I'm a man, I mean what I say. There aren't any double or treble or hidden meanings with me.'

'And then?' Sophie asked him, bewildered by how quickly it had come to this between them.

'I don't know, you answer that one,' Louis told her. 'You're the one who left.'

Sophie struggled with the hundreds of things that she wanted to say but that somehow wouldn't form themselves into a sentence.

'I think you should go and find Seth,' she said instead, feeling somehow as if she was breaking an invisible bond for good. 'It's late.'

'OK.' Louis nodded. 'We'll probably be all night, so I'll ring you in the morning.'

'Fine.' Sophie bowed her head.

'Right, I'll get Wendy.'

As Louis went to stride past her Sophie reached out and grabbed his arm. It was the first time they had touched each other since he'd arrived. He stood and after a moment looked at her.

'Louis, I have to tell you something.' Sophie swallowed. She simply could not find the words to tell him she was pregnant. Not now, not when things were like this between them, and she was sure that the news would serve only to drive them further apart. 'I really think you should tell the girls who Seth is and why you are looking for him so hard.'

'I know you do,' Louis said.

'If Bella finds out another way she'll be so hurt and angry. I'm worried about how she'll react, especially after she took your phone . . .'

'She what?' Sophie realised belatedly that Louis probably still didn't know about that.

'She borrowed your phone to call me one day; they wanted to speak to me and they didn't understand why you wouldn't let them call me. Neither do I, for that matter. You know how much I love Bella and Izzy. No matter what happens between us, I will always be there for them.'

'They are my daughters, I know them. I know what's best for them.'

Sophie nodded, realising that he was in no mood to listen to her and let go of his arm. 'I hope you find him.'

'Me too,' Louis said, opening the door that unleashed a cacophony of canines into the room, excited all over again to find new people there. 'Me too.'

As Sophie lay in the middle of the double bed in the perfectly nicely appointed guest room where the girls were to sleep, she wondered vaguely why her mother had insisted on putting her in her old bedroom despite the fact that it was now used more as a kennel and a store cupboard and came complete with an extra layer of dog hair and no heating. It had to be habit, she supposed. Her mother couldn't imagine her sleeping anywhere else but in the room she had grown up in. Still she was glad that the girls had this nice cosy room to stay in which was relatively free from pet invasion unless you counted Tripod, who Iris let sleep in here, and he was really only three-quarters of a dog.

'So, then,' she said, finishing that night's story. 'Petal the Fairy Pony Princess got on the boat and sailed off into the sunset looking for the World of the Mermaids.'

'No, it's the *Land* of the Mermaids,' Bella, the principal author of the story, reminded her.

'Sorry, the Land of the Mermaids, and tomorrow we will follow her wonderful adventures in the Town Under the Sea.

Sophie looked down to where Izzy was already fast asleep in the crook of her arm, her thumb plugging her mouth, her long lashes sweeping the tops of her cheeks. Just to look at her, already so lost to her dreams, made Sophie feel very, very tired.

'Aunty Sophie,' Bella said, drawing Sophie's attention to her large, dark and very wide-awake eyes.

'Yes, darling?' Sophie stifled a yawn; she had the feeling she was quite a way off getting any sleep yet.

'Who is Seth really?' Bella asked her. 'Why is Daddy helping that Wendy woman, whom you don't like and neither do I?'

'I wouldn't say I don't like Wendy,' Sophie said cautiously. 'I don't really know her that well. It's just sometimes you meet someone and you don't really get on with them that well. I'm sure Wendy is a nice person really to . . . to some people.'

'But why is Daddy bringing us all up to London to find Seth if he's got nothing to do with us? He is a grown-up, he probably doesn't need finding.'

'Well, sometimes grown-ups need looking after too,' Sophie said, noting Bella's thoughtful expression with weary dismay. It meant that, unlike her sister, the child was not at all sleepy. She was in a questioning, getting-to-the-bottom-of-matters and solving-a-puzzle kind of mood. And that in turn meant that Sophie was either going to have to go against Louis and tell Bella the truth about Seth or lie to Bella and risk losing her trust for ever.

'But why is Daddy helping Wendy, because they weren't even friends before a week ago and you and Daddy were doing the wedding and now no one is talking about the wedding and Daddy is helping that Wendy woman and I don't understand why.'

Sophie closed her eyes; it was warm and cosy in the double bed, snuggled in between the two children. It would be so easy to simply drift off to sleep with her girls in her arms, but she had to find a way to answer Bella, otherwise she knew the little girl would be staring at the ceiling in the lamplight keeping herself awake with wondering.

'Well, you know my mummy,' Sophie began a little uncertainly.

'*Yes.*' Bella seemed equally sceptical about the direction the conversation was taking.

'She loves me and worries about me a lot, even though I am properly grown up. And Wendy is Seth's mum, and she worries about him, too, even though he's an adult, because mummies never stop worrying about their children, not ever. And poor Seth is feeling angry and worried and upset and Wendy hasn't really had a chance to talk to him, and see if he's OK. And sometimes when you're worried you need another person, a friend to help you get through it. I know Daddy and Wendy haven't been friends for a long time but really good friendships never fade away, they last for years and years even if you never see the person, because you know how much you care about them, come what may. Like your mummy was – is – still my best friend even though I'll never see her again, because I won't forget how much I love her.'

'So does Daddy love that Wendy woman?' Bella looked alarmed.

'No, no, he cares about her and that's why he's helping her,' Sophie hoped she was right about that. 'He's helping her to be kind.'

'And that's the only reason.' Bella scrutinised her, her dark eyes quizzical.

'Yes,' Sophie confirmed uncomfortably.

She watched the frown between Bella's brows relax as she turned her body towards Sophie and rested her head on Sophie's shoulder. Bella trusted whatever Sophie told her.

'Can you stay here and sleep with us tonight?' Bella asked. 'Like I sometimes used to sleep with you on the sofa in your flat and we'd listen to the sound of the traffic and pretend it was the sea, remember?'

'Yes, I remember,' Sophie said, feeling guilty that it was her half-truths that had soothed Bella at last. 'And yes, I'll sleep here with you two tonight. There's nowhere else I'd rather be.'

Chapter Sixteen

Sophie knew that it was the right thing to take Bella and Izzy to see their grandmother when they were up in London, but despite herself she had been glad to leave Mrs Stiles's flat, even though she suspected that this might be the last time. Mrs Stiles had diminished considerably since Sophie had last seen her, almost as if half of her was already gone, and it didn't help the overall atmosphere of finality that there was something so timeless about Mrs Stiles's home, as if you stepped out of life the moment you walked in through its door and the world only started turning again when you left.

Although the children loved their grandmother and were always delighted to see her, Sophie noticed them change whenever they were around her. Subtle differences: Izzy's natural ebullience ebbed away and the bright, curious spark that was always present in Bella's eyes dimmed. They instinctively adjusted their behaviour to fit in with the kind of woman she was, a woman who Carrie always said thought that enjoying life too much was a sin. Mrs Stiles was always very sweet with the girls, pouring them the ancient, lemon barley water she kept just for their visits and giving them boiled sweets from a paper bag with a twist in the top.

As Sophie watched her give each child two sweets she tried to reconcile this thin, fragile woman with her bold and beautiful daughter. Carrie had fought almost all of her life against the strict, emotionally repressive atmosphere her mother had brought her up in, determined that her daughters should have the childhood that she didn't, one full of laughter, fun and freedom. And so although it was Sophie's duty to bring the children to visit Mrs Stiles as often as possible, there was something about the volume of the ticking clock in the silent living room and the dustless china figurines that paraded along the mantelpiece, Victorian dancing ladies swirling to music only they could hear, that made her think of Carrie and long to be free.

To the delight of the children Mrs Stiles brought out her tin of vintage buttons that she had been collecting since she was a girl and put it out on the table for the girls to play with, where they would make pictures, or host button balls picking out the finest and glitteriest buttons to name as princes and princesses.

'And how is he?' Mrs Stiles asked her as they watched the girls from the small kitchenette. She was referring to Louis.

'He's well, thank you,' Sophie said. It was all she ever said. Carrie's mother had always disapproved of Louis, even before he found out about Carrie's affair and ran away to Peru. But after that point she'd had him down as a weakling and a coward and barely bothered curtailing her thoughts for the sake of the children. If she found out about Seth, about their engagement, or the baby, Sophie wasn't sure how she'd react. Carrie used to tell dark gothic tales of her mother losing her temper, shouting and screaming and locking her in her room for hours on end, but Sophie never was sure how much of that was Carrie's love of a good tale and how much was based on fact.

'Are you and he still . . . ?' Mrs Stiles never liked to refer to her relationship with Louis directly either.

Sophie nodded, suspecting that now was not the ideal time

to discuss their ups and downs, not that she'd dream of talking them over with Mrs Stiles anyway. She watched as Carrie's mother warmed the pot before pouring boiling water on to loose leaves, and compared her to Grace Tregowan. Mrs Stiles had to be at least fifteen or even twenty years younger than Grace, but Sophie could no more imagine Mrs Stiles having four husbands, and a good many lovers to boot, than she could imagine Mrs Tregowan ever bothering to warm a teapot when one-cup tea bags were so much quicker. Old age is not a great leveller, Sophie realised. It doesn't gently usher you into an age of peace and reflection when somehow your heart and mind is cocooned from the world, at least not unless you let it.

For Mrs Tregowan old age meant swearing and sex talk and living in the hopes of husband number five. For Mrs Stiles there was only quiet respectability, waiting out the last of her days under the radar without a hope of a final swan song, or any last rail against the fate that took her daughter from her before she ever really knew her.

'Still working, is he?' Mrs Stiles sniffed as she stirred the tea leaves around the pot.

Sophie nodded. 'Yes, the photography business is doing really well now.'

'He did well out of Carrie,' Mrs Stiles observed bitterly. 'Her death set him up nicely.'

'The girls got the security of a home and he got to establish a business that meant he'd be able to look after them. It's no more than Carrie would have wanted,' Sophie said, lowering her voice, keeping an eye on the girls in case they were listening. Fortunately, they both seemed entirely absorbed in the world of buttons. She watched Mrs Stiles's hand tremble as she poured a cup of pale and insipid-looking tea into a fine bone-china cup.

'And how are you?' Sophie asked her, forcibly brightening her voice as she took the cup and saucer. 'Are you keeping well?'

'I'll be gone soon,' Mrs Stiles said, looking into the living room where the girls were chattering, their heads bent together over the mosaic of buttons.

Almost since Sophie had known her Mrs Stiles had been declaring that she was about to die. Even when she and Carrie had been teenagers and it was clear that the woman was as fit as a horse she'd been citing her blood pressure or migraines or family history of heart attacks as grounds for her imminent demise. This time, thought Sophie as she watched her in the cold afternoon light that somehow fought its way through her heavy curtains, it was almost as if part of her had gone already, leaving a demi-ghost, so frail that she was almost transparent, and Sophie had the feeling that if you held her up to the light you'd be able to see your fingers through her flesh, just as you could through her old bone-china teacups.

'All I want to know is that those two are properly settled, properly cared for by someone I can trust not to disappear.' Mrs Stiles turned to look Sophie up and down and gestured at the ring that Sophie hadn't managed to bring up just yet. 'You marry him, you be a mother to them like Carrie would have been, like she was. And you promise me that even when that one comes along you will treat them exactly the same way that you do now, that you will never make them feel left out in the cold or alone.' Mrs Stiles nodded at Sophie's stomach, lowering her voice as she spoke.

'That one? You mean? Oh no, I'm not—' Sophie stopped, caught under Mrs Stiles's steady gaze. 'No one knows,' she whispered. 'No one.'

Mrs Stiles nodded. 'Well, it's not as if I'm going to tell anyone, so you've no worries there.'

'Thank you,' Sophie said briefly pressing the palm of her hand against her belly, an unconscious protective gesture.

'I've had lot of time to think since Carrie went,' Mrs Stiles went on, keeping her voice low, under the range of the girls' hearing. 'I wasn't a good mother, perhaps I was never supposed to be either a mother or a wife. I drove her father away because I was never content and after he'd gone I constantly tried to pin Carrie down, to trap her like a butterfly – but what for? I'm glad she fought against me and had the life she wanted, even if it was difficult and hard sometimes and I'm glad she gave those girls all the spirit and fire and imagination that she got from somewhere, though God knows it wasn't me. She's gone now and soon I will be and as far as I'm concerned you are the only person that those girls can rely on . . .'

'Mrs Stiles, really, Louis's not like that . . .'

'No, let me finish. I don't know what he's like or what he's not like and I don't want to know. But what I do know is that at the first sign of trouble he ran out on Carrie and the children. Perhaps she deserved it, but those girls didn't. And if he can do it once he can do it again. So you marry him, you have that' – Mrs Stiles nodded once more at Sophie's stomach – 'but you look after my grandchildren. Swear to me that you will always look after them.'

'I swear,' Sophie said, reaching out to touch Mrs Stiles's brittle shoulder. 'I swear to you, the same way I swore to them that they will always have me. Always, for ever, whatever.'

Mrs Stiles inclined her head. 'Thank you,' she said. 'That comforts me.'

Sophie placed her hand gently over her abdomen. 'How did you know about this?'

'Just being old,' Mrs Stiles said, treating Sophie to a rare smile. 'You get to my age and there's not much gets past you.

Besides, you've got that look about you, you look like a mother.'

Sophie pressed her lips together hard, determined not to cry now before the very person who would appreciate it the least. It was the only tribute she knew she could pay to this woman whom she hardly understood.

'Just you make sure he looks after you the way he never looked after my Carrie,' Mrs Stiles said, patting Sophie on the back of her hand, fully appreciative of her determination not to let her emotions show. 'Don't let him run out on you.'

At last, when it was time to go, Mrs Stiles delighted the girls by allowing them to take the ancient tin of buttons away with them.

'When I was your age I used to play with these for hours and hours with your great Aunty Evie, just like you and Bella do,' she told Izzy. 'And your mother used to play with them too when she was little,' she said as she solemnly gave the tin to Bella, whose expression was wide-eyed as she received the treasure. 'Some buttons in here belonged to my grandma, which makes them a hundred years old.'

'That's as old as God, nearly!' Izzy breathed in wonderment.

'Well, not quite, but anyway, you promise me that you will take care of them and that you will never lose them, and that when you see or find a very interesting or special button you will add it to the tin. And then one day you will be able to pass it on to your children.'

'I'm not having children, I'm having cats,' Izzy told her.

'We will look after them,' Bella told her grandmother, sensing the gravity of the situation a little better than her sister. 'Mostly I will.'

Mrs Stiles nodded and with some difficulty bent to kiss both girls, holding them close to her until they wriggled to be free.

'Goodbye, my beautiful girls,' she said with a finality that Sophie found uncomfortable.

'Goodbye, Grandma, see you next time,' Izzy said, hopping off towards the car.

'Goodbye, Grandma, thank you for the buttons . . .' Bella paused. 'I love you.'

'Sophie,' Mrs Stiles said as Bella raced off to join her sister, 'keep Carrie's memory alive for those two, won't you?'

'Always,' Sophie said. 'I'll see you in a month or so.'

'Perhaps,' Mrs Stiles said, kissing Sophie briefly on the cheek. 'Perhaps.'

As Sophie climbed into the car she looked at her phone; it was almost lunchtime and she still hadn't heard a thing from Louis. She wondered about calling him, but then decided against it. He said he'd call if he had anything to tell her. If she called him now then it would look like she was pestering him, like she didn't trust him to do as he said he would. It would be like she felt about him the same way that Mrs Stiles did, that she expected him to run away at the first sign of trouble, and Sophie did not believe that. So she had no choice, she just had to sit it out and wait for him to get in touch.

At least the afternoon held a better prospect for distraction and cheerful company while she waited.

Cal had invited them all out to lunch with the man he loved.

'This actually defines the term "out to lunch",' Sophie whispered as Cal, she and the girls were seated at a table that was strictly for four. 'This is actually what they were thinking of when they coined the phrase "You have gone mental".'

'I have not gone mental,' Cal hissed back, as the waiter unfolded his napkin and laid it over his lap. 'I said we'd be dining with Steven, not actually at the same table with him. I was round his a couple of days ago and he told me that his boyfriend, partner, whatever vile term he uses to describe the whore, was back from France for the weekend and that they'd be having lunch here in the place where they'd first met. Well, the thought of it makes me sick. If it wasn't for you I'd have run away to Cornwall again for the weekend to get away from the torment, but you blew that plan out of the water by still being here. And now I've gone and given into my natural instincts to stalk him, so if I am out to lunch then it's your fault. Fortunately, you and the girls make excellent cover. Hardly anybody goes stalking with a straight woman and a couple of kids.'

'What does stalking mean?' Izzy asked loudly as she stuffed another piece of bread and butter into her mouth.

The restaurant that Cal had chosen to stage his psychotic episode in was a very popular but exclusive vegetarian Far-East-inspired place on the outskirts of Islington. It was popular with writers, artists and actors and people who wanted to be writers, artists and actors, and Sophie got the distinct impression that little girls weren't usually expected for lunch, particularly not ones who were so dedicated to meat. The tablecloths were starched a brilliant white and there were a lot of very breakable cut-glass things on the table that were sure to get tiny pairs of hands into trouble. To give him his due their waiter had almost entirely hidden his alarm when he set eyes on the children and had been perfectly polite when he seated them, even though Izzy had managed to drag a table-cloth and half of the condiments off a table they were passing when the legs of her favourite stuffed toy cat got caught in its voluptuous folds. And he had been patience personified ever since, even though during the twenty minutes that they had been seated Bella had capsized a glass of cranberry juice, turning the tablecloth pink and Izzy had eaten her way through at least a loaf and a half of complimentary bread, which Sophie guessed would be the only thing she would be eating.

Then Sophie had asked him where Steven was going to sit and Cal had broken the news that Steven didn't actually know he was going to be here.

'Stalking means following a person around obsessively and inappropriately because you love them even though they don't love you,' Sophie said far too loudly for Cal's comfort.

'Does that mean I stalk Artemis, then?' Izzy asked. 'Because I love her and I'm always trying to get her to play with me, but she never will.'

'That's because she only likes me in the whole world, even more than Aunty Sophie and she's even her cat,' Bella said from behind the menu where she was searching for something she liked.

'Yes, I suppose you are stalking Artemis a bit,' Sophie smiled at Izzy, 'but because you are four and Artemis is a cat, that's OK. It's when you are a grown man and you know better that it becomes a problem.' She shot Cal a glance. 'So you decided that you'd just happen to be in the same place that he told you about on the day and time he's going to be here having a romantic reunion with the man he loves. He'll know it's not a coincidence, Cal. He'll know that you've become mental and that you are following him around like a love-sick puppy on day release from a secure psychiatric facility.'

'Is it all right to stalk puppies?' Izzy mused. 'I'd like a puppy.'

'Artemis wouldn't like a puppy,' Bella put in. 'She doesn't even like Tango.'

'Except I saw them do hugging,' Izzy said.

'Look, I know that I've become mental,' Cal told Sophie miserably. 'I know that I'm a pathetic freak of a man. But I love him, Sophie, and it hurts. So I just want to see them together. I just want to see what his lover's got that I haven't.'

'The power of rational thought, probably,' Sophie said. 'And I can tell you one thing, you'll have what he doesn't if you're not careful.'

'Go on,' Cal prompted her miserably.

'A restraining order,' Sophie said. 'Look, come on, it's not too late. He's not here yet and we haven't ordered anything more than bread and juice. If we sneak out now he'll never know you are a nutter and your dignity will remain intact.'

Oh!' Cal shielded his face with a menu and slid down in his seat. 'It's too late. Nobody look – they're here. All three females turned around and stared at the couple.

Of the two men one was a little taller than Cal, quite a few years older, in his mid forties with reddish brown hair that was thinning at his temples and a few freckles across the bridge of his nose. He was wearing brown corduroy trousers and an actual cardigan. The other man was around Cal's age, blond, tanned and clearly well built under the thin white cotton shirt he was wearing despite the chill in the air.

'Oh my God, he's an Adonis, I don't stand a chance,' Cal moaned as he peered over the menu's edge. 'Fuck.'

'You're not supposed to swear in front of us,' Bella reminded him.

'Besides, he's no Adonis,' Sophie scoffed. 'He's old and a bit bald. You beat him any day of the week.'

'No, idiot, the gingery baldy one is Steven! He's the one I love. That other one is his boyfriend. He's the one I hate.'

'You love . . . ?' Sophie was momentarily speechless. 'Oh my God, Cal – you love an old gingery bald bloke!'

'Love isn't all about looks, you know,' Cal told her.

'It's not, you know, Aunty Sophie,' Bella said. 'Look at Beauty and the Beast.'

'Or Tango and Artemis,' Izzy said, drawing a puzzled expression from everyone at the table.

'Artemis is beautiful and grey and Tango is ugly and fat and orange,' Izzy said. 'But they love each other. I told you, I saw them do hugging.'

'I expect it was fighting,' Sophie told Izzy. 'I know that sometimes it's hard to tell the difference, but I can promise you that Tango and Artemis don't love each other.'

She looked over at Steven's table and then leaned towards Cal. 'I'm sorry, but they look really, really happy.'

Cal sighed; it was true. The two men sat at a table in the corner, holding hands across the table, never taking their eyes off each other.

'They look like they've missed each other,' Sophie said sadly, suddenly yearning for Louis.

'It's a sham,' Cal said. 'There's no way that my Steven could ever really love that shallow, vain, superficial man. I bet he's even a sham vegetarian.'

Sophie looked at him. 'Are you a sham vegetarian too?' she asked.

Cal hung his head and nodded. 'I want him to love me,' he groaned softly.

'Oh Cal, if he was going to love you, he'd love you whether you ate dead animal or not.'

'Sophie,' Cal pleaded, 'what am I going to do? Somehow I've gone temporarily insane and brought you and two children to help me stalk the love of my life who is going to realise I'm here any second now and my life, my social standing, everything, will be finished for . . . Oh Steven, what a lovely surprise!'

Cal stood up and kissed Steven on either cheek. 'What are *you* doing here?'

'I'm having lunch with Brian,' Steven smiled, 'remember? I told you last week when you came over to play chess.'

'Chess?' Sophie attempted rather too late to stifle her astonishment.

'*Did* you?' Cal overacted, while doing his best to ignore Sophie. '*That* must be why I thought about coming here today! It must have lodged in my subconscious and when I realised that my dear country friend Sophie and her two lovely girls were going to be in town I thought what better place could there be to bring them.'

'Except that they don't do meat,' Izzy complained. 'Or even chicken nuggets.'

Steven beamed at Cal's three female companions and as Cal seemed to be frozen to the spot Sophie took the initiative and introduced herself.

'Hello, I'm Sophie.' She reached out and shook Steven's hand. He had a lovely smile, she thought, and a sensitive air about him that a girl (or boy) could definitely fall for. Sort of quiet but fascinating with rather striking hazel eyes. Yes, she could see how he might hold Cal's attention for the first time. 'This is Bella and this is Izzy.'

'You are a man who goes out with other men,' Bella informed Steven as if he might not know. 'That's perfectly OK, because sometimes men love men and women love women and it's all fine.'

'And I love chicken nuggets,' Izzy said looking mournfully at the menu she couldn't quite read.

'It truly is delightful to meet you,' Steven said. 'Cal told me a lot about you and your heroic journey to the coast to find love . . .'

'Oh did he now?' Sophie raised an eyebrow.

'Don't worry, he is full of admiration for you, as am I. It takes a lot of courage to go out and grab your happiness.'

'I know!' Cal jumped up picking up his glass of wine with him. 'Why don't all of us come and join all of you?' He beamed at Steven.

'Well, of course normally that would be lovely, Cal,' he said softly. 'It's just that I haven't seen Brian for over a month and we were sort of looking forward to some alone time.'

'Of course.' Cal sat down again, sloshing some of his wine on the tablecloth. 'Of course, you want to be alone. Silly me. I tell you what, we'll go find somewhere else to eat. Leave you in peace.'

'Don't be silly,' Steven said. 'There's no need for that.'

'Yes, there is,' Cal said. 'There's every need. I'm really sorry, Steven. Come on, girls, there's a McDonald's down the road.'

'Hooray!' Izzy cheered, knocking over a glass of orange juice.

'Um, waiter – can I pay for what we've had so far please?' Sophie asked as Cal marched out holding a child in either hand.

'I'm very sorry we disrupted your lunch,' Sophie told Steven as she handed over some cash to the waiter.

'Don't be, I'm just sorry that Cal felt so awkward,' Steven said, watching Cal waiting with the girls outside of the plate-glass window, tapping his foot impatiently. There was something unreadable in his eyes, something more than a passing interest that made Sophie take a chance.

'Look, I know it's none of my business at all, but Cal is a brilliant person and a fantastic friend.'

'I know,' Steven smiled, 'I've discovered that.'

'And so what if he's not really a vegetarian and he's never played chess in his life . . .'

'Hold on, the chess part I guessed – but he's not a vegetarian?'

'No, he just wants you to like him and he's never ever wanted anyone to like him before, you're the first. So please don't hold this against him. He's not normally a stalking, obsessed mentalist who turns up at restaurants just to get a glimpse of someone, it's because he's never been in love before and he's not sure how to handle it.'

'In love?' Steven's eyes widened and Sophie realised she'd said far too much.

'You mean to say you really thought we'd turned up here by coincidence and not because Cal's madly in love with you and just wanted to see what your partner looked like?' she asked him.

'I did, sort of,' Steven said, with a tiny smile. 'Perhaps I'm not as intuitive as I thought I was.'

'Oh dear,' Sophie said anxiously. 'Please, please never tell him I spilled the beans. Who knew that all men, whatever their sexual orientation, were idiots when it came to picking up signals?' Steven's smile broadened.

'Thank you, Sophie,' he said. 'I understand a lot now. Including him thinking that a haiku was a type of sushi . . .'

'Good, I hope. Just be kind to him. He deserves it. He's a sensitive soul.'

'Are you coming? We want meat,' Cal said extra loudly as he burst back in the doorway, clearly hoping to shock as many vegetarians as was possible. 'Loads and loads of bloody, dead, innocent animal meat!'

'Like I said,' Sophie said to Steven over her shoulder as she left, 'a sensitive soul.'

'I'm going to have to leave the country,' Cal said miserably over a quarter pounder with bacon and cheese. 'I'm going to have to change my name and go and live abroad somewhere where the culture accepts you even though you have the social skills of a particularly boorish plank of wood. Denmark, maybe.'

'No, you don't,' Sophie said. 'It's not that bad. Everybody at some point in their life has behaved inappropriately while trying to attract the attention of someone they can never hope to be with.'

'Oh thanks, thanks for cheering me up. There's nothing like a shot of optimism when you're feeling down.' Cal pushed his burger to one side and Izzy picked it up.

'You need to eat, Cal,' Sophie said, nodding at Izzy who reluctantly put it down again. 'You can't control your life through food.'

'No, but I can control my waistline,' Cal said. 'You want to take a tip from me in that department.'

'Listen, I'll have you know that I'm—' Sophie remembered just in time that there were two other sets of ears present, even if they were momentarily distracted by chips. 'A very healthy weight for my height.'

'Yes, if your height included the four inches on your heels,' Cal retorted, but without his usual bite. 'I'm going to have to move at the very least. I'm going to have to go south of the river. I can never look Steven in the face after this, or anyone else.'

'I've got a feeling you will be able to,' Sophie said, a little smugly.

'Why – what did you say to him? Sophie Mills, if you told him that I love him then I swear I will kill you right now and hang the consequences.'

Izzy and Bella paused mid-nuggets, their eyes wide with alarm.

'Only joking, sweeties,' Cal told them, but his glare told Sophie otherwise.

'I didn't say anything of the sort,' Sophie lied. 'It's just that he seemed to me like the kind of man who wouldn't disown you just because you behaved well within the normal realms of psychosis in terms of unrequited love. He likes you, I could see it in his face when he was looking at you. You make him smile, even when you're acting like a total idiot. And if he still likes you after all of that then it means that he likes *you*, the actual you – not the chess-playing, Russian-literature-loving, vegetarian you. The trouble is, Cal, that you haven't done this before. You don't know what it's like to be in love. You don't know that it's horrible, miserable, painful, depressing, debilitating and destructive.'

This time Bella and Izzy were staring at her.

'Only joking,' Sophie said with a smile. 'Look, all you can do is go on as normal, hold your head up high and act as if nothing's happened and just wait and see what happens.'

'I'll be the laughing stock of the world, that's what will happen.' Cal groaned.

'You never know, just supposing Steven didn't realise that you liked him that way and now he does. You never know how that might change things.'

'Sweetheart, the only thing it's going to change is my social status. From "it" boy to pariah in one easy step. I might as well come back to Cornwall with you, my life is over anyway.'

It was almost getting dark when Sophie finally got the girls back to her mother's and she still hadn't had any word from Louis. Louis had been out of contact for nearly twenty-four hours and most of that overnight. She had no idea what had happened to him, if he'd found Seth, or even if he was OK. For the first time since she'd known him she found herself worrying that he was dead in a ditch somewhere, but at least the worrying masked the hurt, the pain that it caused her to realise that he could so easily shut her out of his life. That hours and days could go by without him needing to talk to her or be near her, especially when she longed to spend every waking moment with him.

Taking her phone out of her bag, Sophie looked at it, willing it to ring. She knew she shouldn't phone him, she knew she should leave it to him to get in contact with her. That she should play it cool, give him his space and let him work things out, but when it came down to it she couldn't wait any longer. After all, she loved him and she was having his baby. If that didn't give her the right to call him whenever she wanted, even if he didn't want to hear from her, then she didn't know what did.

The phone rang for a long time and Sophie was on the verge of hanging up when Louis finally answered.

'Hi,' he said, sounding tired and emptied of emotion.

'Are you OK? What's happening? Where *are* you?' The rush of questions poured out of her before she had a chance to stem them.

'I'm . . .' Louis paused, probably while he looked around. 'I'm in a café in Tottenham. I've been here for hours, just waiting.'

'Waiting? What for? Did you find Seth?'

'Yes, we tracked him down late last night.' Louis wasn't forthcoming with any more detail than that and Sophie realised that was why she should have waited for him to contact her, she should have waited till he was ready to talk because right now he seemed too tired or upset to want to say anything. Yet still she couldn't let it go, she had to know.

'So, what happened? Did you sort anything out?' There was a long silence on the other end of the line and for a while Sophie thought that Louis had hung up.

'Are you still there?' she asked.

'Yes.' Louis sighed. 'It was pretty bad. Seth was drunk when we found him and on something. He was very agitated. He got angry with Wendy for springing this – me – on him. He kept asking her what she was playing at, what she wanted this time . . . I don't really know what he meant by that . . .' Louis paused as he collected his thoughts. 'And he's angry with me for existing, for even trying to be part of his life. There was a lot of shouting and then he . . . well, he tried to punch me. The last thing I wanted was a fist fight with my own kid so I left Wendy to try and talk to him, calm him down. I told her I'd wait for her to call me and I've been hanging around in Tottenham all day, but I haven't heard. I'm knackered, Soph, and I miss you and the girls.'

Sophie caught her breath. It was the first time he had said anything to indicate that he'd thought about her at all since she'd left St Ives. She clung on to the throwaway sentence like a life raft.

'Well, then, get on a bus or in a cab and come over here,' Sophie pleaded with him. 'It's barely half an hour away and if Wendy calls and she needs you, you can be back there in no time.' Louis was silent. 'Please, Louis, come back here, have a hot bath and some food and a hug from your girls, because it sounds as if you need it.'

'Can I include you in that description?' he asked her. 'Are you one of my girls still?'

Sophie paused as she struggled to marshal the sob that suddenly constricted her throat.

'Of course I am. Of course I'm your girl. I miss you. Come over here and let me hold you, please.'

'I'm on my way,' Louis told her.

Sophie had to wait for several minutes while Louis was overwhelmed by a pile of happy girls and welcoming dogs all keen to get a piece of him – quite literally, in some of the dogs' cases.

'Daddy, we missed you!' Izzy cried. 'I'm glad you're back even though you smell funny. Where have you been?'

'Did you find him?' Bella asked. 'Did you find Seth? Is he OK?'

'Yes, we found him and he's OK,' Louis said as Sophie

318

dragged Scooby off him and then ushered him plus a few other dogs out into the hallway.

'So can we go home, then?' Bella asked. 'Because it's fun in London but I don't want to miss school; we are doing the past – I like the past, especially the Romans.'

'Um . . .' Louis looked at Sophie.

'I'll take you back home tomorrow, OK girls?' she said. 'I think Daddy might need to stay and help Wendy for a bit longer.'

'Ohhh,' Bella moaned. 'Daddy, I wish you would hurry up and stop helping that Wendy woman – we're never going to get married in time if you don't *focus*.'

'I know, I know, darling, I'm sorry.' Louis hugged her. 'That's what I want more than anything too.' He looked at Sophie over the tops of the girls' heads, his eyes asking a silent question.

Sophie sat down next to him and found his hand in amongst the tangle of children.

'It's what we all want,' she said, feeling the tears of relief sting her eyes as he squeezed her fingers in return.

It seemed to take an age to get the girls to bed and settled. There had to be the Petal the Fairy Pony Princess and her Adventures in the Land of the Mermaids story from Sophie, then another story from Louis, then a brief discussion as to why adults didn't go to bed at the same time as children and then a certain amount of toing and froing concerning glasses of water, lights to be left on and the exact gap that the bedroom door should be left ajar.

Finally, when they were settled at last, Sophie and Louis waited downstairs sitting on opposite armchairs as Iris did her make-up in the mirror of the mantelpiece.

'Sorry,' she said to both of them through lips stiffened to

receive a second coat of red lipstick. 'It's just that the light in the bathroom is terrible and I want to look nice for Trevor.' She spun round. 'Will I do?'

'You look great, Mum,' Sophie said, having to concede that, despite what she considered to be a rather inappropriate shade of red lipstick for a woman of a certain age (a category she included herself in), Iris did look good. Trevor had certainly set her glowing.

'I don't normally go to his place,' Iris said, checking herself once more. 'It feels like a bit of a dirty weekend.'

'Oh Mother,' Sophie buried her head in her hands, 'no details remember?'

'That's not a detail, that's an observation,' Iris told her. 'Are you sure you don't mind me going out?'

'We're sure,' Louis and Sophie said together, catching each other's eyes and smiling as they spoke.

'It's nice to know when you're wanted.' Iris smiled at them, turning to Louis. 'And I am very, very glad to see you here, young man. Don't go dashing off now for a bit till you and Sophie have talked properly. You've got a lot to talk about. A lot of very important things—'

'Goodbye, Mum,' Sophie said firmly.

'Right, yes, well, goodbye. And good luck.'

Once Iris was gone they sat for a few moments just looking at each other.

'Are you OK?' Sophie asked him eventually, and he nodded.

'I'm a bit shell-shocked, I suppose. I don't know what I expected when I found out about Seth. So much has happened so quickly that I still haven't really had time to think about it, about what it means. Maybe I expected some big reunion and some sort of father-and-son bonding. Perhaps I thought I'd take him down the pub and we'd have a few beers and get to know each other. But I didn't expect him to hate me, simply

320

for existing. And I didn't expect that my turning up would send him off the rails quite so spectacularly.'

'Don't forget you don't know him, you don't really know Wendy any more,' Sophie said softly, tentatively. 'I haven't had much to do with Seth but from what I can tell I think he's had a pretty hard time of it; he seems fragile and unsure of how to be. Yes, he's a great big hulking man, but he's still very young,' Sophie said. 'Did you know who you were or what you wanted when you were twenty? It's a lot for him to deal with, a father figure in his life just when he's working out what it means to be a man.'

'You know what, you're probably right.' Louis looked at his hand for a moment. 'I don't know why I haven't talked this through with you more – I've cut you out of everything that's been happening, and I don't really understand why. Maybe it's because I can't get used to having someone who will always be on my side. But I do know that it was stupid of me. I need you.' Louis's eyes met hers. 'Please, can I come over there? I really want to hold you.'

'Please,' Sophie said, holding out her arms and then she was in exactly the place she wanted to be – in his arms, inhaling his smells, listening to the sound of his heartbeat slowing and relaxing.

'This has been the most stupid, awful week of my life,' Louis whispered into her hair. 'Remind me to never, ever let you go again. Nothing is right when you aren't around. I can't think, I can't do anything without you. I don't want to do anything without you, ever again.'

He bent his head, searching out Sophie's mouth and kissing her as she curled her arms around his neck, pressing her body into his, sighing as she felt the heat rise in her veins. And then she remembered she had something really quite important to tell him.

'God, Sophie, I love you,' Louis told her, his hands finding their way under her top as he ran them down her back, reaching for her bra strap.

'Hang on,' Sophie said, pushing him away from her a few millimetres with the palm of her hand.

'Am I going too fast?' Louis asked her, his finger stroking her back. 'I'm sorry, I just want you so much. And we're together, alone . . . on a sofa. It seems like old times.'

'No, it's not that, I want you too, but there are things that we still haven't talked about, things I need to say . . .'

'Everything you've said to me since this happened is right.' Louis sat back, pushing the hair out of his eyes. 'I'm so sorry if I've let this business with Seth get in the way of us and getting married. I've been talking utter rubbish and Bella's right, I need to focus. I don't want a break from you, I need you. You're the person who can help me get through this and, more than that you're the person I long to be with. I just need you, babe. I just need you.'

'I know.' Sophie smiled. 'I don't need a break from you either. If anything, I need you now more than I ever have. I love you. I want to marry you. So who cares if we don't know what the future holds? It doesn't matter because I can't wait to be married to you and living with you and the girls.'

'You don't how happy that makes me,' Louis whispered, brushing back a strand of hair from her face.

'I'm glad,' Sophie said. 'Because, Louis, there's something else I need to tell you . . .' She paused. Now was the moment, now was the time for her news and she wanted to make sure she chose exactly the right words to convey it.

'I know what you're going to say and I think you're right,' Louis said, stopping Sophie in her tracks.

'Really?' she asked him, catching her breath. 'What about?'

'About telling the girls the whole truth about Seth. I need

to talk to them. I need to explain that he's not just some random boy I'm helping. I need to tell them that I'm his father and he's their half-brother.'

There was an audible gasp from the other side of the living-room door and the sound of glass smashing on the hall tiles.

'Oh no,' Sophie whispered as the living-room door slammed open, sending Scooby scrambling to his feet and racing up the stairs.

'You LIAR!' Bella shouted at the top of her voice, broken glass around her bare feet, her face red with rage, her eyes molten with fury and betrayal. 'You liar, you liar, you liar – you said Seth was just a lost grown-up boy. You liar!'

'Bella, darling, don't move,' Sophie said, but it was too late, Bella ran into the room across the glass without seeming to feel anything. Louis jumped to his feet and tried to catch her, but she flew at him, beating him with her balled fists, causing them both to sink to the floor.

'Why didn't you tell us, why?' she howled as she attacked him. 'Are you going to leave us again? Are you going to live with that Wendy woman and Seth now? Are you going to leave us again, like you did before?'

Bella screamed and kicked and hit out as Louis tried to restrain her. Seeing that the soles of her feet were bleeding, Sophie knelt down trying to reach out to soothe Bella, whose blows caught her arms and chest.

'Come on, now,' Sophie said softly. 'Come on, baby, calm down. Come to me and let me look at your little feet. I think you may have cut them.'

Her fury burning out as suddenly as it had flared, Bella turned to Sophie, flinging her arms around her neck and sobbing, her expression as she watched Louis one of pure hurt and disbelief. Carefully, Sophie lifted her off the floor and carried her over to the sofa. It had been a long time since she had seen Bella like this, it had been months ago, when she was first readjusting to having her father back in her life. Sophie and Louis had taken them to London Zoo and Bella had gone mad at Izzy because she'd naïvely looked forward to their daddy taking care of them now that their mummy had gone. Bella's hurt and fury had shocked Sophie then; it had been a terrifying glimpse of how the little girl was really handling her grief and the upheaval. In the intervening months Sophie had hoped that Bella now felt safe and secure, certain in the knowledge that she was cared for and loved. She knew how obsessed the seven-year-old was with knowing all the facts and she understood why. But even she was stunned at how insecure and precarious Bella still must feel. At how much pain and fear she had been hiding all this time. The poor child still wasn't certain that her world was a safe place to be, and perhaps after her losing her mother so suddenly, she never would be.

Slowly, as Sophie stroked her back, Bella stopped trembling, her breathing evening out into regular sobs. Sophie met Louis's eyes over Bella's head as he knelt on the floor looking at his daughter in despair.

'I knew it, I knew it.' She turned from Louis and wept into Sophie's hair. 'I knew he was going to go again, I knew he'd leave us again.'

'I'm not, Bellarina, I'm not leaving you – I'd never leave you.'

'You did before,' Bella said accusingly, half turning her head to look at him. 'And now you're going again and I don't want you to. It's not fair, Daddy!'

'No, no, sweetheart – it's not that way. I'm not leaving. I'm going to marry Sophie and we're all going to live together for ever.'

'Don't lie,' Bella shrieked at him, the lull in her rage over abruptly. 'I don't care. I don't want you. And Izzy doesn't want you. You . . . you didn't care that we were on our own in places we didn't like for weeks till Aunty Sophie found us, and you didn't care that you left us with Mummy, and you didn't care that Mummy was dead and there was no one . . . and you're a liar and I don't want you. I want . . . I want my *mummy*. I want my mummy back.'

'Oh, darling,' Sophie whispered into her hair, rocking her against her shoulder. 'Poor, poor baby.'

'I want to go home,' Bella sobbed, the words broken up on each ragged breath. 'Please take me home.'

'Of course I will. First thing in the morning we'll go straight back home.'

'Bella, listen,' Louis tried again. 'Let me explain.'

Bella burrowed even deeper into Sophie's body as he gingerly sat down next to her. 'I didn't know anything about Seth. I didn't know I had another child, a grown-up son till just a little while ago. The only reason I didn't tell you about him was because I was finding out about him myself. Not because I wanted to leave you or live with him or anything like that. I love you and Izzy and Sophie. I'm never going to leave you.'

Bella was unresponsive, her face hidden in Sophie's hair. Sophie looked at Louis and shook her head, signalling that he should wait before he said anything else. Louis nodded and sat back on the sofa, pale with shock.

'Come on, my baby,' Sophie said, lifting Bella slowly up in her arms, a little unsteady under her weight. 'I'll take you back up to bed and we'll find some plasters for those feet. You need to sleep, and in the morning I'll drive you all home, OK?'

Before Bella could respond, Louis's phone rang. Woman and child watched as he checked the name, hesitating for a fraction of a second before answering.

'Hi, you OK?' he asked. 'Yep, Yep, OK.'

He put down the phone and looked at Sophie. 'I have to stay on in London a bit longer.'

'I knew it,' Bella sobbed. 'You like that Seth and that Wendy woman now. You're leaving us again.'

'No, no, darling. I've just got to stay for one more day . . .'

'Stay for ever!' Bella told him, weary with anger. 'I don't care. I don't want you. I hate you.'

'Just wait,' Sophie said to Louis. Carefully, she walked over the broken glass and carried Bella to the bedroom where Izzy was still blissfully asleep, her mouth a perfect round 'o' where her thumb had been. She laid Bella gently down on the bed and went to the bathroom to search out antiseptic spray and plasters.

'It's not too bad,' she said as she gently examined Bella's feet. 'No glass, just a few little cuts. These plasters can come off in the morning.'

'Want to keep them on,' Bella grumbled as Sophie tucked her back into bed.

'OK, then, keep them on,' Sophie said, smoothing the child's hair back from her face so that she could plant a kiss on her seldom-seen forehead.

'Bella – you trust me, don't you?'

Bella nodded.

'I promise you Daddy isn't going to leave you,' she told Bella. 'He didn't mean to keep the truth about Seth from you. He thought he was protecting you and Izzy till you were ready to find out about Seth. Perhaps he was wrong but I know one thing. He loves you and your sister with all of his heart. And the biggest regret – the thing that makes him saddest in all the world – is that he ever left you before. I know now that he would never ever leave you or Izzy or me again. I promise you.'

'Do you?' Bella asked her, her lids swollen and heavy. 'Do you promise, because you promised never to leave us – but you did. You came here.'

'I know,' Sophie said, her heart aching. 'I shouldn't have done that, I was wrong. But I do promise you that I will never leave you again and neither will Daddy.'

'Because you said always, for ever, whatever and that's the rule, isn't it? You can't leave us now you've said that, can you?'

'No,' Sophie said. 'And I never will, come what may.'

'Want to go asleep,' Bella mumbled, tears still wet on her cheeks as she drifted into unconsciousness, with the sudden release that only a child can have.

Sophie took a deep breath as she walked back down the stairs preparing what to say to Louis, how to help him deal with what had just happened and work out what to say to Bella. It meant that she'd have to wait at least another day before telling him she was pregnant, but as long as she could get things between him and Bella on an even keel again that didn't matter. She stepped over the broken glass and pushed the living-room door open and her heart sank.

Louis had made a liar out of both of them.

He'd gone.

Chapter Seventeen

It was just after four on Sunday afternoon when they finally drove into St Ives and Sophie decided they should head to Ye Olde Tea Shoppe before they did anything else. As taking up smoking again was definitely not an option and gin was off the table even if she could stomach it, she decided that a cream tea for two all to herself was the only option.

She hadn't seen the point in waiting in London for Louis to get in touch. For one thing, she'd tried his mobile phone the moment that she'd realised he'd gone and found it ringing behind a cushion on the sofa. And he hadn't called her since he'd left without saying goodbye.

It had still been dark when she packed up the car that morning, the chill in the air seeping through her coat and sweater. As she slammed the door of the car shut she stood perfectly still for a second, watching the rising sun streak the dirty sky with gold over the chimney tops, and tried to work out exactly what had happened last night.

Everything had been going so well, everything had been almost perfect, and then suddenly her plan to tell him about the baby, Bella's whole life, and even the image of Louis that she thought she knew so well, had shattered all around her just like the glass smashed on her mother's hall tiles. What she couldn't understand was that Louis hadn't even stayed to see that Bella had gone to sleep, to check that her feet weren't too badly cut, to tell her where he was going and when he'd be back. He'd just left, without his phone, and Sophie had no idea why.

Suddenly afraid, she had sat down in the chair and wept. She was frightened for Bella and Izzy, scared of the loss that was still damaging them and that she barely understood. And she was fearful for herself and her baby, the tiny life inside her that had to be constantly battered by the torrents of emotions that had racked her body recently. But the thought that made her most afraid was that Mrs Stiles was right about Louis: he would run away from trouble when the going got hard just like he had when he had found out about Carrie's affair. Sophie thought back to the night he had described how he'd felt and why he'd left, the night they'd first slept together. He'd seemed so genuine, so plausible – a vulnerable man who had made a mistake and bitterly regretted it. But what if he'd said what he knew she had to hear in order to get her into bed? What if he'd just run out on Bella because he couldn't cope, given up on Carrie because he didn't have the guts to fight for her? Sophie shook her head, that wasn't her Louis – that wasn't the man she loved, the man she knew – it couldn't be. She was tired and upset and hormonal and Mrs Stiles's warning was echoing around her head like a siren, tempting sailors on to dangerous shores.

Sophie had picked up Louis's phone, her thumb hovering over the key pad as she contemplated reading his texts and checking his messages, perhaps trying to find out something that might tell her where he was, and then, before she knew what she had done, she'd thrown it hard against the wrought-iron fireplace, smashing its fragile plastic casing to pieces.

And on that cold morning Sophie realised that, for the first time since she'd met Louis, she was angry with him. Her blood was boiling, her heart was pumping, her teeth were grindingly furious with him, and she knew that if he turned up on the street at that moment she would happily punch his lights out.

Even so, on the drive back down to Cornwall she had kept her phone by her side, and her hands-free plugged in, convinced that he would find a way to call her eventually, full of apologies for dashing off with news of a genuine emergency, and wondering what had happened to the phone he'd so stupidly left behind. But as the journey wore on and the girls' enthusiasm and collection of songs wore out, Sophie's phone remained silent. She kept glancing at it furiously, willing it to make a noise, but still it didn't ring and that made her angrier still.

She was too old, and too pregnant, to be waiting for her boyfriend to call her at this stage in her life. Now was the very time that she should be feeling secure and happy, not wondering if she even still had a relationship. But the fact was that Louis was gone and he'd left her to pick up the pieces of his daughters again.

'When is Daddy coming home?' Izzy asked, just as they hit Devon. It was a question that Sophie had endeavoured to answer several times on her journey down, but her trite answers of 'Soon, sweetie' and 'Before you know it' had not satisfied the four-year-old and succeeded only in drawing sighs from Bella.

'He'll be back when he's finished helping Wendy with Seth,' Sophie told her, hesitantly. It was the grain of truth that Bella had been waiting to pounce on.

'Because Daddy is Seth's daddy and Seth is our half-brother,' Bella informed her little sister without ceremony. Sophie had tried to persuade Bella not to tell Izzy about Seth until after they got back, but even as she had asked her, she knew it was unfair to ask a child for such restraint and she counted herself lucky that they'd made it this far before Bella blew the story wide open.

In the driver's seat Sophie braced herself for Izzy's reaction.

'Oh,' Izzy said, thinking for a moment. 'But isn't Seth a grown-up man? And Daddy's a grown-up man, so he can't be Seth's daddy – that's just silly! Grown-up men can't be grown-up men's daddies!' The idea seemed to tickle Izzy, making her giggle. It wasn't quite the reaction Sophie had been expecting.

'That Wendy woman is Seth's mummy,' Bella went on, determined to make her sister understand. 'Daddy and that Wendy woman used to do kissing when they were young. So even though Seth is a grown-up man he is still Daddy's son and our half-brother.'

'How can he be half a brother?' Izzy quizzed her, her giggling rubbing Bella up exactly the wrong way. 'Hasn't he got any arms or legs!' She doubled over in her car seat with laughter, finding herself utterly hilarious.

'He's our half-brother because he's only . . .' Bella trailed off at a loss as to how to explain. Sophie decided it was time that she stepped in.

'Half-brother means you have the same mummy or daddy. You and Bella have the same daddy as Seth, but there are two different mummies. Your mummy and Seth's mummy, who is that Wendy woman,' Sophie explained, using Bella's phrase for her without thinking and gaining some small satisfaction from it.

'So we really have half a brother, then?' Izzy asked, perplexed.

'Yes, and that's where Daddy is,' Bella added darkly. 'With him.'

'And when is he coming back?' Izzy enquired, her voice suddenly trembling.

'We don't know.' Bella scowled out of the window. 'He might not come back at all, not if he prefers them to us.'

'Bella . . .' Sophie warned as she caught sight of Izzy's face in the rear-view mirror on the brink of crumbling into tears.

'Of course Daddy's coming back.' Sophie glanced at her dark and silent phone and added through gritted teeth, 'Eventually.'

'So tell me all about it, then,' Carmen encouraged her as soon as she had the girls settled at a table by the window with a pile of pens, a colouring book and a plate of sandwiches.

'I don't really know where to start,' Sophie said bleakly, spreading jam on her second scone. 'The long and the short of it is that Bella overheard us talking about Seth when she came down for a glass of water and found that he's their brother. She went ballistic – it was so frightening, Carmen. I thought the girls were settled, that they were moving on with their lives, coping without Carrie. But I was a fool to think that it could be so simple; I lost a parent and I'm still not over it and I was much older than them when it happened. Bella is terrified that her whole world is going to get pulled out from under her again, and as for Izzy, she's always laughing and chuckling away but sometimes I look at her and I don't think that she really understands that Carrie isn't coming back one day.'

'Poor little mites,' Carmen said, glancing over at the girls who were frantically drawing picture after picture of mermaids and fairy ponies. 'They've had it harder than most, but they're lucky, too. Lucky that they've got you and Louis there for them.'

'But have they? I mean, I panicked and went off to London

and left them more or less at the drop of a hat and now Louis's disappeared into the night. I have no idea where he's gone, who he's with or if he's even coming back. I don't know anything and that means I have nothing to tell the girls. And add that to the fact that he hasn't called me and I've wrecked his mobile phone, not to mention that I'm pregnant, and then you've got a right old mess.'

'You're pregnant!' Carmen gasped, clapping her hand over her mouth just in time to stifle the salient word before the girls heard it. 'You're *pregnant*?' she asked again in a whisper.

'Yes.' Sophie nodded. 'It came as something of a shock to me too.'

'Well, I don't know why, what with all that shagging you've been doing. One of the little buggers was bound to get through eventually. After all, if there's one thing we know about Louis, it's that he's fertile.'

'Thanks for that,' Sophie said through a mouthful of cream and jam. 'Anyway, what do I do now?'

'Stop eating cakes for a start,' Carmen said. 'I've heard that pregnancy pounds are the hardest to shift afterwards. I can't believe that he left you in lurch knowing you're pregnant! That just doesn't seem like Louis at all.'

'No – he doesn't know. I haven't had a chance to tell him yet. But please feel free to beat him up on the grounds that he has generally left me high and dry with his two angry and confused daughters. He definitely deserves a slap or two for that.'

'You're pregnant,' Carmen repeated, her eyes wide with wonderment. She reached out a hand to cover Sophie's. 'Oh my God, babe – that's immense.'

'I know!' Sophie said. 'It's taking me a while to get my head round it but I think that I am, or at least I will be, really pleased. Me pregnant with an actual child, who'd have thought it?'

'At least now you have a reason to eat for two,' Carmen joked, but there were tears in her eyes.

'Oh Carmen, I'm so sorry. I'm being completely tactless,' Sophie said, remembering only then what Carmen had told her just before she left St Ives.

'Don't be so silly.' Carmen shrugged off any pain she might be feeling. 'If I tried to avoid every pregnant woman around here I'd never go out. Thank God I'm not still in Colchester – the place is crawling with them. Besides, I've had a lot of time to get used to the idea and I'm fine with it. Really I am.'

'And how are things between you and James?' Sophie asked her. 'Is that still all OK?'

'Yes, of course it is. Me and James are as tight as a drum.' Carmen smiled. 'For now, at least. What we need is a plan, a plan to find Louis and get him back down here looking after his girls and wife-to-be, like he should be.'

'Short of hiring a private detective to find him again, I honestly don't know how to do that,' Sophie told her. 'Chances are he didn't know my phone number off by heart, because it was stored in his mobile which is now well and truly dead. And I don't know Wendy's number. I think the only thing I can do is wait for him to get in touch . . . and I bloody hate it.'

'I know!' Carmen said. 'He'll have left a message for you on the phone at his house. He knows that number.'

'You're right,' Sophie said, sitting up. 'That's probably what he's done.'

'Well, then, go home and check it now and then phone me and tell me exactly what he says.'

Sophie glanced at the girls who were still eating.

'I'd better wait for them,' she said, tapping her fingernails on the gingham tablecloth.

'Leave them here with me, they'll be fine,' Carmen offered. 'They can help me close up and then I'll take them out the back for a bit of telly.'

'No,' Sophie said. 'Thanks, Carmen, but no – I promised I wouldn't leave them and for today, at least, I think that means not even for five minutes.'

The girls were tired and irritable when Sophie finally let herself into Louis's house. She made herself wait to check the phone for messages while she got them undressed and washed and into bed.

'I'm glad I'm home,' Bella told her as she kissed her goodnight. 'And I'm so glad we've got you.'

'Always,' Sophie promised her.

Downstairs she stared at the phone, hopeful that it would contain some news of Louis and his whereabouts. She picked it up and heard the altered dialling tone that signified there was a message. Sophie found her heart was racing as she dialled 1571 and waited to hear the one new message.

'Hello, Mr Gregory, this is Mrs Tallen from St Ives First School, calling on Friday afternoon. Bella and Izzy weren't in today and we were just calling to check that everything is OK. We hope they're not sick. If you could call back and confirm, we'd be very grateful and they will need an absence note when they next come in.'

'You have no further messages,' the automated female voice told Sophie primly.

She hung up the receiver and sat down on the bottom stair with a bump. Her mum had promised to call her if she heard anything from him, so he couldn't have been there. Where was he?

Suddenly weary to the bone, Sophie climbed up the stairs and fell fully dressed on to Louis's bed. She dragged the covers over herself and hugged her arms around her shoulders. Dimly she became aware of another presence on the bed and opening one eye saw Artemis turning in three circles before settling down next to Sophie, her back pressed against Sophie's belly. It was so odd, so uncharacteristic of the cat to ever seek Sophie out for any kind of companionship, that Sophie worried that she was sick. Hesitantly she reached out a hand and ran it along Artemis's sleek back, expecting a tooth and claw protest at any second. But Artemis remained still, her breathing steady and sedate beneath Sophie's hand and far from seeming ill, Sophie noticed she looked better than she ever had, her natural, always hungry feral thinness, had seemed to disappear, and her ribcage had filled out to pleasant housepet plumpness. Sophie smiled to herself as she let her heavy-lidded eyes close once again; there were four mixed-up females in this house and somehow they had all found a place in the world with each other. Whatever else happened, all four of them would always have that.

Sophie's shattered brain had been halfway through forming yet another question when she fell asleep, all her worries and fears still unanswered as she drifted into fretful dreams.

'Sophie ... Sophie*eeeeeee* ... Aunty Sophie, wake up! It's a school day!'

Slowly, painfully, Sophie prised her thick-lidded eyes apart to find Izzy's face looming millimetres from hers, her big eyes out of focus as she peered at her.

'Oh God,' Sophie moaned, rolling on to her back and rubbing her eyes. 'What time is it?'

'Eight forty-five,' she heard Bella say somewhere on her periphery. 'It's a really good job you went to bed with your clothes on, otherwise we'd be *really* late for school.'

Sophie sat upright too quickly, the blood rushing from her

head and leaving her dizzy, the corners of the room wheeling around her as she weighed her heavy head in her hands.

'Right,' she said, waving her arms at the girls, her eyes still closed. 'Go and find cereal and I'll get you some clothes together ... we'll be late, but we can blame your father ...'

'But we've had breakfast already,' Bella informed her. 'We had Coco Pops and a Cornetto each from the freezer for pudding, because we were thinking that breakfast is the only meal without pudding and we didn't think that was fair. Plus, we've been dressed for hours.'

'And hours and hours,' Izzy reiterated.

Sophie blinked her eyes open and looked at the girls. Sure enough they had cobbled together an approximation of their school uniform, with a few customised touches gleaned from the dressing-up box. Izzy was wearing one of Bella's school jumpers pulled over a yellow sundress, which she'd accessorised with her grey school tights and topped off rather optimistically with Perspex play high heels that Sophie wasn't keen on her wearing in the house, never mind out of it. Bella had done a little better, squeezing herself into one of Izzy's school jumpers, the sleeves of which ended just below her elbows. She wore it over a blue and white checked summer school dress with pink socks and her trainers that flashed lights every time she jumped up and down.

Sophie looked at her watch and weighed the pros and cons of delivering the girls in their own take on the school uniform on time versus getting them changed and scrubbed and taking them in an hour late. Trying once more to shake the sleep out of her head she stretched her arms up and looked at Bella and Izzy.

'You'll do,' she said. Painfully, Sophie hauled her body out of bed, briefly running her fingers through her tangled and unwashed hair.

'You know, Bella, you're right, it *is* lucky that I'm already dressed.'

If Sophie had not been exhausted, angry, confused and pregnant when she dropped the girls off at school she might have felt a little paranoid, given the looks that some of the mothers and guardians gave her as she shepherded the girls through the sea of shiny newly washed hair and perfectly turned-out uniforms.

But for once she was too preoccupied with her own thoughts to indulge in paranoia or to care what other parents might think about her, the interloper, the girlfriend. Besides, Bella and Izzy were the toast of the school, drawing crowds of admirers around them as they showed off their unique styling. As Sophie headed out of the gate, still rubbing last night's sleep from her eyes, she knew there would be a message left on Louis's answer phone detailing the unsuitability of the Perspex play shoes and asking for a replacement pair to be brought in. And no doubt when she picked them up this afternoon there would be a letter in their book bags reminding Louis of what the school dress code was and their policy on glitter gel eye make-up, but Sophie didn't care.

Louis had gone, he had walked out on her in the middle of the night. He'd made her fall in love with him, enticed her away from the life she knew and understood, forced her to feel and experience delights in a way she'd never known before *and* got her surprisingly pregnant before disappearing into the night to help his rediscovered first love find his long-lost son, the selfish bastard. And if getting him into trouble with St Ives First School was the only way she could strike back at him for all he had done to her, then she was damn well going to take it; she wasn't proud.

Desperately in need of some clarity, Sophie decided to

walk, leaving her car parked on a double-yellow line outside the school gate as she headed towards the B&B to find some sanctuary in her twin room, a place where she could think and look in the mirror and stare at her own reflection once again.

It was a brilliant chilly morning as Sophie walked into the heart of the town. The sky dazzled her, reflecting light off the flat and glassy ocean that ricocheted in turn off the white-washed houses. This was the light that Carrie had loved so much, Sophie thought as she headed instinctively for the shoreline, the magical radiance that seemed to bend over the coastline throwing even the smallest rock into sharp relief, making it seem possible to see every blade of grass or grain of sand from miles and miles away. Sophie had lived in the St Ives light for a long time, but it was only now, when her head was so muddled and brimming with confusion, that she really felt that particular atmosphere, that sensation that you were just a little closer to the sky here than anywhere else in the world. She paused, taking a moment to breathe in, feeling the cold air numbing her from the inside.

The tourists had dwindled to almost nothing now, and the cobbled streets were largely empty, so Sophie decided to take the long way round to the B&B, walking through the town and around the harbour, stopping briefly at the tacky gift shop, its entrance garlanded by pirate hats and slogan T-shirts, where Izzy had been pestering her father to buy a life-size inflatable dolphin for weeks.

She paused in the crook of the harbour looking out at the boats that were bobbing on the high tide. In a few hours the tide would be out and the boats would be stranded on the soft golden sand, beached on their side, many of them, their fat bellies billowing skyward, waiting for the water to come back and make them beautiful again. Only a couple of months ago she and Bella and Izzy had walked in amongst the boats almost every day, when the tide was out, collecting rocks and interesting shells. The girls had liked to imagine that they were mermaids swimming beneath the surf, in and out and under the hulls looking for treasure. It had been only a few weeks, but it seemed like centuries ago, so much had changed since then.

'Where are you?' Sophie whispered into the wind, absently hoping that it would carry her words to wherever Louis was. 'Please, Louis, don't do this to me now. Don't disappear on me now that I finally know how much I need you.'

Chapter Eighteen

'You never know, he might be lying in a hospital bed somewhere.' Mrs Alexander patted Sophie gently on the shoulder, offering her own unique brand of comfort as she set an extra-large cooked breakfast down in front of her. 'From the sound of things it doesn't sound like he's really left you, love. It'll be something to do with the boy and that Wendy woman.'

'Of course he hasn't left you,' Grace Tregowan affirmed. 'Not for good, anyway. He might be having a final fling before he settles down with you, that's not uncommon. You can't move at the Wednesday-afternoon tea dances for fellers feeling you up in the hopes of getting their end away one last time before they pop their clogs. It might be a bit like that for your young man – although in his case he had sowed a fair bit of his wild oats already.'

'Oh great,' Sophie said, poking at the scrambled egg with her fork, feeling her stomach turn at the thought of it. 'So he's either dead or groping up some woman under a mirror ball. What on earth am I worrying about?'

'I didn't say dead,' Mrs Alexander reminded her, refilling the salt and pepper cellars. 'I said lying in a hospital bed. He doesn't necessarily have to be dead.'

'He doesn't necessarily have to be anywhere!' Sophie's anger flared like a lit match. 'He should be here with me, looking after his *daughters*. Looking after his *pregnant fiancée*, that's what he should be doing.'

'Pregnant?' Mrs Alexander gasped.

'He's got you up the duff, has he?' Grace asked her. Sophie nodded, pushing the plate of bacon and eggs away from her.

'I knew it wasn't like you wanting the decaffeinated tea,' Mrs Alexander said. 'Pregnant. Well, I'll say one thing for Louis. If there was a sperm Olympics that man's stuff would win gold.'

'You poor love,' Grace said, covering Sophie's hand with her own, her palm feeling tight and cold against Sophie's boiling skin. 'But he won't have walked out on you.'

'Won't he?' Sophie asked her in dismay. 'After all, he's done it before. He did it to Carrie.'

'Well, yes, that was a scandal,' Mrs Alexander said, thoughtfully.

'You knew about that when we first met?' Sophie asked her. 'You've never mentioned it before?'

'Didn't really seem appropriate to mention it before, and besides, it was gossip and you know I'm not one for gossip,' Mrs Alexander said. 'Besides, you were my guest here then and now you're my friend. I know Louis now and I know that he's not the sort of man who'd just run off and leave his little girls and pregnant wife.'

'Oh he's left a pregnant wife before, has he?' Mrs Tregowan said. 'That doesn't look good.'

'Yes, but this is different, totally different,' Sophie said desperately. 'Carrie told Louis to go. She told him that she wanted to start a life with another man. He was hurt and shocked and overreacted by going halfway around the world and not coming back for three years. But he didn't run out on her because she was pregnant. And anyway, he doesn't even know that I'm pregnant. In fact, Louis is probably the only person in the entire world that doesn't know I'm pregnant. I was just about to tell him when he walked out on me. And now I don't know what to think. What if he worked out I'm pregnant by himself and did run a mile. He was only saying the other day that he didn't want any more kids.'

'Don't be so silly. You two are getting married, of course he was going to want kids,' Mrs Alexander told her. 'I know Louis now and you and those girls. You're a family. A little unit. Louis wouldn't mess that up; he's been through too much to get you.'

'Don't you worry, he'll turn up,' Grace said. 'Mr Tregowan always turned up in the end. Well, except for the last time . . .'

'So what was he up to, then?' Sophie asked her, a little hysterically. 'Was he an international spy or an octogenarian Casanova or both? What was he getting up to when he disappeared?'

'Alzheimer's,' Grace Tregowan said, nodding once. 'He'd go out and forget where he was.'

'Oh God, I'm sorry,' Sophie said, aghast at her thoughtlessness.

'Don't be,' Grace told her, rubbing her hand. 'I'm not sorry. I had the happiest years of my life with my William. And he was taken from me before it got really bad, before he lost all of himself to the disease. I often think it was for the best.'

'Was he . . . I mean, did you know he was ill when you married him?' Sophie asked her. Somehow she felt that Mrs Tregowan's marriages held the key to her understanding of her own relationship. She had been married so many times, had so many lovers and different experiences of love, that Sophie was sure that somehow she'd help her to understand her own feelings.

'No, dear me no,' Grace said. 'Which is a good job too, because if I'd known I might not have married him and that would have meant I wouldn't have had the wonderful time with him that I did have.'

'But why, why wouldn't you have married him if you loved him so much?' Sophie asked her. Grace looked thoughtful.

'I'd lost too many people in my life already. I don't think I'd ever have chosen to be with someone I loved and knew I would lose again one day, I think that's an impossible choice to make. But that's the way our life turned out and I don't regret a moment of it.'

'How long were you married to William, Grace?' Mrs Alexander asked. She removed Sophie's untouched and congealing full-English breakfast and replaced it with a plate of lightly buttered toast.

'You've got to eat something, my girl,' she added as she sat down at the table with her two remaining guests.

'William and I were married seven years,' Grave told her steadily. 'Three of them, he was fine for. Just like the man I met down there on the harbour wall, a real gentleman, a real stud. Perfect man, really.'

'You just picked him up on the harbour wall?' Sophie asked her. 'Like some townie on the pull?'

'Well, I was bored,' Grace winked at her. 'I was living on my own then, in the bungalow. Frank was always on at me to sell and move in with him, but that was only because he wanted my money. He wanted me locked up in some bloody annexe while he and that bloody awful wife of his cruised round the Med on my cash. Well, I told him, I don't feel old, I don't feel like being bricked up in an annexe. My body might look like it's come out of Tutankhamun's tomb, but in here I'm still eighteen.' She tapped her chest with the heel of her hand. 'I'm still a young hot-blooded girl ready for love and danger.'

'Really, you said exactly that to Frank?' Sophie asked her. Why she never had the knack of saying exactly what she wanted to people, Sophie didn't know. But for some reason she was doomed to never be able to get to the point. For example 'I love you' and 'By the way, I'm pregnant' seemed especially tricky.

'Well, he always was a stuffy so-and-so,' Grace said. 'German father; no sense of humour. I'd been on my own for years by then, I'd had a few affairs, you know. That cribbage club at the community centre is a hotbed of sexual desire, let me tell you. But there hadn't been anyone special and no matter how much fun no-strings sex can be, I'm still a woman. I still wanted the romance and the companionship. But no one I met really lit my fire and when you get past sixty you really need a lot of kindling to get it stoked up, if you know what I mean.'

'Goodness me,' Mrs Alexander said, rolling her eyes at Sophie and pouring more decaffeinated tea. 'Personally, I've never known what all the fuss was about when it came to sex. Mr Alexander and I never really bothered with it all that much.'

'Well, I did,' Grace said. 'I bothered with it a lot. Sex for me was about feeling alive, *being* alive. The heat of a man's body on yours, the feel of his hard cock throbbing inside . . .'

'OK.' Sophie held up her palms. 'OK, let's get back to Mr Tregowan, shall we? The romance and the companionship part. So you met him on the harbour wall?'

'Yes.' Grace's smile was full of tenderness. 'It was early spring, but still really warm even though it was late evening. The sky was as clear as a bell, the stars were out all over the place. So I thought I'd take myself for a little walk to look at the sea. I could get about a lot better then, before this dammed arthritis got into my knees. A lot of the old girls in the bungalows don't even open their door after six, but I've never been one of those. I always think if I get mugged or murdered at this point of my life then so what? I've done everything a woman could ever have wanted to in life, any time I have left now is a bonus and I'm not spending it cooped up behind closed doors if I can possibly help it.'

Mrs Alexander and Sophie exchanged a look. Grace hadn't been out of the guest house, except to sit in its gardens on a sunny morning, since the day she'd arrived. It was a fact that nobody ever mentioned.

'So there I was on the harbour wall, looking at the full spring moon, and it was almost as if I could feel my blood pumping through my veins. I felt like I used to when I was in France during the war. Like every second might be my last so I'd better live it as best I could. And that's when I noticed William watching me. He was tall, I liked that about him, and he still had all his hair – well, most of it, anyway. He carried himself like a young man, like a man who still had a lot to give.'

'I always thought that about Louis,' Sophie said wistfully. 'I always thought he had a lot to give, I just didn't plan on him giving it to someone else.'

'We don't know he's given anyone anything yet,' Mrs Alexander said, patting her on the shoulder.

'Except his sperm,' Grace put in. 'He's been pretty generous with his sperm.'

Sophie pressed her lips together. 'So, go on, tell us how you pulled Mr Tregowan, then.'

'"You're thinking about loves lost", that's what he said,' Grace told her. 'Smooth as you like. "A beautiful girl like you shouldn't be thinking like that," he goes. "Come for a drink with me and we'll talk about love found instead."

'Well, it was the best offer I'd had since the Christmas bingo, so I wasn't exactly going to refuse. He took me to the Anchor and bought me a whisky Mac. It was such fun, he made me laugh out loud and he had this twinkle in his eye and a particular way of looking at me . . . And then towards the end of the evening, just as last orders were called, he put his hand on my knee, kissed me on the cheek, and asked me if he could see me again. I agreed.'

Grace's smile was as coy and as sweet as the eighteen-year-old she had once been and for a second Sophie saw her in all her former glory, a vital battling force of nature who would let nothing stand in the way of her quest for living. A beautiful frail girl with violet eyes and black hair who would let fate bend her to its will without a fight and love every second of whatever was in store for her.

'Well, when you're my age you don't hang about so we got married six weeks later. Frank was furious. Went up the wall, he did, said that William was after the bungalow and my money. Well, of course he wasn't, because he had his own place up on the hill. Big double-fronted Victorian pile that he'd lived in all his married life and beyond, even though he and his first wife never had any kids. We could have lived there but that was her place and, besides, I didn't fancy being that far out of town. William said he liked to be cosy so he moved in with me. It was a proper honeymoon, those first few weeks, we hardly ever got out of the bedroom, once . . .'

'More tea?' Mrs Alexander interrupted, filling Sophie's mug. 'Eat that toast, love. That baby needs some food.'

'I know,' Sophie said, reluctantly picking up a slice of cold toast and nibbling at its edges. 'So what happened, Grace?'

'Those first few years were the best I'd ever had,' Grace told her. 'It's strange to say it, but it's true. William was the first-ever man I spent time with when I really felt like me. With him I didn't have to pretend to be anyone else to try and fit in with him, he loved me exactly how I was. And we laughed and laughed every day, he was a tonic.' Grace took a sip of her stone-cold tea. 'Then one morning he called me by his first wife's name, Alicia. I didn't mind, we joked about it, even. And it was little things like that at first, a misplaced word, or forgotten pan on the hob. He'd leave the bath to overflow and I'd find him out in the garden digging up weeds, and he'd have forgotten that he'd started to run a bath at all. That was nothing, senior moments we called them. We all have them, the silly little things that sometimes slip by you when your brains are on the brink. Then one afternoon he called me from a payphone in the town. I'll never forget it, he sounded so frightened and so lost. He told me he couldn't remember how to get home. It was just as if the little bit of his brain that remembered the way to my bungalow had been wiped away. He could remember how to get back to his house, but he knew it was empty and boarded up, he knew Alicia didn't live there any more and that he lived with me in our bungalow. But he couldn't work out how to get there from the town. So I went and found him and I took him for tea and cake, and by the time we got back that afternoon we were just as we had always been, just as if nothing had happened.'

'You must have been so frightened,' Sophie said.

Grace shook her head. 'No, not really. He was fine again, you see, as soon as he saw me. He was completely fine again. But he decided to see the doctor anyway, just to be on the safe side. We thought he'd tell us it was nothing, just the Grim Reaper creeping a little bit nearer. It was quite a shock when we found out it was Alzheimer's. That day, when we came home from the hospital, we sat on the bus and he held on to my hand ever so tightly and he said the thing he couldn't stand was that he was going to forget me. He was going to forget how much he loved me. Well, I told him I'd love him enough for the both of us, but I don't know that it helped all that much. The illness took a long time to get worse. There were months and months of hardly noticing anything and you'd almost let yourself believe that the doctors had got it wrong. Then, one morning, he'd wake up and it would be twenty years earlier and I'd be Alicia. And some afternoons he'd go out and get lost again and have to phone me for me to come and fetch him back. I even got him one of these mobile telephones with just my number in so he didn't have to try and remember it. But towards the end he kept on forgetting he had it or what it was for.'

'How did you cope? Sophie asked her. 'With seeing someone you love fall apart like that.'

'You don't cope, really,' Grace said thoughtfully. 'Or at least I didn't. I've done a lot of coping in my life, got through a lot of things. Hardened my heart, stuck my chin up in the air and got on because that's all you can do. But losing William that way, so slowly, so painfully . . . losing his love for me – I couldn't cope with that. I just went from day to day, minute to minute, the best way I could.

'Then one night he got out, I don't know how. I'd bolted and chained and double locked the door and hidden the key, but no matter how much he was losing his marbles he could always find a way out. He was never a man who liked to be penned in and that was one part of him that stayed the same to the last.

'I was so exhausted trying to keep track of him during the day that I slept like a log that night and didn't realise he'd gone till the morning. I still think to myself if only I'd stayed up, kept an eye on him, I'd have had a few more years with him . . .'

'But you can't think like that,' Mrs Alexander said. 'You can't blame yourself for sleeping, you must have been worn out.'

'It was icy, icy cold that night,' Grace told them, hugging herself as if against the chill of a day long past. 'There was frost on the ground and I knew he didn't have his coat or shoes on. I phoned the police. They had everyone out looking for him, the coast guard, everyone. But I knew where he was. I knew he'd go back to the place where he felt comfortable and at home, where he could talk to Alicia. I found him sitting on the doorstep of his house, the silly old fool. Sitting there in the frost and the ice like he was sunbathing in the Bahamas.'

'Oh no,' Sophie breathed. 'Was he . . . dead?'

'No, not quite. He'd got hypothermia and he was dehydrated. His kidneys failed first and then the other bits of him began to go. He was in the hospital for two days. I sat by him the whole time. They tried to make me go home and rest but I said what's the point of resting while my husband is dying? I have to be with him for every last second that he's on this earth. He spoke to me before he went. Or at least he spoke to the woman he'd loved before me and he looked at me the way he would have looked at her and I took comfort in that. "Alicia," he called me. It was the last thing he said.

'I couldn't go back to the bungalow after that. I didn't want the house. So I sold it and came here. And here's where I've been ever since and it does me very nicely too, especially now that I have you two. My children have never been up to much, I don't know why – I always tried to get them to love life the way I did. But you two, you've been my family now and I couldn't hope for a better one.'

'Oh God,' Sophie said as Grace smiled at her, tears streaming down her cheeks. 'Oh Grace. I'm so sorry.'

'Don't you be sorry for me,' Grace said. 'I've not a single regret in my life. Not one. Maybe I could have had a safer life, a more stable one. Married some nice steady man and stayed with him ticking all the moments of my life away. Maybe that's what being alive is about for some. But it's not for me.

It's never been that way for me. William was my swan song, my last great love. I'm not sorry I found him and if there's one thing that I know because of him it's that love doesn't waver through the hard times. It sticks fast and it grows stronger than ever. And I know your love for Louis will stick fast too. Even through all of this and just like that baby in your belly it will grow and it will flourish.'

'Especially if you eat the toast,' Mrs Alexander reminded her gently.

'But what if his love doesn't stick fast for me?' Sophie asked, chewing on the bread that tasted like burnt cardboard in her mouth.

'It will,' Mrs Alexander said. 'He'll be back.'

'And when he gets back,' Grace told her, 'you can bloody kick his balls in, the insensitive git.'

Sophie wasn't sure if it was the pregnancy itself, or simply the fact that she now knew about it, but suddenly she was exhausted. There didn't seem to be enough hours in the day or night for her to sleep sufficiently as her body laboured over making another human life and her head and heart tried to reconcile everything that had happened to her since that wet morning months ago when she'd found out that Carrie was dead and she was responsible for her two little girls. Telling her she was far too pale for her liking, Mrs Alexander had sent Sophie up to her room soon after she'd finally eaten her toast for a lie down and Sophie had fallen asleep before she'd even had chance to take a shower.

'I'll call you when it's time to get the girls, OK? You and that baby get some rest.'

She had been deep in a dreamless sleep when Mrs Alexander had come to wake her, having to resort to gently shaking her shoulder to get her to open her eyes.

'Sophie, it's time to fetch the girls.'

Sophie sat up and rubbed her eyes. 'Really? Is it one o'clock already?'

'No, love,' Mrs Alexander said slowly. 'It's just before three. I thought I'd leave you to the last minute, you looked like you needed it.'

Sophie had to think hard for a moment or two why that was a bad thing and then it hit her. Izzy finished school at one o'clock, not three. She was more than two hours late to pick her up.

'Oh God,' Sophie said, pulling on her shoes. 'The school is going to kill me. They must have tried phoning Louis's house and his mobile and not had any luck and they don't have my numbers! How am I ever going to cope with a baby when I can't even get them to school and pick them up on time?'

'I'm sorry, I didn't think,' Mrs Alexander said, as Sophie raced past her and ran out on to the street to her car.

'It's not your fault,' Sophie called back. 'I should have said. I should have remembered.' But when she reached the curb she remembered that her car wasn't there, she had left in outside the school on the double-yellow line and now she had less than five minutes to cover a twenty-minute walk.

'Oh no, no, no, no, fuck, no!' Sophie cried, stamping her feet on the pavement in despair. 'No fucking car!'

'Calm down,' Mrs Alexander said, hurrying down the path in her slippers. 'I'll call you a taxi.'

'No thanks, a taxi will take twenty minutes just to get here. Look, I'll just run up there – you call the school, tell them I'm on my way.'

This time Sophie took the most direct route to the school which was all uphill. She felt the sweat trickling down her back on the chilly afternoon even as her breath misted in the air. The sharp jab of a stitch lodged in her side and her heart pounded as she powered up the hill forcing the deadweight of exhaustion to the back of her mind. She was perhaps ten minutes away when the children from the school started filtering past her, in ones and twos at first and then a steady stream of excited children chattering about their day to their grown-ups, some of them scooting down the hill a little too fast for a mother's comfort, ducking in and out of the trees that lined the road, hopeful for some early conkers. As the hill steepened, and the downward flow of children thickened, Sophie's progress slowed even further and it seemed like an age for her to make the last five hundred yards. But as weary and as worn out as she was, once she was in the playground she ran to the school entrance where she was sure she would find the girls waiting in reception for her and a cross-looking teacher with her arms folded.

'I'm here,' she announced breathlessly as she skidded to a halt on the parquet tiles. But the reception was empty except for the school secretary doing some photocopying and one of the cleaners.

'Oh, sorry, excuse me,' Sophie asked the secretary. 'I'm Sophie Mills. I'm late to pick up my . . . my fiancé's daughters, Izzy and Bella Gregory. I'm really late to pick up Izzy, and I'm so, so sorry. I'm pregnant, you see, and I've lost their father and apparently the ability to stop talking when appropriate. And now you're another person who knows about the baby when he doesn't.'

The school secretary blinked at her.

'Anyway, if you could just tell me where they're waiting?'

'They haven't been brought here,' the secretary told Sophie hesitantly. 'I haven't heard about any late parents or . . . helpers today. And I would have been the one to make the calls if Izzy had still been here at one. Are you sure their father didn't fetch them today? After all, if you've lost him . . . ?'

'I . . . I don't know,' Sophie said, battling the rising wave of nausea and frustration that was surging through her.

'Try their classrooms,' the secretary suggested. 'But really, I'm sure it's nothing to worry about. We're very careful here. We don't let our children run off on to the streets on their own, you know. I bet their daddy's got them and he just forgot to tell you. Men, hey? They never tell you anything.'

Could Louis have come back without letting her know and picked the girls up? Sophie wondered as she turned on her heel and headed towards the classrooms. That had to be what had happened, the secretary was right. The school wouldn't just let Izzy wander off with no one to look after her. It had to mean that Louis was home. The thought flooded Sophie with a sense of relief and fury in equal measure. What was he playing at, not letting her know he was back in town?

Sophie knew the nursery would be long empty so she went to find Bella's classroom where her teacher Mrs Sinclair was pinning some artwork to the walls.

'Hello,' Sophie called out, breathless.

'Hello?' Mrs Sinclair looked up, not best pleased to be interrupted.

'I just wanted to confirm that it was Louis Gregory who picked up Bella today, wasn't it?'

'No,' Mrs Sinclair spoke to her like she was ever so slightly stupid.

'No?' Sophie's heart stopped beating for a few terrifying seconds. 'Then who was it?'

'It was her big brother,' Mrs Sinclair said. 'He came at lunchtime and took Izzy; I know, because young Miss Aster was quite flustered by him. When they came back at three to pick up Bella they had a huge inflatable dolphin in tow. I asked Bella about him and who he was and she told me that he was her brother and that he was picking her up today. It came as a surprise to me, as I didn't know that she had a big brother, but she seemed very excited about going with him. All three of them went off together.'

'Her brother picked her up,' Sophie repeated wide-eyed with horror and a million other half-formed thoughts running through her head that she didn't quite understand yet.

'Yes,' Mrs Sinclair slowly. 'Is there some kind of problem?'

'Yes, yes,' Sophie said. 'There is the rather large problem that she has never met her brother before,' she said. 'She doesn't know anything about him. I don't know anything about him. The last thing I knew was that he was in a squat in London off his head on drugs and alcohol and you just let her go with him?'

Mrs Sinclair stood frozen to the spot. 'But Bella told me he was her brother and she's such a sensible girl, not the sort of girl to go off with a stranger at all.'

Sophie thought of Bella's plan to sneak out of school and make a phone call. She had been worried how she would react if Louis pushed her too far and now she knew. Izzy was tiny and trusting, Seth probably charmed her out of the young and inexperienced nursery teacher's arms as easily as he would have charmed birds from a tree and Izzy would not have denied that he was her brother or said she didn't want to go with him. If anything, she would have been delighted to meet him. Bella, on the other hand, would know that Seth was not supposed to pick them up from school. Perhaps she wanted to be the one to solve the mystery and find him, or perhaps she just wanted all of her own questions and fears answered. Maybe she saw that he already had Izzy and decided she had to go with him to protect her little sister, but either way she had made the decision to go with him. Whether she knew it consciously or not, Bella had made a decision to show her

355

daddy what happened when he walked out on her. Sophie found that she had stopped breathing.

'I had no reason to be suspicious. Izzy had already been with him all afternoon. He didn't look like he was drunk or on drugs, he was smart and clean. He looked fine.'

'No adult told you that they were going to be picked up by their brother, you shouldn't have let them go with anyone but me or their father!' Sophie shouted at her.

'But Bella told me he was her brother, she wanted to go.'

'She's seven years old and Izzy is four. They don't know when or where they should be going. Oh God.' Sophie turned away from Mrs Sinclair as the enormity of what had happened finally hit her. 'Oh God, I don't know what to do.'

'I would never have let her go – but he already had Izzy and she looked so happy with her dolphin. And Bella told me it was fine. She said he was her brother . . .'

'Oh God . . .' Sophie struggled with the fact that she couldn't get through to Louis, that she didn't know Wendy's number and that she had no idea what Seth was like except that he was angry and confused and possibly on drugs and he had her two girls.

'I've got to find them,' she said. 'I've got to. I've got to find them.'

She turned on her heel, suddenly desperate to be out and looking for them, even if she didn't have the faintest idea of where to start.

'I'll call the police,' Mrs Sinclair called out after her. 'I'm so sorry! Bella said he was her brother . . . I thought it would be fine.'

Sophie ran to her car, pulling the ticket off the window and screeching when she saw that it had been clamped.

'No, no, no!' she shouted, kicking the car and immediately feeling it kick back through her toe and spine.

Where was Seth? Where had he taken them?

Sophie had no idea about Seth, except that his mum lived in Newquay and he went to college in Falmouth. She didn't know if he could drive, or if he had a car. And she had no idea what he wanted with her girls. She had to think, she had to get her body and her brain moving. She had to get to them as soon as she possibly could.

Grabbing her phone she dialled Carmen's numbers and held her breath while she waited for her to pick up.

'Ye Olde Tea Shoppe?' Carmen snapped as she picked up.

'Carmen, I'm at the school and . . . and Seth's back, he's — he's got the girls, my car's clamped. I don't know where they are, I don't know anything or what to do . . .'

'Stay there,' Carmen said. 'I'll be with you in five.'

True to her word, Carmen walked out of the Tea Shoppe leaving a regular customer in charge and was at her side in seconds.

'Right, let's think,' Carmen said as Sophie scrambled into her car. 'Now we know he's not a nutter or a pervert. He's not going to hurt them. He's just a messed-up kid who's done something stupid.'

'Do we know that?' Sophie asked Carmen, her heart gripped with icy fear as the car pulled away from the roadside. 'Do we know he's not going to hurt them, because if anything happened to them because of me, I'd never . . . I couldn't . . .'

'Shush,' Carmen told her. 'The police are already looking, they were already asking around when I left the Tea Shoppe. I've told all my customers to keep an eye out. He won't take them out of St Ives, I'm sure of it. Bella wouldn't let him, she's done stranger danger, she knows what to do.'

'But he's not a stranger, he's her brother and she'll be trying to find out about him, trying to get to know everything – you know what she's like.'

'No, I'm sure he'll have taken them somewhere they know. What about the park? Let's try the park.'

Sophie hadn't known that the passing of time could be so agonising. As Carmen drove her to the park, each second that passed without her being certain of the exact whereabouts of her girls dragged over her, rasping at every inch of her skin as she battled with the fear of the unknown, and every moment passed too quickly, too much time slipping by between the last time she had known they were safe and now, as if they were gradually falling out of her reach.

The park was empty, except for some disconsolate teenagers, leaning against the swings and spinning slowly around on the roundabout as if they were gang members in L.A. and not a bunch of kids from Cornwall.

'Excuse me,' Sophie marched over to them, aware that the tone and pitch of her voice would instantly alienate them, high and angry as it was. 'Have you seen a man, tall and dark with longish hair and two little girls in here this afternoon?'

'Why?' One of the boys asked her as he kicked one more revolve out of the roundabout. 'He a pervert or something?'

'No ... no, they're my ... I'm looking after them and I need to find them, please,' Sophie pleaded. 'If you've seen them—'

'Pigs have already been round here asking,' another kid spoke up, from the top of the climbing frame. 'We've been here since four and we've not seen them.'

'Really?'

'What, you saying I'm lying?' the boy challenged her.

'Sophie, come on,' Carmen called her from across the park.

'Yeah, Sophie, go on,' one of the boys called out.

'Hey, Sophie, got any fags?' another one called as Sophie hurried back to Carmen.

'What else you got under that jacket, Sophie?' she heard as she shut the car door.

'Take no notice of them,' Carmen said. 'They're just idiot kids. I was thinking we should go and check the house. Bella knows the neighbour's got a key.'

But when they got back to the house it was standing quiet in the twilight, no lights on in any room, no outward sign of life. Just to be certain, Carmen waited in her car with the engine switched on as Sophie raced through the house checking every room, pausing in the girls' bedrooms to look at the clothes strewn thoughtlessly across the floor, the school shoes discarded in a corner. The house had never seemed more empty. She picked up the phone and listened to the single monotonous dial tone. There were no messages waiting.

As she scrambled back into Carmen's car, the sun was already low in the sky.

'Seth hasn't thought this through, he doesn't know what he's doing,' Sophie said anxiously. 'It will be dark before long – and then what? He's never been to Louis's house, he doesn't know where they live. What's he going to do then? What if he panics and realises how much trouble he's in? Then what's he going to do? Wendy said he was impulsive. The last time Louis saw him he was agitated, on some sort of drugs. Sometimes violent . . . oh God, Carmen.'

'There's no point in thinking about that now, he's just a kid, a boy. He's not going to do anything stupid. All we have to do is think . . . where else might they go? Would he take them to one of the beaches? Maybe they're at one of those having an ice cream or something. Think about it, he's doing it to find out about Louis, to find out about being a big brother. He'll want them to like him, to be impressed by him. He'll have taken them out for ice creams somewhere, I bet you. He won't have thought about all of this pain, he's just a kid himself. He'll have thought he was doing a good thing.'

'The beaches,' Sophie said, quietly, willing herself to believe in Carmen's logic even though it was cold and getting dark and the likelihood of a cone of Mr Whippy on the sand seemed ever diminishing, like the beaches themselves as the tide came in. But it was something to do and she had to do something. 'Let's check them.'

They drove from beach to beach as the sun sank in the sky, stopping to talk to dog walkers and hard-core swimmers in wetsuits, most of whom said that the police had already asked the same questions. All of them said they hadn't seen the girls or Seth. They'd been walking along the wall of the harbour when Sophie sighted her first woman police constable speaking to some die-hard tourists sitting huddled on benches warming themselves over fresh pasties.

'I'm Sophie Mills,' she told them. 'The girls' guardian while their father's away. Has anyone seen them?' The constable was very young, her face smooth and round. She didn't look older than Seth himself and her discomfort at talking to a distraught woman was palpable.

'It would help if you had a photo to give us,' she offered the advice apologetically.

'No,' Sophie said, shaking her head and glancing at her watch as moment after moment separated her further from the children.

'Yes, madam, it really does help to have a photo,' the young woman told her. 'Hold on here and I'll radio through to the station, get the sarge to come and have a word with you about protocol.'

'*No!*' Sophie found herself shouting. 'No, because . . . it's not that bad, it's not that serious. They haven't been abducted. They're just somewhere around here. We just need to *look*.'

'A photo would help,' the policewoman told her, unable to look her in the eye. 'Seriously, it's something to help jog people's memories. It doesn't make it any more serious. It will help.'

'This is a waste of my time,' Sophie gasped as she dragged her purse out of her bag and handed them the school photo that she kept in the clear plastic part of her purse, the first photo of anyone that she had ever carried anywhere. It had been taken at the end of last term, Izzy with her hair sticking up vertically because she'd insisted on styling it herself that day and had a very individual idea on how a headband should be worn, and Bella sitting alongside her, her smile prim and proper, her shoulders straight as she posed for the camera.

'It's my only one,' she said reluctantly as she handed it over.

'We'll find them,' the policewoman told her, with the self-assurance that a girl of her age could not possibly have.

'So he's not taken them for ice cream,' Carmen said as soon as Sophie shut the car door. She kept her eyes ahead on the road, determined not to let Sophie pause for thought as she pulled away and headed out of the town centre. 'And he wants to get to know them, he wants to find out about them. He'll ask them about Carrie, about what it was like when Louis came back. Where would Bella take him? Where would she show him to explain everything? Maybe Carrie's grave?'

'Carrie doesn't have a grave, she was scattered over the . . . oh my God.' Sophie looked up at the cliffs that rose up behind the town.

'They could be up there, they could have taken him to meet their mummy.'

*

Carmen had pulled the car up as near as she could to the footpath that led up to the cliff edge, dragging her four-by-four much further over the rough terrain than was strictly allowed, but the rest of the way had to be walked and as Carmen waited in the illegally parked car, once again Sophie found herself labouring uphill, against the clock, her heart pounding in her chest as she strove for the crest of the hill. As she finally reached it she expected to see nothing but the empty expanse of the jagged edge of the land as it jutted into the sea, and the faint embers of the day dying in the sky.

She caught her breath as she saw the silhouette of people on the horizon. They were sitting on the rough grass, and she couldn't be sure how many of them there were or how old they were. They could as easily have been a courting couple or a pair of bird watchers as two small girls and their confused older brother.

Slowly, quietly – fearful of the sound of her own heart hammering in her chest, Sophie crept towards the group, holding her breath as the small huddle of humanity finally fell into focus. She stopped by an outcrop of rock about fifteen feet behind them, standing in the shadows, and let out a long silent sigh of relief. It was Seth. Seth and her girls, sitting at a safe, but still frighteningly close, distance from the cliff edge.

Sophie edged carefully around the rock till she could make out what they were saying. She had to pick her moment, she had to make sure he couldn't hurt them before she let him know that she was there.

'Mummy's out there, somewhere,' Izzy was explaining. 'And she's in the trees and the sky and the lamp-posts and the bushes and the . . . sea and the boats and stuff. She's every-where, Aunty Sophie says, keeping an eye on us and loving us. But this is our best place to talk to her, here, because this is her most favouritest place.'

'Shit, you must miss her a lot.' Sophie heard Seth say as she crept closer to him. He didn't sound like a crazed loon who had just kidnapped two children in order to hurt them. He didn't even sound angry, just tired and somehow relaxed.

'I've always had my mum,' he explained. 'Mum's always been around, but I never had a dad, except for a bit and that turned out to be shit too.'

'We didn't have our dad for a bit either,' Bella told him. 'He left us when I was little and she wasn't even born. I don't think he meant to but he went and . . . then it was just us and Mummy for ages.'

'But he's back now, yeah?' Seth asked her. 'And that's cool, right?'

Sophie squinted into the gloom, afraid to move any closer. She could see evidence of sandwich wrappers and a Styrofoam cup of something warm lay on its side on the grass. Hot chocolate, probably, if Izzy had had anything to do with it.

'He was back until he found out about you,' Bella said, her tone darkening. 'And then he went away again to find you. He kept going away and leaving us and now we don't know where he is. Because he's not with you.'

'He was, babe,' Seth said, ruffling her hair. 'Fuck, I'm sorry, I messed all your shit up. I didn't really think about you lot. I was just angry with him, and Mum, you know? For thinking it was cool to drop that on me out of nowhere. I went off on one, acted like a fool. My mum and your dad have been chasing me round the bloody country and they haven't finished yet. I never told them I was coming back down here today. I just had to get away from her, always telling me how it's going to be. I'm not a kid any more. I don't need anyone to tell me how anything is going to be. I'll decide that for myself.'

'You're not supposed to go anywhere without telling your mummy where,' Bella chided him. 'They told us that in stranger danger.'

'And does your mummy know where you are?' Seth asked her uncomfortably.

'Yes, cos we just told her,' Izzy said, pointing at the darkening sky. There was a moment's silence.

'I've never had a big brother before,' Izzy said. 'Is there hugging? I hope so, because I'm a bit chilly.'

Seth was quiet for a moment; Sophie was unable to see his expression as he looked out to sea.

'Fuck, I don't know,' he said, eventually. 'I've never had little kid sisters and shit before. I don't even know *any* kids. But I guess a quick hug should be all right.' Sophie watched as he put his arm around his four-year-old half-sister and rubbed her shoulder briskly.

'I should get you back really,' he said. 'The shit's really going to fucking hit the fan, if it hasn't already.'

'But why? You're our big brother,' Izzy said. 'That's allowed.'

'Suzanne Dean's big brother picks her up every Thursday for football practice,' Bella added.

'Yeah, but she probably lives with her brother, she probably knows all about him. You'd never met me before today.'

'You look a lot like Daddy,' Izzy said. 'Only smoother.'

'You don't look much like that Wendy woman at all,' Bella added.

Seth chuckled. 'Is that what you call her?' he asked. 'That Wendy woman – it suits her.'

'Are you cross with your mummy?' Izzy asked him, just as Sophie was about to make herself known. She paused, waiting to hear Seth's answer.

'She does my head in a lot of the time,' Seth said. 'It's like, I know that she went through hell having me so young and on her own. And she's done a fucking lot with her life, considering. Got her own business, got her own place, pays her own bills and got me to art college. She's always done her best for me. But sometimes it feels like she thinks that, because she's done all of that, she owns me, you know? And this thing with your dad, my dad . . . It's not like it's the first time she's tried to spring a bloke on me and told me this is the way it was going to be. She was married once to this decent enough bloke when I was a bit older than you. She told me he was my dad, she told me to think about him like my dad and love him and shit. I didn't want to at first, but I did want to make her happy, you know, and she said that if I could love him then I would make her happy. So I tried, I got to like him. Love him, even. It was a big deal for me, to have this bloke in my life, to share him with her and to trust him . . . and then it didn't work out with her and he was gone. We never heard from him again because that wasn't what she wanted. And I was supposed to forget all that stuff that I felt about him, supposed to forget that he was my dad and act like it never happened. And now she's trying the same shit on me again. It's like, I'm an adult – I don't need a dad now. I don't need anyone fucking telling me what to do. Do you know what I mean?'

'Not really,' Bella said carefully. 'Not exactly. But also she is four and I am seven. You're not supposed to swear in front of us.'

'Shit, sorry,' Seth said. 'I forgot you were such little dudes.'

'I loved Daddy and then he went way,' Bella told him. 'I was little, littler than her, but I remembered him and I missed him, even though I was really small. Then Mummy *died*.' She spoke the word carefully as if she were aware of how important it was, how that single word and its meaning had altered

365

the course of her life. We were very, very sad and Aunty Sophie came and got us from Grandma's and took us home and looked after us.'

'And let us eat nuggets,' Izzy remembered fondly.

'And then Daddy came back,' Bella added.

'I didn't even know he was my daddy,' Izzy giggled. 'That was a bit funny.'

'But I did, I knew,' Bella said. 'I didn't like him very much. Because he'd been away so long and I felt funny and angry and shy, but not funny in a funny way. Funny in a bad way.'

'You shouted at him,' Izzy reminded her. 'And do you remember when we made that tent out of Aunty Sophie's coat and I got stuck in the toilet!'

Seth chuckled as Izzy collapsed into giggles against his shoulder.

'She does that,' Bella explained. 'She laughs about things when she's worried. I'm the only person who knows that. And you now.'

'Cool,' Seth told her. 'I think that's a cool thing to do if you're worried. Like whistling in the dark.'

''Cept I can't whistle,' Izzy said.

'Man, I'm totally top at whistling.' Seth grinned at her. 'I'll teach you, babe.'

He turned to Bella. 'So what happened to make things cool with your dad, then?'

'Aunty Sophie said that sometimes grown-ups are stupid and do stupid things too and that him not being there didn't meant he didn't love us, it just meant he was stupid. And we came back here and when we got here he looked like my daddy again,' Bella said.

'Till you were invented,' Izzy told Seth, matter-of-factly. 'Then he went off with that Wendy woman.'

'It's a right fucking mess for all of us, then, isn't it?' Seth said, shaking his head. 'Sorry, forgot not to swear again. She's cool, then, is she, Sophie?'

'She goes to sleep in her clothes,' Izzy giggled.

'She made us a special promise to look after us,' Bella told him. 'She's not used to being a mummy, but she's tried really hard to be our mummy even though she doesn't know it and even though we have a mummy that we love, we love her like she's a mummy. An extra one that's here to do us teas and give us hugs.'

'And she talks to us about Mummy whenever we like,' Izzy said, suddenly thoughtful. 'Daddy never really talks to us about Mummy, but Aunty Sophie does all the time and it helps us to remember her.'

Sophie pressed her hand against her chest, desperate to run up to the girls and hug them and tell them how grateful and glad she was to have the chance to love them. But they had never spoken to her this way, and she was beginning to realise that there was so much about how they thought and felt that she had no idea about. For some reason they could talk to this brother they barely knew and she wanted to hear more.

'And she loves Daddy a lot, they do a lot of kissing,' Bella added.

'So before I rocked up it was all pretty cool for you kids, then,' Seth said.

'Yes,' Izzy said. 'We're getting married to Aunty Sophie and there will be wings.'

'So you don't really need me around fucking it all up for you, do you?' Seth said, standing up suddenly, making Sophie's body tense as she stood in the shadows. Bella and Izzy stood up too, the safe distance between them and the cliff edge shrinking as Seth strode nearer to the cliff's edge, the girls in his wake. 'What would be best for you little dudes is for me to get out of here, fuck off and let you get on with your lives.'

'No! Stay!' Izzy ran full pelt towards Seth and the thin air just behind him, catching hold of his hand at the last second and breaking her speed against his weight.

'Yes, stay,' Sophie spoke finally, raising her voice just enough for it to be heard above the sea breeze that whipped through the grass, keeping it calm and friendly. Keeping all the fear and anger and shock at bay. 'Stay there, Seth, and don't go any closer to the edge, please.'

'Aunty Sophie!' As she had hoped, Izzy let go of Seth's hand and raced towards her, closely followed by Bella. She clasped them into her arms, pressing their small bodies against hers as if she could somehow fold them into her flesh and keep them safe from harm for ever.

'We've been with Seth,' Izzy said. 'We had chocolate for tea.'

'You came for us. Are we in trouble?' Bella asked her, her arms wrapped tightly around Sophie's body.

'No, no . . . no one's in trouble,' Sophie said carefully, aware of the distant sound of police sirens growing ever louder. She wondered if Carmen had been worried about how long she had been gone and alerted the police. 'I was very worried about you, but you're not in trouble.'

'I'm sorry,' Seth said, his back to the sea. He looked like a little boy who'd been caught with his hands in the sweetie jar.

'You bloody stupid boy,' Sophie said, her voice low, as she clung on to the girls. 'You should be sorry. You can't just rampage through people's lives because you're having a hard time. No matter how difficult or messed up you think your life is, you have no right to drag two small children into it and put them in danger.'

'Was there danger?' Izzy asked her, suddenly alarmed. 'What, monsters?'

'Leave Seth alone,' Bella said indignantly. 'He's been kind to us, not bad. Not a monster.'

'I know, darling, but he shouldn't have taken you away without asking. I was so, so worried.'

'I'm sorry, Sophie, about everything . . .' Seth took a step closer to her. 'But I would never hurt them. I wanted to meet them without Mum and Louis on my back. Louis said I should meet them so I decided I would. Today. I didn't think, I didn't get how much you'd worry. I thought you'd be cool once you knew they were with me.'

'You brought them here, to the top of a cliff, and you're standing there talking about disappearing for good!' Sophie exclaimed. 'How on earth would that make me feel cool?'

'What, you think I'd . . .' Seth shook his head. 'I meant, like, transferring courses to Manchester or something, not topping myself. Those two are proper cool. I don't want to wreck things for them. Or you, you seem like a decent kind of woman, taking them on when they had no one. Looking after me when I'd got a bit out of control. I want you to get your wedding with your wings and be happy before me and my bloody mother mess it all up for you. Look, I'm stupid. I'm really bloody stupid, but I'd never . . .' He paused, the trouble he'd caused just registering in his face. 'Oh God, I'm so sorry.'

'Sorry?' Sophie let out a ragged rage-filled breath. 'You bloody, bloody idiot, Louis,' she sobbed, collapsing on to the cold, wet grass the girls still in her arms.

'Aunty Sophie!' Izzy's giggles echoed in her ears. 'Don't be silly. That's not Daddy, it's Seth.

'I can't breathe,' Sophie gasped. 'I can't . . .'

'But it's OK, we're OK now,' Bella, said placing her palms

either side of Sophie's face as she lay on the ground dimly aware of the wet grass on the back of her neck.

'I feel . . . I can't . . .' Sophie felt the heat of the girls' bodies in her arms as she pulled them closer to her, determined never to let them go again, and then nothing.

Then there was nothing.

Chapter Nineteen

Someone was holding Sophie's hand as she came round in the back of the ambulance, its rocking motion as they headed towards the hospital bringing her back to the world. She tried to sit up but her head spun and her eyes blurred whenever she tried to move. She could see the drip in her arm and feel its cool fluid circulating through her veins.

'I'm pregnant,' she blurted out. 'Please, don't give me anything that's going to hurt my baby.'

'You're pregnant?' A male voice spoke. 'Like with a baby?'

'Yes, Seth, I'm pregnant and your antics with my children haven't exactly helped matters, thank you very bloody much, so just get the fuck out of my ambulance ... oh Louis, it's you.'

Sophie concentrated very hard, forcing her eyes to focus on Louis's face. 'But how ... when did you arrive ... have I been out for weeks or something? Is the baby born and I didn't notice? Where are the girls, are the girls OK – are they here?'

'Hello,' Louis said, staring at her as if he wasn't quite sure he knew who she was. 'Hello, Sophie. The girls are fine, they are safe, Mrs Alexander and Carmen are taking them home. The police had a word with Seth, but they let him go home. You've been out for about half an hour, but the paramedic says you're going to be fine. Seth had got himself into trouble, got himself arrested for being drunk and disorderly – trying to pick fights in a part of town where every other kid carries a weapon. He'd got drunk again and told Wendy he didn't care what happened to him. Wendy was so frightened for him that she called the police and they kept him in a cell overnight to sober up. We went back the next day to pick him up but they'd already let him go. I never thought he'd come back down here. Bloody student rail discount cards, I blame them.' Louis attempted a smile but Sophie just stared at him, somehow detached from what he was telling her, from everything except for the lull and sway of the ambulance, as if she were still unconscious and dreaming, only with her eyes open.

'Seth called Wendy this morning, told her he was coming back to Cornwall to meet his family. We followed him down as quickly as we could. But when I got back the house was empty, Mrs Alexander said you had rushed off to find the girls, the school said their brother had them. I didn't have my bloody phone, did I? But I found James at the lifeboat house. He told me you were with Carmen, and I rang her. She was worried when you didn't come back quickly so she followed you up the hill. She arrived just as you collapsed. I came straight to you, babe.'

'You came too late,' Sophie told him, coming around ever so slowly as everything he said to her began to sink in. 'Where were you, Louis? You walked out on us!'

'I know . . . I know . . .' Louis closed his eyes, his face an expression of pain. 'When you took Bella upstairs to clean her feet Wendy phoned back. She said she was really worried about Seth. Said he'd gone off into the night and she didn't know what he might do . . . she said she thought he might hurt himself. She begged me to come and help her find him. I kept thinking that it was all my fault and I knew the girls would be safe with you. I just went. I didn't know I'd left my phone. I didn't think you'd be gone before I had a chance to speak to you. I didn't think and . . . Sophie, did I imagine it or did you just say you're pregnant?'

Sophie turned her face away from him.

'Listen, mate,' the paramedic told Louis. 'We'll be in Penzance in a minute. The girl's just fainted. Give her a bit of space, OK?'

'I'm sorry,' Louis kissed the back of Sophie's hand. 'I'm really, really sorry. We can talk about it whenever you want. But Sophie, please tell me, are you really pregnant?'

Sophie nodded slowly, biting her lip fearfully.

'I'm just over three months gone,' Sophie told him wearily. 'I'm sorry.'

'You're sorry?' Louis asked her, 'Why in God's name are you sorry?'

'Because you've already got three children. And you said you didn't want any more. And I didn't even realise I was pregnant until my mum told me when I was in London. You'll have another child with a useless mother who can't get children to school on time and leaves them to be kidnapped by their unhinged brother.'

'Listen, that was scary, but it wasn't your fault,' Louis said. 'And the girls weren't ever really in any danger.'

'I didn't know that, and neither did you until you got here,' Sophie said. Swallowing as she remembered the fear that had consumed her, she turned to look at him. 'And you got here too late, you bastard!' Without warning she punched Louis hard in the arm, making him yelp and the paramedic whistle through his teeth. 'You should have been there, you should have been there to look after your daughters and take care of me. That's what you're supposed to do and you left, you bloody left again. Because that's what you do, isn't it?'

'It's not . . . honestly, it's not. I know that's how it looks, but it's not how it is,' Louis said. He glanced at the paramedic then unstrapped his seat belt, so that he could lean on the floor next to the trolley she was strapped to.

'Sophie, you're pregnant. You, Sophie Mills, are pregnant with my baby – that's . . . that's amazing, it's incredible. It's the best, most brilliant news I've heard in a long time. I know I fucked up, I've really bloody badly fucked up and I'm sorry. I didn't know how to handle things with Seth and Wendy and instead of talking to you about it, relying on you like I should have, I shut you out. I let you down, and I let my daughters down – something I swore I'd never ever do again. You don't have much reason to believe me right now but I promise that I will look after you and Bella and Izzy and our baby. And Seth, if he'll let me. And I know I don't deserve it but the only news you could give me now that would make me any happier is that you will still marry me despite what a bloody prick I've been.'

Sophie stared at him, chewing her lip.

'Seth kissed me,' she told him. 'That night that he came back to the B&B, he kissed me and I let him. It was only a few seconds but it probably wasn't appropriate under the circumstances. I'm telling you because I'm trying to think of all the skeletons that could possibly be in my closet before we go any further.'

'OK,' Louis said. 'That's a bit weird but it doesn't matter. Nothing matters as long as you'll still have me.'

'And when I was in London I had lunch with Jake and he told me I was incredibly sexy and beautiful and he kissed me too. Against a wall, which was wrong, I know, but it helped me realise that I don't want to be kissed by anyone but you. Not even a younger version of you.'

Louis breathed out a long, slow breath.

'OK,' he said. 'I'm pretty fucked off about Jake and I may

have to track him down and kill him, but I get it. I wasn't around. I wasn't there for you and you were confused. And as for Seth, well if there is one thing I've learned about him it's that he's impulsive, he acts first and thinks later. Plus, I'd try to kiss you if I were him, you're the most beautiful girl in the world. So it's OK, none of that matters. I forgive you.'

'Oh, mate,' the paramedic said as they pulled to a halt in the hospital car park, 'you were doing so well right up till that moment.'

Sophie stared at the murky mass of shadows on the monitor. Amidst the grey, like the churning clouds of a stormy night, lay a small black pearl, perfectly round, a serene dark world, the world her baby inhabited.

'It's too early to see much,' the nurse told her. 'But everything looks good so far and if you squint really hard . . . you can just about see the heartbeat. See that little flicker there?'

Sophie peered at the image, feeling as if she were attempting to divine her own future and then suddenly she saw it, just as images of animals and faces used to emerge from the pattern on her mother's Formica kitchen table top, it was there. Just a scrap of life, the merest flicker of a candle that might snuff out at any second except that it kept on burning.

'Wow,' Louis said from the doorway, where Sophie had told him to stand unless he wanted another thump. 'Look at that, Sophie, that's amazing.'

He edged a little closer and bent over so that he could get a better look.

'Can we have a photo?' Louis asked the technician.

'Well, you won't see much, but you can have one.' The nurse smiled at him. Tentatively Louis reached out and picked up Sophie's hand. She withdrew it immediately.

'I'm sorry,' he told her. 'It just sort of came out. You're the one who should be forgiving me, not the other way round. I know that now, especially after you slapped me. You slap hard for a recently unconscious pregnant lady.'

Louis rubbed his jaw gingerly.

'The thing is . . .' Sophie looked at the nurse.

'Don't mind me,' she said, handing Sophie a wad of tissue to rub the gel from her stomach. 'I'll just pop out and let the doctors know the results. You two have a few minutes to get straight.'

'The thing is,' Sophie said once they were alone, 'if we were solid, if we were the kind of couple that should get married, then things wouldn't have happened this way, would they? You wouldn't have cut me out of what was happening with you and Seth and that bloody Wendy woman. I wouldn't have run away to London at the first possible opportunity and thought about kissing Jake . . .'

'And actually kissed Jake,' Louis added, a little darkly.

'And if we hadn't been so wrapped up in this bubble of us, and being in love and thinking that the whole world would just fall into step with us because we want it to, then maybe I wouldn't haven't got accidentally pregnant.'

'You're not the first woman in the world that this has happened to,' Louis told her. 'It's not as if you're some kid, on your own without a father on the scene . . .' Louis trailed off, obviously thinking about Wendy, a fact that spiked Sophie's jealousy. At this moment in time she didn't want one second of his thoughts to stray from her.

'Actually, since the moment I found out that I was pregnant, there has been no father on the scene,' she told him sharply. 'I've been coping with this alone, Louis. We've all been coping alone because you weren't there.'

'I know, but, Sophie – you were the one who left first. When you walked out I didn't know what to think.'

Sophie was silent for a moment. 'You're right. That was a mistake. I let you and the girls down and I'm so sorry for it. I should have told you how I was feeling, but you seemed impossible to talk to.'

'I know, but I've been stretched so thin recently. I've been trying to do the right thing and ending up getting it wrong all of the time. I should have listened to you about Seth, especially about telling the girls about him, and I shouldn't have shut you out of what was happening. But I couldn't ignore him and Wendy either, could I? You were the one that told me that. You said I had to find out about my son and you were right. You have to see all the mistakes I've made weren't because I was being a coward and running away. I made them because I want to get things right. I want everything right before you and I start our married life together. And anyway,' Louis went on, 'so what if we were wrapped up in a bubble of love, that's what being in love is about, isn't it? Being happy, experiencing the joy of being with someone who is so perfect and so right for you.' Louis caught Sophie's wrist as she stood up to button her jeans. He pulled her close to him, entwining the fingers of his free hand in her hair.

'You make me so happy, happier than I've ever been,' he told her. 'I thought I made you happy too.'

'You did, you do,' Sophie insisted. 'Most of the time. I've never felt so happy, but it shouldn't be at the expense of everyone else.'

'What do you mean?' Louis asked her.

'We thought that because we were happy that everyone else was too – but they're not. The girls aren't happy. Yes, from day to day they're OK, but deep down inside they aren't over losing Carrie or the trauma they went through, of course they're not. Their mother died. How could we let Carrie down so badly? You saw Bella when she thought you were going to leave her. She still doesn't feel safe or secure, Louis. She still thinks you might abandon her at any moment. And did you know that if Izzy is frightened or worried she hides it by laughing and being silly? I didn't know that, I didn't know it till Bella told Seth, someone she barely knows, about it on the cliff top. She told him, but not you or me, and now I think about it, it makes perfect sense. Little sunny Izzy, always so full of fun even in her darkest hour, but that's not true. All she was trying to do was keep the shadows at bay. Neither one of us noticed that. Because we didn't want to. We didn't want reality crashing in and spoiling things for us.'

Sophie shook herself free from Louis's grip and went to the door. 'And now this, and now a baby. What's that going to do to them? You want me to say that everything's going to be fine. That I'll marry you and we'll have our baby and all live happily ever after. But I just don't know if that is possible any more.'

'What are you saying, you're saying you'd consider . . .' Louis put his hand on Sophie's belly.

'No, God, no – of course not.' Sophie said.

'Then what?' Louis asked her.

'I'm just not sure that I can marry you,' she said. 'That's what I'm saying.'

'OK, so the idea of marriage freaks you out, I get that, I think. And if you really don't want to do it we don't have to. We can live together, you me, the girls, the baby – like one big happy family.'

'I love you,' Sophie said. 'But I don't know. I don't know if we are ready to do that yet. It would be easy to say that we are because of the baby, but I don't want Bella or Izzy or our child to have to go through any more upheaval, any more confusion or loss because you and I aren't as strong or as close as we need to be to really make this family work.'

'Are you saying that you'll stay in the B&B for ever with our baby?' Louis asked her.

'I don't know,' Sophie said. 'Maybe I am.'

They were silent on the way home, Sophie staring bleakly out of the taxi window.

'Well, I'm telling you one thing, you're not going back to the B&B tonight,' he'd said as they climbed into the car. 'I want you with me and the girls where we can keep an eye on you.'

'You heard what the doctor said, I'm fine. My blood pressure is fine, the baby is fine. I don't need keeping an eye on.'

'Sophie, you are having my baby. Bella and Izzy's and Seth's half-brother or half-sister. Whatever you decide about marrying me, we are a family, wherever you live, and I love you. I know you're upset with me and you're worried about the girls, but for tonight at least you are coming home with me and that's that.'

'I'm coming because I want to see the girls,' Sophie told him. 'Not because you said so.'

Carmen opened the door and Sophie found herself engulfed in a mass of hugs.

'You're alive!' Bella cried, burying her head in Sophie's stomach.

'I told them you were going to be fine,' Carmen said. 'But they got themselves in a right state, especially Izzy.' Carmen nodded towards the front room where Izzy was sitting on the sofa sucking the sleeves of her pyjamas as she watched *The Little Mermaid*. She didn't even look up at Sophie standing in the doorway.

'It was the ambulance that made her scared,' Bella said, her voice muffled somewhere in Sophie's middle.

'The ambulance?' Sophie hugged Bella to her ever so tightly and then released her.

'There was an ambulance after the car accident,' Bella said slowly, entwining her fingers in Sophie's. She looked up at her father.

'I see you are back,' she told Louis.

'I am. And I'm back for good now, I promise,' Louis told her. Bella said nothing, following Sophie towards the living room to find Izzy, leaving Louis and Carmen standing in the hallway.

'Come in the kitchen,' Sophie heard Carmen say gently to Louis. 'Mrs Alexander is making us all a bacon sandwich. It was the girls' special request.'

Followed closely by Bella, Sophie walked into the living room where Izzy stared doggedly at the screen, her knees tucked up under her chin, her toes curled in on themselves as if she were clinging on for dear life.

'Hello, sweetheart,' Sophie said softly as she sat down carefully next to her, Bella sitting on her other side. Izzy didn't waver.

'Are you OK?' Sophie asked her, brushing a curl from her forehead. 'You've had a very long and busy day, you must be ever so tired.'

Izzy shook her head from side to side once.

'Did you have a nice time with Seth?' Sophie asked. Izzy nodded.

'You must have been worried up on the cliff when silly Sophie fainted. Were you worried, Izzy?'

Izzy kept her eyes on the screen but she took her thumb out of her mouth. 'They took Mummy in an ambulance. I was in the car still when they took her. I was left behind with the other lady and Mummy went in the ambulance and she didn't ever come back. I was very shaken up.'

Sophie nodded.

'I remember. You must have been very scared when I went

in the ambulance, but I was fine. I was just a bit silly and forgot to eat and I fainted. They had to take me to the hospital to check me out, but I was OK. Ambulances help people.'

Izzy turned to look at her, her features still and serious, just like Carrie in the few precious moments when she was quiet and thoughtful.

'We've got a new old brother,' Izzy explained. 'His name is Seth. He came to get me from school and I went with him. I shouldn't have, but I did. He bought me a giant inflatable dolphin but I think I left it on the cliff . . . he's going to teach me to whistle.'

'Is he?' Sophie asked. 'That's good. It will be fun to get to know him, won't it? And I expect that once you know him a bit better you'll do all sorts of exciting things with him.'

'I would probably like to go to a circus with him,' Izzy said thoughtfully. Then without warning she hurled herself at Sophie, flinging herself into Sophie's lap, tightening her arms around her neck.

'You must stay now,' Izzy told her. 'And not faint again.'

'I promise not to faint again,' Sophie said.

'Or go away in an ambulance.'

'I won't,' Sophie said.

'At the circus, will there be an elephant like Dumbo with huge enormous ears?' Izzy asked her, quite tickled at the thought.

'An elephant that can fly?' Sophie asked. 'With huge enormous floppy ears?'

Izzy giggled. 'Yes, I'd like to go for a ride on one of those.'

'Well, you never know,' Sophie said.

She looked into Izzy's eyes. 'Listen, poppet, you can always tell me if you're worried about anything ever.'

'Or me,' Bella said, patting her sister on the knee.

'I am worried about one thing,' Izzy told them darkly.

'Tell me, sweetheart,' Sophie braced herself.

'What if Daddy eats my bacon sandwich, too?'

Sophie sat on the edge of Louis's bed fully dressed and looked around the room. This would be only the third time she had slept here. The first time she had crept in and taken her clothes off before seducing Louis, the second time she had crashed fully clothed and confused. Now as she sat on the edge of the bed, Louis took off his clothes, set his watch down on the side table and went off to brush his teeth in only his boxers. It was like being part of a couple. A proper grownup couple, and it felt strange, alien.

Sophie sat perfectly still, fully dressed and looking around the room, the wardrobe that was half empty, the wall devoid of pictures, only the faint ghost of the last owner's artwork where the wallpaper had faded in the sun leaving an impression of the past.

'Are you getting in?' Louis asked her dropping his boxers in front of her. Inexplicably, Sophie blushed, looking away.

'Are you shy?' Louis asked her, smiling a little as he knelt down in front of her. 'Are you scared to see me naked? I mean, I know that I have an impressive physique, but it's probably a little too late to be scared of it now.' He put a hand on either side of her on the bed.

'Sophie,' he said quietly. 'We are OK, aren't we? I mean, you're angry with me and I deserve it and you've been through hell all alone these past few days, but we are OK? Aren't we? Because if I think I've messed this up when it's all almost so perfect, then I'll never forgive myself. I know you said you didn't want to marry me and you wanted to live in the B&B with our baby and just visit every now and then, but that was crazy talk, wasn't it? You didn't mean it, did you?'

Sophie looked up into Louis's eyes.

'I love you,' she told him. 'I want to marry you. I just don't know if I can. Bella and Izzy are so scared that something bad is going to happen again. And Seth, he barely knows who he is or who you are and just as you're getting to know him then a baby comes along.'

'Listen,' Louis said, sitting back on his heels. 'If Bella and Izzy are scared that something bad is going to happen then we have to make them see that a baby is one of the *best* things that can happen. And the very best thing we can possibly do for them is to give them the stability they need. To get married and all live together here as a family, proving to them that nothing bad is going to happen. And as for Seth, well . . . I'll find a path with him. Maybe now is the right time for him to join the family, because he won't be the newest one for very long. Soon there will be this one.' Louis nodded at her belly. 'Our baby, yours and mine.'

As he looked at her his eyes lit up and Sophie felt her heart quicken.

'You really are pleased about the baby, aren't you?' she asked him.

'Pleased? Sophie, I'm over the moon. You're having my baby. You, the love of my life.' He leaned towards her and kissed her. 'Now, listen, you've had a very long and difficult day and you need to rest.' He lifted the hem of her T-shirt, pulling it over her head, pushing her gently back on to the bed. Sophie did not resist. 'You just lie there and I'll put you to bed,' Louis whispered, unbuttoning her jeans and pulling them off her hips and legs. Gently he lifted her legs on to the bed, running his hand lightly over her belly and the tops of her thighs as he looked at her.

'You are incredibly beautiful, you know,' he told her, rolling her on to her side so that he could unhook her bra strap.

Gently he slid the straps off her shoulders, the tips of his fingers running over her breasts as he removed the garment.

'The most perfect being that I have ever seen,' he said, kissing her stomach as he eased her underwear off.

Naked in his arms Sophie looked into his eyes. 'I love that you see me that way,' she whispered.

'Well, of course I do,' he whispered back. 'It's the way you are.'

Carefully he pulled back the quilt and then threw it over her, climbing in bed next to her, pulling her body into his, wrapping his long legs and arms around her.

'Are we going to have sex?' Sophie murmured hopefully, even though sleep was already nudging her towards unconsciousness.

'Nope, you need to sleep,' Louis whispered into her hair. 'And to not worry about a thing because I promise that I'm going to make it all OK. And I'm going to be here. I'm going to hold you all night and when you wake up I'll be waiting for you, hoping that you're going to tell me that we're still on for our New Year's Eve wedding.'

'And we can have sex then.' Sophie nodded.

'Oh Sophie,' Louis kissed her, 'you're such a romantic.'

Chapter Twenty

'Aunty Sophie, Aunty Sophie, quickly, wake up, it's an emergency!'

Sophie prised open her eyes to find Bella's face millimetres from hers, her big brown eyes shining in the half-light, brimming with tears. 'Come quickly,' Bella half whispered half sobbed.

'What's happened?' Sophie sat bolt upright, 'What is it? Is it Izzy?'

'No,' Bella dragged Sophie out of bed, 'it's Artemis, I think Artemis is dying.'

Sophie grabbed a dressing gown from the back of the door and wrapped it hastily around herself as she followed Bella into her bedroom.

'Dying? Bella, what do you mean – where is she?' Sophie asked her, the last dregs of sleep trickling slowly away.

'She's under my bed.' Bella knelt on her carpet and pointed underneath her bed, her face stricken with fear. 'I knew it was strange because she never usually comes in at night, she's usually out killing things. But I was just going off to sleep when I heard her coming in, but she didn't say hello, she just went right under my bed, I heard her scrabbling about in my spare blanket and then she went quiet and I must have gone to sleep, but I shouldn't have because ... because I woke up and she was crying . . . I looked under the bed with my Barbie torch and I thought I could see blood. So I tried to fetch her out and see where she was hurt but she scratched me.' Bella offered Sophie the back of her hand where four long and painful-looking red welts were forming. 'I think she must be dying because she's never ever hurt me before.' Bella let out a sob. 'She can't die, Aunty Sophie, please don't let her die. I need her.'

Sophie put her hand over her mouth and took a breath to compose herself. In her head she had visions of Artemis hit by a car or a truck, crawling in up the stairs in the night to find a safe place to lick her wounds. Just as fearful as Bella of how badly hurt her precious cat might be she braced herself and, taking Bella's torch, knelt down on the carpet and peered under the bed. Artemis was breathing heavily, lying on her side, her head towards Sophie, so that she could not see the bulk of her body.

'Hello, girl,' Sophie said. 'You're not looking too good there, are you? I'm just going to see if I can get you out and we can have a look . . .' But the second that Sophie's hand approached Artemis, the cat lashed out at her, her panting and distress apparently increasing.

'What shall we do?' Bella asked her, gripping on to Sophie's nightgown with clenched fists. 'What shall we do to save her?'

Sophie fought to control the tremble that shook her voice, desperate not to show Bella just how afraid and upset she was. 'I'll just see if I can see anything one more time so we know where she's hurt and then we'd better call the vet out. Run downstairs, Bella, and get Daddy's phone book from the hall table. Go on, quickly, and bring me the phone too.'

Carefully Sophie took the torch and on her hands and knees peered under the bed, but this time instead of approaching Artemis directly she tried to look at her from one end of the bed at an angle to see if she could see where and how she was injured. She blinked, trying to make sense of what she was seeing amidst the rucked-up blanket that Artemis had ensconced herself in.

'Hang on a second,' she said as Bella arrived back with the phone book and phone. 'Something's happening she's . . . what is that?'

Sophie stared as Artemis half sat up and began licking at something soft and slimy. At first Sophie thought it might have been a dead mouse or a bird, but she had never seen her cat be so gentle with another living thing. And then as Artemis licked away the slime and gunk from the tiny creature Sophie realised it was furry and orange. For a second she thought that the injured animal had taken comfort on Izzy's toy cat but then it stirred, wriggling closer to Artemis. Sophie stared as Artemis continued to lick at the little creature, tenderly loving, washing its face clean of any muck as it took its first breath.

Sophie gasped, clasping her hand over her mouth, tears springing to her eyes. She sat back on her heels and handed the torch to Bella.

'It's OK,' she told Bella, grinning from ear to ear. 'It's fine, Artemis isn't dying. Oh, look, Bella.' She hugged the little girl hard. 'Artemis is having kittens!'

'Right.' Sophie came back into the room armed with supplies. 'The vet says we need towels in case she needs a bit of help with rubbing them awake, dental floss in case Artemis doesn't cut the cords properly, and some yoghurt. He says she might fancy a spoonful of yoghurt to keep her going. Oh, and a big box to put them all in once she's finished. I thought that old packing box in the shed would do. We have to line it with shredded newspaper.'

'There are two now!' Izzy exclaimed, as she lay on her

tummy in front of the bed. Louis had taken Bella's bedside lamp and laid it on its side next to the bed so that they could all get a clearer view without using the bright flashlight. 'The second one looks grey to me . . . oh, they are soooo cute. We can keep them all, can't we?'

'What I don't understand,' Louis said, keen to gloss over that subject as he hunkered down next to Izzy, 'is how Tango ever got near enough to her to make this happen, the old dog. The old cat dog. Artemis has hated him from day one and he's always avoided her.'

'I told you I saw them hugging,' Izzy said, triumphantly. 'They are in love!'

'What I don't understand is that Artemis is a rescue cat,' Sophie said. 'She's supposed to be spayed. I'd have never let her move in with an un-neutered tom, even one as soppy and hopeless as Tango, if I hadn't thought that.'

'Well, someone, somewhere, made a mistake,' Louis said. 'Because that cat is most definitely fertile.'

'And now they are married!' Izzy said, clasping her hands together happily and rolling on to her back for a moment. 'Married and having babies. Just like you and Daddy are going to, Aunty Sophie.'

Sophie's and Louis's eyes met above the girls.

'How many kittens do you think she will have?' Bella asked. 'I'm hoping for about twenty.'

'The vet said four or five, most likely,' Sophie said. 'He said if she's still in labour in another few hours then he'll come over and check her out, but he expects she'll be able to manage perfectly well on her own.'

'Look at her, look, Aunty Sophie.' Bella dragged Sophie back down on to the carpet to peer under the bed again. 'Look, she loves her kittens.'

Sophie watched as Artemis licked the two kittens that

already nestled at her nipples. She looked so gentle and so tender with them, like an entirely different cat from the one that Sophie knew and loved. This Artemis knew exactly how to be a mother, how to break the membrane sac so that her kittens could breathe, how to lick them clean and bite off the umbilical cord. The fierce, angry loner cat had been transformed into a mother, all of her natural instincts flooding in just when she needed them.

'She's going to make a wonderful mother,' Sophie said, wincing slightly as she straightened up, her body still stiff and aching from lack of sleep.

'And so are you,' Louis told her, his cooling hand on the back of her neck.

Bella looked up at him sharply.

'What do you mean?' she asked him.

Sophie and Louis looked at each other and Sophie nodded. She didn't want to keep any more secrets from the girls.

'I mean,' Louis said reaching out to hold Sophie's hand. 'That Sophie is going to have a baby. And I'm the baby's daddy and you and Izzy are going to be big sisters.'

'That's awful!' Izzy cried out horrified. 'You're not even married yet!'

Sophie watched Bella's face very closely as she took in the news.

'It's OK, Izzy – you don't have to be married to have a baby.'

'You do,' Izzy said. 'Tango and Artemis are married. How long will it take for the baby to get here? Will it take longer than the wedding? If I am big sister will I get to boss the baby around, like Bella bosses me around? Will I get a bigger bedroom? I want a bigger bedroom if I am going to be a big sister and my own Nintendo DS. Is that why your tummy is so fat, Sophie, because there's a baby in it. How big is the baby in it now?'

'Just hold on for a second,' Sophie laughed, holding her

hand up to stave off any more questions as she kept an eye on Bella, whose gaze was fixated under the bed.

'The baby is going to be here in May,' Sophie told Izzy. 'It's not very big at the moment, hardly anything to see at all, really, although I have got a picture I can show you later if you like. So I'm afraid that all of this' – she patted her tummy – 'is mainly cream teas and jam.'

'Can I name the baby?' Izzy asked her. 'I would call it Petunia.'

'Oh well . . . maybe,' Sophie said.

'What if it's a boy, dummy?' Bella said, her eyes still fixed on Artemis.

'If it's a boy then I would call it Rufus,' Izzy said. 'Like next door's dog, that way when we take it to the park we can call after it "Here boy, here Rufus".'

Izzy giggled which once Sophie would have found re-assuring, but now she wondered if Izzy was really showing shock and anxiety with her jokes.

'Bella?' Sophie said easing herself up on to the bed. 'What do you think about me having a baby?'

Bella sat back on her heels and looked at Sophie.

'I'm not sure,' she said slowly. 'I like things how they are. With just us. I like you looking after us.'

'I liked it too, but that won't change,' Sophie told her. 'I'll still look after you. I'll still always be here for you. I promise.'

'But that baby will be your baby,' Bella said, pointing at Sophie's middle. 'You will love it more than us.' She glanced at Louis. 'He will love it more than us because it's your baby.'

'You are all my children,' Louis said. 'I'll love you all the same.'

'Even Seth?' Bella challenged him.

'Eventually,' Louis said. 'Given the chance then yes. I'll love him too.'

Izzy sat up, watching Bella, her face still and thoughtful as she listened.

'And as for me,' Sophie told both the girls, 'it's not possible for me to love anyone more than I love you.'

'Isn't it?' Bella looked uncertain.

'Mitchell Lambert in my class has four brothers and a sister and their mum loves all of them the same,' Izzy said.

'Yes, but Aunty Sophie isn't our mum, is she?' Bella said. 'She'll be the baby's mum, but she won't be ours.'

'Oh, I forgot that,' Izzy said, sadly.

Sophie rubbed her hand over her face and looked at Louis, who reached out and stroked Bella's hair.

'The thing is,' she said slowly, 'I know I am not your mum but I *feel* like you're my daughters. I feel like you are *my* girls. Carrie was your mummy, and she always will be – but when you were gone and missing and I didn't know where you were all I could think about was *my* girls, my daughters. About getting you back and keeping you safe. Artemis is lucky, she's got animal instincts to tell her how to be a mummy, the second that her first kitten was born. But I realise that I've been even luckier. I've had you two to show me what being a mummy is really about. So that when this baby comes, when your little sister or brother arrives, then I'll be able to do nearly as good a job at it as Artemis.'

'Will you bite off its cord thingy with your teeth?' Izzy asked her, in awe.

'Probably not,' Sophie said. 'But apart from that, I think I'll be better at looking after this baby because I've got you two. You're my daughters and I love you and nothing, nothing on earth, will change that. I promise you.'

Bella peered under the bed again, 'Now there are three!' she exclaimed. 'This one looks tortoiseshell.'

'Anyway, I've been thinking,' Sophie went on, treading carefully, 'the last thing on earth I want is for you and Izzy to worry about anything, so if this is all happening too quickly for you, if you feel that everything is changing too fast, then Daddy and I don't have to get married. I can stay in the B&B with the baby and things can go on as they are.'

Louis dropped his head.

'But if you do get married, then what?' Bella asked her.

'Well, then I'd come and live here, and the baby would live here too eventually and we would all be together every single day.'

'And Seth would sometimes visit too,' Izzy added. 'To teach us to whistle.'

Bella got up and sat next to Sophie on the bed.

'I don't want you to move in after you've got married,' she said, and Sophie felt her heart sink with disappointment that she hadn't fully appreciated till she had heard Bella's verdict. 'I don't want to wait that long. I want you to move in now. After all, Artemis will need help with the kittens and you'll need extra looking after and if you're here then . . .'

'Then?' Sophie asked her, on bated breath.

'Then we'll be a family,' Bella said. 'Our own, silly, strange, mixed-up, special family.'

'And you're happy for me and Sophie to get married?' Louis asked both of the girls.

'We are,' Bella and Izzy said together.

Louis looked at Sophie. 'And what have you got to say?' he asked her.

'I have this to say.' Sophie was radiant. 'Louis, Bella and Izzy – will you marry me?'

Soon after Artemis's fourth and final kitten was born Louis sent Sophie and the girls to bed, just before eight a.m.

'You need rest,' he said kissing Sophie on the forehead,

'And you two could do with at least one day off school, what with all the excitement you've had. I'll sort out Artemis, get her box ready and all the business.'

Sophie and the two girls had curled up in Louis's bed and drifted off to sleep the moment their heads touched the pillow.

It was midday when Sophie finally woke, feeling refreshed for the first time in ages. The girls had already gone and she found them down in the kitchen, cooing over Artemis and her kittens who Louis had put in a box next to the boiler.

'Good morning, Sophie,' Louis said, encircling her with his arms. 'Good morning beautiful woman and bride and mother to be. The vet popped in to take a quick look at Artemis and she says she is fighting fit. Tango even turned up for breakfast and tried to have a look at his offspring but Artemis sent him away with his tail between his legs, which is pretty much all he will have there soon. The vet says we have to have them both done if we don't want a repeat performance.'

'That's great that she's doing so well,' Sophie said as she sat at the table and looked into the box at Artemis with her kittens. 'That's really, really wonderful.'

'Well, probably not for Tango, the poor feller,' Louis said, wincing. 'But I have got more good news. We have been busy, haven't we, girls?'

'Yes!' Bella jumped up excitedly, resting her palms on Sophie's knees. 'We have got surprises . . .' she said, wiggling her fingers in what Sophie assumed was an indication of mystery.

'Really?' Sophie asked her, a little cautiously. 'I'm not entirely sure that I'm up to surprises.'

'I called Finestone Manor this morning and they still have New Year's Eve free,' Louis told her.

'They don't!' Sophie exclaimed delightedly, before her brow furrowed. 'But why do they? Are they a rubbish place that no one wants to get married in?'

'No, they are a wonderful place that lots of people want to get married in. It just seems that very few people decide to get married so soon before the ceremony and no one else booked it. They're thrilled we still want it, they've promised me candlelight and music and they'll do all the catering – we just need to look at menus and give them numbers.'

'That's a fantastic surprise – but New Year's Eve – it's only a couple of months away – there's so much to do. I need to find a dress that won't make me look like a house.

'Or a horse,' Izzy interjected.

'Ah well, that's our other surprise,' Louis said grinning at Bella. 'I phoned Carmen earlier to tell her about the kittens and Finestone Manor and to ask her about the cake and all that and I asked her if she knew of any dressmakers in the area that might help us.'

'Did she?' Sophie asked.

'She did better than that. She knows *the* dressmaker, the one who designed the dress you saw and loved at the fair? Apparently after it all kicked off Carmen decided to phone the organiser and find out about the designer, got her number, address – everything. She said she would have mentioned it sooner but everything seemed a little bit up in the air.'

'A long way up in the air,' Izzy commented as she gazed happily at the kittens.

'Anyway, they're a small outfit based in Plymouth. I called them today and Ellen, that's the designer, said if you go in tomorrow they can fit it for you extra loose and then just before the wedding take it in or let it out so that it flows perfectly over all of your curves. I tried to get her to tell me what it would look like but she refused.'

'Quite right too,' Sophie said and then, 'oh my God, I'm so happy.'

'I should have known it would have been a fashion item that would have made you happy.' Louis smiled.

'But what about invitations?' Sophie thought suddenly. 'We need to invite people in a couple of weeks which means we need invites now.'

'I know,' Louis said. 'And I've got the perfect idea for them. I'll take a photo of all of us, the whole family. I'll get my mate Jack down at the printers to print us up the invites with the photo on the front. We'll be telling everyone that this is a new start, not just for you and for me, but for all of us. That we're a family now and that's the way it's going to stay for ever.'

'I love that idea,' Sophie said, reaching out to touch his face.

'I'm glad, because the girls and me have been talking. And there is one more person that we'd like to ask to be in the photo.'

Sophie nodded. 'Seth.'

Wendy's house was remarkably unlike the bawdy bordello style that Sophie had imagined it. It was a modest semi in a suburban part of Newquay, tastefully decorated in pastels and white. Her kitchen, in which Sophie sat opposite Wendy, sipping a weak cup of tea, was largely painted lemon with glittering white units. Wendy might be an evil old relationship wrecker, but it turned out that she liked to keep a clean home.

'Thanks for inviting me in,' Sophie said, keen to break the silence that hung in the air between them. 'Louis would have come in too, but we thought that under the circumstances he and the girls had better stay in the car.'

Wendy nodded. 'I can see why. I was going to call today, anyway, to say thank you to you and Louis for helping sort things out with the police. Seth's in bits up there. When I got him home and he'd realised just exactly what he'd done, all the thoughts that must have been going through your head and how frightened you must have been, he was gutted. He is gutted. He knows he's blown it.'

'Blown it?' Sophie asked her. 'What do you mean?'

'Blown getting to know Louis and his sisters, he knows that after yesterday there is no way you will want him anywhere near them.'

'But that's not true,' Sophie said. 'Yes, it was stupid and frightening and if I'd've had the chance to get my hands on him yesterday then I probably would have killed him. But nothing's changed. He's still Louis's son, he's still the girls' brother. They – we want him in our lives.'

'I see. Did Louis tell you?' Wendy asked Sophie. 'Only I think if we're going to move on from this then you should know.'

'Know what?' Sophie asked uneasily.

'In London, that second night, the night that he left you and came to help me, after the police had Seth, it was God knows what time, really late. Louis took me back to my B&B. I tried to get him to stay with me, tried to get him to come to bed with me. Threw myself at him, really, made a right fool of myself. But he didn't want anything to do with me, not even for a second. He told me he loved you, he told me he'd sleep in a chair downstairs and he did, all night. I got into my bed and I thought about Seth in a police cell and Louis downstairs on the chair, and it hit me, what a bloody stupid selfish cow I'd been, putting Seth and Louis and you through a lot of pain that there didn't need to be. I'm sorry, Sophie.'

Sophie sat back a little and glanced down at her lukewarm tea wondering if this was all some sort of evil mastermind confession and that in a second Wendy would announce she'd sweetened it with cyanide.

'You're sorry?' Sophie felt it was best to check.

'I got angry and jealous and insecure. Angry that suddenly my nice stable little life was going to be turned on its head, jealous that you seemed to have everything that I never had without even having to try, and furious that Louis was about to waltz into my son's life, and get to be his dad without having to do any of the hard stuff, without having to go through the years and years of struggling that I had gone through. It didn't seem fair and I blamed it all on you. It's me that Seth gets his rash and angry side from.'

'Oh, right,' Sophie said, cautiously. 'I'm sorry, Wendy. I don't know exactly what to say. I mean, I know this must have been hard on you. But you're the one that turned it into a fight over Louis, I still don't really get that. Why?'

Wendy sighed. 'Look, my life's been what's it been and I can live with that. It's my choices that have brought me here. I chose not to tell Louis about Seth, although I think my dad probably had a lot to do with that. I chose to keep him, when I could have had him adopted. And it's been tough. Mum and Dad were there for me but I never had those years of being young that everyone else had. No nights out down the pub, no real boyfriends to speak of. It's really hard to get a boyfriend when you've got a baby to look after. I loved Seth, with all of my heart. But I never felt like I lived my life. I didn't realise it till I saw Louis again but I hadn't felt as happy, or at least not that same sort of happy, as I did that last summer with him. Seth made me happy and proud, of course he did. But there was always the rest of life, responsibilities, bills to be paid, sitters to be found, so that I could go out to work, banging on my door and wearing me down. I made mistakes, married the wrong man, pushed him far too quickly on Seth and then took him away again when things didn't work out. That hurt Seth a lot. And I've always

397

known that. I just didn't want to admit it. I've got things wrong, but I've always tried to do my best for him. Always worked my bollocks off to give him the kind of life he deserved even if I haven't always got it right. But, if I'm honest, I think that last summer with Louis, that was the last time I was ever really carefree and happy. And it seems like a long time ago.'

'You've been through a lot,' Sophie agreed. 'Seth told me how much he admires you, how much you've done for him. Though I don't know if that quite gives you the right to try and steal my fiancé.'

'I know that now.' Wendy shrugged. 'When I saw Louis that morning, all of those feelings came back to me, the way I felt with him, how happy I was, and I suddenly realised that I had his son. I didn't want those feelings coming up and dragging me down again, I'd got used to my life, I was content. But then you saw us at the fair and put two and two together and I knew I didn't have any choice any more. I'd have to face the way I used to feel about him. I thought I wanted him back. I used this whole thing with Seth to try to get him back; I thought that the more time he spent with me and worried about Seth the more likely it was that he'd start to feel about me the way he used to. But that was never going to happen. He was never going to leave you. I'm sorry.'

Sophie nodded. 'Well, for what's it's worth I'm sorry too, for turning your life upside down when you asked me not to.'

'I don't suppose you had a choice,' Wendy said.

Sophie shrugged. 'I probably didn't have to do it quite so abruptly. I'm the one who started this whole roller coaster. I'm sorry for that.'

The two women sat in silence for a moment and Sophie looked towards the front door, thinking of Louis and the girls waiting in the car.

'What about Seth?' Sophie said. 'Will he come down? I'd really like to talk to him.'

Wendy went to the foot of the stairs and called up to him.

'Seth, come down and talk to Sophie, love. Come on, she's not angry.'

Sophie waited for the heavy footfall on the stairs and finally Seth emerged into the bright kitchen, blinking under the strip lighting, the sleeves of his jumper pulled down over his fingers. His eyes looked red rimmed and swollen, he looked pale, scared and very, very young.

'Hello,' he said, unable to look Sophie in the eye as he sat down at the breakfast bar. Wendy put the kettle on.

'Are you OK?' Sophie asked him gently.

'I am,' he said. 'I'm fine – are *you* OK? I'm so sorry about what happened. No one said I couldn't take the girls at the school. I mean, I thought if it was a problem they would have stopped me. But no one did.'

'I know,' Sophie said. 'Look, I'm not going to pretend that yesterday wasn't the most horrible, stressful and sickening two hours of my life ever but I understand why you did it, I think. And Louis understands too. We just want to put it behind us all and move on.'

'I know,' Seth said. 'And you don't have to worry. I won't be hanging around any more. I'll stay away, I promise.'

'No . . . we don't want you to stay away. We want to get to know you . . . if that's OK with you. I know it will be really strange to begin with, but Louis is a good man and a great dad and . . .' Sophie glanced at Wendy. 'I'm going to marry him on New Year's Eve.'

'That's quick,' Wendy said. 'You pregnant?'

'Yes, I am actually,' Sophie said, making Wendy spit out her tea. 'But that's not why we're getting married. We're getting married because we love each other.'

Seth grinned and then his face fell. 'God, you're pregnant and I put you through all of that, I am such a fucking wanker.'

'Well, it wasn't your finest moment, but I'm fine and the baby's fine and now we all want to move on. Focus on the wedding and the baby. Focus on this strange and wonderful new family that we're creating that will hopefully include you.' She looked at Wendy. 'Both of you.'

Seth and Wendy exchanged glances, the meaning of which Sophie couldn't quite determine.

'I came here to ask both of you to the wedding and Seth – Louis and I would love if you would be in our wedding invitation photo along with me and Louis and the two girls. Would you think about it at least?'

'Where is he?' Seth asked her.

'He's in the car with the girls,' Sophie said. 'We didn't want to rush you or crowd you out. I think you've had a bit much of that recently.'

'They can come in, if you like, for a bit, can't they, Mum?' Seth asked Wendy. 'Have a cup of tea?'

Wendy nodded. 'Of course,' she said. 'Of course they can.'

'I said I'd teach the girls to whistle,' Seth explained. 'Got to start somewhere. It's a complicated business, whistling.'

'I'll go and get them,' Sophie said with a smile. Glancing at his mother Seth followed her into the hallway and stopped her at the door.

'Listen, Sophie, this person you've seen, the person who kisses their dad's fiancée, gets drunk, gets into brawls and wanders off with his kid sisters, that's not me. That's not all of me, anyway. It is a part of me but it's a part I'm sorting out, you know, getting under control. I'm growing up. I am.'

'I know you are,' Sophie said.

'Being a big brother is going to be cool,' Seth told her. 'Having little kid sisters and another one, too, maybe it'll be a boy and me and Louis will be able to take it fishing and shit.'

'Do you like fishing?' Sophie asked him in surprise.

'Can't stand it, but that's big brother territory, isn't it?' Seth replied with a smile.

'I don't know,' Sophie said. 'This is new for me too, you know. Brothers, fathers, being a mother. I think the best thing you and I can do is take one step at a time and see how we go.'

'I'm up for that,' Seth said as he opened the door and waved at Louis and the girls in the car. 'I'm definitely up for that.'

Epilogue

'Well, I've seen worse, I suppose,' Cal said as Sophie stepped out from behind the screen in her wedding gown.

'What? Shut up,' Carmen cried, crossing the bridal suite to take Sophie's hand in hers. 'Oh darling, you look beautiful. That dress is so perfect. You'd hardly know you were five months gone.'

'I don't care if anyone does,' Sophie said, turning to look at herself in the mirror and smoothing the cream silk satin over her bump. 'I want the whole world to know.'

'You look like a princess,' Izzy oohed as she ran into the room, followed closely by her sister, both of them wearing dresses made out of yards and yards of dusky rose pink net, each with a pair of specially made beaded wings attached to their backs.

'No, like a queen,' Bella said. 'And we're your princesses.'

'And how about me?' Cal asked them, gesturing to his suit that had been dyed to exactly match the bridesmaids' dresses. 'I think you'll find that as fifth joint-head bridesmaid how I look is just as important as the bride. Steven's out there, you know. This is our first official date since he broke up with his ex. I want him to be blown away by me. I want him to get ideas.'

'You look nice too,' Bella told him. 'Even if I'm not exactly sure about a boy as a bridesmaid . . .'

'Plus, if you really want a man to marry you, then you have to ask him, it's the safest way,' Christina said, handing Sophie a glass of water. 'I'd like to offer you champagne but, well, what with the bump and all, water will have to do.'

There was a knock at the door which Carmen went to answer.

She picked up Sophie's bouquet of pink winter roses and handed it to her.

'Right, they are all ready out there for you. Are you ready, darling?' she asked her. 'Ready for a new year, new life, new baby, new husband?'

'I am,' Sophie said steadily, looking at the door. 'I am so very ready.'

The candlelight reflected in the chandeliers, making the room flitter and sparkle as Sophie slowly walked down the aisle on her mother's arm. Izzy and Bella walked in front of her, supposedly to scatter rose petals, but actually waving at people and, in Izzy's case, stopping for a chat when she saw Grace Tregowan, holding everything up for a few seconds.

Then finally Sophie found herself standing opposite Louis, with Bella and Izzy either side of her and a rather nervous Seth at Louis's shoulder, clutching the rings.

'I didn't think you could look more beautiful,' Louis said. 'I was wrong.'

'We're here,' Sophie whispered as the celebrant prepared to start the ceremony. 'We're doing this at last. You and me getting married!'

And it seemed like a dream to Sophie, as she stood in the candlelight with all her family and friends around her, Izzy's hand tucked into hers as Louis made his wedding vows, Bella standing by her side, her arm around Sophie's waist. She saw Grace Tregowan and Mrs Alexander sitting in the front, Grace resplendent in red and Mrs Alexander ploughing her way through a box of tissues. She saw her mother standing behind her, determined not to cry, and Trevor waiting for her a few rows back with what Sophie happened to know was an engagement ring in a box in his pocket, because earlier that morning he'd come and asked her if she would mind if he proposed to her mother while they were down in Cornwall.

Best of all she saw the man she loved, she saw Louis telling her and the whole world that he was going to be by her side for ever. That he was her husband.

'And do you, Sophie Mills, take this man to be your husband?' The celebrant asked her. Sophie smiled at Louis and hugged his two daughters close to her.

'I do,' Sophie said. 'Always, for ever, whatever.'

The Accidental Mother

Rowan Coleman

Sophie Mills has worked her Manolo Blahniks off to reach the near-top of her profession. And she's very happy with her priorities in life – her job, her neurotic cat Artemis and her passion for shoes. After all, relationships only get in the way. And as for children? She hasn't even begun to think about them yet. Until one day an unexpected visitor brings news of a strange inheritance and Sophie is suddenly, out of the blue, in sole charge of two children under the age of six. But motherhood can't be all that hard, can it?

Within twenty-four hours, her make-up is smeared all over the bathroom, Artemis has taken up residence on top of her wardrobe, and Sophie is in despair. And all her unconventional mother can suggest is Dr Roberts' *Complete Dog Training and Care Manual*.

Determined to rise to the challenge, Sophie soon realises that she'll need more than a business plan to cope with all this . . .

Praise for Rowan Coleman

'A witty, wonderful, warm-hearted read' *Company*

'Touching and thought-provoking' *B*

arrow books

ALSO AVAILABLE IN ARROW

The Baby Group

Rowan Coleman

Meet The Baby Group: Natalie ran her own design company until baby Freddie unexpectedly came along. Now the capable person she once was is trapped inside a crazy woman's body, longing for just one decent night's sleep and words of more than one syllable. Meg is onto her fourth child but still feels she has to take notes. Meg's sister-in-law Frances organises her little boy like he's a private in the army, but underneath her rather prickly façade she longs for the kind of friendships others seem to find so easy. Former career girl Jess sees danger lurking in every corner, doubting she'll ever be a good mother. Stay-at-home house-husband Steve is just glad to have the opportunity to spend time with his daughter. And sixteen-year-old Tiffany is the youngest – yet possibly the wisest – of them all.

Six very different parents. Six very different lives. But when Natalie's dodgy wiring leads to a series of chance encounters they rapidly discover – through Baby Music, Baby Aerobics, coffee and more importantly cake – that there's safety in numbers. And their own unofficial baby group is formed . . .

Praise for Rowan Coleman

'Highly amusing' *OK!*

'A sweet tale' *Closer*

arrow books

The Accidental Wife

Rowan Coleman

How do you know if your life has taken a wrong turn?

Alison James thinks she might be living the wrong life. She loves her husband Marc and their three children but somehow, in the process of building a perfect life for her family, she seems to have lost herself. And sometimes she worries that she's being punished for how it all started – for the day she ran away with her best friend's boyfriend.

Catherine Ashley knows she's living the wrong life. She adores her two daughters, but she'd always thought that at thirty-one she'd be more than a near-divorcee with a dead-end job. In those dark middle-of-the-night moments that come all too often these days, her mind still flicks back to the love of her life: Marc James. And she still wonders whether Alison stole her life as well as her boyfriend.

Alison and Catherine have been living separate lives, a hundred miles apart, for fifteen years – since Alison and Marc ran away. But now Alison's moving back to Farmington, the town in which they both grew up. And they're about to find out just how different both their lives could still be . . .

arrow books

THE POWER OF READING

Visit the Random House website and get connected with information on all our books and authors

EXTRACTS from our recently published books and selected backlist titles

COMPETITIONS AND PRIZE DRAWS Win signed books, audiobooks and more

AUTHOR EVENTS Find out which of our authors are on tour and where you can meet them

LATEST NEWS on bestsellers, awards and new publications

MINISITES with exclusive special features dedicated to our authors and their titles

READING GROUPS Reading guides, special features and all the information you need for your reading group

LISTEN to extracts from the latest audiobook publications

WATCH video clips of interviews and readings with our authors

RANDOM HOUSE INFORMATION including advice for writers, job vacancies and all your general queries answered

Come home to Random House

www.randomhouse.co.uk